OTHER BOOKS BY ROBERT BARNARD

The Masters of the House

A Hovering of Vultures

A Fatal Attachment

A Scandal in Belgravia

A City of Strangers

Death of a Salesperson

Death and the Chaste Apprentice

At Death's Door

The Skeleton in the Grass

The Cherry Blossom Corpse

Bodies

Political Suicide

Fête Fatale

Out of the Blackout

Corpse in a Gilded Cage

School for Murder

The Case of the Missing Brontë

A Little Local Murder

Death and the Princess

Death by Sheer Torture

Death in a Cold Climate

Death of a Perfect Mother

Death of a Literary Widow

Death of a Mystery Writer

Blood Brotherhood

Death on the High C's

Death of an Old Goat

The Bad Samaritan

•A NOVEL OF SUSPENSE•
•FEATURING CHARLIE PEACE•

Robert Barnard

SCRIBNER

NEW YORK   LONDON   TORONTO   SYDNEY   TOKYO   SINGAPORE

SCRIBNER
1230 Avenue of the Americas
New York, NY 10020

Manufactured in the United States of America

10 9 8 7 6 5 4 3 2 1

Library of Congress Cataloging-in-Publication Data
Barnard, Robert.
The bad samaritan : a novel of suspense featuring Charlie Peace / Robert Barnard.
p.   cm.
I. Title.
PR6052.A665B3   1995
823'.914—dc20   95-16383
CIP

ISBN 0-684-81334-3

For
Margaret Burton,
who knows the problems

PART I

ROSEMARY

CHAPTER ONE

A Loss

Rosemary Sheffield backed her husband's car out of the garage and through the gates, then parked it by the side of the road pointing in the direction of St Saviour's. She got out, blinking in the early spring sunshine. Feeling rather silly she dabbed with a cloth at the door handles. For some reason she could not fathom, her husband was fussy about the appearance of his car when he went off to take service. It was presumably a form of vanity, since in other respects he had no illusions about cleanliness being next to godliness. Anyway, there it was waiting for him: clean, sleek and shining.

Her husband sailed out, clerical collar gleaming white over pale grey, folder clutched in his hand. From time to time the folder exploded, scattering all over the driveway, and when that happened, and they scrabbled together on the driveway bumping heads, Rosemary had to tell herself she wouldn't have wanted an orderly husband. Today the folder remained intact. Her husband pecked her on the cheek.

"I'll be there tonight, Paul," Rosemary said, and he nodded, put the car into gear and drove smoothly away. He loves that car,

11

Rosemary thought, though without any feeling of jealousy. The sun felt warm on her cheek, wonderful after the long, bleak winter months. She felt she ought to go indoors and get down to things, particularly as she had told Paul how busy she was. Instead, relishing the clear morning light, she crossed the road on to the grassy open spaces of Herrick Park.

The turf felt good under her thin-soled shoes. There were the usual dog-walkers, and she thought again it was time to get another dog: getting a puppy immediately after Bo'sun had died had seemed wrong to her, a sort of unfaithfulness, though everyone had said it was the only way to get over her grief. She still missed him, missed their walks and games together. If it had happened when the children were still young, there would have been more to take her mind off it. She looked over to the tennis courts, where two students were playing a strenuous, rough and ready game. In the distance she saw one of the usual Sunday morning joggers approaching.

And suddenly, in the warmth, surrounded by shimmering light, she felt something lift from her, leave her. It was as if a worry had suddenly evaporated—she could almost physically feel herself being rid of it. She said to herself: "I do not believe." There was no need to add to the sentence. There was nothing to add. Suddenly she knew that she no longer believed. She had lost her faith. She stood there feeling free and happy—feeling, indeed, almost lightheaded. She no longer believed in God: not the Christian God, not any God. She felt she ought to feel desolate, deprived, but she didn't: she felt liberated, joyful, full of the most enormous potential. The road ahead of her seemed suddenly wider, taking her through an entirely different landscape.

The jogger approached down the path from the woods. It was a young black man she had seen often in the park. She raised her hand and he raised his in return. As he passed her she was conscious that he was looking at her curiously. She ought to feel bad about that: clergymen's wives should not do anything that made people look at them curiously. But she did not turn and go back into the house. She stood there in the godless sun, savouring her new freedom.

When she thought about it later in the morning, going about her accumulation of tasks, she realised that her loss of faith could not have come suddenly, as it had seemed. It must have been led up to, must have been the culmination of a process involving worries, niggling doubts, shifts in patterns of thinking. But, puzzle as she might, she could not remember any occasion when doubt had tried to force a way into her mind and had been repressed. There had been no incident—no accident or massacre, no personal loss—where she had questioned whether a benign God would allow such a thing to happen. So then and later Rosemary saw her loss of faith as a sudden thing, a quite unexpected *lifting*, as if she was standing on a mountain and suddenly the cloud had gone, revealing wonderful new perspectives.

As usual she timed the Sunday lunch for two. Paul sometimes went off for a pint with some of his male parishioners after the service, or liked time for a sherry at home with her—something, anyhow, to relax him after the tensions of taking the service, for tensions, even after all these years, there still were. As she peeled and scraped she meditated the totally unexpected questions: When would she tell him? How would he take the news? The first question was easily answered: not until after he'd enjoyed the pork, his favourite roast. The second question was not easily answered at all. She felt she simply didn't know. That was odd, after all these years of marriage, parenthood, and the usual vicissitudes of modern life. She felt she knew her husband very well, but this was a totally unexplored terrain, and she lacked a compass. She trusted Paul and loved him, but this . . .

13

The pork was tender, the roast potatoes crisp as he liked them, the peas just like frozen peas always are. Even with just the two of them there was an air of well-being hovering over the table. After pudding, a bread-and-butter one, and when she had put cheese and biscuits on the table, Paul said he could do no more than toy with them.

"Wonderful meal," he said. "I would say I've had an elegant sufficiency, but I've had a good deal more than that."

Rosemary smiled, her mind working away.

"Who went along to the Game Cock with you?"

"Oh, Jim Russell, Arthur Beeston and Dark Satanic Mills."

"What did *he* want?"

Her husband smiled tolerantly.

"You always ask that. The poor man's been coming to church for nearly fifteen years and you still suspect his motives."

"I certainly do. I won't say 'You've only got to look at him' because I know how you'll react."

Paul Sheffield nodded.

"I'll say you have a conventional as well as a suspicious mind."

"Questioning, anyway. . . . A funny thing happened to me today, Paul."

"That sounds like the beginning of a bad joke."

"No, it's not. . . . Or I don't think so." She swallowed. Now for it. "After you drove off to service I went for a little walk in the park, it was so nice."

"It *was* nice, wasn't it? Lucky you."

"And I suddenly realised . . . that I don't *believe* any longer."

Her husband's mouth dropped, just as he was about to pop a piece of crumbly cheese into it.

"You're joking."

"Not at all."

He put the cheese down and swallowed.

"You mean you've lost your faith?"

"Yes."

"Rosie, how awful for you."

She left a pause before she answered.

"Maybe. But oddly enough it doesn't feel awful."

"How does it feel?"

"Liberating. As if a cloud has lifted."

Paul frowned. He's quite bewildered, the poor lamb, thought Rosemary.

"But your faith and the Church are so important in your life, so central. Surely you must feel . . . empty?"

"I would have expected to, if I'd thought about it, but I don't." She added carefully: "perhaps it was the Church that was central, rather than the faith."

"We must all try and help you as much as we can."

"I won't have you publicly praying for the return of my faith, Paul."

"No, of course not, if you feel like that," he said hurriedly. Then he added, with a quick glance at her: "perhaps it would be better not to say anything at all about it for the moment."

Rosemary considered.

"Maybe you're right. I don't want to make it a dark little secret. On the other hand, to announce it does seem to give *me* a lot more importance than I actually have."

"A lot of people in the parish will be very upset. And the children will be."

"Oh, the children are tougher than you think—children have to be these days. Janet will probably imagine it's my time of life, knowing her, and Mark certainly will pray for me. I only hope he keeps *quiet* about it, that's all."

"Perhaps you need time off—time away."

She frowned at him.

15

"You're not trying to get rid of me, are you, Paul?"

"No, of course I'm not."

"Shuffle me out of the way, so that people don't *talk*. You're horribly afraid of people *talking*."

"I don't like people talking nonsense, which you are now."

"Because eventually the parish is going to have to know, and then they're going to talk."

"I'm sure everyone will be very sympathetic."

"Golly yes—that's what I'm dreading. And those will be the nice ones, not the troublemakers."

"But you're talking as if it's gone for good and is never going to come back."

"You make it sound like a skin disease."

"Well, is it gone for good?"

Rosemary pondered.

"I really don't know. How could I know? How could anyone? It *feels* that way, that's all I know. I suppose it may *descend* on me again as suddenly as it lifted. But I have to say I don't expect it to."

"Will you come to church?"

"I'll come tonight, as I said I would. I'll see how it feels. I'm not sure I want to *pretend* to pray."

"You could just close your eyes."

"That *would* be pretending to pray. Anyway, people know how I pray. People notice me—as the vicar's wife. More's the pity. One of the things I hate about Dark Satanic Mills is the way he looks at me."

"What about the Harvest Festival Committee and the Mothers' Union meeting?"

"Oh, I won't have any problem with the social side. Why should I? They're all quite useful activities, or pleasant enough. I'll do them as your wife, as I've always done."

"That's a relief. I do think you ought to keep coming to church as well. It might help."

Rosemary laughed.

"You show a touching confidence in your own powers as a spiritual leader," she teased him.

"You know I don't mean that. I mean the experience—the prayers, the hymns, the communion."

"Of course I'll have to stop taking communion. Then everybody will know."

"Yes, they'll know then."

"And *won't* there be whispering!"

Paul Sheffield looked very unhappy. The uncharted territory that seemed exciting to Rosemary only bewildered him. He had always been a consolidator rather than an explorer.

It was certainly an odd experience going to church that evening. As usual, there were far fewer there than at Holy Communion—fewer to notice, Rosemary thought. She sang the hymns enthusiastically: she was a would-be choral singer who could imagine no joy greater than singing in the *Messiah* or the *Sea Symphony* but had somehow always failed in her attempts to learn to read music. But for the rest it was going through a charade—quite empty. She occupied her mind with thought: had it been going towards this for some time? Had religious observance gradually had its significance drained out of it for her? She had certainly not been conscious of it if so. There seemed all the difference in the world between her participation in Holy Communion the Sunday before and the pantomime performance which was all she could manage now—like an actor playing his part in an empty theatre.

But the thing that struck her most was that she did *not* feel empty, did not feel a sense of loss or deprivation. She felt good; she felt stimulated; she felt free. Have I been living a lie all these years, she wondered? Can one live a lie without knowing it? Can one think one believes when in reality one doesn't? What was she going to say to Paul about the service? She imagined him asking her, "How was it for you?" and had to suppress a giggle. She looked round to see if anyone had noticed, and rather suspected that Mrs Harridance had.

After the service she waited for Paul by the car. He stood in the porch exchanging pleasantries, parish small talk and gossip with the members of his congregation. In the past she would normally have stopped with him and participated in the chat, but tonight she felt awkward. He's a good parish priest, thought Rosemary, looking at him. I hope this doesn't spoil things for him. Of course logically there was no reason at all why it should, but logic wasn't always operative in parish affairs.

Paul freed himself from his little knot of admirers and came over to let himself and her into the car. He put it into gear and drove off towards home.

"Did the service do anything for you?" he asked. Again she had to suppress a giggle.

"Absolutely nothing. Do you realise you're sounding like a doctor again?"

"Sorry. It's obviously going to be a long process."

"If there is a process at all. I think it's something I and everyone else are just going to have to accept."

Paul looked genuinely upset.

"Oh, I hope not."

"I'm beginning to feel *observed*—do you know what I mean?"

"Not entirely."

"Beginning to feel that people—you mainly, of course, but the sharper-eyed parish members as well—are observing me, as if they know I've got something terminal and they're watching for symptoms of my approaching demise."

"You're being absurd. Nobody knows. And who's talking in medical terms now?"

"I know I am. . . . Still, I think I *might* go away after all."

That cheered Paul up.

"I do think it might be a good idea. We can afford it."

"Oh, I wouldn't go to anywhere grand. But I could think things out without any of the people I know watching me."

"The Lakes?"

"Hmmm. I don't think so. I'd feel Auntie Wordsworth looking over my shoulder and telling me to experience God through nature. I think the sea would suit me better. Brid or Scarborough. There wouldn't be anyone much there at this time of year."

"What will you do?"

"Walk on the beach, walk on the cliffs, sew, read a detective story, put flowers on Anne Brontë's grave."

"Scarborough, then?"

"Yes, Scarborough, I think. There's more to do there if the weather is vile."

"And you'll . . . think things over?"

She patted his arm.

"Yes, I'll think things over. But you can't *think* yourself into a faith, you know."

"I'm sure many people have done just that."

"Not me. That wouldn't be my kind of faith."

He left it there. They had a cosy, joky evening together, with television and music. When they went to bed Rosemary was afraid she was going to get the feeling that Paul was praying for her, but if he did he did it discreetly. They made love and he was as warm and tender as he had ever been. In the morning Rosemary looked in her address book and rang a guesthouse they had stayed at three summers before on St Nicholas's Cliff in Scarborough. She felt perhaps she ought to feel cowardly, as if making a strategic withdrawal. Instead she had an exhilarating sense of going off to pastures new.

"Have you ever known anyone have a mystical experience?" Charlie Peace asked his superior Mike Oddie, as he slogged his way through a mountain of paperwork in the CID offices at Leeds Police Headquarters the next morning.

"Can't say I have. What does a mystical experience consist of?"

"I'm not sure I know."

"Why do you ask?"

"Because I saw a woman in the park yesterday, and it looked as if that was what she was going through."

"What did it look like?"

"Like she'd had a revelation. Like she'd suddenly discovered God."

"Bully for her," said Mike

"Only I don't think it was that."

"Why?"

"Because I think she's a clergyman's wife."

CHAPTER TWO

A Friend

Rosemary walked from the Scarborough station to her guesthouse. The journey had been uneventful, except that on Leeds station she had bumped into Dark Satanic Mills, who had leered at her as if he knew something about her—a knowing, conspiratorial look that she had tried to freeze but failed. Her case was not large or heavy because she did not see her holiday as an opportunity for a display of fashion, even had she had the wherewithal for one, so walking the short distance was no problem. She did notice as she loitered along that there were shops in Scarborough that sold the sort of clothes that she liked. She wondered whether she might take the opportunity to branch out into an entirely different sort of clothes, but she decided it was too late. It was not a change of *life* she was embarking on, but a change of *thought*. Anyway, now was hardly the time to start feeling uneasy about what she was wearing.

Scarborough was mildly bustling in a watery, uncertain sunshine, and Rosemary congratulated herself on picking it. Bridlington would have been dull at this time of year. Brid was dull at any time of year. At Scarborough there was usually plenty going on.

It was lunchtime when she arrived at the Cliff View Guesthouse, set in a commanding position on St Nicholas's Cliff opposite the bricky horrors of the Grand Hotel. The proprietress welcomed her as someone she already knew, said she'd given her one of the bedrooms with a sea view, and asked if she would be taking lunch. Rosemary had had a tasteless sandwich on the train and shook her head.

"I expect I'll generally have dinner as my main meal," she said, having booked half board. "It fits in better with my husband's work to have the main meal in the evening, so that's what I've got used to."

"Isn't your husband a clergyman?"

"That's right."

"Awfully demanding on their wives, I've always thought."

"Yes. . . . Yes, I've never thought about it, but I suppose it is. Restricting, certainly."

"Anyway, you can forget it for a bit and enjoy yourself, can't you?"

"Oh, I expect I'll have a very quiet time."

Rosemary took her case up to her room, which did indeed have the most splendid view out to sea. That was the joy of coming out of season: you got the best rooms. She unpacked everything and set out things as if she had come for a long stay.

Once she had freshened up she went out to the shops. She just browsed in the clothes shops, but in the bookshop she bought a biography of the Sitwells and a detective story set in ancient Rome. "I'm here to think, not to shop," she chided herself. "No I'm not," the other side of her mind said, "I'm here to get away from people." No part of her said, "I'm here to regain my faith." She took the funicular down to the beach and had a long walk along the headland. She must have been thinking as she walked but, oddly enough, when she got back to the Cliff View Guesthouse she had no idea what it was she had been thinking about.

She took a book in to dinner that night. It was the sort of place where you could, and eating alone is never easy. You wait, try not to look around, and hope the other diners aren't feeling sorry for you. She was just beginning to enjoy the manifest impossibility of the Sitwells' father (as one does enjoy on the printed page people one would run a mile from in life) when she felt a shadow at her shoulder.

"You like the meat or the fish? The meat is pork fillet and the fish is salmon. Is also a veg'tarian dish, but is not nice if you not veg'tarian."

"I can imagine," said Rosemary. "Or even if you are one, probably. I'll have pork."

He smiled, as if that was what he would have advised if he had been allowed to guide her choice. When he came with the meal Rosemary found it was indeed the sort of meal she might have cooked herself at home. She put aside her book and looked around her. The dining room was sparsely peopled: two middle-aged couples and three elderly ones, three other single ladies and one single man. The waiter was managing to cope on his own, banging happily in and out of the swing doors leading to the kitchen.

After she had enjoyed the pork, Rosemary took up her book again and managed to continue reading while eating a remarkably boring fruit salad. She congratulated herself on choosing a place where you could do the kind of thing that you did when you were at home without disapproving eyes being fixed on you. Rosemary was just finishing her coffee when the waiter darted up to her from the foyer, a question in his dark eyes.

"You Meesa Sheffield? There phone call for you. Thees way."

Rosemary followed him, thinking it must be Paul, then realised he would be at a Parochial Church Council meeting. When she picked up the phone in the foyer it was her daughter's voice she heard.

"Hello Mum. We wondered how you were."

That medical metaphor again, as if spiritual and physical health were inextricably muddled in everyone's mind but her own. How much did Janet know?

"Hello Janet. Lovely to hear from you. Who's 'we'?"

"Kevin and I, of course. And Mark is here as well."

"Good Lord." Her daughter and her son Mark never fought, but they had never seemed to have much in common and seldom got together except at home. "What are you two cooking up?"

"Just got tickets for *Carousel*, that's all. Mum—Dad says you're going through some kind of crisis."

"I'm sure he told you exactly what kind of crisis, dear, so there's no point in beating about the bush. Actually I'm not sure I regard it as a crisis at all."

"Well, it's your life, Mum. I hope you manage to think things through. We wanted you to know we're right behind you."

"That's good of you, dear."

"Mark wants a word."

Why did her heart sink?

"Mum?"

"Hello, Mark dear. I do hope you all enjoy *Carousel*."

"I'm sure we will. Mum—you've really got to work at this thing, you know."

Rosemary was conscious of a sharp but not unexpected twinge of irritation. It wasn't just being told what to do by her son. It was the quality and tone of her son's voice: the quality was plummy and the tone was—what? Condescending? Forbearing of human frailty? Parsonical in the worst sense?

"Oh?" she said coldly.

"You mustn't think your faith will just return, you know. You've got to work at it—pray hard, think things through, try to work out where you've gone wrong to make God leave you in this terrible way."

"Thank you, Mark. I think I have things under control. I should have thought even you would have realised that it's not easy to pray when you have no one and nothing to pray to. Don't let me keep you from *Carousel*."

And she put the phone down, feeling angrier than she had done in years. What had she and Paul done to produce a sermonising prat like Mark, and him only twenty-two years old? She retrieved her book from the empty dining room and wandered into the lounge. *The Bill* was on, watched by a bored and uncomprehending elderly guest. She sat down, but found the television did nothing to soothe her fuming mind. Drug trafficking on a run-down and violent Council estate was not a restful subject. There was a bookcase in the corner with a lot of old Companion Bookclub books in it, and a few standard classics. She didn't feel like starting a new detective story—she always read fiction before she went to bed—so she went over, inspected the stock, and took out *A Tale of Two Cities*. She hadn't read it, to her recollection, since she was at college. It wasn't as soothing as a Jane Austen, but she felt she wasn't cool enough for sly Jane.

On the landing she was caught up with by the slim waiter, bounding up the stairs.

"You have nice telephone call?"

"Yes thank you," she lied. "It was my son and daughter."

"Very nice." He paused, and then said: "I have a little girl—back in Bosnia."

"Oh dear—how awful for you. Are you Bosnian?"

He shrugged.

"Bosnian, Serbian, Croatian—what does it matter? I thought I was Yugoslavian."

"Do you get news from your wife?"

"I not talk to her for many weeks—months. Is no lines. Sometimes I have letter from my wife, but not often." He patted the breast pocket of his jacket. "I not talk about my problems no more. You here on holiday."

"I'm very interested, er—sorry, I don't know your name."

"They call me Stan here."

Rosemary was about to say that didn't sound very romantic, but she thought she might give the wrong impression, so she simply said, "Good night, Stan," and watched him open an unmarked door and bound up the poky stairs to his room in the attic.

The next morning, after a leisurely breakfast in which she admired Stan's dexterity with five or six plates and his excellent memory for orders of great complexity, Rosemary walked down to the lower part of the town. Here she could see the other Scarborough: whelk stalls, fortune-tellers, amusement arcades and streets littered with takeaway cartons. Come the summer holidays and there would be people in funny hats with slogans on them, fat women in skimpy cheap dresses, screaming children with snotty noses. "There is nothing for me here," Rosemary said to herself and walked on to the beach and down to the sea's edge.

The sea should have put her in mind of eternal things, but it did not. She was niggling away at her previous thought: *why* had the lower town nothing for her? It was a loud, vulgar, happy kind of place in its way, yet she shrank from it, hated the harsh music with the heavy bass issuing from the arcades, hated the misspelt and mispunctuated hand-painted advertisements and shop signs. Here am I, a vicar's wife, she thought, someone who ought to be in touch with all sorts of people. But the sort of people who come on day trips here in summer are totally alien to me—or if not alien at least foreign. There are no people like that at St Saviour's—there are in the parish, but they don't come to church. Of Paul's parishioners the people I like and the people I dislike—Dark Satanic Mills and Mrs Harridance, for example—are all middle-class. Am I simply a snob? And if so have I always been one, or have I been made one by Paul's congregation?

She was struck by a horrible thought: people seeing me here, standing by the water's edge, could probably guess that I am a vicar's wife. I dress like a vicar's wife: sensible jumper and skirt, with flat or low-heeled shoes. I have my hair done like a vicar's wife: sensibly tied back so as not to need too much attention. I make up like a vicar's wife: very discreetly. I am a vicar's wife *type*. I can be pigeonholed.

Disturbed, she turned and walked in the direction of St Nicholas's Cliff.

She walked very slowly, keeping close to the sea, stopping now and then to look at the boats. How much more activity, she thought, there would have been out to sea in Anne Brontë's time. And when the Sitwells used to spend their summers here as children. She reached the bottom of the funicular railway and was just wondering whether it was warm enough to sit and read for a bit before finding somewhere for a sandwich and a cup of coffee when she saw the figure of Stan, sitting on an anorak spread out on the sand, gazing abstractedly out to sea.

He looked slight, sad and very vulnerable. Her heart was touched by pity for him, and she felt maternal in a way she could no longer feel for her own son. He was so far from home and so terribly separated from his loved ones. How could one explain what was going on in Yugoslavia? How could European, educated, civilized people do such things to each other? What did it feel like to be one of these people and to have loved ones caught up in the conflict? She found she could not stop herself going over and sitting beside him.

"Hello," she said. "It's a lovely day, isn't it?"

He looked up at her and smiled shyly.

"Yes, lovely. For England."

"Would you rather be home in Bosnia?"

"No!" He said it violently, and there was fear in his voice too. "How could I want to be there when things are as they are now? But I would like very much my family here with me."

"Of course."

"I would even like to know where they are."

"You don't know that?"

"No. The last I hear, they are in a camp, my wife and little girl. But that was nearly three months ago. And it was not very far from the fighting. You see why I am so worried?" He shrugged. "What people we are."

"*How* can that kind of thing happen today?" asked Rosemary passionately. He shrugged again.

"It go back to the war. More back, to when we became Yugoslavia. More back, to the Austrian Empire. More back, more back. Too much history, too many people, too much religions. We all have—what is the word?—things we want revenges for."

"Grudges."

"Grudges, yes. We have so many. We want to pay back things our fathers suffered, things our grandfathers suffered. Too many peoples, too much history."

Rosemary thought it all sounded much like Scottish history in Stuart times. Or Irish history at any time since the Settlements. To change the subject she said, "Have you got a picture of your little girl?"

He nodded, dived into the pocket of his threadbare jacket and shuffled through a pile of snapshots in his bulging wallet. He handed a picture to her. It was a baby in white at its christening, a crucifix in the background.

"She looks lovely. . . . Are you a Christian?"

"Oh yes. But my grandmother is Moslem. We are a bit of every-thing in my family. Is true of many families in Bosnia. That is what is so mad, you see: when we fight each other we also fight part of ourselves."

He put the snapshot tenderly back in the pile of memories and stood up.

"I must go and get ready for lunch. I have one hour free only in morning."

"They work you hard."

He shook his head.

"Is good. I not complain. It stop me thinking."

"Thank you for talking to me, Stan. . . . Do I have to call you Stan? It's a slightly ridiculous name. No young man is called Stan these days."

"I am Stanko. Call me Stanko."

"That's better. I'm Rosemary."

"You not come to lunch, Rosemary?"

"No, I'm on half board. I prefer dinner."

"Is sensible. Lunch is often offle!"

He raised his hand and disappeared into the tiny station just above the beach. Rosemary stayed on the rock, looking out to sea. She did not take out her book, but for some reason her thoughts strayed to her reading of the night before: to Dr Manette reverting at moments of crisis to the shoemaking he had done for years during his long incarceration. This had reminded her of things learnt at teachers college: of Dickens's own obsessive returning, over and over in the books, to his months in the blacking warehouse. We are all prisoners of the most terrible times in our past, she thought. The child victims of sex abuse, the adult victims of rape, seem never able to put it behind them. What chance was there for Yugoslavs of all races in the future? What chance of Stanko's little girl ever managing to put the experiences of civil war behind her?

That night she decided she ought to ring her husband. She left it till after ten, when she knew he would be back home, and since she preferred to be entirely private she went out into the street and used the nearest phone box.

"Fine," she said, in answer to her husband's first questions. "Lots of fresh sea air, not too many people, food perfectly acceptable. . . . I had a phone call from the children last night."

"Oh dear, I rather thought you might," said Paul, sounding terribly guilty. "Both of them?"

"Yes, they were apparently off to see *Carousel* together. I suspect Mark had mainly gone to London to make sure the new boyfriend, Kevin, is totally acceptable."

"I'm sorry about saying anything to them, but Janet rang, and was curious, and . . ."

"That's perfectly all right. Janet I love and can cope with. I did object, though, to being given good advice by Mark. How did we manage to produce a son with such a plummy voice and such a smug manner?"

"He *has* blotted his copybook! You sound very out of love with him."

"Of *course* I love him. . . . Oh dear, I sound like so many parents I've heard saying *of course* they love their children but they don't actually *like* them very much. Do you think it's possible to love someone without liking them?"

"I'm sure it is. A lot of married couples feel that way about their partners."

"It sounds very uncomfortable. I'm glad I don't feel that way about you."

"That's a lovely thing to say. Thank you." Paul hesitated. "Mark's coming up on Friday."

"Is he? I hope you told him not to bring his washing."

"He's welcome to bring it and do it himself in our machine. . . . I rather think he wants to have a serious talk about you."

"You don't surprise me one little bit."

"Shall I tell him you're working at the problem?"

"No, tell him to get lost. . . . Oh, I am thinking about it on and off, Paul. But I won't have either of you, and especially him, acting as my spiritual physiotherapist. Prescribing spiritual exercises and suchlike."

"Have I?"

"No. But if I hadn't taken a strong line from the beginning you might have."

She finished her phone call as she saw Stanko wandering down the street. She left the phone booth, smiled at him, and together they walked back to the guesthouse.

"I walk about a bit at night," Stanko told her. "Is nice—quiet and nice fresh air. You been phoning someone?"

"My husband. I've been off-loading my irritation at my son. Children—who'd have them?" She saw his face and immediately began apologising. "Oh Stanko—I *am* sorry. How thoughtless of me. I wouldn't for the world . . ."

"Don't you worry, Meesa Rosemary. Don't you think about it again. You have a nice day today?"

And they went upstairs talking naturally and normally, as if, Rosemary thought afterwards, they had known each other for years.

CHAPTER THREE

People Talking

In the next few days Rosemary settled into a comfortable routine, varied by special treats. The treats included a visit to the theatre (an Ayckbourn, of course) and the first film she had seen in a cinema in years (she found she had simply lost the habit). She visited the art gallery and took some trips out of town by bus, sometimes walking back to the guesthouse.

Otherwise she read, relaxed on the beach or the cliffs, had long afternoon naps if the weather was rainy or windy, and watched some television.

She found she liked to be down in the lounge either for the twenty to six news or the six o'clock one on the BBC. This often meant exposure to Australian soaps in the minutes before. She decided that the appeal of the soaps was that everyone seemed healthy, good-looking and clean—they depicted a sort of hygienic Elysian fields. All the young people had rather nice manners too: she actually saw one ask to get up from table at the end of a meal. Did young people in Australia, she wondered, really ask to get up from table? Did they still sit down at table for meals?

She was watching for news of Bosnia. At home she tended to turn away or turn off, finding the scenes unbearably painful. Now she wanted to know where the fighting was, and who was fighting whom. This was not easy to discover from the television reports. On some days there was no item from what she still thought of as Yugoslavia at all. On others a situation was focussed on, but with hardly any background information, as if knowledge of it was assumed—or perhaps because the reporter had despaired of ever explaining the situation to viewers, or even of understanding it himself. It was like the Schleswig–Holstein dispute: everyone who could explain it was either dead or mad or had forgotten the explanation.

She asked Stanko where the camp was from which he had last heard news of his wife and child. She listened for it, but never heard it mentioned. Finally she bought a pocket atlas and asked him to point out its location to her. Then she listened for mentions of the nearest towns, but when they came they were unilluminating. Some days she bought the *Times* and the *Guardian*, but their reports were mostly about the peace talks in Geneva, and since the only people who seemed to want peace were outside Yugoslavia these seemed futile and doomed. Had the newspapers no longer got reporters where things—horrible things—were actually happening?

"Do you understand what's going on?" she asked Stanko.

"I know *who* is fighting who," he answered gloomily. "I not understand *why.*"

They got into the habit of having little talks together. Rosemary would go down late to dinner, so that by the time she was drinking her coffee she was the only one left in the dining room. Stanko would sit opposite her and together they would swap little tidbits of information about their former lives until the proprietress came in looking disapproving. Sometimes they would meet out walking. Once they found they had the television lounge to themselves in the evening after Stanko had finished work for the day, and there they had a good talk which Rosemary felt she really learnt something from. They were falling into a routine.

"I must remember I've got to go home," said Rosemary to herself.

She was reminded of this on the seventh day of her stay by a phone call. It was Sunday, and she had not gone to church, enjoying instead a breezy walk on the North Cliff. She was savouring a better-than-usual pudding when the proprietress, Mrs Blundell, came to tell her there was a phone call for her.

"Probably my husband," said Rosemary, spooning into her mouth the last of the crème brulée and getting up.

"No, it's a . . . woman," said Mrs Blundell. Rosemary knew she had been about to say the word "lady" but had been prevented from doing so by her strict standards of gentility. Rosemary suspected it would be one of Paul's more militant or more gossip-hungry parishioners.

"Rosemary Sheffield," she said cautiously.

"Rosemary, it's Florrie here. Florrie Harridance."

She needn't have given a name. The wheeze and the slow, somewhat threatening delivery identified the caller.

"Oh yes," said Rosemary neutrally. "Hello Florrie."

"Well, we've heard about your problem in the parish, and we're all very sorry," the voice laboured on. "There's a lot of sympathy for you, but there *is* something odd about a clergyman's wife who doesn't believe—there is in my book, any road."

The voice was pure Lancashire, and seemed to spin out the long O in "book" to eternity. Rosemary pictured her at her phone, with her whiskery face, her voracious expression, and her enormous bosom stretching out before her like some kind of personal continental shelf.

35

"It's certainly not an ideal situation," she said, to say something.

"It certainly is not! Coming at a time when we need a new chair for the Mothers' Union."

Oh yes, thought Rosemary. Now we're getting there.

"Is Mrs Munson really giving up this time?" she asked.

"She is. No question. The arthritis has got her so bad—crippled, she is. Tragic! Oh no, this time she's really going. And of course with you being the vice-chair . . ."

"Oh, I've never regarded myself as Mrs Munson's successor, necessarily," said Rosemary truthfully. "There's many others could do the job. I know Mrs Macauley would like it."

"Hetty Macauley!" This was not at all the name Florrie Harridance wanted to hear, as Rosemary well knew. "Hetty Macauley hasn't got the energy, she hasn't got the vision, and she hasn't got the common touch. . . ."

Well, if it's the common touch that's needed, you've got it all right, Rosemary thought. She sank gratefully into a chair thoughtfully placed near the reception desk.

"Now you know me, Rosemary: I'm North Country, and I'm blunt with it." Brutal more like, and totally insensitive to others' feelings, Rosemary thought. "I *don't* think it would be suitable for a nonbeliever to take the chairperson's job, and I don't think Hetty Macauley's the person for it either. Now this is going to look like pushing myself forward . . ." It is, Florrie, it is. ". . . but there is a body of opinion in the Mothers' Union that wants me in that job. I'd call it a sort of current of opinion. And since in the present circumstances, if rumour is correct, you couldn't take the job, not in my opinion, then I don't think I'd be doing myself justice if I didn't let my name go forward. And if you found you could support me, nobody would be happier than me. . . ."

And so it went on. Through the wheezy display of Florrie's

hcavy artillery Rosemary interjected the odd banality, and when the whole business drew towards a close she said briefly that she would think over what Florrie had said and put the phone down without giving her any further chance to draw out the process of self-aggrandisement. She reminded Rosemary of a heavily armed tank advancing into a country where there is no opposition to the invasion.

She sat on in the foyer for a while, thinking over the phone call. So Florrie knew, and was using her knowledge to further her ambitions to take over the Mothers' Union. Others would use the knowledge, doubtless, to further their aims and schemes. Fine by me, Rosemary thought. All the formal positions she held in the parish she had taken on because pressed to or because no one else wanted to take them on. She set much greater store by the more informal aspects of her life as vicar's wife—visiting, helping, cheering.

But she wasn't happy at the knowledge that her present godless state was known to Mrs Harridance. Because if it was known to her that meant it was known to the parish as a whole. The twenty-four hour news service that the BBC has for so long wanted to set up nationally had been anticipated locally by the service provided for St Saviour's and Abbingley generally by Mrs Harridance.

How had she heard? Not from Paul, that was certain. Behind his civilized, concerned facade he was embarrassed and upset by the turn of events. He didn't know how he would cope with the sort of comment that inevitably would follow news leaking out. And if not Paul, who? Rosemary's suspicion immediately fixed on her son. Either Paul had not warned Mark strongly enough or Mark had deliberately gone against parental instructions out of some obscure sense that he knew best how to bring his mother back into the Christian fold. If the latter, he very much mistook his mother's nature. She could not be tricked or badgered back into the faith. Opposition merely aroused her to greater obstinacy. She told herself sadly that children often think they understand their parents but really know nothing about them at all. Perhaps that was because the parents had a life *before* parenthood which remained submerged but waiting to come up once the more arduous duties of being father or mother were over.

Then another thought occurred to her. Florrie had referred to her loss of faith, and had implied that it was generally known. But she'd also said "if rumour is correct." In Florrie's mind rumours went from possibilities to probabilities to facts with the speed of lightning, and in this she did not greatly differ from many other men and women in Paul's congregation. Had her sudden departure from Abbingley sparked off rumours in the parish? She was in no doubt that the rumours would have to be sexual. Rumours were always sexual or financial, and since she had no connection with anything financial beyond managing the tiny bit of money she had inherited, sexual it would have to be. Who might she be thought to be having an affair with?

The only figure who sprang to her mind was Dark Satanic Mills, and as the image of his saturnine good looks, his small-town Clark Gable handsomeness, came to her mind her mouth screwed into a pout of distaste. She would hate her name to be coupled with his. She wondered whether to ring her husband, and her hand had strayed towards the telephone when she thought again. Paul was always the last to hear rumours: even the most eager bearer of ill tidings to the one most affected would be abashed by his patent decency. She'd give it a day or two: by then someone would have summoned up the courage or the effrontery.

In the event, she rang Paul the next evening, Monday night. She was just too curious to know what was being said in the parish to wait any longer. After some friendly preliminaries she said, "How did Mark's visit go?"

"Oh, fine," said her husband, a touch of constraint in his voice. "I didn't see all that much of him because he was around visiting old friends much of the time. But we did, I'm afraid, have a long talk about you. He insisted upon it."

"That boy is becoming a moral steamroller," said Rosemary, aware of an unmotherly sharpness in her voice. "Couldn't you try to dissuade him from going into the Church?"

"You only say that because you've lost your faith."

"On the contrary: it's the good of the Church I'm thinking about."

"Now you are being unfair."

"No I'm not. It's not clergymen who go off with other men's wives or who collect pornography who do the Church harm—well, it *is*, but more harm is done by pompous prigs like Mark who act as if the Church still had the central part in people's lives that it had in 1850. He thinks he's going to be an important man by going into the Church, poor silly boy. In fact the Church is hardly even marginal any more."

"Well, *I* know that."

"Of course you do. I wish you could get it across to him. . . . Paul?"

"Yes?"

"Did you make clear to Mark that this—this about me—was to be kept under his hat?"

"Ah . . . well, yes I did but . . ."

"Go on."

She could just picture him swallowing and stuttering.

"Well, I got in a bit late. And when I made it clear to him a sort of shifty look came into his eyes."

"I know it well."

"You see, he got here while I was at evensong, and he walked to the Church, and when I came out he was talking to—"

"Florrie Harridance. All right. That explains how she knew. I gather it's all over the parish by now. I rather got the impression there might be other rumours as well."

"If so I haven't heard them. What kind of rumours?"

"Don't know. Maybe that I'm having a mad, passionate affair. Whether this is seen as a reason for or a consequence of my loss of faith I don't know."

"I think you're imagining things. Anyway, you can't blame Mark for *those* rumours."

"He's a blabbermouth. I don't know why he thinks his mother's spiritual state should be the concern of the whole parish."

"Well you *are* a clergyman's wife."

"Don't I know it!"

There was a brief pause.

"Nothing's er . . . ?"

"Happened? No pretty pink cloud of faith has descended? No, Paul, I'm afraid it hasn't. I think that's something we're going to have to live with."

She was being uncharacteristically brutal, and she heard Paul sigh at the other end.

After the phone call she did something unlike her. She left Cliff View, found an off-licence and bought herself a chilled bottle of white wine. She felt oddly embarrassed about it and was glad it was well disguised in an anonymous plastic bag. The phrase "secret drinker" kept coming into her mind. It was still early evening and, once in her room, she poured herself a glass, sat thinking, then sipping, reading a little, and thinking again. Soon after nine she finished *A Tale of Two Cities* and slipped down to the TV lounge to get a replacement. There were three old people in a comatose state watching a sitcom. Wasn't it fun in the old days when we actually *laughed* at the comedy programmes on television, Rosemary thought? There wasn't much joy in the shelf of classics either, but she selected *The Prisoner of Zenda* and took *Adam Bede* just in case the Hope book, which she had never read, proved too awful.

Outside, going up the stairs, she found Stanko, out of his white jacket and black trousers, in the sad and shoddy civvies he wore in the evening. She caught him up.

"Tired?"

"A little. A little bit sad."

"Do you feel like a quick drink? I went out and bought a bottle and I couldn't possibly drink it all."

He smiled the little-boy smile which was his off-duty one and nodded, but put a finger to his lips. At her door he said, "Goodnight, then, Meesa Sheffield," and went to his obscure staircase. Then he came back, treading only on the floorboards he knew did not creak. Rosemary shut the door behind them, not sure whether she felt schoolgirlish or immoral.

"Not approved of?" she asked, fetching a second tooth-mug and speaking quietly.

"I think it would not be," said Stanko carefully. "Is no need to speak quiet. The next rooms is empty."

"You mustn't think I sit here drinking every evening," said Rosemary, pouring. Stanko shrugged. "Well, whether it matters or not, I *don't*. But I felt like it tonight."

"You have problems?"

"No. Well—nothing important like your problems. I just wanted to think something through."

"And you have?"

"I've thought *about* it. I don't think I've thought it through. It's just a little difficulty, really."

"With your husband to do?"

"With Paul? Oh no. Well, not as you mean it. More to do with his job."

"You told me he was a—a priest. What is your word?"

"Clergyman. Priest sounds too grand, though we do use it in the North."

"So what is your husband's problem?"

"Me. I suddenly . . . lost my faith. Or suddenly realised I didn't have it any more. I really can't describe how or why it happened. But I find I don't believe in God any more."

Stanko leaned forward, his liquid eyes warm and concerned. He looked like a spaniel who has realised his master is in pain.

"Is very sad."

Rosemary hedged.

"Would you be sad if you lost your faith?"

"Of course," he said, surprised. "Is what I . . . *hold*. What I—I have not the word—"

"What you cling to?"

"Yes. Cling to. I lose everything, all I own, all the peoples I love. Is what I cling to."

"Yes, I suppose it would be." In her new mood Rosemary found his words sad and pathetic, where before she would have been moved and admiring. "I hope you will always have it."

"But you do not feel sad?"

She decided to be honest.

"Not at all, I'm afraid," she said briskly. "I sometimes tell myself I will be when my loss sinks in, but so far I haven't felt sad in the least."

"But what is your husband's problem? He has not lost his faith?"

"Oh no. It's not catching. But there will be problems—with his parishioners, and so on."

"What is that word par—?"

"Parishioners. The people who go to his church."

"Why don't he tell them to mind their own businesses?"

"Good question. I wish he would. But Paul's not like that."

"So what will you do?"

"Go home and face them, I suppose."

"You could pretend."

"I could. On anything else I might, but the thought of pretending to be a Christian rather shocks me. Anyway, from what I hear, my dark secret is out."

"I will miss you when you go."

"I shall miss you, Stanko. I wish you had had news from your family while I was here."

"Sometimes I wish . . . "

"Yes?"

"I wish I had *any* news. Even bad." He looked at her to see how she was reacting. "You understand? That it is almost better to know something terrible has happened than to be . . . like this. Uncertain. Knowing nothing."

Rosemary nodded.

"I understand. My mother said she felt like that during the war, when my father was fighting in North Africa."

"I seem to be living in a dream here," said Stanko, his eyes miles away. "No reality. My wife and little girl they are at war. And I? I serve at table." He stood up. "I go now. You very kind to listen to me. I never met so kind person."

Rosemary had stood up too, worried by his face, which seemed about to crumple. Perhaps to hide it he took her hand and raised it to his lips. She had never had her hand kissed in that Continental way before and hadn't expected Stanko to do it, but as he dropped it she realised that his face was indeed crumpling into tears, and the next thing she knew he was sobbing into her shoulder—long, anguished, racking sobs, and she could only put her arms round his thin shoulders, murmur words of comfort and encouragement, say she understood, that it was very natural, and all the banalities with which one tries to soothe terrible grief. It occurred to her that she had been in such a situation only with children before. She also wondered where it might end.

It ended with his taking out a grubby handkerchief and dabbing at his eyes.

"You very kind," he said. "I go now."

He was looking straight into her eyes. Rosemary nodded.

"I would like to hear if you get news of your family. I'll give you my address."

"Is not necessary. Is in the book."

"Of course."

"Thank you again. Thank you for so much kindness."

He was at the door now. He looked as if he was going to burst into tears again. Rosemary said firmly, "Good night, Stanko," and he wrenched open the bedroom door and fled out into the corridor. Rosemary heard him running up the stairs to his attic room, but she also heard steps on the main staircase from the ground floor that passed her bedroom and finally went into another room further down the corridor.

She poured herself another large glass of wine and sat in the armchair, thinking hard. This time she thought things through, and came to the conclusion that it was time for her to go home.

CHAPTER FOUR

Homecoming

Rosemary fixed her return home for Wednesday. By then she would have been away for ten days, and if anything was going to "happen" (about her loss of faith, of course, not in her relationship with Stanko) it would surely have done so by then. All that had happened, in fact, was that she had shaken down into her agnosticism: it had become more comfortable, like new clothes after a few wearings. The holiday in Scarborough to find herself had in reality been no more than a pleasant break away from home. Now it was time to return to normality.

Things with Stanko had gone no further. He had seemed a little embarrassed by his breakdown in her room, and at breakfast the next day they only exchanged conventional greetings. Rosemary had an uncomfortable feeling, though, that some eyes in the room were fixed on them. At dinner on Tuesday he had dropped a small, square snapshot on to the table, something that looked like a passport photograph. It was a pretty, dark-haired young woman.

"Is my wife," he said.

"She looks very nice," said Rosemary, thinking how staid and middle-class she sounded. But it was quite true: she did look nice. Where was she now, and what had the war done to her?

On Wednesday Rosemary felt no need to hurry home. Paul would be at a Rotarians' dinner that evening, so there was no chance of eating together. She decided to have a last long walk on the beach and then lunch at Cliff View. This was a mistake. When Stanko came to offer her a choice of braised lamb and cod and chips he bent down and hissed in her ear, "Both is offle." She chose the awful cod and chips and settled down to read about the last years of the various Sitwells: eccentricity ripening into sheer awfulness. When, at the end of an extremely boring culinary experience, Stanko brought her coffee he said, "You forgive me for Sunday night?"

"Stanko, there's nothing to forgive."

"Is very not English."

"Sometimes being un-English is a very good thing to be."

"Un-English. Is good word. I learn."

But she felt very English when, as she left, she shook his hand and said, "Keep in touch."

He looked bewildered for a moment, as if her words had something to do with touching her. Then he understood and beamed. "Oh yes, I keep in touch," he said. As she settled her bill she heard him whistling around the kitchen.

She carried her own case again as she walked back to the station, taking a last look at the shops that sold the sort of clothes she wore—she, the wife of a Church of England vicar in a reasonably well-to-do parish, wearing the uniform of her order. The thought still depressed her a little. The train was fairly empty for the first stretch of the way home, but at York she had to change trains, and as she was walking over the bridge she saw ahead of her the figure of one of her husband's parishioners, Selena Meadowes. Rosemary slowed down and looked around her airily, as if seeing the beauties of York station for the first time. But as ill luck would have it, just as Selena was about to board the train she looked around at the station clock and in the process she spotted Rosemary.

"Oh, super!" she said, waving energetically. "Someone to share the journey with."

Without a hint of a query to *her*, Rosemary thought resentfully, as to whether she wanted her journey shared. But then, clergymen and their wives were generally regarded as always on tap, and not to have needs and preferences of their own.

"Hello Selena," she said in neutral tones. "I wondered if I would see anyone I knew."

Selena breezed ahead, her smile cleaving a way through the bustle of travellers till she found a good double seat facing forward. She was her usual bright, spick-and-span self, all her clothes brightly patterned and sparklingly clean, as if she were dressed for a soap powder ad, and in her usual nice-young-mum style that made the heart sink. She always reminded Rosemary of the heroines in fifties musicals, and she imagined her as anxiously awaiting the return of the dirndl skirt.

"Here we are," she said in her bright soubrette voice. "Golly, you *do* look well, Rosemary. Blooming. Your break away has really done you good."

Probing, thought Rosemary. In fact she was aware that she was being watched very closely.

"Thanks," she said noncommittally.

"So what did you do?"

"Oh, the sort of thing one does at seaside places out of season: walked, read, took in a play. It was an old Ayckbourn—quite funny."

Selena looked as if she was not after drama criticism.

"Well, whatever it is it's certainly agreed with you, I can see that. Did you, er . . ." Here we go, thought Rosemary. "Did you come back any happier?"

"I wasn't suffering from depression, Selena."

Selena looked the tiniest bit embarrassed.

"Oh, I know, but people were saying—Mrs Harridance was saying—"

"Mrs Harridance says a great deal, as you know, and very little of it is to the purpose."

"Oh Rosemary, she means well."

Rosemary raised her eyebrows skeptically.

"When people say that about anyone they usually mean that they blunder about bringing disaster in their wake with the best possible intentions but not an ounce of common sense. I don't see Mrs Harridance like that at all. Florrie Harridance has one thought and one thought only: herself."

Now Selena Meadowes looked shocked. Rosemary had violated a code. One did not make out-and-out condemnations of people if one was a clergyman's wife.

"Rosemary! How unkind of you. You'd never have been so uncharitable . . . before."

"Wouldn't I? I'd have thought it even if I didn't say it, which comes to much the same thing. You were saying that Mrs Harridance said—"

"Well . . . that you were having . . . *problems.* Spiritual problems."

"You could call it that. I lost my faith."

Selena looked terribly concerned, as if she had said that her puppy had disappeared.

"And the break away didn't . . . change anything?"

"No. I never really thought it would. What is that saying about travellers changing the sky above them but not themselves? I don't see why anyone should expect to find God in Scarborough, in any case."

"You must be *awfully* unhappy," said Selena soulfully. Since she had just been trying to convey exactly the opposite, Rosemary was annoyed.

"Not at all. I'm perfectly happy."

"But your whole life was centred on your belief in God."

"Was it? I think you must have been under an illusion about me, Selena. It had become not much more than a routine. Now it's gone it's as if a blanket has been lifted from over my head. Now I can breathe properly at last."

"Oh Rosemary!"

"It's as well to speak the truth, isn't it? That is precisely how I feel."

"But what will you *do*?"

"Do? I don't see that I'm called on to do anything."

"But . . . maybe I shouldn't say anything."

"Do. I'm quite unshockable."

"Mrs Harridance feels you shouldn't play any part in parish affairs as long as you're an unbeliever."

Rosemary smiled grimly. "Back to Victorian values, eh? Ostracise the unbeliever. Well, that will give me a lot of spare time, which will be very welcome. I wonder what I should do with it? Take up macramé, perhaps, or study for an Open University degree. I wonder what Mrs Harridance would advise."

"I'm not saying everyone agrees with her, of course."

"I should hope not," said Rosemary, in tones that were becoming positively grim. "I should be sorry to think that the spirit of Mrs Harridance had infected the whole parish."

"You *are* unfair to her, Rosemary."

"Could we talk about something else, Selena? I'll have quite enough talk about this when I get home to Paul."

"Oh, I am sorry!" Selena's face was quite guileless, which showed what faces could do. "I thought you'd *want* to talk about it. I know I would."

"Well, I don't. And please tell anyone who asks that I don't. Has anything else happened while I've been away?"

"I don't think so, Rosemary. Stephen Mills has agreed to talk to the Mothers' Union on 'Business Ethics and the Christian Religion.' "

"What would he know about either?"

"Rosemary! You *are* changed."

Rosemary kept up her brisk, unkindly tone, which she found very palate-cleansing.

"Now don't pretend you don't know there are lots of people in the parish who are extremely suspicious about Mr Mills."

"Well, I think they're very unfair. You shouldn't be suspicious unless you've got good, concrete reasons. . . . And he's so dishy!"

"Do you think so?"

"Well, you can't deny *that*. Film-star looks. When he looks me straight in the eye I go positively weak at the knees."

"I have a physical reaction, certainly, but not that one."

"Don't tell anyone, will you?" Selena was not listening to anything said to her and gave a tiny giggle. "Me, a happily married woman!"

"Your secret is safe with me. I'm just glad you're not one of those whose knees go to jelly at the sight of Paul. I don't know what it is about a clergyman that *gets* to some women."

"Your husband is *awfully* attractive for his age."

"I'll tell him you said so. He'll be terribly grateful. Now I think about it, maybe you'd better keep quiet about some of the things I've said today. I don't want to cause him more trouble than he'll have from me anyway."

"Of course, Rosemary! Silent as the grave."

On the way home on the bus Rosemary wondered why she had bothered attempting to ensure Selena's silence. She belonged to the Florrie Harridance Broadcasting Corporation, and everything Rosemary had said would be round the parish by the next day. By the time she had settled herself comfortably in at home, deciding that it really *was* nice to be back among familiar things again, she was starting to ask herself why she had said anything to Selena Meadowes at all. She knew what she was like, she had no liking for her, yet she had blabbed to her as if she was discretion itself. Had she got some kind of parochial death wish? Did she see her work with Paul in Abbingley as at an end? If so, Paul ought to have been the first to be told. And when she really got down to hard thinking, she was not at all sure that this was what she wanted.

Paul was in and out quickly at six, kissing her warmly and saying it was wonderful to have her home, then changing into black tie and decrepit dinner jacket and going out looking infinitely seedier than he would have in a lounge suit or clericals. Rosemary listened to a Nielsen symphony, watched the ten o'clock news with her usual hunger for reports from Yugoslavia, and waited for his return. When she heard the car pull into the garage it was clear he had someone with him.

"It's just Stephen," Paul called as he came through the front door. "Come to get the Rotary Club books."

He bustled in and went to his study and over to the bookcase, where the account books had been piled in readiness. Dark Satanic Mills came in to the hall and stood in the living room doorway with his usual smooth confidence.

"Hello Rosemary," he said. "Welcome back."

He did look handsome, Rosemary thought, against the half-light from the hall. In fact, he stood there posing as handsome, exuding the confidence of handsomeness, *broadcasting* his handsomeness. He was not tall, in fact he was almost stocky, but he had shiny black hair, each strand immaculately in place, and perfect features set in a sallow skin. Women notice me, his bearing announced. And if they have anything I want, I notice them.

"Hello Stephen," Rosemary said.

"Here they all are," said Paul, coming through and handing over a small pile of heavy books. "I couldn't be happier about handing them over. You'll make a much better job of it than I could ever do."

"Nonsense, you've done a wonderful job," said Stephen Mills, hardly bothering to put conviction in his voice. "Now, I'll make myself scarce. You two will have a lot to talk about, and I'll only be intruding if I stay for coffee."

Which you have not been offered, Rosemary thought, and your mentioning it is your way of drawing attention to the omission. When Paul came in from showing him out she said:

"The church mouse handing over to the church rat."

"The Rotary Club has nothing to do with the Church," said Paul pedantically. "I will admit that Stephen would not have been my first choice as treasurer, but h—"

"But he offered. Of course he did."

"Don't make too much of it. I don't think for a moment he'll do anything improper."

"Nor do I. Too many shrewd financial brains among the Rotarians. But he'll milk the job for all it's worth as far as contacts and mutual favours are concerned."

"True. But enough of Dark Satanic."

"More than."

"Is it good to be home? Would you like a nightcap?"

"It's lovely! Do you mean an alcoholic one?" Paul nodded. "Is there any red wine open?"

"There is. I cooked for myself last night and compensated for the awfulness of it with a glass or two." He went to the kitchen and came back with a half-full bottle. As he was pouring her a glass he said casually, "Situation still as it was?"

"Oh yes. I don't think there's much point in talking about that, Paul, if you don't mind. It is as it is, and if it changes it does, but it won't be through anything we've done. . . . I met Selena Meadowes on the train from York."

"Brightly sparkling as ever?"

"At least."

"Did she say something that worried you?"

"Isn't marriage dreadful?" said Rosemary, sipping her wine. "Each partner is the nearest thing to a thought policeman there is. . . . Not worried, exactly, but she did make me think. Apparently Florrie Harridance is spreading it around that since I'm now an unbeliever I shouldn't play any part in parish affairs or any of the groups and activities."

"I'm sure Selena has got it wrong."

"I don't think so."

"Florrie's a very silly woman if she's saying that kind of thing. People don't take kindly to witch hunts these days."

Rosemary thought that over seriously.

"*Most* people. . . . And actually I'm not even sure that that is true. Witch hunts are what the tabloid press is based on."

"St Saviour's isn't a tabloid parish."

"Don't you believe it! The *Sunday Times* delivered, and the *People* bought surreptitiously while walking the dog. Anyway, the *Sunday Times* is just a tabloid for the upper-middle classes."

"Would it worry you, taking a back seat?"

"I think what she wants is to push me out of the car. No, not at all. Or not much. I'd been thinking anyway about what I might do, and I was coming to the conclusion that the Open University was made for people like me, whose children have left home. But something in me really dislikes being pushed."

"Good for you."

"And I don't like the thought of the spirit of Florrie Harridance taking over the parish either."

"Don't make a bogey-woman of her, Rosemary."

"I don't need to. She's done that herself."

Paul swerved from the subject.

"So you'll fight. I think that's excellent. You'll try and stay on as vice-chair of the Mothers' Union."

"It's not just offices like that. I'm not mad about the Mothers' Union. They always remind me of a line in a song we used to sing at school: 'They laugh, and are glad, and are *terrible.*' But I am going to resist her, generally. I am going to try to get across what a mean, restrictive, vengeful sort of attitude hers is. Not to say self-promotional."

"Good for you."

"I'm not sure *how* I'm going to fight her. It will be difficult to oppose her without saying precisely what I think of her, which would make things difficult for you."

"Turning the other cheek is excellent advice, you know."

Rosemary smiled at him. He didn't give up.

"You'd have to say that," she said.

"No, I mean it. If you prefer to put it in worldly terms, it's a wonderful *ploy.* It puts the other person so wonderfully in the wrong and gets sympathy immediately on to your side."

"How Machiavellian of you, Paul. I've never thought of you as that before. You may be right, but turning the other cheek is not something Christians often do, is it? I've never seen such a belli-cose lot, in general, or such dirty fighters."

"It's not unusual, is it, for people not to live up to their reli-gion? It happens in all of the faiths. Christians haven't realised yet that returning good for evil, as well as being right, is an extremely clever move. If you stay meek and mild while Florrie

54

Harridance gets more and more dogmatic and extreme, you'll soon have everyone on your side."

"It's a thought," said Rosemary. "I'll consider it."

But she didn't tell Paul that, if turning the other cheek was to be her strategy, she had made a very bad start on the train that day.

CHAPTER FIVE

The Other Cheek

Rosemary had always seen it as her job as vicar's wife to provide a practical backup to her husband's ministry. Paul went round to see the sick and the dying, providing them with spiritual comfort and a shoulder to cry on. Rosemary dropped in on the same people to make sure they had home helps, meals on wheels and plenty of reading matter. The young mothers mostly ran their own groups in the church hall or the vestry, but Rosemary went along to them now and then and was always in the background willing to give advice when problems arose. They seldom did, because the young mothers were too busy for the rumour-mongering and backbiting that the older members of the congregation went in for. Thus, her role was practical, and she tried to avoid involvement with any of the parish groups or diocesan bodies. Those were the sorts of activity she found boring and shouldered with reluctance.

Nevertheless she was vice-chair of the local Mothers' Union branch, and she was on the various committees that arranged such parish events as the harvest festival, fêtes and bring-and-buy sales. They were positions she would have relinquished very readily if it had not been Florrie Harridance who was trying to shoulder her off. She kept in the forefront of her mind a mental picture of Florrie, with her bustle, her bulk and her endless steam-kettle monologue, as she went about her business as Paul's pastoral adjunct.

She called next morning on Violet Gumbold, a Mothers' Union stalwart, though her children, like Rosemary's, were grown up and had moved away. Mrs Gumbold had broken her leg on the day Rosemary went to Scarborough, and as her husband was a commercial traveller and away much of the time, she needed all the help from the parish that she could get.

Rosemary took away a list of shopping basics Violet needed and three library books to change, repressing the feeling that Stephen King and Robert B. Parker were not the sickbed reading she would have chosen. When she came back Violet Gumbold had hobbled round to make tea and biscuits. Together they sat down comfortably over them.

"Did you enjoy Scarborough?" Rosemary was asked.

"Yes, I did. Lots of fresh, clean air and good walks."

"They say you're going through a sort of . . . crisis."

"You could say that. Do you mind if we don't talk about it, Violet? I seem to have done nothing but talk it over with Paul and others in the family."

"I'm sorry, Rosemary. I should have thought. Will this make any . . . any difference?"

"I really don't know. If people want me to *withdraw*, then there are plenty of things I could do."

"Oh no, Rosemary, nobody wants *that*." Rosemary waited for her to say what they did want, and Violet began to flounder and go rather red. "You do the parish work so wonderfully well we couldn't possibly manage without you. We'd all be at sea. . . . Mrs Harridance came round the other day."

"That was nice of her, to come and help," said Rosemary, meekly and maliciously.

"She didn't actually h——. Well, but while she was here she said she thought, since you had lost your faith, maybe you shouldn't stay on as vice-chair in the Mothers' Union, and the way she put it it did seem . . ."

Mrs Gumbold's attitude appeared to be akin to saying it was all right for her to muck out the stables so long as she didn't try to ride the horses. She was not the strongest brain in the parish, though Rosemary had always found her well-meaning. She just said, "I'll leave that entirely up to the members. I wouldn't dream of staying on if that wasn't what they wanted."

Mrs Gumbold looked relieved, as if she had in some way done her duty, or done what she had been told.

"Oh well—that's all right then. I'm sure . . . Mrs Harridance was talking about the chairmanship as well."

"Of the Mothers' Union? Yes, she rang me about that."

"I believe Mrs Munson is adamant that this time she *will* go."

"She's done a wonderful job over the years. I'm sure everyone will understand."

"And if it goes by hard work then Mrs Harridance has worked like a Trojan too, and you could say . . ."

She faded into silence and looked at Rosemary. Once again Rosemary had the sense that she had said what she had been told to say. She also had the feeling that Violet Gumbold didn't actually like Mrs Harridance any more than she did.

"We're so lucky in the Mothers' Union, aren't we?" Rosemary said brightly, feeling herself an awful hypocrite. "There's so many who are willing to work hard for us. There's Mrs Macauley, and there's Mrs Bannerman, who can never do enough, and—"

"Oh, do you think Mrs Bannerman could be the chairwoman of the Mothers' Union? That would be nice—she's such a pleasant person, and very efficient." Mrs Gumbold frowned, uncertainly. "But she's not an educated woman."

"I don't see what that's got to do with it," Rosemary said briskly. "What we need is someone hard-working and capable, and she certainly is that. So is Mrs Harridance, of *course*, but she's hardly an educated person either."

"No. . . . Do have another biscuit, Rosemary."

That conversation was the first of several Rosemary was to have over the next few days. She never brought up the subject of her loss of faith or her position in the parish, but when it came up she always expressed herself quite happy to abide by the views of the majority. She suspected that her apparent determination not to put up a fight meant that many resolved to put up a fight for her. She became quite certain Mrs Harridance wanted her off the committee because she knew her opinion of her. She accordingly never wavered from her expressed belief that Mrs Harridance would make an *excellent* chairwoman, and that they were lucky to have so many hard workers who would all do a splendid job if they were to think of putting up for the chairwoman's position.

"I do think a real election is often a good idea," said Mrs Munson, the retiring chair. "Rather than its just going to someone by default."

"It does clear the air," Rosemary agreed.

Such conversations were always conducted with the utmost meekness (which was a bit of a strain). They did seem to Rosemary after a time to be bearing fruit. Her antennae were keenly attuned to the niceties of parish opinion, she having been among these people for the last twelve years, and when she saw people talking together in muted tones she could tell from their stance and the way they looked at her whether they were on her side or against her. She rather thought that by and large they were on her side. It occurred to her that Mrs Harridance, for all her appearance of steamrolling forward and never hearing a word anyone else said, also had antennae that were at least sensitive enough to get the same message. If they were, she suspected that she might be getting a social call from her.

It came when she had been home a little more than a week. She saw Florrie approaching from the direction of the park, her ample figure wrapped in a bright blue coat, with a large, flowery hat covering her tight curls. Her somewhat protuberant eyes had the glint of purpose in them, but then they always did. Florrie had something of the purposive air of an outsize rodent.

Rosemary did not rush down to let her in, but waited till she heard the doorbell, then walked down to her visitor in a leisurely fashion.

"Rosemary, you do look well."

"Thank you, Florrie."

"People have been saying you did, but we don't run into each other like we used to, with you not coming to church."

"No, we don't," said Rosemary neutrally.

"It's a pity, that. Means you're bound to be a bit out of touch."

She had taken off her hat and come through to the living room, where she sat down determinedly on the sofa. Rosemary did not offer her coffee or tea because Florrie always refused them (they interfered with her monologues). Rosemary sat opposite her in the big armchair, wondering which cheek was the other one that she ought to turn.

"Because naturally we've all been thinking about you and your position, Rosemary—in a Christian spirit, of course . . ." She stared at Rosemary, as if daring her to object, or to laugh. "Because of course we all hope you'll be back with us *fully* before long, I mean in *spirit* as well, but really what we do feel is that the Mothers' Union is a *church* group, a *Christian* group. So we understand your still wanting to be part of it, but on the other hand . . ."

Rosemary sat back and let it roll over her. It wasn't pleasant, but these days one's ear was used to unrelenting noise: one had only to go into the centre of Leeds to be assaulted by sounds of diggers, demolition trucks, high-speed drills and chain saws, and every pub she knew had music in various degrees of loudness in the background. Florrie in a small room produced much the same effect as the drills and the chain saws. Sometimes Rosemary made an effort to check her flow, but on this occasion she knew that eventually Florrie was going to have to get to a question that demanded from her an answer. After ten minutes or so it came.

"Now, what I'm sure would be best, Rosemary dear, would be if you resigned now as vice-chair, just went quietly. Everyone will understand, and there certainly won't be any criticism, and that way there won't be any nastiness, and I'm sure that for Paul's sake—who we all respect so much—that's what you'd want to avoid."

Rosemary wanted to object that bringing Paul into it like that was fighting dirty, but she kept the other cheek resolutely turned. The monologue went on a bit longer, but eventually Florrie had to draw to a close and look interrogatively at Rosemary.

"I'm just going to leave it to the members," she said.

There was a silence of several seconds. Florrie glared, then smiled forgivingly.

"I don't think you've been following, Rosemary dear. What we felt was there'll be so much less nastiness if you—"

"There's been no nastiness, Florrie. You've all been very nice about it. So there'll be no need for any in the future. I'll just go to the next full meeting, tell them the problem (though of course everyone knows by now) and then leave the meeting and they can take the decision."

"Oh Rosemary dear that is *awfully* unwise. Because if you were quietly to resign now saying it's because after all it is a *church* organisation and you'd feel out of place *now*, you wouldn't get the same feeling of rejection as you will if—"

"I'm sorry, Florrie. I won't feel rejected at all. I've made up my mind. I'm afraid I have to go now. I've said I'd go and do some shopping for Mrs Gumbold. I believe you've been helping her since she's been laid up. She told me about your visit. So kind. She needs everyone rallying around now . . ."

And she ushered her to the front door, through it and out to the gate, leaving her time for only a few parting shots.

"I *wish* you would think again Rosemary, because we've all got your interests at heart and—"

Rosemary was just turning to go in again when she realised that a BMW had pulled up in the road opposite, on the park side, its windows down. Dark Satanic Mills got out and lounged over the road, a smile playing on the corners of his lips.

"Good for you, Rosemary. I like a woman who fights."

He didn't say it sexily, but somehow there was sex in the background.

"Good morning, Stephen. What can I do for you?"

He left a pause, to suggest that there was a variety of things he could think of. That was the trouble with overtly sexy people: almost anything one said seemed capable of a second meaning when one talked with them.

"I think Paul has missed out on one of the account books for the Rotarians," he said easily. "Not important, but I need it to get the whole picture. I should think it will be in his study. Any chance of my coming in to have a look for it?"

Rosemary led the way in, and then watched him as he rummaged around for it. As she was watching she considered her reactions to him. Of course the "Satanic" epithet was absurd. No one imagined him indulging in devil-worshipping rituals with children, or dipping his hands into disembowelled animals or birds. Still, the word somehow did seem to fit him: there hovered over him the *possibility* of evil. In fact, Rosemary could imagine all sorts of nastinesses, shading off into outright evil, and could fit them in with his character. And yet, as Paul said, he had been a regular churchgoer in the parish for well over a decade now.

Why did he come? There was not the slightest suspicion of anything spiritual about him. Yet on consideration Rosemary would have had to admit that the same was true of quite a number of the St Saviour's regulars. Yet about Dark Satanic Mills there hung an air of earthiness, greed, sensuality and a total lack of scruple, and *that* was not something that could be said of the other less-than-spiritual communicants. He's not at all *churchy*, she said to herself. He's amoral, outside any code of ethics, totally self-absorbed. Perhaps in the nineteenth century such a man would go along to church to establish some kind of credentials, leading enthusiastically a second life of sin and corruption. But at the latter end of the twentieth century? Today nobody could be *bothered* with that sort of hypocrisy. So why was Mills?

"There it is," said Stephen Mills, making a quick dart and taking a heavy ledger from among books of theology and paperbacks of popular devotion. "What an odd shelving system your husband has."

"It's all his own," agreed Rosemary, waiting for him to go. He stood there, clutching the book to his chest, smiling at her— *knowing* she was wanting him gone.

"So what are the old biddies on about?" he asked.

Rosemary played for time, unwilling to discuss her personal position with him.

"Mrs Harridance wouldn't thank you for calling her an old biddy. She's a woman in the prime of life."

"You haven't answered my question."

"I don't think I need to, Stephen. You always have your finger on the pulse of the parish."

He smiled, almost purred, in self-satisfaction.

"So it's your sudden godlessness, is it? I guessed as much. What do they want? For you to parade down the Ilkley Road in penitential sackcloth?"

"They want—Mrs Harridance wants—me to give up any parish positions I hold."

"And you?"

"I'm just leaving it up to the members."

"Isn't that good enough for her?"

"No. Because she's afraid they'll support me. She wants me to resign quietly so there's no contest."

"Why?"

"Because she wants to be chairwoman of the Mothers' Union, and she wants one of her cronies as deputy, not someone who knows her for what she is—on the make."

She regretted saying that as soon as it was out of her mouth. What *was* it about Dark Satanic Mills, that he could screw things out of you even as you felt distrustful and repelled? And what else was Mills himself but on the make?

"What is there in these jobs?" asked Mills, seemingly genuinely curious. "What's in it for them?"

"Nothing in your sense," said Rosemary. "Nothing in the way of money or contacts or suchlike. But position, prestige, something to bustle about, be self-important about."

Mills had nodded when she talked about money and contacts, the little smile playing around his lips as she showed him how she viewed him—which was probably why he had asked the question in that form in the first place. As usual, he'd got what he wanted. Now he started for the door.

"Very odd, that's what I say. Well, I must be on my way. Tell

Paul I've collected this, will you, Rosemary? And—" he put his
face close to hers—"go on fighting back. Show them what you're
made of."

But over the next week Rosemary found very little call for
fighting or for showing what she was made of. If anybody brought
up the matter of her loss of faith she repeated the formula of
"leaving it up to the members" of any organisation she was
involved with to decide whether it made any difference. But very
few people brought it up. It was increasingly accepted: it had
happened, it was nobody's fault, and Rosemary was just the same
person she had always been. It had been a nine days' wonder, and
the nine days were over. Rosemary could imagine that when she
brought the matter before the Mothers' Union committee the
members' main reaction would be to wonder why she had raised
it at all.

She was told by a friend that Florrie Harridance had tried to get
a local *Yorkshire Post* reporter interested in the matter as a news
story. But in the reporter's view it had not had the human interest
to compete with the declining fortunes of Leeds United or the
total hopelessness of the Yorkshire cricket team. It lacked sex,
passion or fanaticism, and news stories involving clergy and their
families had to have at least one of those. The reporter had
shaken his head and gone on his way.

Rosemary went about her parish work as usual, but she no
longer went to church on a Sunday. This meant that she saw
much less of Florrie Harridance and her cronies. She did bump
into Selena Meadowes one day in the library, and they fell into
their usual topic of conversation, the needs of several elderly
members of the congregation. For once, though, Selena gave the
conversation a personal twist.

"You can't tell me anything about the decline of the elderly,"
she said, still in her bright tone which seemed so inappropriate.

"My poor old Mum seems to have less and less interest in life every time I see her or call her."

"I didn't know you had elderly parents, Selena."

"One, just the one: my mother."

"You must have been a late child."

"I was. What can you do, Rosemary, if they just seem not to want to go on living any more?"

"I don't know. My mother's still very lively. Isn't she interested in the grandchildren?"

"Not very. Oh—I'm being unfair. She likes to *see* them, but then quite soon she's had enough and wishes they'd go away. I wonder whether I shouldn't try a change of scene for her."

"Where does she live?"

"Near Skipton. She used to go to Morecambe for her holidays when my father was alive, but she says she wouldn't want to go back, with all the changes, and from what I hear it's a depressing place now. I wondered whether to try to get her to Scarborough."

"Well, I certainly enjoyed it. But it might be less attractive for someone who's less active. All those hills."

"Where did you stay?"

"It's a place called Cliff View. On St Nicholas's Cliff, near where Anne Brontë died."

Selena Meadowes bridled a little.

"That's literary, isn't it? We're not a very literary family, I'm afraid. Is the food good—traditional, I mean? She's very conservative."

"Yes—anyhow it's perfectly decent."

"I think I might try taking her myself. Then she might stay a fortnight, if I got her really settled in, and I could go and fetch her and take her home."

They smiled and parted then, and the conversation passed from Rosemary's mind as she went about her usual duties, which did not get any less onerous. It was over a week later, when Selena Meadowes's name came up in conversation with Paul over dinner, that Rosemary said:

"I didn't realize she had an elderly mother, going towards senility."

"Really?" Paul said, looking up. "That is sad. I met her once, a year or two ago. Perfectly spry and interested in everything—I wouldn't have said she was more than sixty."

Rosemary knew, from more than one case in the parish, how sadly early Alzheimer's disease could strike. It was a horrific stalking-horse, a terror more actual to most than AIDS. She said no more, but the subject of Selena's mother—or, more particularly, Selena's motives—remained in the back of her mind.

She rang her own mother that evening, while Paul was out at a Parochial Church Council meeting. Her mother was a lively old lady living in Lincoln, very much taken up with clerical controversies and quarrels, of which there were an inordinate number in Lincoln. Rosemary had been keeping her loss of faith from her, but thinking of Selena Meadowes's mother made her decide that this was the sort of misplaced consideration that the old could do without—that it was, in fact, positively insulting. Her mother took the revelation in her stride, was almost dismissive.

"Probably your time of life," she said. "It will pass. It's probably due to your having *so much* to do with Christians. They can be very depressing, you know. How are the children?"

The question made Rosemary think how much more sensibly her mother had reacted than her son. There was a lot to be said for experience—she hoped Mark would be able to learn from it when it came to him. She was just telling her mother about her son, and trying to keep her irritation with him out of her voice, when the front doorbell rang.

"Must go, Mother. Someone at the door."

It was half past nine—late for a parishioner to visit. She put down the receiver, hurried to the door and put on the front light. Not a shape she recognised. But she had no apprehensions and opened the door. It was Stanko, an appealing, apologetic smile on his face.

"Rosemary, can you help me please? I am in much trouble."

CHAPTER SIX

Place of Safety

Rosemary drew Stanko inside and led him through to the living room. She looked at him in the better light there.

"You look tired," she said, "and hungry."

"A little," said Stanko. "I was told I must go middle morning. I went to do packing—" he gestured towards a pathetically small and ill-filled knapsack—"and then I said good-bye and went to coach station. Coach is cheaper, you see. When we get to Leeds I have great difficulty finding bus to Abbingley—everybody very kind and try to help but I go wrong."

"Well, sit down. I'll get you a hot drink, and then I'll make you an omelette or something."

Rosemary found she rather enjoyed fussing over Stanko, as he had fussed over her in the dining room at Cliff View. She lit the gas fire because the evening was getting chilly, made him a pot of coffee, then made a big mushroom omelette with a salad and opened some tins to make some kind of sweet. She was just sitting down opposite him and saying, "Now," when she heard Paul's key in the door. She smiled at Stanko encouragingly, said "Don't worry" and slipped out into the hall.

71

"We have a visitor," she said.

An unexpected visitor was not an unusual occurrence in a vicar's life. Paul nodded and waited.

"It's the waiter at the guesthouse in Scarborough—I told you about him."

"Good Lord, the Yugoslav boy? What's he doing here?"

"He says he's in trouble."

Paul nodded again, and went in and introduced himself. Rosemary felt herself blessed in having so unflappable and unsuspicious a husband. Stanko was looking less drawn and lean now, and she thought Paul was liking him already.

"Well, what's the trouble, then, Stanko?" Paul asked, when they had all sat down.

Stanko put the bowl with fruit and cream in it down on the table in front of him and sat with his hands in his lap.

"I get the sack," he said.

"Is that so terrible?" asked Paul. "Surely there must be lots of jobs in seaside places at the moment, with the summer season coming up."

Stanko nodded.

"Is true. But Mrs Blundell she say the police is getting very strict. Always before I have—what do you say?—been a jump in front of them." He gave Paul a shy, conspiratorial glance from lowered eyes. "You see, I have always heard when they have started to make enquiries—in Whitby, at Robin Hood Bay and so on—so I get out before they come. But Mrs Blundell says they are making a . . . a *drive* she calls it, in all the seaside towns, in the smaller restaurants and hotels."

Paul had not stiffened up his easy stance in his chair.

"What you're saying is you've no work permit."

"No. I got passport, but I not got work permit."

There was silence in the room for a moment. Neither Stanko

nor Rosemary was looking at Paul, but Rosemary's heart was in her mouth, wondering what he was going to say next.

"I wish we had more contacts in the hotel or restaurant trade."

Rosemary blamed herself for doubting him. Of course he would take the humane decision. He always had in the past. It could only have been a slight twinge of guilt on her part that had made her doubt he would this time.

"There's no one in the congregation that springs to mind," she said, keeping the relief out of her voice.

"It's something we'd better think about tomorrow," said Paul, who could take snap decisions when necessary but tried to avoid them. "There's no problem about a bed, is there?"

"No—Mark's is still made up from his visit while I was away. If you can put up with it tonight I can change it tomorrow, Stanko."

"No, no—you go to no trouble. Is fine."

"I think," said Paul slowly, "it will be best if you lie fairly low while you're here. A clergyman is not exactly in the public eye, but he is observed by his congregation. Someone they don't know—and an obvious foreigner, as you are—coming to see me would cause no comment, but someone coming and going and obviously living here might."

"That's true," said Rosemary, who knew all too well parish habits of mind. "What we really need to find is a job with some kind of living accommodation thrown in."

"A room, a shared room—anything!" said Stanko. "If the police catch me they send me straight back to Gorazde—anyway to Bosnia. Back to fighting and being bombed. You understand, Rosemary, I *can't* go back there. I'd rather die!"

Paul touched his arm.

"Yes, we *do* understand, both of us. We'll do what we can, but we need to think carefully first. You really do think the police in

Leeds are likely to be less active in hunting down illegal immigrants than those on the coast?"

Stanko nodded quickly. He had obviously thought about it.

"I think so. I hope so. Is in London and the seaside towns we mostly work, and in London is only in the small, not very nice hotels. I think they will not look very hard in Leeds."

"You have contacts with others?"

He nodded hesitantly.

"With a few. Is my countrymen, you understand? They speak my language."

"Of course, of course. Now—I think it's time for bed for you, my lad."

Rosemary noticed that Paul's tone had become fatherly—and fatherly as if towards quite a young child. Yet he knew Stanko was married with a child of his own. Somehow his reaction was not unlike her own to Stanko's air of well-meaning bewilderment.

In bed later on Paul said, "you know, I've been thinking, and I think the personal touch is called for here. I think we should go to Gianni's for lunch."

Rosemary frowned.

"I suppose it's the best we can do. Gianni is a dear, of course, but we can hardly pretend that we're regular customers."

"Gianni gives me a little of the respect he would give to one of his own priests," said Paul, amusement in his voice. "I don't expect him to offer the boy a job, but he could wise us up on the best avenues of approach."

"That's true. I'll give Stanko the run of the cupboards and the deep freeze for his lunch and we'll go out. It seems ages since we had lunch out together."

"You think I was right about his lying low while he's here?"

"Very much so. There are eyes watching us—cat's eyes."

"It's sad for the lad to be cooped up."

"Oh rubbish, Paul: Think what he'd be if he was in Sarajevo or Gorazde. And he knows that, poor man, only too well. . . . Oh, and thanks, Paul."

He looked at her in astonishment.

"You didn't think there was any question of my handing him over or showing him the door, I hope, Rosemary?"

"No," she said, not entirely truthfully. "But I'm just saying 'thank you' to *some*body, *some*thing, for having married me to a man who wouldn't consider doing that."

The next day they went to Gianni's late on, leaving behind a Stanko who looked much better—less hungry, more relaxed—and was anxious to be useful around the house. They suggested it was best if he didn't answer the door or the telephone. Gianni's was an unpretentious but warm and inviting trattoria off the Ilkley Road. It was moderately full with lunchtime eaters when they arrived at one fifteen, to a genial but respectful welcome from Gianni himself. By the time they had had their soup and pasta it was two o'clock, and most of the customers had disappeared back to work.

"You not like something else? Ice-cream? Zabaglione? Coffee?" Gianni enquired.

"Two coffees, please—cappuccino," said Paul. "And we would like a word with you if you have a moment." Gianni nodded, apparently pleased and flattered, and five minutes later he came back with the coffee and sat himself at their table.

"How can I 'elp? You want to come over to the Cat'olics, like a lot of your priests and politicians?"

"Not this week, maybe next," said Paul. They all chuckled. Gianni was a genuinely devout Catholic.

"Woman priests! What an atrocity!" He saw a look in Rosemary's eyes, and quickly said, "But we don't quarrel, eh?"

"I'm sure we won't," said Paul, ever the conciliator. "I'm sad about the priests, but you're welcome to the politicians. What we want is advice. We want to know—" he looked around him and lowered his voice—"how to go about finding a job in the catering or hotel trade for someone who . . . who doesn't have all the necessary paper work."

Gianni shot him a quick, suspicious glance, but seemed reassured by the clerical collar which Paul had taken care to wear. It was a useful piece of superstition and seemed to work even though Paul had his wife with him.

"Forgive me. One 'as to be careful."

"Of course. We're trying to be."

"Not that I myself—" Gianni leaned back expansively in his chair, once again the genial host—"not that I myself would need to employ such a person. A business which is doing very nicely does not need to—*capisce?*" He exuded proprietorial satisfaction. "But I tell you this: when the recession was at its worstest, I think of it, eh? I consider. Because then it was all 'cut this cost, cut that cost,' otherwise—" he brought his hand down like a guillotine on to the table.

"We thought you might know *something* about it, even though not from experience," explained Rosemary guilefully. "You're the only person in the trade we really know."

Gianni paused to say farewell to a departing party of regulars. Now they were the only people in that part of the restaurant.

"You have a person in this country, and you want to find him a job—maybe a place to stay, a room over?"

"That's right. That would be ideal."

"You not want to talk to your Mr Mills?"

"Stephen Mills?" said Rosemary sharply. "Why would we want to talk to him? Stephen doesn't have anything to do with the restaurant trade."

"No, no. But he is a good—how do you say?—organiser. He know how to get things done."

"He's a fixer," said Rosemary.

"Exactly! A feexer!"

"I would *very* much rather not bring in Stephen Mills," Rosemary said.

"Right. I understand." He looked amused and smiled slyly. "Is a man who the ladies like very much or not at all. Maybe not at all is wisest. So, you do it yourselves, eh? Now let us talk turkey, like you say. Hotels in Leeds, they are not like seaside hotels. In Leeds there is not a hundred and one little guesthouses that are very difficult to investigate. On the other 'and, little takeaway food places—"

"Pizza takeaways?"

"*Esattamente*! 'Pizza and Pasta,' 'Pizza Pronto'—that kind of thing. They are all over the place. Some is family establishments—the big family, you understand, with distant cousins brought over from Sicily to learn the trade and learn the language, though mostly they don' learn the trade and they don' learn the language. Is not suitable, such places. But other places, where there is one man, who has seen an opportunity, an opening you say, where there is perhaps an area with many many students and no takeaway—such a man with no large family behind him . . ."

"That sounds just the job," said Paul.

"Your man—he can make pizzas?"

"I'm sure he can," said Rosemary firmly.

"Is silly to ask. Anyone can make pizzas, pizzas that students will eat. They just want to be filled up, as cheap as possible because they're living on loans. Now, I give you four names, just to start with." He wrote rapidly on the back of their bill. "You try Signor Gabrielli first. Is a very nice man, good Cat'olic, but not very wealthy. Struggling a little bit, you know? He try to help if he can. Ring him up maybe eight, half past eight. When the early evening peoples is gone and the late supper peoples isn't come yet. Don' mention my name. Is delicate, you understand? Tell him you are a priest."

They left Gianni's on the whole well pleased with their work. They walked home, talking over the options, and when they arrived back at the vicarage they found that Stanko had spent the time vacuuming over the entire house. Their threadbare carpets hadn't looked so good for years.

"Just so long as he doesn't start clearing up my desk," said Paul, ruefully glancing at the chaos there.

They rang up Signor Gabrielli that evening, having been assured by Stanko—he regarded the question as almost insult-ing—that he made an excellent pizza. Paul took Gianni's advice and introduced himself as the "priest" of St Saviour's. Signor Gabrielli, amiable to start with, became positively friendly.

"Ah, you want pizzas? You want pizzas for a party?"

"Not at the moment, though it's an idea. Definitely an idea. No, it's a question of someone I'm trying to help."

"Yes?" Still friendly.

"He's not an Italian, but a Yugoslav. Bosnian, I suppose we should say. He's an excellent cook, makes a splendid pizza, and it's a question of whether you might have a job at Pizza Pronto."

There was a pause, and then a somewhat cautious response.

"I could do with some help, certainly some evenings."

"There are reasons in his case to be . . . discreet about the fact that you are employing him, if you understand."

"Ah yes," said Signor Gabrielli, his voice now low and conspir-atorial. "Now I *do* understand."

"Particularly we need to be discreet because of where he comes from. The consequences of his being sent back there would be very much more serious than if he were sent back to Italy."

"*È vero*. In Italy we are not quite yet in the civil war. Maybe soon the North fight the South, but not yet. But the police they do send back to Yugoslavia, that I know."

"So we've heard. The important thing you understand, Signor Gabrielli, is not wonderful pay, but having enough to live on, and maybe a bed to sleep in. I don't suppose . . ."

"There is a room upstairs. Is not nice, is partly storeroom, but it has a bed in it. Another boy—this is boy from Tunisia, you understand?"

"I understand."

"He has the other room. Is a nice boy, very clever with languages. So he is a companion. But perhaps I should talk to this man."

"Yes, of course. We wouldn't dream of suggesting you give him a job simply on my recommendation."

"Tomorrow evening, about this time, is possible he could come and we could talk?"

"Very possible. I shall be at a meeting, but my wife can bring him. Look, it might look best if we ordered a couple of pizzas. My wife can collect them, say at eight thirty, and Stanko can stay and talk when it's convenient for you."

"Excellent. What you like?"

"Let's say a Bologna sausage and a *quattro staggione*."

"Right. I talk to your lady tomorrow."

Paul put down the receiver rather pleased with his work. He turned to face the others.

"It sounds very promising," he said to Stanko, who had followed with great relief the progress of the conversation. "There's a room above and another member of staff living there. In the same position as you, but it will *look* perfectly natural and normal. We don't want to be inhospitable, but—"

"You have been wonderful!"

"—but well, the fact is that everything a clergyman does is observed."

"And everything his wife does," said Rosemary. "By hawklike eyes."

The next night, when Paul was out at a meeting of Leeds clergy discussing the theme of "targeting young people," Rosemary and Stanko walked to the Ilkley Road and along to Pizza Pronto. As they neared the brightly painted little takeaway, Stanko, at Rosemary's suggestion, dropped back a few paces, and entered the warm, friendly place just behind her. As Rosemary went up to the middle-aged man behind the counter with a meaningful smile on her face, Stanko ducked under the counter and went to stand casually among the hot ovens and the table with bowls of chopped sausage and chopped mushroom and large tins of peeled tomatoes.

"Mrs Sheffield," said Rosemary. "The two I ordered."

Signor Gabrielli was friendly and respectful, but in a quite nonchalant way. Rosemary paid her money and went out bearing her comfortingly hot burden. She did not notice that among the little knot of people waiting for their orders was Selena Meadowes, and she certainly did not realise that Selena had been watching their approach all the way along the Ilkley Road.

CHAPTER SEVEN

Whispering Campaign

Stanko came back to the vicarage an hour later, but only to collect his clothes and belongings.

"I don't want to go," he said. "You have been so kind, both. But is better for you. The job is fine, the room is fine. I shall be quite all right."

"But you'll keep in touch," Rosemary insisted. "If you get any news from home you'll come round or ring? I'll give you our phone number."

"Is here," said Stanko, tapping his head.

He looked so slight and pathetic standing in the doorway that Rosemary wanted to give him a hug, as she might have hugged a son going off to school for the first time. But she resisted the impulse and told herself it was absurd: Stanko was experienced in the ways of the world—more experienced in its nastier byways than she was, in all probability. For a moment his gentleness and bewilderment seemed to her something like a triumph of the human spirit.

In the next few days Rosemary went about her business in the usual way, with that significant exception that she did not go to church. The omission, now several weeks long, left a hole in her life, but she found it difficult to pin down the nature of the void: was it a spiritual one or a social one? Or was it, perhaps, simply a matter of *time*? Sometimes she tried to fill the hole by walking to church to meet Paul as the service finished. That way at least she met some of the people she had been accustomed to meet. Mostly they were very kind and relaxed, but one evening she did note Timothy Armitage, an elderly and very devout parishioner, scurrying off in an unaccustomed direction, and she wondered whether he was trying to avoid her. Again, Mrs Mulholland, a middle-aged battle-axe, walked past her stony-faced one evening, but that was the sort of thing she did after the most trivial of slights: an omission to thank her for some small service, forgetting to enquire after her health when she'd been ill. Rosemary did not give it a second thought.

One evening, when Stanko had been gone nearly a week, after she'd been to tea with a housebound young mother, she turned aside from her shortest route home and went to see him in Pizza Pronto. Signor Gabrielli greeted her with a smile and took her hands in his.

"The boy makes a very nice pizza. He's very handy. You want to talk to him? I take over a bit."

And he went to where Stanko was juggling with little bits of this and that, scattering them blithely on to the dough base and laying shreds of ivory-coloured mozzarella on top. Stanko looked up, saw Rosemary, and came over, his face suffused with smiles. He had the gift of making people feel special.

"Rosemary! You are very kind."

"I wanted to see you. They said on the news there'd been an outbreak of fighting near Petrinje."

"Yes, I hear."

"You've had no news from your wife?"

"Nothing. I have a letter from my mother, but she hear nothing either."

"Is your mother in that area?"

"No. She is now in Zagreb. Is in safety."

"But she's no way of contacting your wife?"

"None." He looked up at her, with pain in his troubled eyes. "Is horrible—not knowing anything."

"It must be." She bent down, speaking earnestly. "*Please* ring us or come round if there is any news. The job here is all right, is it?"

"Is very nice. Always busy—that's what I need. I good friends with Hanif, and Mr Gabrielli is very kind. Don't you worry about me, Rosemary."

She smiled, said a hearty, encouraging good-bye, and left. She did not recognise anybody sitting waiting on the chairs around the counter: most of them were probably students or members of families where both parents worked—anyway, not members of the St Saviour's congregation. When she got home Paul was already back from one of his eternal meetings.

"I dropped in on Stanko on the way home from Maggie Pauling's," Rosemary said.

There was a tiny pause before Paul said, "Good. How is he getting along?"

Rosemary and Paul had been married for more than twenty-five years. Both of them knew in all its intricacy the grammar of marital discourse. Rosemary understood perfectly the significance of that tiny pause, and Paul knew that he had let something slip and that she had understood what it was. Both of them decided it was something best not pursued until it was absorbed and all its implications comprehended.

It was a case, Rosemary decided, in which the best thing was to watch for signs and then interpret them. There had been talk, obviously, about her and Stanko. How did they know about Stanko, and how much did they know? She was more worried about that than anything they might imagine about the relationship between her and him. Dirty minds she could cope with, but there was the possibility that as soon as his nationality was known, someone would put two and two together and decide he was an illegal immigrant, or at least working illegally. Paul's was an intelligent rather than a warm-hearted parish.

The signs that she had decided to look for were not slow in showing themselves. They were ones that were usual in well-bred English circles: increased reserve or reticence in conversation, constraint in greeting, avoidance on social occasions. This was the British way not only of expressing disapproval of a supposed sin or crime, but also of sparing the disapprover the embarrassment of being open in their condemnation. It showed Rosemary that the person concerned had heard that she was having a fling, but it did not in any way pin them down as far as future conduct was concerned: if in the future the gossip proved groundless they could resume their relationship with her as if nothing had happened. In Italy ugly names might have been shouted at her in the street. In England people found urgent reasons for crossing to the other side of the road.

Rosemary observed and absorbed, as if she were studying British habits for a sociology course. She viewed this development surprisingly dispassionately as far as she personally was concerned. She was mainly worried about Stanko's plight. She rang Signor Gabrielli, who assured her that in the pizzeria Stanko was referred to as Silvio and that they conversed in the presence of the customers in an elementary kind of Italian.

"He speak a little, you know. We are neighbours, Italy and Yugoslavia, is a lot of tourism and he learns quickly. Is the same with my Tunisian. The buyers like to think these are Italian pizzas made by Italian boys—is natural."

Armed with this knowledge Rosemary felt she could talk the rumours over with somebody before she thrashed the matter out with Paul, in an attempt to decide whether to confront the gossip or just let it ride. She chose to visit Violet Gumbold, whose own marriage had been the subject of innuendo, based, so far as Rosemary knew, on little more than the fact that her husband was frequently away from home. Violet was getting around a bit more now but was still visited a lot by female parishioners, who stopped by for tea, biscuits and a spot of character assassination—in this respect parish behaviour had changed little over the last two hundred years. Rosemary found her in the middle of limb-strengthening exercises which she was very ready to discontinue. The pair of them sat in the kitchen, and Rosemary circled around the delicate subject.

"You'll soon be able to come back to church," she said.

"Next Sunday, I thought. People have offered me lifts, but I want to get there under my own steam when I do go. Pity you won't be there."

Rosemary grimaced.

"I have considered just going along—as a sort of habit, or in the hope that something will 'happen,' as I think Paul still hopes it will. It would fill a gap. But the idea of spending a lot of time on what has become an empty observance just doesn't appeal to me. There've got to be better ways of using my time."

Mrs Gumbold looked dubious.

"I suppose that's the practical view. But I do think it's sad. I hope you don't mind me saying that."

"Not in the least. But I have to say that for some reason—and it's odd, when you think how much of my life has been given to the Church, in one way or another—it's not sad for me. I feel *freed* from something."

"Well, I hope it doesn't last."

"I almost hope it does. Maybe it's the pleasure of being freed from some of the sort of people who do go to church."

She looked at Violet Gumbold out of the corner of her eye and saw that she took the point.

"Rosemary!" she said, beginning to blush. "You've always got on so well with us all in the past."

"Yes—well enough. But the relationship has never really been challenged on either side. Now it has been."

"By your loss of faith?"

"That, and this notion that I'm having an affair." Mrs Gumbold looked down into her cup. "And now that it is challenged, I'm afraid I'm weighing a lot of people in the balance and finding them wanting."

Violet Gumbold made no reply, though she was clearly trying to think of one.

"Is the whole parish talking about it, Violet?"

"Well, yes. I'm afraid they are." She seemed quite ready to talk as long as they stuck to facts.

"Without coming to talk to me about it?"

"I suppose they think you'd just deny it, there wouldn't be any point."

"Ah—the 'he would, wouldn't he?' syndrome. They must feel they have some pretty good evidence."

"I don't know about that. You have been seen to go to Pizza Pronto just to talk to him."

"Gosh! How sinful!"

"And it's said you introduced him to Mr Gabrielli and persuaded him to give the young man a job."

"Again, gosh. Come off it, Vi. They must be throwing around nastier stuff than that." Violet Gumbold was silent. Rosemary sighed.
"All right, let's get on to the who. Who started all this talk?"

"Really, I couldn't say, Rosemary."

"You mean you won't tell me."

"No, I won't. But I will tell you what they're saying about how
it started." She was still looking down at her cup, but she felt she
had to look Rosemary in the face when saying it, so she raised her
eyes. "They say it began when you went to Scarborough, and that
he got the sack when he was seen coming out of your room one
night."

Rosemary laughed.

"Right. Thank you, Violet. That's really what I wanted to
know. You know, if it wasn't for poor old Paul and his position in
the parish I think I'd find it rather flattering that someone my
age could snap her fingers and have someone St—Silvio's age
come running. But it doesn't seem much like real life."

"I don't know, Rosemary: affairs between older women and
younger men seem very common these days."

"Only in the soaps. And they're *not* real life."

"It's not just the soaps. You read about it all the time. Show biz
people and that. You're still a very attractive woman."

"The 'still' says it all."

"And he's a charming young man."

"You know him?"

"Well, I saw him when I was driven by Mrs Harridance to get
a pizza."

Rosemary allowed herself a malicious smile.

"Funny, I've never thought of you as a pizza sort of person, Violet. Or Florrie, come to that. One good result of all this is probably that Signor Gabrielli's business has picked up no end."

"Oh Rosemary, you're being unkind. I don't *want* to believe these rumours, truly."

"Then don't. The trouble with rumours is that people get the idea that if they hear them often enough they must be true. This one is being circulated vigorously, you'll hear it often, but it is nonetheless a lie."

Leaving Violet Gumbold's Rosemary felt delighted that she'd pumped her: the information she had got was just what she wanted. It gave her, too, several possible avenues for further activity, at least one of them very enticing. It was by no means clear to Rosemary, though, how best to investigate the Scarborough connection, and it was not till the following afternoon, when she was alone in the vicarage, that she felt confident enough to ring up the Cliff View Guesthouse.

"Hello, that is Mrs Blundell, isn't it? This is Rosemary Sheffield—I stayed with you a couple of weeks ago."

"Oh yes, Mrs Sheffield." Cautious—not a good start. It threw Rosemary off course, and she blundered on less circuitously than she had intended.

"Mrs Blundell, I wanted to ask something about Stanko—"

"Oh, I couldn't possibly discuss any of my staff with you, Mrs Sheffield."

"I don't want to *discuss* him, Mrs Blundell. He's here in Leeds at the moment, and I can talk to him any time I want."

There was a slight access of warmth, as she added: "I hope he's found a job."

"Yes—he's working in a pizzeria."

"Good. I always *liked* him greatly."

"He says he was sacked because the police were clamping down on people working illegally."

"I couldn't possibly comment on that."

"Mrs Blundell, let's stop being cloak and dagger about this, shall we? I very much doubt if my telephone or your telephone is being tapped. I know and you know that Stanko has no work permit. Was this why you got rid of him?"

There was a brief silence, then some sign of cautious co-operation.

"When summer comes the police tend to get more interested, with all the hotels and guesthouses taking extra people on. I always make sure that all my staff have their papers in order during the peak months."

"Meaning July and August. So that wasn't why you got rid of Stanko now, in May?" There was silence at the other end, and Rosemary plunged on. "Mrs Blundell, there is a nasty rumour being spread around the parish, very distressing to my husband and me, that Stanko was sacked after being seen coming out of my room. The implications are obvious. Is that true?"

This time, after a pause, Mrs Blundell replied.

"No, that's not true. I can assure you of that, Mrs Sheffield. As you know, there was quite a while between your visit and my suggesting to Stanko that he move one."

"Exactly. But am I right in thinking that there was some kind of an incident?"

"Well . . . the fact is, Mrs Sheffield, that he *was* seen coming out of your room one evening—not late, as you will know, but—well, old people talk, and often they have rather nasty minds. When it came to me, this talk, I took no notice, because I knew you took an interest in him and his problems. But a lot of my guests are long-term in the winter months, and when the same people came to me with another incident of the same kind—"

"You mean Stanko coming out of a female guest's room?"

"Yes. Such a nice woman, really sweet, here for a few days with her mother. So anyway I felt I didn't have a leg to stand on, when it happened a second time, particularly as I'd told him to be careful, so I asked him to move on."

"You didn't talk to Mrs Meadowes about it?"

"No, I didn—" There was a shocked silence. "I did *not* mention any name, Mrs Sheffield."

"No, Mrs Blundell, you didn't need to. I am *so* grateful to you for clearing the matter up."

"So far as I know, Mrs Meadowes knows nothing about it—she and her mother left the next morning. I wouldn't want—"

"I shall be very careful, Mrs Blundell, very tactful. I can assure you of that. It goes with being a vicar's wife."

So that was that. Thinking about it as she put the phone down she wondered whether her closing remark hadn't been misleading: she was tempted to be very tactless indeed. In fact she was tempted to spread the rumour, or rather the news, that Stanko had been sacked after he had been seen leaving Mrs Meadowes's bedroom. That would certainly signify an end to turning the other cheek, but it would be both satisfying and poetically just.

A moment's thought convinced her that such a move could spell disaster for Stanko. The more attention that was focussed on him, the more likely it would be that he would be forced to make another quick move. The only safe course for Stanko was to fade into the background, and the really unfortunate aspect of Selena Meadowes's gossip was that it prevented him doing that. But how much did she know about him? Did she know anything about his place of origin?

Rosemary decided to find out. She also determined to have a showdown with Selena.

She had just made this decision, and was turning her mind to the when and where, when Paul came in from evensong. He seemed in fine good humour.

"I made a suggestion about the party after the spring fête," he said, rubbing his hands.

"Some genteel version of the rite of spring?" Rosemary enquired. "With me as sacrificial victim?"

"Ah yes—well, it did have something to do with that. All this silly talk—I know we haven't discussed it—"

"But we both know it's been going on."

"Exactly. Well, I thought that for refreshments, as a change, instead of going to the Cosy Nook people to do quiche and salad as usual, we'd get a big order of pizzas from Pizza Pronto. Everybody likes them, and it will make a change."

"*And?*"

"And I've organised with Signor Gabrielli that Stanko will bring them along to the parish hall. I'll be conspicuously friendly, I'll introduce him to people—as Silvio, of course—and *that* should stop people's tongues."

Rosemary saw no option but to kiss her husband and seem to applaud his notion. It seemed the only possible reaction to his puppyish, pleased-with-himself air.

"Dear old unsuspicious Paul! When I *do* decide to have an affair your simple trust will be an invaluable asset."

"You think it's a good idea?"

"Excellent. But don't imagine it will stop people's tongues. Nothing ever does that. But it may slow them down a bit."

But privately she thought that they would be drawing attention to Stanko, just when they ought to be letting him fade from people's minds. Because she was determined that Selena Meadowes was going to withdraw her slanders, and well before the spring parish party.

CHAPTER EIGHT

Party Going

Rosemary bearded Selena Meadowes next day in her bland semi off the Otley Road, distinguished only by looped satin curtains in the front room, which made the bay windows look like a toy stage at which Selena might be expected to appear as Maria von Trapp and sing of her favourite things.

Rosemary marched up to the front door and gave a single businesslike ring on the doorbell. When Selena opened it with a nervous smile Rosemary said, "Hello Selena. I want to have a talk about what you've been saying about me."

Selena seemed inclined at first to bar her entrance, but Rosemary marched straight past her, down the hall and into the sitting room. Selena was alone in the house, luckily: her anonymous-looking husband was at work at his bank and her 2.5 children at school. She could be taken on in single combat.

Rosemary sat down in a fat armchair and had to resist the impulse to gesture to Selena to do likewise. Truth to tell, she was going to use to the full her seniority and her moral superiority. She felt rather like a headmistress preparing to give an almighty dressing-down to an unsatisfactory pupil.

"Right, Selena," she began, "let's not beat about the bush. You and I both know the rumours about me that have been put around the parish."

"Well, Rosemary, I have heard," said Selena, in her littlest voice, "but of course I would be the *last* person to spread anything like that."

"Don't pretend to be above gossip, Selena. Very few of us are that. And if not you, who else? You got the idea that I had been up to something in Scarborough—whether this was because you felt that someone who had lost her faith was bound to feel free of all restraint and go wild, or because you saw me happy and relaxed and put your own interpretation on it I can't guess. The last thing I'd care to do is go into your thought processes. But you went to Scarborough intending to find out any dirt that was going, and you succeeded. You heard—or by dint of questioning you learnt—that there had been comment on the fact that Silvio had been seen coming out of my room during the evening."

"Well, I must say Rosemary I was *most* surprised—"

"You were delighted, Selena: be honest with yourself for once. It was exactly the sort of information you'd hoped for. And then, when Silvio turned up in Leeds some days later, and when he and I were seen together, you put two and two together and made the sort of fantastic number people do come up with when they try to work out that particular sum."

Selena Meadowes dabbed at her eyes, which were dry.

"You're most unfair, Rosemary."

"I am, on the contrary, unduly charitable, since I haven't gone into your motives. Now, I have no intention of defending myself or explaining myself to you, Selena. I would only ever do that to someone I respected. What I insist on is that you use the same energy and devotion you've been using in spreading this story to retracting it. I want you to tell everyone that you've made a terrible mistake, that it was a result of a complete misunderstanding of what happened at Cliff View, and that you've been assured by the landlady that there's no question of Silvio having been sacked after being seen coming out of my room."

"But Rosemary," said Selena, a cunning look coming into her eyes, "that wouldn't be true, would it? I know the man—Silvio, is that his name?—*was* seen coming out of your room. And I haven't spoken to Mrs Blundell about it. You wouldn't want me to tell lies, would you?"

"Selena, after stretching the truth in the way you have in the last week or two, you can hardly jib at stretching it an inch or two further. You knew perfectly well, and ignored the fact, that there were weeks between my visit and Silvio being sacked. If you want to you can ring Mrs Blundell at Cliff View and find out the truth."

"Oh, that would be rather awkward."

"It would be *very* awkward for you. Because by chance you did hit on the truth about Silvio. He was asked to leave after being seen coming out of a guest's bedroom. Unfortunately the bedroom in question was yours, Selena."

For the first time she showed real emotion.

"Rosemary! It wasn't!"

"Oh but it was. No doubt you'd been asking probing questions about him and me. I haven't discussed that with him, not wanting to embarrass him. But it's unfortunate for you, isn't it? Because if you do not start retracting your story—vigorously, comprehensively, totally—I shall tell people the truth about Silvio's dismissal with a great deal of pleasure."

"You wouldn't!"

"You think not? I don't know how stable your marriage is, Selena. That wasn't something you thought about when you started spreading stories about me, and I won't greatly concern myself with it if I have to start spreading stories about you. But I wonder how Derek would feel if all the parish was talking about his wife and an Italian waiter. A bit conventional, your Derek, isn't he? And a bit of a snob as well, I would guess. Think about it, Selena, and if you're wise you'll start spreading your retraction, and making it as convincing as you know how. Time to do a bit of grovelling, I think, Selena."

So much for turning the other cheek, Rosemary thought, as she left the Meadoweses' bijou residence. Perhaps turning the other cheek needs to alternate at times with the threat of strong-arm tactics to be fully effective. In any event she decided not to give Paul anything but a very generalised account of her conversation with Selena.

There was one other reason for being satisfied with the interview, and this she could share with Paul. It was obvious that Selena had never bothered to find out Stanko's name when she was at Scarborough, or even his nationality. One less thing to be explained, one more dangerous possibility avoided. The main thing was that talk should die down, and Stanko be allowed to fade into the background.

Die down it did, somewhat to her surprise. Perhaps it had something to do with the fact that she had always been liked and respected in the parish, both for herself and as the vicar's wife. The retraction, as it progressed (much more slowly, inevitably, than the gossip), was believed: people stopped avoiding her, snubbing her, pretending she wasn't there. Though the retraction lacked the specificity of the original gossip—inevitably, since Stanko and his situation had to be kept out of it—it was accepted by most of those who had heard it. Perhaps it was the deadly earnestness of Selena Meadowes that did the trick.

Rosemary took the renewed warmth as she had taken the quiet ostracism, but just once she did say something. She had walked in the pale sunshine to meet Paul from St Saviour's and perhaps go with him to the Five Hundred Tavern when Timothy Armitage, emerging with the congregation, saw her waiting and made a point of coming over and greeting her.

"So good to see you, Rosemary. It's nice that you're not shunning us."

Remembering his scurrying off to avoid having to talk to her she said, "I won't shun you if you don't shun me, Timothy."

He looked down at the pavement.

"Oh, my dear, you noticed!"

"Of course I did. Gossip's so easy to believe, isn't it, even when you don't want to?"

"You make me feel very small, Rosemary. I feel that I've let you down."

"No hard feelings." To soften her words—because Timothy was really one of the nicest members of the congregation, and she had spoken as she had only because he was one of the ones who would understand—Rosemary added: "Remember me when Lassie has her litter. I think I'm ready for another dog."

"You *have* been out of things, Rosemary. She had them last week. Come round and see them when they're a bit bigger."

The shift in parish opinion gave Rosemary the hope that Stanko's appearance at the party after the spring fête would be unsensational. It couldn't be too much of a nonevent from her or from his point of view: talk about Stanko almost inevitably meant questions about Stanko. Or Silvio, as she tried to call him, even in her own mind.

Meanwhile her children were coming up for the weekend of the fête and party.

It hadn't been planned like that. Or had it? Janet had certainly promised to bring her new boyfriend up during his half-term. Mark had said nothing about coming, but now suddenly he was too. Had there been collusion between the two? Recently there seemed to have grown up a closeness between them, which somehow Rosemary didn't like. Stop being paranoid, she told herself. Still, there was the possibility that Mark's antennae had caught the new gossip and he was coming up to smell out the lie of the land and give her a thoughtful little lecture in the phraseology of a *Times* leader. A *Times* leader of the Rees-Mogg era. If so, he could expect an explosion. There is just so much lecturing that parents can take from their children, Rosemary said to herself.

They arrived on the Friday before the fête and party. Janet and Kevin arrived in Kevin's old banger. Kevin was a cheery, fresh-faced young man, very different from Janet's former boyfriends, who had tended to be saturnine, smouldery types who seemed to be auditioning for roles in prewar films set in Ruritania. Whether there was anything *to* Kevin, Rosemary couldn't decide. There certainly hadn't been anything to his predecessors.

Kevin was sleeping at friends'. Rosemary was sure this was to spare her and Paul embarrassment. She rather resented this sort of cossetting. She felt she could have coped with the idea that her daughter and her daughter's boyfriend were sleeping together.

Mark arrived by coach from Oxford with a prim little suitcase and a large bag of dirty washing. He was much as usual, only more so. He brought up Rosemary's loss of faith almost at once and at every subsequent opportunity thereafter. He was very dissatisfied with Rosemary's explanation that "it just went," but he failed to get much more out of her. He clearly had ambitions to be a Torquemada without any of the necessary skills.

Paul and Rosemary had agreed that something had to be said about the recent rumour-mongering. The opportunity came up on Friday night at dinner, when Mark asked how things were going on in the parish.

"Buzzing," said Rosemary, helping herself to more potatoes. "Someone has been spreading the rumour that I'm having an affair with a fast-food chef."

"Mother! You're joking!" said Mark.

"How exciting," said Janet. "I presume you're not."

"I don't think I'm flattered that you should presume that, but no, I'm not."

"How did the idea get around, though?" asked Mark, increasingly headmasterly.

"Let me see," said Rosemary, pretending to think. "I got him his present job. He was a waiter at my guesthouse in Scarborough. He was seen coming out of my room there at around half past nine one evening."

Mark puffed out his cheeks, already plump, and looked very concerned. Or looked, to be precise, like a turkey about to lay an egg.

"Mother, you haven't been silly, have you?"

"As a matter of fact I think I've been very responsible."

"You do realise, don't you, that with your loss of your Christian belief, people in the parish will be on the lookout for falling standards in other matters as well? You will need to be very careful not to do anything that could give rise to scandal. You should think about that."

"What does give me pause for thought, Mark, is the question of how it has come about that your father and I have somehow produced a pompous and sanctimonious little prat like you."

There was a silence, Mark went tomato-red, and Paul stepped into the breach.

"Would anybody like some more carrots?"

Later that evening, when she was helping Rosemary with the washing up, Janet said, "That was glorious, Mother. Absolutely spot-on."

But reaction had set in, and self-doubt.

"It was rather cruel, I'm afraid, and premeditated as well. I knew I was going to get a sermon from him."

"Yes, that was easy enough to guess."

"Anyway, why the congratulations? I thought you and he were rather close at the moment."

"Close? Good heavens, no."

"You just seem to be seeing more of each other."

"Well actually . . ." Janet shuffled a little, then gave her mother a little grin. "Kevin, you see, writes these little plays, one-acters, for his kids to perform at the end of term. The first time he met Mark he started badgering me to invite him to this and that— hence *Carousel*. He's put this wonderful prat, to use your word, Mum, into his present play, and Mark keeps providing him with wonderful things to say."

"Well, it's nice to know he has his uses. Good for Kevin," said Rosemary, thinking that there must be more to him than to all those gigolo types who had preceded him. "Golly, I do hope this is just a dreadful passing phase with Mark. What I really worry about is the Church."

"The Church?"

"Well, I *do* care about it, in spite of what's happened to me. It's been my life up to now. Mark will be the most terrible clergyman if he goes on the way he is going—the congregation will defect in droves. There's no chance of his leaving over the ordination of women, is there?"

"None at all. He thinks it provides the most wonderful opportunity for renewal and revival."

"Oh dear. The Catholic Church does seem to be able to embrace awful people much more easily than the Anglican one. Look at all those dreadful politicians. Paul was talking about them only the other day. We seemed to give them a platform, whereas now they're Catholics they keep wonderfully quiet. . . . Tell Kevin he'll have to come to the church party tomorrow night. We can introduce him to lots more terrible types for his plays."

That night they all watched the ten o'clock news together. The peace processes in the former Yugoslavia were gathering momentum, and the guarded optimism of recent months was giving way to a sturdier hope. Rosemary was conscious that she was making an almost physical effort not to show more than a normal humanitarian interest. The truth of the lines about what a tangled web we weave was neatly illustrated in her case, though she told herself that her deceptions were quite selfless, designed only to benefit Stanko. Still, it didn't feel good to hold back such an important part of her recent life from her own children.

Fête days had an ordained pattern, an almost mechanical routine, like coronations or (for all Rosemary knew) bar mitzvahs. Who did what was known, and was varied only by illness, retirement or death. The fact that some members of the congregation were beginning to feel that they had done their bit would lead to changes in the Mothers' Union next year, but did not yet mean changes in the arrangements for the fête. The various ladies had their usual stalls, and the men understood their various backup functions without even being asked.

Rosemary, of course, had her allotted part in all this activity: fetching, carrying, filling in during tea breaks and pee breaks, getting change, transporting takings to the all-day safe at the bank, encouraging, exhorting and generally exhausting herself. The St Saviour's fête was genuinely popular, and people came in droves. It had a reputation for cheapness and quality, and Rosemary always saw people she did not recognise as residents of the area, let alone members of the congregation. Students came in large numbers too, in quest of cheap food. The hungry student was one of the phenomena of the nineties that Rosemary was saddest about: one of those revivals of an old tradition, like the worn-out working-class woman, which the country could do without.

She did manage—again, this was by tradition—a brief rest back at home around about five o'clock. Then it was up, change into her vicar's-wife uniform (olive-green woollen dress, calf-length, with a chunky necklace) then off across the park to the parish hall, where the party was always held, and where the preparations were already under way.

"Florrie! How nice to see you!"

Social occasions, in Rosemary's experience, generally began with a lie.

"Rosemary, you are looking well. But we've all said so all along, ever since you—"

"Are you doing the soft drinks as usual?"

"That's right: soft drinks free with the price of the ticket; glass of wine seventy-five pee." She paused, thrusting out her bosom. "Mr Mills has got some very good value Bulgarian and Rumanian wines, I believe. Are you going to supervise the food as usual?"

"Yes I am."

"Pizza, I hear. So good that awkward little business is sorted out. I never believed it. Some people have terrible minds, don't they? Makes you ashamed to be human—"

Rosemary moved on mid-flow. The woman disgusted her, and she had the excuse of going about her business, which there was plenty of. Turning away she realised the encounter had been watched and overheard by Dark Satanic Mills.

"Good for you, Rosemary. I'm glad you stood up to them."

"*Did* I stand up to them?"

"I heard rumours of a visit to Selena Meadowes."

He nodded towards the centre of the hall, where the Meadowes family—Selena, Derek, and little Matthew and Flora—

102

were clustered with some of the other younger people, having all the smiling anonymity of a family in a TV commercial.

"You know everything, Stephen. Is Dorothy here?"

"I expect she will be later, if the cat turns up. It went missing this afternoon, and she insists she's staying at home until it reappears."

"I know the feeling."

"She worries more about that cat than she does about me. It's not having children. . . ."

He said it resentfully, blamingly. Coming to the defence of a woman she hardly knew, Rosemary said, "If she'd had children she would worry about them more than about you. And quite right too, though you're probably the sort of husband who would resent it. Excuse me—I must go and get the plates and cutlery ready."

The long table had plates with serviettes at one end and knives and forks at the other. Rosemary had always resisted disposable plates and cutlery—the latter would have been even more than usually useless with pizza, and Rosemary expected that most people would use their fingers. She had three or four helpers already waiting behind the table, Violet Gumbold among them, and she chatted with them while observing how things were going in the hall. The party was filling up, with quite a lot of people paying at the door: as with the fête, the party had a reputation for offering good value. The congregation was actually outnumbered by nonworshippers, which suited Stephen Mills, who was standing by the table talking to local businessmen. Rosemary heard words like "cash flow," "liquidity" and "reserves." It occurred to her that she had only the vaguest idea what Stephen *did*, but she certainly associated him with expressions like "cash flow." She noticed how much more at ease he was with men of his own kind: with women, and with men like Paul, he tended to be actorish, conscious of being on display, with something of the difficult temperament of the peacock. With businessmen he shed all this and got down to brass tacks in a completely normal way. She decided he was a very old-fashioned kind of man.

Her nose twitched. Through the main door, where people were still strolling in and paying, Stanko had arrived, almost obscured by a great pile of large cartons from his hands to his chin. How good pizzas always smelt! Someone directed him to Rosemary's table, and he staggered over, smiling at her with his eyes. It was with relief that he lowered them on to the table.

"Thank you, Silvio," said Rosemary. "Can you help for a bit with cutting and handing out?"

She summoned her helpers round, and they began opening boxes. She noticed Paul approaching for his display of friendliness to Stanko for the parishioners' benefit. Stanko had grinned at her, nodded, and started round to her side of the table. He was passing Stephen Mills and his group when he realised he was being watched, and stopped. Rosemary looked up from her work of slicing pizza and saw too. Mills had broken off from his conversation and had his eyes fixed on the new arrival.

"Hello, Stanko," he said.

CHAPTER NINE

An End and a Beginning

There were many accounts given subsequently of what happened next. There was no great disagreement about the facts, which were unexciting. What happened was that there was a moment or two's silence, in which Stanko seemed to be struggling to find something to say. Then he turned to Rosemary.

"I cannot stay to help. I sorry. Is many customers back at Pizza Pronto."

And he turned and hurried out.

Rosemary told the police (conscious that she was on the very outer verges of the truth, but without any guilty feelings about it) that Stanko had delivered the pizzas and left because they were busy back at the takeaway. Others recounted the encounter between him and Stephen Mills; but there were various versions of what Mills actually said, and the descriptions of Stanko's demeanour varied enormously: dumbfounded, guilty, outraged, angry, embarrassed were among the words used, and many suggested that Stanko was surprised to meet someone from his past whom he had betrayed or double-crossed, or by whom he himself had been betrayed or double-crossed. The encounter was so brief, it involved so few words, that there were as many accounts of it as there were witnesses. Rosemary, if she could have heard them, would have been surprised at the parish's holding so much imaginative energy.

She found it impossible to put the encounter out of her mind as she went through the mechanical business of slicing and distributing pizzas, but this did not prevent her from absorbing other things as well: how the party was going, how people were behaving. She noticed that her rebuke to her son had not significantly altered his manner: it was avuncular—avuncular at twenty-two!—and orotund. A certain tolerance was extended to him as the vicar's son, but she noticed that the people he talked at quickly found that there was something else it was imperative they do, or someone they simply had to talk to. Whereas her husband always had a crowd around him, her son mostly had a space.

When there was a lull in the work, when everyone was eating and before the washing up started, Rosemary was surprised to find herself bearded by Derek Meadowes. She had smiled at him, greeted him, often enough before, but this was the first time she could recall having anything approaching a conversation with him. He always reminded her of a minor public schoolboy, quite useful with a bat lower down in the batting order, with a mind the consistency of well-boiled cabbage.

"It's all going very well," he said.

"Yes, isn't it?"

"Everyone's worked very hard," he continued, dipping into his ragbag of clichés.

"It's a good parish for workers," Rosemary agreed.

"You seem to have been reinvigorated since your break in Scarborough."

"It was good to get away," said Rosemary, dipping into her own conversational ragbag but wondering all the time where all this was leading.

"Yes, Selena found that. It was nice of you to call on her the other day. You must have found a lot to chat about."

"Yes, we did." Rosemary, having found out where the conversation was leading, had no intention of obliging him with further information. For something to say she asked: "Did your mother-in-law feel the benefit of Scarborough too? I believe she's failing."

"Mum? Failing? Good Lord, no. Plays golf three times a week and as strong-minded as they come. She's only sixty-one, you know. Prime of life."

"I must be thinking of someone else," said Rosemary meekly, but smiling to herself. "It's easy to get people mixed up in a large parish like this one."

"Good heavens, yes. I'd be doing it all the time if I was in your position. Er . . ."

Derek looked as if he was going to probe further, but then shut his mouth, obviously unable to find a suitably anodyne question that might lead Rosemary to tell him what had passed between his wife and her when she had called.

Pizzas had been eaten, quite a lot of wine drunk, and the washing-up beckoned. It was something she felt she did quite enough of at home. St Saviour's was a very forward-looking parish, but somehow this had never resulted in any males being part of the washing-up team. Rosemary took a deep breath, summoned her helpers and they went through to the kitchen and got stuck into it. Even working full out, with the efficiency born of long practice, it took them more than half an hour.

By the time they had finished, the party was thinning out a little but still had plenty of life left in it. There was a healthy queue
at the wine table (did Britons drink more than when she was
young, Rosemary wondered, or just drink more white wine?), and
at the table where the pizzas had been served, there were a couple of students eating discarded fragments.

Her son Mark, Rosemary saw, had exhausted his store of other
people's patience and was now talking to Janet and Kevin. His
manner to them was much the same as his manner with other
parishioners. She saw Kevin on occasion move back a step, to get
a better look at his stance and his gestures. Sometimes she saw his
eye flicker, as if he had heard something he wanted to remember.

It was cruel—both Kevin's using him for caricature and her
own delight in it. And yet . . . Rosemary thought again about the
cliché parents used, particularly when their children were going
through "a certain stage": that they *loved* them but didn't *like*
them very much. Was that possible? And if in fact she didn't love
Mark, how had that come about?

Then she saw something that really put her on the alert. Janet
was standing a little apart from her brother and her boyfriend,
sipping at a glass of wine. Stephen Mills detached himself from
a little knot of businessmen, came over to her and bent his face
close to hers. She fixed him with a stare of outrage and revulsion,
then conspicuously turned away from him and went to stand
closer to Mark and Kevin. Mills shrugged, smiling, and went off
to find other people to talk money with.

The encounter troubled Rosemary. She had never before had
reason to associate Janet with Stephen Mills in any sort of relationship at all. She had shared—she *thought* she had shared—the
family's skepticism, that was all. But to account for that look,
there *must* have been something else. It was worrying. She looked
around her: her job was over. The party was going with a self-gen-

108

erating force towards its close. She decided to do what she often did when her parish duties were over: slip away home without any fuss. Paul was near the door, talking to Florrie Harridance. As she passed she winked at him and then passed out into the night.

She enjoyed the cool air and the quiet. She stuck to the road rather than crossing the dark park—these days an elementary precaution even for a far from nervous woman such as herself. As she walked on, her mind was going through the monotonous round of a single preoccupation: Janet and Stephen Mills. Stephen Mills and Janet. Why did the idea disturb her so much, she wondered? Because she so disliked and distrusted Dark Satanic Mills, of course.

All was quiet at home. She poured herself a glass of milk from the fridge, then went straight up to bed. She felt totally exhausted and knew she would go straight to sleep and not wake up even when Paul joined her.

Nor did she. She slept right through until after eight. Paul, who presumably had been a lot later, was still fast asleep beside her. She slipped out of bed, put on a dressing gown, and started downstairs to get the morning tea. At the turn of the stairs she paused. Through the little window there she could see out to the park. At the wooded, hilly part to her left she could see police cars. There was a large area cordoned off, and a couple of uniformed men were keeping early-morning joggers and dog-walkers away. As she watched, another police car sped along the road beneath her on its way to the scene.

Rosemary shivered and went on down to the kitchen to make the tea.

PART II

CHARLIE

CHAPTER TEN

Local Body

Charlie Peace had been called on duty an hour before his shift was due to start. He lived with his girlfriend in a small flat about ten minutes from where the body was found. When he arrived there he found the area already cordoned off, with a small knot of uniformed men urging sightseers to move on, which they did with the unabashed reluctance of natural ghouls. The photographers and other scene of the crime men were hard at work in the immediate vicinity of the body. Charlie looked around for anyone from CID and saw on the other side of the fenced-off area his preferred boss, Mike Oddie, who was being approached by one of the S.O.C.O. men. Charlie went over to his side and surveyed the scene.

"You've cordoned off a big area," he said.

"Blood," said Oddie briefly, looking at the things he had just been handed. "There was a trail of it."

"Long time dying? Long-running fight?"

"Maybe the latter. But it seems to have ended with his throat being cut."

"Unusual."

"Distinctly odd."

Charlie stood quietly, his eyes still fixed on the body and its sur-roundings. He was in a part of Leeds that in theory he ought to know well: it was close to home and he ran there three or four times a week—not obsessively, merely keeping fit for his job. But running does not encourage you to survey the scene. Mostly you keep your eyes on the ground, watching for muddy patches, glass or dog dirt. The body was on the rising ground at the far end of Herrick Park, where tended grassland shaded off into woodland. The body was on grass, but the cordoned-off area included the wide pathway between the trees. All this was no great way from the road, but if the killing took place at night the darkness made it unlikely that any passing motorist would have seen anything. Or indeed would have done anything if he had. Charlie looked over the expanse of green towards tennis courts and the rather fine old buildings of Her-rick College beyond. He knew that few students went through the park area after dark—almost no female ones.

"Who is he?" he asked.

"According to his wallet someone called Stephen Mills. Ring any bells?"

"None."

"His business card is for European Opportunities Ltd. Private address and office address given. Know anything about the firm?"

"Never heard of them."

"Me neither. Look at this." He showed him a printed ticket for the St Saviour's spring party, for Saturday, May 15. Admit one. "Last night. Presumably that's where he'd been. Hardly the sort of rave-up you might expect to lead to this."

Charlie shook his head vigorously.

"Don't you believe it. Religious people are the biggest bearers of grudges around. Don't you know any churchgoers?"

Oddie thought.

"As a matter of fact, I don't. No regular ones, anyway. Sign of the times, I suppose."

"Well, they are. And they're very good at justifying themselves in their grudges." Having delivered himself of this wisdom with some relish, Charlie thought for a little. "Well now, we're getting to know our body: Stephen Mills, assaulted and killed on the way back from the St Saviour's spring party. I know about that party. My girlfriend told me that some of her friends were going."

"Oh? Religious? I didn't know Felicity was a churchgoer."

"She's not. The St Saviour's party is cheap, with lots of grub. There'd been a fête earlier on. It's known as a place where you can get good things at knockdown prices—jams, cakes and that sort of thing. Students are always on the lookout for cheap food. Any idea when this chap was killed?"

"Doc is cagey, as ever, but he says he's been there hours. I could have told him that. He's been rained on."

"The vicar of St Saviour's lives over there," said Charlie pointing to a part of the road a few hundred yards away. "I think his name is Sheffield. I could find the house easily enough. Want me to go and have a word?"

But as he spoke a figure in clericals came out of one of the houses, with a woman beside him. As they watched he kissed her, got into his car and waited for a moment. Two young people came out of the house in a hurry, got into the car, and it drove away, leaving the woman on the pavement.

"That's his wife," said Charlie, not afraid to state the obvious. "She sometimes comes out on to the park when she's seen him off to church." They watched as she crossed the road and walked towards the tennis courts, casting occasional glances in the direction of the police presence, as if she would like to join the curious public if it weren't for the fact that it was not the done thing. "Want me to go and have a word with her?"

115

"Do you know her?"

"Nodding acquaintances."

"Well, why not? Can't do any harm." Oddie thought for a moment. "I'll send someone now to this address to see if there's a wife and break it to her. Be a bit careful what you say to the vicar's lady, but see what you can find out about the church bash last night."

Charlie headed towards her, and when he saw her turn and start back towards her defiantly ordinary vicarage, he broke into a run. She heard him, looked around and, when she saw who it was, smiled.

"Hello. We sort of know each other, don't we?" she said.

"To nod and smile to."

"Were you wanting my husband?"

"Well, I may have to speak to him later."

"Births, marriages or deaths?"

"None of those at the moment, thank you. Actually it was you I wanted to speak to."

"Oh?"

"I'm from up there." He turned and pointed towards the impressive police presence on the knoll. Comprehension dawned in Rosemary's face.

"Oh, you're a policeman!"

"Detective Constable Peace."

She frowned.

"I don't know that I can help, I'm afraid. I slept well, didn't see or hear a thing."

"I thought you might have been at the St Saviour's party last night."

Rosemary raised her eyebrows.

"I was. I was helping with the food. What on earth can that

have to do with anything?" She looked him in the eye. "What are you investigating up there?"

"I . . . can't be too specific—" Charlie began.

Light dawned on Rosemary.

"Of course. There are so many of you. It couldn't be anything but a body, could it?"

He returned her look guilelessly.

"If you could just tell me a bit about the party, Mrs . . . Sheffield, isn't it?"

"That's right. Of course you have to be careful, I can see that. Well, there's not a great deal to tell. It went off very well, as usual. I slipped away early."

"How early?"

"I don't remember exactly. A bit before ten, I think."

"Did you notice a Stephen Mills at the party?"

"Oh yes, I—oh dear. Is it him? But I suppose I'm not allowed to ask."

"You did notice him?"

"Yes, he was there. He was close by the table when I was going to serve the food. Then I saw him again later. Both times he was with a little group of men—businessmen."

"They were close to you at the table, were they? Did you hear what they were talking about?"

"Oh, the usual things I imagine when business people get together: the dire state of the economy, whether there are any signs of things picking up. I caught some phrases suggesting that. It wasn't the sort of talk that interests me."

"It didn't develop into any sort of row?"

Charlie noted Rosemary looking up at him sharply.

"Good heavens, no."

"How did the group break up?"

"The food arrived, and everybody got plates and we began to serve it."

"And the later group?"

"I was too far away to hear anything."

"Was he still there when you left?"

Rosemary had a sudden sharp picture of Mills going up to Janet, and the surprising rebuff he had received.

"Yes, I'm pretty sure he was still there," she said.

"Could you tell me the names of the businessmen he was talking to, if I should need them?"

"One or two. They weren't all churchgoers by any means, but I expect if I were to get together with the other women who were serving the food we could come up with most of the names."

"I got the impression . . ." Here Charlie paused, having difficulty in finding an appropriately roundabout way of putting his impression into words, "that when you made your assumption about Stephen Mills you—well, let's say either you weren't surprised, or you weren't upset."

In spite of the tentativeness of his words Rosemary suddenly sensed something formidable about Charlie and realised she had to go very carefully.

"Certainly I was surprised," she said. "Sudden death is always surprising, isn't it? . . . If that's what it is. . . . But yes, if that's what it is I suppose I shan't be too upset. It sounds unfeeling, but that's the truth."

Charlie smiled encouragingly. He had not expected such honesty from a vicar's wife.

"You didn't like him?"

"Not much. And didn't trust him either."

"Why not?"

Rosemary paused before replying.

"Oh dear—this is going to sound silly. Because he was *too*

118

handsome, *too* smooth, *too* ingratiating. He always had for me the air of a fraudster, a con man, a sharper."

"But you've no evidence that's what he was?"

"None at all."

"And he was a member of your husband's congregation."

"He was indeed. He'd been coming to St Saviour's for years. . . . Congregations include all sorts."

"Of course they do. What did he do for a living?"

"Business of some kind—I've very little idea what."

"Did he have a family?"

"He had a . . . Goodness, we have gone into the past tense, haven't we?" She registered Charlie's expression of annoyance with himself and went on hurriedly: "That's between ourselves. He has a wife. She comes to church now and then, but she isn't regular, not these days at any rate."

"But he is? Every Sunday?"

"Pretty much so. And quite active otherwise. Also in with other bodies such as the Rotarians, helps with the local youth groups, and so on."

"Sounds a model citizen."

"Oh, no doubt he . . . is. Don't take any notice of a cynical old body like me."

"But you think he's in it for what he can get out of it?"

"Yes, I'm afraid I do."

"What could that be?"

"Well, with groups like the Rotarians and the Masons it's pretty obvious, isn't it? No need for me to spell it out. With the Church I'm not at all sure. I've often asked myself, but I've never come up with an answer."

"You sound as if you've thought a lot about Mr Mills."

It was a sudden, sharp jab. Rosemary said, too hurriedly: "Oh, that's putting it too high. But he intrigued me. Intrigues me."

119

"I must be getting back," said Charlie. "My boss will probably want to talk to you and your husband later." But he paused in the act of turning away. "I saw you standing here one Sunday about a month or so ago. This sounds silly, but you looked . . . quite strange. As if you were having some kind of experience. Or maybe a vision. Something mystical, it looked like."

"Yes, I remember. Goodness, how embarrassing. Was it so obvious? I remember thinking I was making an awful exhibition of myself. How awful! It makes me feel sort of spiritually naked."

"I was right? It was a mystical experience?"

"In reverse. Very much in reverse. I suddenly realised I no longer believed in God."

"Just like that? Belief just . . . left you?"

"Yes. That exactly describes it. When you saw me I was suddenly alone, without God. That was the beginning. . . ."

She stopped. He watched her closely.

"Of what?"

"Oh, of a lot of nastiness in the parish. You can imagine what people have been saying. I mustn't keep you. I'll tell my husband you may want to talk to him."

She walked on towards her semidetached vicarage, and Charlie wondered why he had been given what amounted to a dismissal. It was as if she had declined to enter what could be an area of danger. When he got back to Mike Oddie and the activity around the body, he said, "Interesting."

"What she told you, or the woman herself?"

"Both. But she's keeping something back."

"She knew him, did she? Maybe she disliked him. Murdered people tend to be disliked."

"She did know him, but she's not keeping back the fact that she disliked him. She made that perfectly clear."

"What did she tell you about him?"

Charlie ticked off each piece of information on his fingers.

"Local businessman, business unknown, keen churchgoer, reason unknown but probably not ardent faith. Smooth, good-looking, likes to keep in with people, particularly other businessmen. Has a wife but no family."

"And he was at the parish party?"

"Yes, and still there when she left, towards ten."

"Anything else?"

Charlie thought for a moment, feeling he was not yet at the heart of Rosemary's reticence.

"There seems to have been something going on in the parish recently. Some nastiness or other. It seems to have started with Mrs Sheffield—the vicar's wife, that is—losing her belief in God."

"Good heavens, that must be awkward. Like a surgeon's wife taking up alternative medicine."

"Yes. I get the impression the nastiness in the parish is not just about that, though. Some other factor has entered in. And she doesn't want to talk about it. She chatted quite happily about the loss of faith, but she cut the conversation short when we seemed to be straying towards other matters."

"Then we'll have to talk to some of the parishioners, won't we? In the meantime we'll have to talk to Mills's wife. As soon as we find out how she's taken the news I'll decide if it's worth going there when we finish here."

"I have the feeling that his wife was a bit of an irrelevance in Stephen Mills's life," said Charlie thoughtfully. "A sideshow, an optional extra."

"Why do you think that?"

"I got the impression he was the parish Lothario."

"Good Lord—I find it difficult to imagine any such thing."

"You just don't know anything about religion," said Charlie.

121

CHAPTER ELEVEN

The Little Wife

The Millses lived in a substantial, square Victorian house which gazed out at the world like one of the industrialists of the time: hard, confident, holding his secrets. Bentham Road was a "good" street off the Ilkley Road. The house had ample gardens around it and was shielded from curious gazes by trees and hedges. The imposing bay windows, curtained, on either side of the front door clearly belonged to large, formal rooms; further back the symmetry of the facade was lost, giving way to a more rambling, built-onto structure. It was a large house for two people and, built in a cul-de-sac, very quiet. It was even quieter than usual that day.

Mike Oddie had ascertained by telephoning the WPC on duty there that Mrs Mills would talk to them. He was told that she would prefer to get it over. When they rang the front doorbell the young woman who had fulfilled the traditional role of comforter opened it to them and beckoned them into the living room.

"She's upstairs—a bit upset, I think."

Oddie raised his eyebrows at the inappropriate cliché. He and Charlie looked around them. The room was not quite what they expected, being full of old furniture, including bookshelves with well-thumbed books and worn carpets and rugs. Charlie wondered whether it was a room that Stephen Mills had come into, rather than one he had made himself. It certainly wasn't a room that suggested the usual modern businessman, still less the parish Lothario.

"How did she take the news when you broke it to her?" Mike Oddie asked.

"Very well . . . more dazed than anything else," said Constable Morrison. "Kept asking questions about the details, but not crying or anything. When I told her you'd be coming soon she said she'd go upstairs and get tidy, but she went into the bathroom, and I've heard crying."

"That's a pretty common sequence."

"Oh, I don't need you to tell me that," said the woman, with a trace of bitterness in her voice. "I've had my share of breaking bad news and holding hands afterwards. It's a burden that ought to be shared more equally."

She looked at Charlie, who bared his teeth in one of his more fearsome smiles, designed to suggest in this case that as a comforter he was a nonstarter.

"Should I go and tell her you're here?" Morrison asked. But even as she spoke they heard the sound of soft footsteps coming down the stairs.

When she entered the room their first impression was of someone small and insignificant. She had put on a dark grey skirt and a cream blouse with halfhearted bits of frill here and there. Her eyes were red and she had no makeup on, though her hair, nondescript brown, had been neatly combed back into a little bun at the neck. It was only when Charlie looked into the reddened eyes that he saw how large, dark and beautiful they were. It was like diving into a pool and discovering it was bottomless.

124

"Hello. I'm Dorothy Mills."

Oddie shook her hand.

"I'm Superintendent Oddie, and this is DC Peace."

"Please sit down. I'd like to get this over so I can be alone and start to come to terms with it." She gestured them to seats, worn but comfortable like the rest of the furniture, and sat down herself. "Could you perhaps tell me a little about what happened? Constable Morrison has been very kind, but she couldn't tell me much. I do need to know where he was found and what . . . what had been done to him."

"Of course I'll tell you what I can," said Oddie. "He was found on the edge of Herrick Park by one of the early-morning joggers. He had had his throat cut. He'd been dead for some hours when he was found."

"I see." The words came out calmly, but she dabbed at her eyes as if the calmness was an effort. "Oh it all seems so . . . incredible, so *impossible*! I mean, Stephen was perfectly capable of looking after himself. How could he—this sounds silly—how could he *let* someone cut his throat? Was it someone who came up behind him? Was it someone he knew and trusted?"

"There had been a fight."

There was silence. She looked down into her lap.

"Oh dear. I wish it had been sudden. . . . I suppose he was on his way home from the St Saviour's party?"

"That's certainly what it looks like."

"I should have gone." Her hands began working as she started to blame herself—pudgy, unglamorous hands, hands that worked around the house. "Not that I could have done much, I suppose, if there had been a fight." She looked up at them again. "But we wouldn't have walked back through the park if I'd been with him, would we?"

"Why didn't you go?"

"The cat was missing, and I didn't want to go out before he turned up. . . . To tell you the truth, with these church do's Stephen usually bought two tickets to support them financially, but I was never frightfully keen."

"Aren't you a churchgoer?"

"An occasional one. I *used* to go, because Father was keen, but I suppose I got bored. It was the opposite of the usual in our household. Stephen was the churchgoer, and he'd take Dad when he was up to it."

"Your father lives with you?"

"Yes—he has a little flat at the back."

"So you and he were together last night?"

"Not together, but I was in and out to see how he was, and to give him a bit of supper and a cup of Ovaltine."

"You didn't go out looking for your cat?"

She looked at him with her unfathomable eyes and then over to Charlie Peace.

"No, I didn't, except just up and down the road here. If you go further you just find him by the front door when you get home after hours of looking and calling. . . . I do see where these questions are going, Superintendent. I wouldn't have gone to Herrick Park to look for him. He never goes that far away, and he'd have had to cross the Ilkley Road to get there. He's scared of busy roads, and he'd never have done that."

Oddie nodded, neutrally.

"He's home now?"

"Yes. I found him in the front garden about half past ten."

All this was delivered in a firm but dull voice, but one that occasionally broke, paused for a moment, then resumed again its apparently calm course.

"Mrs Mills, what did your husband do?"

She sat back in her chair as if expecting the question, acknowledging his right to ask it.

"He ran his own business, advising manufacturing firms about export opportunities in Europe and around the world. It was his own idea, and he built it up from nothing. He thought British businessmen fall behind because they are poor at foreign languages and they don't understand the needs and preferences and customs of other countries. They treat Budapest as if it's Whitehall and get nowhere as a consequence. He offered the sort of expert advice they needed. Stephen was very widely travelled, and he had friends and contacts everywhere."

"He was often away from home?"

"Not so much in recent years, but earlier, when the business was starting up. In the last few years, with everything in place, he's found he can do much of it by telephone or fax."

"Was it a business in which he would make enemies?"

"*No!*" At that the voice really broke. "No! Why should it make him enemies? He was just giving a service. He wasn't competing with anyone. . . . I keep trying to make sense of this in my mind. It would have been so much easier if he had been ill, if he had died naturally. Stephen didn't have enemies. He was so active, busy in all sorts of things, and he made friends, not enemies!"

He didn't make a friend of Rosemary Sheffield, Charlie thought to himself.

"How did you get to know him?" he asked.

"Through the church, mainly," she said, turning to him her deep eyes and unremarkable face. "As I say, I used to go much more regularly because I went with Dad. He's always been keen, particularly after Mother died. That was when I was ten, and I suppose he was looking for an interest to fill the gap. So it was at St Saviour's that Stephen and I met."

"Where was he from? Did he have any family?"

"Not still alive. Both of his parents were dead."

"Where was he from?"

"London. South of the river."

"Was there any special reason why he moved to Leeds?"

"To get out of London, but still to have city amenities—theatre, music and so on." She smiled reminiscently. "I remember talking to him about that when we were engaged. Stephen had a very sharp eye. He could see then that Leeds was a much better proposition for the future than Manchester or Birmingham."

"And so he set up his business, and it did well," Charlie continued. "Was it still doing well? Businesses are going to the wall everywhere."

"It was—is—doing wonderfully well. There are all these new markets opening up in Eastern Europe. They want business know-how, and the British want to get into their markets. Oh no, the business is going better than ever."

"Who will take it over?"

She shook her head.

"Oh dear. I hadn't thought about that at all. . . . There's Brian Ferrett, his second in command. Perhaps he'd buy me out, or go on running it for me. . . . I can't say anything about that because I simply haven't had time to consider."

"I shouldn't have asked," Charlie said quietly. "Of course it's much too early for you to have thought of that."

"You see we're in a quandary," resumed Mike Oddie. "Someone has murdered your husband, and yet you can't think of anything that he's done that might have made him enemies."

"But I can't! It was a unique business where he had no competitors, and he and Brian Ferrett got on very well. . . . I just can't think of anyone who'd do *that*."

Oddie tried to put the next question tactfully.

"There are areas in his life you don't know so well. If he travelled a lot . . . and of course the church."

An expression came over her face that could only be described as mulish.

"I went to church now and then. I know the people there. Stephen did a lot of work for the church in all sorts of ways. If anyone resented him, then they'd be very ungrateful. But I don't believe for a moment they did."

"And the travelling?"

The mulish expression remained set.

"As I said, he'd done much less recently, now the business was up and running. Probably not more than three or four times a year, short trips, within Europe."

"Your husband was a handsome man," put in Charlie.

She had to suppress a flush of irritation.

"Please don't treat me as if I were stupid," she said sharply. "I can see the direction of these questions. You are a good-looking man, Constable. Does that mean I should take it for granted that you are stringing along five or six women at once?"

"No, but it means that if I wanted to I'd find it easier than someone who wasn't. I'm sorry if I offended you. I just meant that if he travelled a lot he might have had . . . relationships you knew nothing about."

"You're not making things any better, Constable."

"We weren't just thinking of . . . that kind of relationship," said Mike Oddie, stepping in quickly. "Eastern Europe is a pretty murky area at the moment. Take Russia, for example: gangsterism is rife there—big-scale, highly organised gangsterism. There are some seriously rich people, and most of them didn't get that way by straightforward capitalist enterprise."

Mrs Mills shrugged.

"That's the sort of thing I've just read about in newspapers. I'm quite sure Stephen would never get involved in it."

"The big men there need contacts in the West."

"They'd find they couldn't use Stephen—if they ever tried."

"Your husband may have found that, with his job, he couldn't keep out of involvement."

"You can always keep out of crime if you're firm about it. I think you're straying into fantasy, Superintendent."

"I'm just trying over possibilities in my mind, Mrs Mills."

"Talk it over with Brian. Look at the firm's records. I know you'll find everything was above board because that's the sort of man Stephen was. He was sharp, competitive and totally honest."

"I've heard mention of the Rotarians," said Charlie.

She turned to him, this time more openly hostile.

"Good heavens—are they considered suspicious now? Britain's Cosa Nostra?" She thought. "Stephen had been a member of the local branch for about seven years. A week or two ago he took over as treasurer from the Reverend Sheffield. That does not suggest that anyone in the Rotarians thought he was a dodgy character. But of course if you regard the whole organisation as suspect that won't cut any ice with you, will it?"

"I'm sorry. I seem to have the knack of offending you," said Charlie, with no obvious contrition.

"I'm sure you know your job," said Dorothy Mills. "But you don't know my husband."

"No, we don't know your husband yet," said Charlie quietly. He laid no particular emphasis on the last word, and she gave no sign of having registered it, but her next words seemed to be a response.

"He's hardly cold, and you seem to be scrabbling around trying to find out dirty secrets about him."

"It's what happens in a murder enquiry, I'm afraid," said Oddie.

"Haven't you thought that this may be casual, unmotivated violence?"

"That doesn't usually happen to healthy white males," said Oddie. "It happens to women, and the springboard, one way or another, is usually sexual. But of course we'll keep all possibilities in mind."

She swallowed.

"I suppose you want . . . Do you want me to . . . ?"

"Identify the body. Yes, I'm afraid we will want that, when you feel up to it."

"One gets such a knowledge of things, doesn't one, from the television and books, but you never think it's going to happen to you. . . ." She paused, then made a decision. "I would like to do it now, if that's convenient . . . get it over with, start again, or try to think about starting again. . . ."

"Yes, of course," said Oddie. "Could I just ring and find out if . . . everything is in order?"

"The telephone's over there." She gestured to a corner of the sitting room where it sat on a small table. As Oddie was dialling the number the door to the hall opened and an old man came in. He had been tall, commanding, but his big, lean frame was now bent. His face was Scandinavian—big-boned, with sunken cheeks; but the chin was still firm and determined, like the last stones of a once-proud house.

"What's happening, Dot?" he said, looking from Charlie to Oddie, then back at his daughter. "Why are these men here?"

She got up quickly and went over to him.

"Sit down, Dad. We've had some bad news. Would you like your cup of tea?"

"I've had my cup of tea. You know I can make my own tea,

Dot." He sat down, under a sort of protest, but almost sighing with relief. "What do you mean, bad news?"

She knelt in front of him.

"It's dreadful news, Dad. Stephen had an accident coming home from the party last night. I'm afraid he's dead."

His mouth dropped open.

"Dead? Stephen dead? Dottie, he can't be."

"I'm afraid he is, Dad." She took his hand in hers and stroked it. "We've all got to be very brave. I've got to go and identify the body now."

"Oh Dot, how terrible for you. I can't believe it, though. Stephen dead. Dottie, tell me it isn't true."

He looked at her, bewilderedly, and seemed to see in her face that it was true. First one tear, then another, started coursing down his cavernous cheeks, and he began fumbling in his trouser pocket for a handkerchief.

"Poor Stephen. How can Stephen be dead? He was like a son to me. The only son I had. The best son I could have had."

It was, Charlie thought, the most grief he had yet seen displayed for Stephen Mills. Because he was not entirely convinced that what Dorothy Mills felt was grief.

Mike Oddie gestured to WPC Morrison to stay with the old man, and together they led Mrs Mills out to the car. Twice on the journey into Leeds she made as if to ask something, then stopped herself. It was as they were drawing up at the West Yorkshire Police Headquarters that she said, "Is he going to look very dreadful?"

"They'll have cleaned him up as far as they can," said Oddie. He adopted a businesslike tone because experience told him that was best. He led the way briskly inside. As they passed the desk the duty sergeant hailed him.

"Call for you, Mike."

"Take it, Charlie, will you?" Oddie said, and went on at the same fast pace towards the police mortuary. Charlie picked up the phone.

"DC Peace speaking."

"That's a constable, isn't it? I want to speak to the man in charge."

"Superintendent Oddie is in the mortuary with a witness who is identifying the body."

"Oh, that'll be Dorothy Mills, like as not, I suppose. How is she taking it? Well, I suppose you won't be able to say much, especially being junior, and I'll be brief with you, because I've got a Sunday dinner to cook. . . ."

Lancashire, thought Charlie, whose ear had refined itself in his three years in the North. And he very much doubted whether this lady was going to be brief.

"Now, of course the whole parish is devastated by the news, particularly as he was among us last night, and when you've been speaking to a man—not that I said more than 'hello'—you can't believe, can you, that—?"

"Excuse me, but we are *very* busy here. Could you get to the point?"

"That, young man, is *precisely* what I am getting to. My time is valuable if yours isn't. The point is the incident that happened at the party last night, when the food arrived. I thought you might not have heard about that."

"No, as a matter of fact we haven't, Mrs—?"

"Harridance. Florrie Harridance."

"And address?"

"It's in the book. There's only one Harridance. Don't interrupt me, young man. *Now,* it was pizzas last night, and I can't think why, because it's never been pizzas before, and you can make what you like of that, because the person who brought them was this young man from Pizza Pronto that there's been all this talk about. Not that I give the talk any credence, because I *know* Rosemary Sheffield, and I know she never would, not with someone so young. Though people say it's her time of life, and we all know people do funny things—"

"Did the incident involve Mrs Sheffield?"

"It did *not*. Or not directly. Don't be foolish, young man. It involved Stephen Mills, or why would I be ringing you? The boy came in with cartons of that foreign rubbish piled high in his arms, and he dumped them on the table, and it was then that it happened."

"What happened?"

"He saw Stephen Mills, and Stephen Mills saw him."

"And?"

"They were doomfounded. Well, the boy was doomfounded. Stephen Mills was very cool—he was always very cool, was Stephen—what you'd call a cool customer. Any road, all he said was 'Hello, Stinker,' or that's what it sounded like, and the boy, this Silvio, he just stammered something and turned and ran out."

"I see. Is that all?"

"Well, by all accounts the expression on that young man's face was *murderous*."

"You say 'by all accounts.' Didn't you see it yourself?"

"No, I didn't. I wasn't close enough to see."

"And yet you were close enough to hear?"

"No, I was not, young man. What I've been telling you is what I've been told by those who were, and I've told you because it's not everyone who's public-spirited enough to come forward and volunteer information. If you want to talk to someone who was close by and who could both see and hear, you should go not to Mrs Sheffield, who may have her own reasons for not telling the

134

whole story, but to Mrs Gumbold, that's Violet Gumbold, in Severn Road, and no I don't know the number but it's in the book and it's an unusual name like Harridance, so use your initiative. And now, young man, if you've nothing more to ask me of any consequence, I'm going to go and turn the potatoes over—"

"Feel free," said Charlie, and put the phone down quickly.

CHAPTER TWELVE

Liars

When Oddie came back from the mortuary he ushered Mrs Mills out to the waiting car, driven by a comfortable-looking sergeant, then came back into the headquarters' outer office.

"How did she take it?" Charlie asked.

"Very well. They'd done a good job on him. She just nodded. She's got herself well under control."

"Yes. . . . That phone call—"

"Oh yes. Anything interesting?"

"It was a woman who claimed there was some kind of incident while the food was being served at the party last night. Some kind of encounter between Stephen Mills and the young man who brought the food."

"Anything in it?"

Charlie frowned in puzzlement.

"I don't know. If I'd just heard the story in isolation I'd have said she was making something out of nothing very much. But it's interesting that Mrs Sheffield didn't mention it."

"If it was nothing, why should she?"

"You're being literal-minded, Mike. There was some kind of a situation, an eyeball-to-eyeball thing. The boy was, according to this woman, disconcerted, and fled like a rabbit. Apparently there's been talk in the parish about him and Mrs Sheffield. What were you planning to do next?"

"Go to the offices of European Opportunities Ltd. I've got the address and Brian Ferrett's home phone number. I think I'll just commandeer all the papers I can lay my hands on, then bring Ferrett in here and see what I can get out of him. If I take a uniformed man with me I can give you a couple of hours, if you want to follow up this encounter."

"Done!" said Charlie happily. He turned to the nearest woman with a computer. "There's a Mrs Gumbold in Severn Road. Could you get me her number?"

When Charlie arrived at the Gumbolds' he found both of them at home. Sunday was one day, Mr Gumbold explained, when he could usually get back from his job as a rep for a paper firm. He was overweight, probably from too much driving and sitting. The pair had heard about the murder on the parish bush telegraph, and Mr Gumbold left Charlie with his wife, saying he'd only got back at midnight and wouldn't be of any use.

Violet Gumbold was fadedly pretty, honest if Charlie was any judge, but not too bright and probably easily led. When asked to say exactly what happened at the party when the pizzas arrived, she became hesitant.

"Of course I've talked it over with people, told my husband, but it's so difficult to remember exactly what I saw, putting aside what people have said. . . . The young man came in, with a great pile of cartons, brought them over to the table where we were. . . . I'm trying to *see*. . . ."

"That's good. Picture it all. Where was Stephen Mills?"

There was a pause. She really was trying.

"With two or three other men, to the young man's left. . . . The Reverend Sheffield was coming forward, I think intending to be friendly to the young man. . . . Then Rosemary—that's Mrs Sheffield—asked the young man if he would help cut up and serve the pizzas."

"Did he say yes?"

"I can't remember him saying anything, but he started forward, and then . . . then he saw Mr Mills, and he was—well—*thunderstruck*, I'd say. As if . . . well, as if he was the last person on earth he would have wanted to see."

"Did he look guilty?"

"That must have been it, mustn't it? Someone from his past whom he'd cheated or done down."

She seemed to have seized on that explanation. Charlie said, very gently, "You don't sound entirely convinced. Has someone suggested that to you? Wasn't that how it looked?"

She frowned.

"Well, somehow it wasn't. I can't really say that the boy looked guilty."

"Try to *see* it again. Try hard. How was it he looked?"

After a pause she said, "More outraged. Angry. And yet confused at the same time."

"Thank you. That's very helpful. So what happened next?"

"Mr Mills said 'Hello—' and then what I think was his name. It wasn't 'Stinker,' like people are saying, but something like that. Though people have been saying his name is Silvio. Anyway, the boy stammered something about them being busy back at the pizza place, and he turned and fled, though I'm sure he'd been intending to come and help us."

Charlie thought, fixing the picture in his mind.

"What was the expression on the boy's face as he left?"

139

"I couldn't see that. He turned and went away from us."

Charlie was inclined to put the murderous expression down to the embroidery endemic in parish gossip.

"You said the Reverend Sheffield was coming over intending to be friendly. Why should he take pains to be friendly with the deliveryman?"

Violet Gumbold looked confused.

"Well, of course he's naturally a nice person, and courteous . . ." Charlie fixed her with an unrelenting stare. "And you see there was all this silly talk. . . ."

"Tell me more."

She swallowed and went red.

"Well, actually it was about poor Rosemary and this young man from Pizza Pronto."

"The vicar's wife and the fast-food cook. It sounds like a dirty story. I presume it *was* a dirty story."

"Well, yes. People were saying—"

"I can guess what people were saying. Who was spreading the story?"

"Oh, I don't know about spreading—"

"Let's not quibble. Where did the story start?"

"I wouldn't want to accuse anyone. I'd much rather not say."

Charlie sighed.

"Mrs Gumbold, if this story was going round the parish I can find a hundred people who will have heard it, of whom I guarantee ninety will be willing to tell me who was spreading it. It's all one to me if you want the reputation of obstructing the police rather than helping them."

There was a long silence. Mrs Gumbold was a naturally law-abiding person. Finally she swallowed.

"Mrs Meadowes. It must have started with Selena Meadowes. I'm sure she meant no harm, but she'd been to Scarborough, you sec, at the same guesthouse where Mrs Sheffield had gone when she lost . . . when she lost her faith, and this young man was a waiter there, and she heard talk about . . . about his having been seen coming from her room. That's what everyone was saying. And then he turned up here and Mrs Sheffield found him a job. . . ."

"So this Mrs Meadowes put two and two together and broadcast the result. Sounds like a really nice little congregation at St Saviour's."

"Oh, you mustn't think too badly of us. And I never heard it from her. She probably mentioned it to someone and it just . . . got around. And when she found out she was mistaken she went round to everyone to take the story back and say she'd wronged Rosemary."

Ho, thought Charlie. And there again hum.

"And what was behind all this mudslinging?"

"Behind it?"

"Why were they so keen to do the dirty on Mrs Sheffield? She seems a very nice lady."

"I wish you wouldn't use . . . I couldn't say . . . It's not for me . . ." Fixed by Charlie's stare again, she hurried on: "Well, there are people who say they wanted her out of her parish positions so they could take over themselves."

"They?"

"Well, Mrs Harridance, Selena, and one or two others."

When he left Mrs Gumbold's Charlie felt very much more wised up on parish matters than when he had gone there. A seething mass of ambition, dirty tricks, slander and innuendo, or so it seemed. This didn't surprise him. It would not have been very different in the predominantly black parish in his native Brixton with which he was well acquainted. His mother had fulfilled the double purpose of both spreading and providing the subject matter for a great deal of the gossip.

Charlie parked his car in a cul-de-sac off the Ilkley Road and walked along to Pizza Pronto. It was a takeaway he and his girl-friend had used in their time, though it was not the best in the area. He found it overflowing with waiting customers: word had obviously got around that there was a connection between it and the murder which was occupying everyone's attention that spring Sunday morning. There was a rather dim girl at the cash desk, and two men were working flat out around the ovens. He took out his ID and flashed it in the direction of the proprietor, a slim, worried-looking man in his fifties. He came over, visibly reluctant.

"We're very busy."

"I can see that. Is that Silvio?"

He nodded in the direction of the small, frantically busy young man who was constructing pizzas as if he was aiming at the Book of Records.

"No. Silvio is off today. That boy I have on loan from the Trat-toria Aliberti."

"I see. You normally have two boys, don't you?"

"Yes. Is both off duty today."

"Ah. . . . Right. Well, I'll come round and hope to see him tomorrow."

Hesitantly, uncertainly, Signor Gabrielli said, "Of course. Yes. All right. I'll tell him."

Thoughtfully Charlie walked back to his car. He very much doubted that he was going to be talking to Silvio in the near future. It might be that some kind of alert would have to be put out, though they would need more hard evidence that there was a connection with the dead man. It could be, he thought, that they could use more subtle methods. He looked at his watch. One fifteen. Service at St Saviour's would be long over. However, he drove towards it and cruised along the road that it stood on. The church was a large Victorian construction, abounding in knobs and small spires. He had read a smart journalistic piece once saying how much better Victorian Gothic was than the real thing. He didn't think the author could have been thinking of St Saviour's.

He was just about to speed up towards the vicarage when he saw the door open at the Five Hundred pub, a short way away, and a family group emerge. He pulled his car up beside the kerb and watched them in the mirror as they came in his direction. It was the conventional enough family group—father, mother, daughter, daughter's boyfriend, son—yet somehow ill-assorted: or rather, with one discordant element, one cuckoo in the nest. The one whom he identified as the son seemed not to walk or talk or behave generally in the natural way the others had. It was as if he was conscious of being, or had persuaded himself that he was, on show.

Charlie got out of the car as they approached.

"Hello," he said to Rosemary.

"Hello." He was unsure how much welcome there was in the greeting. She turned to her family. "This is one of the detectives on the Mills case. I'm sorry, I've forgotten your name."

"DC Peace."

"Peace be with you," said the son, and let out a laugh like the last of the bathwater escaping. He laughed alone. Charlie behaved as people do when they have heard every possible joke on their name.

"This is Mark," said Rosemary, in a voice pregnant with meaning. "Janet and her boyfriend Kevin. And my husband Paul."

"I'll probably want to talk to all of you before long—me or my boss. It was just you I wanted to ask about something at the moment," he added, turning to Rosemary. She nodded, though Charlie felt she was suppressing anxiety. They let the others walk on, then followed at some distance behind.

"I'm trying to get something straight about the party last night," Charlie began. "You said you were behind the table that the food was to be served from, and Mills was one of a little group standing about nearby, right?"

"That's right."

"Tell me what happened when the food arrived."

"I thought I had done. Let me see. . . ." Rosemary's voice had been edgy. Now she put on an air of trying to visualise the scene. Charlie was sure that she had thought about it all too often since their earlier talk. "The deliveryman from Pizza Pronto came in, bang on the dot when we had arranged. He had a pile of pizzas up to his chin. He put them down in front of us on the table, then I and the other ladies each took one out of its carton and started cutting them up."

"And the deliveryman?"

"He left, of course."

"There was no . . . confrontation, episode of some kind, between him and Mills?"

"Not that I noticed. I was busy slicing pizzas. It's not that easy if they have a crispy bottom."

"There was no question of the man from Pizza Pronto helping you?"

Rosemary made gestures of just having remembered.

"Ah—that's right. I'd forgotten that. I asked him if he'd like to help—him being so much quicker and better than us, probably—and he started round, then remembered they were very busy at the takeaway and said he'd better not be away too long."

Rosemary was a guileless liar, Charlie decided, but hardly a wise one: she must surely realise that parish gossip about her and the Pizza Pronto boy would get to the police before long. Then a thought struck him: probably she was lying to give the boy time to get away. When she was sure he had, she would come clean. He could of course have challenged her version of events and of the situation, but he preferred to give the appearance of accepting it, if only on the well-worn principle of giving someone enough rope. He smiled down at her.

"Well, that clears that up," he said. They had finished up outside the vicarage. "Are you going to eat straight away? I wondered if I might pop in and have a word with your family. They were all at the party, weren't they?"

"Yes, they were. You won't want me, will you? I've all sorts of little things to do in the kitchen."

The Sheffield family were assembled in the dining room, talking and laughing. They were apparently unconcerned by Mills's death, and by the reappearance of the policeman investigating it. When Charlie asked if they had talked to Mills at the party they all shook their heads.

"He was talking to local businessmen," said Paul Sheffield, who seemed, of them all, the most at ease. "He tended to. If there was no woman he was interested in, he liked to be polishing up his contacts."

"*De mortuis nil nisi bonum*," said Mark. He considerately turned to Charlie and translated in a kindly tone. "One should only speak good of the dead."

"That would make murder investigations practically impossible," said Charlie.

"I've always thought that a silly injunction," said Paul. "Surely it should be while they're living that you shouldn't speak ill of people."

"So none of you had anything to do with him last night?" Charlie asked. He saw a flash of something pass over the daughter's eyes, but her boyfriend jumped in.

145

"I don't even know which one he was. It's very frustrating. Towards the end of the evening Janet introduced me to Mrs Harridance, and the rest of the time passed like a blur."

"I believe he's been a member of the St Saviour's congregation for some time," said Charlie, turning to Paul.

"Oh yes, quite a while. Since my time here, but it must be something like . . . oh, twelve years or more."

"Do you remember how or why he started coming?"

"I can't say. I suppose he'd just moved here—that is the usual reason." He paused, as his wife came into the room. "Do you remember how Dark Satanic—how Stephen Mills started coming to St Saviour's?"

His question had been drowned in a gale of laughter from his wife and daughter.

"Really, Father, you've given the policeman a totally false impression of the man!" protested Mark.

"Not so bloody false," muttered his sister.

"Right," said Rosemary, becoming businesslike again. "How did Dark Satanic Mills come to be a member of St Saviour's congregation? I've asked myself often enough why he was a member at all. . . . I somehow associate him with old Mr Unwin. That's his father-in-law. He was much spryer then, of course, and in complete control. I seem to think either he brought him along, or they were often together."

"He and Dorothy weren't married then, though," put in Paul. "And Mr Unwin wasn't a member of our church. He was a red-hot Evangelical. I married Stephen and Dorothy—what?—about ten or more years ago."

"I rather think that marriage to Dorothy sprang from his friendship with her father," said Rosemary. "Odd way round, that."

"You said to me that you didn't think Dorothy Mills was a very

146

important element in Stephen Mills's life," said Charlie. "What was it that made you think that?"

"It was only an impression," said Rosemary thoughtfully. "It's just that you don't see them around together much. Oh, occasionally she'd come to church, or to one of our do's, but it was occasionally. If we were at a concert or the theatre in Leeds you might see Stephen, but to my recollection we hardly every saw him and his wife together."

"If you had to make any sort of date or arrangement with him," said her husband, "he'd take out his diary and consult it, but he'd never say he'd have to ask his wife. Most men do these days—as a sort of sop, I suppose—but he never did."

"And you implied there were other women," Charlie pressed him.

"That was certainly the impression given. I wouldn't be able to name any names."

Mark nodded wisely, as if his previous strictures had been justified. Charlie could imagine Mark being exceedingly irritating. He turned to Rosemary.

"Could you name any names?"

"No, I couldn't. You might say that if there weren't he should have been sued for false pretences. It was really a question of manner. He exuded confidence in his powers of attraction. If any woman gave the slightest sign of responding he was in there pressing his advantage home. But as to *evidence* of his sleeping with any of them—no, I'm afraid I have none."

"Isn't that odd?" Charlie asked.

"Maybe," said Rosemary, not seeming convinced. "But maybe he took care to keep that side of himself away from the congregation. I've certainly seen him emerging from a pretty sleazy massage parlour in town—The Sinful Sunbed, in Potter Street. He just grinned, quite unembarrassed. So perhaps he didn't want to compromise his position at St Saviour's."

"That suggests his position there was important to him," said Charlie.

"Though there's also the possibility that the ladies there are just not very tempting."

Once again Charlie could have sworn that a shadow passed over Rosemary's daughter's face.

CHAPTER THIRTEEN

Partners

On his way back to base Charlie dropped in at the flat he shared with his girlfriend Felicity. It was a one-bedroom affair, but with a large living room they had already made cheerful and personal by their own choice of pictures and bits and pieces of furniture. Felicity was surrounded by books and was hunched over a blank writing pad.

"So what made them summon you early?" she asked.

"It's a murder."

"It's lovely being a policeman's partner," commented Felicity. "You have such lovely casual conversations about perfectly horrible things."

"I'm surprised none of your ghoulish university friends have rung to tell you."

"They know I'm supposed to be writing an essay. Who was it?"

"Know a man called Stephen Mills?"

"Never heard of him."

"Ask around of your friends—particularly women."

"Particularly a certain sort of woman student, I suppose."

"Yes. . . . Felicity, you go to Pizza Pronto more often than I do."

"Don't I ever! All those nights when you say you'll be home and then ring to say you're working late."

"Would you recognise the boys who work there?"

She frowned, sidetracked.

"The boys? Is it all right to call them 'boys,' I wonder?"

"Spare me the intricacies of political correctness. Would you know them?"

"It's only recently that there's been two. I've only seen the new one once, and there was nothing very remarkable about him."

"And the other?"

"Oh yes, I've seen him often. The proprietor speaks to him in Italian, but I don't think he is. Maybe North African."

"Both the boys have scarpered, or so I suspect. The new one won't be in the Leeds area, if he knows what's good for him, but the other one may be. Neither of them has a work permit, if my guess is right."

"You're not harassing illegal immigrants, are you, Charlie?"

"In my job I do what I'm told to do," said Charlie impatiently. It was an old argument. "But no—the new one is involved some-how in the murder, and I'd like to know if he said anything to the other that might throw light on it. He's quite likely to have gone to some other pizzeria in town. Could you alert some of your stu-dent friends to look out for him?"

Felicity thought, then shook her head.

"I doubt that would work. He's probably gone to a quite dif-ferent area of Leeds, hasn't he?"

"Probably."

"Students change digs, but they don't often move right across town. You hear of something going in your area and you snap it up. . . . Quite apart from the question of whether they *want* to help the police . . . Wouldn't it be better to drive around and look?"

"When we have a spare week, I suppose."

"It wouldn't take that long," said Felicity confidently. "I'll look in the Yellow Pages for likely places and map out a route. I could cruise around myself, just look through the windows. You won't need the car, I suppose?"

"I'll be working all the hours God sends, and then some."

When Charlie got back to headquarters he was told that Oddie had just come in with a witness. He found them in a corridor on the way to an interview room and was introduced to Brian Ferrett. He was a chunky, slightly chubby young man, with thick brown curls framing a moonlike face and a manner that would have been encouraging on a school playing field—cheery, a little too loud. If he showed signs of nervousness, that was to be discounted; it was one of the most common reactions to murder, among the innocent as much as among the guilty.

"It's just incredible," he said to Charlie when they had been introduced. "Mind-blowing. I mean, you couldn't meet a more decent bloke than old Steve. And so full of life."

That was as of yesterday, Charlie felt like saying. But he held his peace and, with Oddie, ushered him through to the interview room.

When the formalities had been gone through, it was Oddie who started the questioning.

"You were Stephen Mills's—partner, was it? Or second in command?"

"Second in command," Ferrett said, readily and unresentfully. "Though he treated me more like a partner. I'd practically worked my way up from office boy."

"In how many years was that?"

"I'd been with him eight years. The business had been going nearly a year when he took me on."

"And I gather you do—you've been doing—a lot of the travelling involved in recent times."

"Yes, I do a lot of that. Stephen still had his places where he had a special expertise, good contacts he wanted to maintain. But yes—a lot of it I'd been getting to do, and developed my own contacts and expertise. Due off tomorrow, as a matter of fact—" He saw something in Oddie's face and said hurriedly, "Nothing that can't be put off."

"How did you come to get the job?"

He leaned back in his chair confidently.

"He wanted someone good with languages. It's something I've never found a problem. I graduated in Russian, but there were no jobs around. I had French and German as well, to Advanced level. Stephen saw that there was use for Russian in all the Eastern bloc countries where it was taught, and when he realised I was very fast at learning new languages he took me on. He was tremendously farsighted: he could see that things were loosening up in Eastern Europe. Hungary, Bulgaria, then gradually the rest—like the old domino theory in the Far East, only in reverse. Steve was just waiting for it to happen, then going in to see how he could help."

"Help?"

"Do business with them. That is helping them. We had what they need—taught them the skills they need."

"Is it in Eastern Europe where most of your business lies?"

"Oh no. But it's the *developing* part of our business. The bulk occurs in the Common Market countries. That's where the money is. In spite of all the processes of standardisation, each country has its peculiarities and quirks, its little hurdles you have to jump. It's those we can advise customers about, as well as putting them in touch with individual firms with marketing interests that coincide with their own."

"I see. And is business flourishing?"

"Oh yes!" he said, with positively boyish enthusiasm. "Brilliant. Of course we were hit by the recession, especially when it really started biting on the Continent as well. But we've weathered it—and now things are picking up in a big way."

It was the first time Charlie had heard anyone outside government claim that things were picking up.

"So you were both busy?"

"No question of that. Still, we're used to it. There was a time when Steve was running his father-in-law's business as well. That *really* took twenty-five hours a day!"

"Not much time for personal life, when you're working that hard," said Oddie neutrally. Ferrett shot him a glance, markedly less confident.

"Well, Steve was more or less only doing it as a favour to his wife's father."

"Somebody commented that Dorothy Mills was something of an irrelevance in her husband's life," put in Charlie. Brian Ferrett spread out his hands in a gesture of coming clean.

"Look, he was a bloke in a thousand. Straight as a die, old Steve. He'd never willingly have hurt Dottie. But maybe—and it *is* maybe, because we didn't discuss it—maybe he realised early on that he'd made the wrong choice. She's a nice enough lady, but she's got no class, to put it bluntly. She's not sexy or elegant, and she was no use at all in the business. Stephen was no monk. Maybe—again, maybe—he got what he wanted elsewhere. But he stayed with her, had her dad living with them, and I never heard him give her a cross word. Not every wife could say the same. Fair's fair. He did his duty to her."

It was a long speech, but Oddie didn't find it an entirely convincing one. He certainly didn't believe this was a subject they had never discussed.

"Where was the 'elsewhere' where he got what he needed?" asked Oddie. Ferrett shrugged.

"Search me. It wasn't something we talked about, like I said. I only know there were times when I didn't ask him where he'd been, know what I mean? My *impression* is that there may have been one or two affairs, but that mostly he got what he wanted by paying for it, if you get me."

"I get you," said Oddie with a man-to-man smile. "Now, obviously in this sort of enquiry we have to look for enemies of the dead man. Do you know of any?"

"Of course I've thought," said Ferrett, engagingly candid. "Thought all the way here. It's what first springs to mind, isn't it? But there's none I know of in his business life. Why should there be? He was providing a service, and there was nothing to speak of in the way of competition. He'd carved out his own little niche."

"Clever of him. What about dissatisfied customers?"

Ferrett shook his head confidently.

"It doesn't do to have dissatisfied customers. If there were any that felt they'd been given bad advice, or hadn't got their money's worth, Steve scrapped the bill or sent them a much smaller one. That was only sensible business practice."

"What about his earlier life?"

"Before he came to Leeds? I've no idea. Never discussed it. I think he came from London."

"But he never mentioned a father or mother? Or other family? Friends from the time before he came to Leeds?"

"Not to me. I've always had the impression that both parents were dead."

"Unusual for a man in his forties."

"Maybe. Could have been some kind of accident."

"Of course. But from all we've found out Mills seems to have emerged in Leeds like some kind of phoenix from the ashes."

"If you say so. By the time I met him he was already married to Dorothy and very much part of the family there. He and old

Unwin were thick as . . . very close. It never occurred to me to ask about his earlier life."

For two people who had worked closely for years there seemed to be many subjects they had kept away from.

"We have to ask, though. *Some*where there's got to be a motive for his murder."

"You don't think it could be sexual? That he was murdered by someone he picked up on the way home?"

Oddie shrugged.

"It's possible. Anything is possible, nothing is ruled out. But if you look at the pattern of that sort of crime you see that homosexuals are sometimes murdered by violent men they've picked up, prostitutes likewise. But a prostitute murdering a client? It may happen, but we'd want to find a pretty strong *other* reason, if you get my meaning."

"But if she wasn't a prostitute—say a student, and if he'd forced her . . ." Ferrett saw his mistake immediately. "But of course Steve wouldn't. It's inconceivable. Wouldn't have needed to, quite apart from anything else. And he wasn't that type at all, not at all."

He subsided, conscious of having put his foot in it. Charlie left a moment or two before he took up the questioning.

"Do you know of any connection between Mills and a young man who works in *Pizza Pronto*, on the Ilkley Road—he goes by the name of Silvio, but that probably isn't his real one."

Ferrett frowned.

"Never heard of him. Doesn't sound likely. Our contacts are all with businessmen."

"What about the vicar of St Saviour's and his family?"

"Oh, he had lots to do with the Reverend Sheffield. They were both very active in Rotary. And of course old Steve threw himself into parish affairs."

"What about Sheffield's family? His daughter, for example?"

"Ah. . . . You mean did she have the hots for him?" Ferrett put on that all-males-together smile again. "There was a time when I thought so. We gave her a bit of typing to do at home, and after that she used that as an excuse for coming to the office whenever she could think of a reason."

"You don't know any more than that?"

"I don't. I've told you, that was an area of his life where I didn't ask questions. There may have been something going on. If so, it didn't last very long. She went off to college—oh, three years or more ago it must be now."

It was becoming clear that they weren't going to get any more out of Brian Ferrett for the time being. When they had shown him out of police headquarters Oddie and Peace turned and looked at each other.

"I don't—" they began simultaneously, then stopped.

"Trust him an inch?" suggested Charlie.

"Not a centimetre. All that 'straight as a die, old Steve' stuff. I never met Mills, but he was employing as his second in command a distinctly dodgy type."

"And if you take on and promote a dodgy type, the chances are you are a dodgy type yourself, and the business you're into is dodgy as well."

"A business that claims to be doing well at the moment *has* to be suspect."

"Especially one dealing with Europe, where everyone's in the doldrums."

"You don't trust the people close to Stephen Mills, do you?" Oddie said, looking at his sidekick. "You didn't trust his wife either, unless I'm mistaken."

Charlie considered.

"That was different. I didn't *believe* the wife. I might have

156

trusted her on other matters, in other circumstances. There's no way I'd trust this joker on anything."

"The question is, what was the dodgy business they were both engaged in? And I have a mountain of paper that I'm going to have to go through to try to find out."

"What's the drill?" asked Charlie, without enthusiasm. "Do we sit down and go through it all together?"

"I thought about that. It has its advantages, but it leaves the 'people' side of the case up in the air. Is there anyone we ought to be talking to now?"

"Ah . . . well, there's the Sheffield children. They seem to be up for the weekend, so we ought to talk to them as soon as possible. I had a hunch the girl knew something about Mills she wasn't letting on about, and now we've talked to Ferrett it's pretty obvious what it was."

"Yes," said Oddie slowly, adding a caution: "though Ferrett was all the time trying to shift our attention to his private life rather than his business affairs."

"Right. Even to suggesting that straight as a die old Steve was a rapist. But, whatever the dodgy business they were engaged in, the possibility is still there that he was killed because of something in his private life."

"Agreed. Anything else?"

"I'd like to track down the other boy who worked in the pizza place. My suspicion is that they've both gone missing but that the other one may still be in the Leeds area. If I'm right they were both working here illegally. If that is so, they'd have had a bond, they'd have talked."

"The priority is to get hold of the boy called Silvio."

"Of course it is. But what chance, with no name and no photograph?"

"And Mrs Sheffield?"

"Is saying nothing. But there is one possibility—"

"Yes?"

Charlie produced his idea without much hope.

"Bugging the Sheffield phone. I suspect he's fond of her and will contact her."

"Put it from your mind. You know it's out of the question."

Charlie shook his head regretfully.

"Any villain can walk into a shop and buy the latest hi-tech bugging device and a whole range of things for industrial espionage or any type of private spying. And we have to go to Home Secretary level."

"But those are the rules. We do. Any evidence we got would be useless if we'd done anything else."

"It wasn't so much evidence I wanted to get. Just where this young man *is*. I suppose the best we'll have to hope is that once the chap is well out of our reach Mrs Sheffield will come in and tell us what he told *her*. Whatever that is, it probably won't be much if he is fond of her and wants her to think well of him."

"Mike!" Somebody was bustling along with a piece of paper, and handed it over. It was a white-coated man from the mortuary. "Preliminary p.m. report."

Mike Oddie skimmed through it, then went back and read it through with more care.

"Well?" asked Charlie.

"Pretty much what we thought. He was attacked, beaten up—there's some evidence of martial arts techniques, maybe from someone who'd learnt a few blows, basic self-protection stuff. He was stunned, unconscious, when his throat was cut. They're not going to stick their necks out—*of course* they're not going to stick their necks out!—but they say it's possible he was unconscious for some time before his throat was cut."

"So, getting fanciful, one of the Sheffields could have beaten him up, gone home for the carving knife, then come back and done him in?"

"Theoretically. It's not a scenario I'd go for."

"I wasn't being serious. On the other hand, if you have a knife and want him dead, why not use it straight away?"

It was something they both pondered as they went their separate ways.

CHAPTER FOURTEEN

Terrible Good Cause

Charlie thought with satisfaction of the mountains of paper Mike Oddie had taken home with him to get to the bottom of Stephen Mills's business affairs. By the time he saw them they would have been filleted by an expert hand, and only the ones of possible relevance to the case would need to be read and pondered. All very much to the good. Charlie's interest in crime was people: faces, attitudes, gestures, signs of hidden woes and hidden passions. The intricacies of financial malpractice could interest him only when they led him to the mind that had conceived them.

And there were other ways of getting into contact with that mind, and other aspects of it that were to him of more interest. As soon as he got to his desk he looked at his watch. It was coming up to half past six. After a moment's thought he got out his telephone directory and rang the Sheffields.

"Oh, Mrs Sheffield, it's DC Peace here. . . . Progressing, but a long way from concluded yet. I wondered, Mrs Sheffield, how long your children were going to be there."

"Oh, Mark is with us till tomorrow evening," Rosemary said,

with no obvious signs of pleasure in her voice. "Janet and Kevin are driving back to London later tonight."

"Then I wonder if I could talk to Janet, please?"

"Of course."

There was a pause before she said it, the involuntary giveaway of someone not used to dealing with the police, then a longer pause before her daughter came on the line with a very tentative "Hello?"

"Hello, Miss Sheffield. This is DC Peace—we met earlier. I thought since you're leaving Leeds tonight we ought to talk about the party last night."

"Oh, should we? Is there any need? I've told you everything I know."

"It's perfectly normal," said Charlie, in his comfortable-copper voice, "just routine. You're the only person that I know of—you and your boyfriend—who'll be leaving Leeds. . . . And we need to talk about Stephen Mills generally."

"Oh." There was a silence of several seconds, and then he detected a note of relief in her voice when she said, "Yes, I suppose we do. I think I'd prefer to come to you."

"Excellent. You'll know the Leeds Police Headquarters, of course. And could you bring—Kevin, is it?—with you?"

"Yes, I suppose so. . . . He doesn't know anything about Stephen Mills."

"Just a matter of routine, like I said," said Charlie smoothly. "I'll hope to see you in twenty minutes or so."

They arrived together at the desk, an appealing-looking couple, humorous and warm, with an air of suiting each other. Charlie thought he might have a lot in common with Kevin. But it wasn't Kevin that was of principal interest, and he resisted the suggestion that he should talk to them together.

"It's never done," he said. "But if you'll wait here, sir, I'll have a chat with you later."

It had been Kevin, not Janet, who suggested that he might talk to them together, and Charlie got the impression she felt a sort of relief that he had vetoed the proposal. Once in the interview room she sat forward in her chair opposite him with a nervous expectancy. She was not a beautiful girl, but she was healthy, sharp-eyed, alert. If the word "wholesome" had not been devalued, she would have been that.

Charlie came straight to the point.

"You knew Stephen Mills a lot better than you've been letting on, didn't you?"

"Yes. Who told you, I wonder? Was it that awful Ferrett person? Oh, never mind. Yes, I did know him better than I've been letting on."

"And a lot better than your mother realises, I would guess."

"Yes, mother never knew anything beyond the fact I'd done some secretarial work for the firm. I'd be glad if you didn't have to tell her now."

"I don't see why I should need to."

"Good. She loathed him. Somehow I'd feel . . . devalued in her eyes if she found out. In our house he was always 'Dark Satanic Mills'—an object of suspicion, though I don't think they ever made up their minds what they suspected him of. I think that probably made him more attractive in my eyes—the Byronic man of mystery, the attractive rotter, that kind of thing."

"Did he turn out like that on closer acquaintance?"

She frowned.

"You know, in one way he *did*. In the sense that he must have *had* a past, like the Byronic hero, but I never found out anything about it beyond dark hints. For example, his speech was very precise, almost old-fashioned, but it told you nothing about where he came from."

"Did you find out what he did?"

She looked surprised.

"Yes, of course. I thought you must have found out about me from Brian Ferrett. I did typing work for Stephen. His business was facilitating the work of exporters, particularly in Europe—finding markets for people, getting things through all the red tape, making contact for them with people who mattered."

"And that was all the company did?"

"So far as I know. . . ." She pondered. "I was hardly at the heart of the business, but all the typing I did for him and Brian was about things like that."

"I suppose it would have been. But your relationship wasn't just boss-typist, was it?"

"No," said Janet flatly. "I threw myself at him, to tell you the truth. Quietly, in private—so there was no scandal. I went through a long phase, I suppose it was a kind of prolonged adolescence, of finding dark, Latin, rather oily men attractive. The Valentino type. They all turned out to be rather awful. When they made love they were really making love to themselves. Mills was one of a line."

"And he was no exception, I suppose."

"No. If anything an intensification of the tendency."

"Where did you go?"

"To make love? All sorts of places. Sometimes in the open air—Ilkley Moor, or on the Haworth–Hebden Bridge moors. This was summer, and there were lots of hot days."

Charlie racked his brains to remember the last hot summer, but failed.

"When would this have been?"

"Five years ago."

"But when it wasn't hot?"

"He had a flat—a small, rather insalubrious little place over a shop in the Ilkley Road."

164

"What kind of shop?"

"A camera shop—Snaps was the name."

"Was it just a flat to take girls to?"

"So far as I know. When we went there I felt as if I was one of a long line and was part of a routine."

She made no effort to keep the distaste and self-loathing out of her voice.

"No signs of business done from there?"

"No. But I wasn't there much—a quick in and out, you might say."

"How long did the affair last?"

"Oh, five or six weeks. The length of the school holidays."

"You were still at school?"

"Yes, coming up to my last year."

"How did it start?"

"Well, I fancied him. Quite shamelessly, I'm afraid. So as I said, I threw myself at him. To that extent he was blameless. After church one Sunday I went up to him and asked him if he had any typing or computer work I could do in the holidays. I could see in his eyes that he had something in mind other than typing and that he knew I had too. Humiliating to look back on."

"So he agreed, and it went on from there."

"Yes. He gave me some work, bedded me, and I kept on going back on the excuse of wanting more work if it was going. I hate myself for it now."

"Everyone has one or two big mistakes in that line."

"I had a whole series."

"How did it end? Did you just go back to school?"

"Not quite. No, that wouldn't have ended it. . . ." She thought before she spoke, making Charlie very aware that this was the most difficult part. "I had had the feeling for some time that he was getting bored. If I'd had any savvy I'd have cooled it, played hard to get, but I was very immature. I kept going round there, supposedly to see if he had any jobs, but in reality . . . well, I suppose I don't need to spell it out. Anyway one day he said 'OK, there's a job for you, but we'll have to fetch it.' So we got into the car and drove to this large house—"

"In Abbingley?"

"Oh yes. Not far. And he opened the front door with his own key, and I was just realising it was his own house when he took me into the sitting room and introduced me—no, it was more like he was flaunting me—to his wife. He said: 'Hello, Dottie. You know Janet, don't you? She's come round to do something for me.' And he . . . he *leered*. And before I knew what he was doing he took me upstairs and into a big double bedroom that I imagine was his and hers, or had been once, and he was stripping off, and stripping me as well and . . . well, I suppose I don't have to go on."

"You didn't resist?"

She stared down at the table, remembering.

"I did . . . but very feebly. Just said things like, 'Stephen, we can't.' Quite useless, really. It was as if he had some kind of *power*. I suppose girls have said that from time immemorial. I think because I was so young and knew so little, and he was so mature and worldly-wise and—*corrupt*, that there was a kind of power he had over me and enjoyed. It was like being mesmerised by a snake."

"You think his wife knew what you were doing?"

"Oh, of course she knew, and that was the point."

"How did she look when he took you to meet her?"

"Oh, it's difficult to describe. Weary. Almost indifferent."

"Was there hate there?"

"Maybe. But she didn't show it. She didn't even show contempt for me, if she felt it. Her look was more . . . pitying."

"Did you see her again?"

"No. When we'd done he just got up and put his clothes on,

and I did the same. Back to business seemed to be the message he wanted to get across. On the way out, in the hall, we met the father—old 'Onions' Unwin, her father. Stephen said, 'Oh, you know Janet Sheffield, don't you, Dad? Paul and Rosemary's girl. She's been doing work for us at the shop.' The old chap sort of bumbled a greeting, Stephen shouted ''Bye, Dottie,' and we left the house. He was oozing with self-satisfaction. He drove me home, hardly speaking, but he gave a nasty grin as he dropped me off at the vicarage as if the fact that I was the vicar's daughter gave added spice—maybe the only spice—to the affair. That was his sort of humour."

"And—?" asked Charlie.

"And that put paid to it. I suppose that was the intention. Nobody was in, and I went up to my room and sobbed and sobbed. You know people nowadays are always talking about low self-esteem? That was the rock bottom of my self-esteem. I bathed him out of me, and by the time I had finished I knew that the affair was over, knew that I wanted it to be over, and knew that I would never ever look at that type again."

"Have you seen much of him since?"

"I've *seen* him often enough. Couldn't avoid that, with him always being at church. I've not exchanged a word until last night at the party. He came up behind me and whispered, 'How come we never get together these days?' I gave him a look and froze him out. I think he only came up because he saw I had a boyfriend and was happy with him. That would have been something worth ruining. And I knew he really hated women who rejected him or showed him that he could never get anywhere with them. It's not very effective after he definitely *has* got somewhere with them, but that's why I froze him out."

"So the fascination had really worn off."

"Really!" She looked him in the eye with what seemed a genuine frankness. "It had become repulsion. But that summer it was like a basilisk. It was only the sheer nastiness and cruelty of what he did and made me an accomplice in doing that saved me."

"What did you feel when you heard he was dead?"

"Nothing. I'm glad I didn't feel exultation, feel my humiliation had been revenged or anything melodramatic like that. I was empty of feeling for him."

"Could you have killed him yourself?"

She thought.

"No. I suppose you'll think, 'She would say that,' but since you thought it worth asking, I'll tell you. I couldn't have killed him, not even *then*. I felt disgust for myself, and I think that's what I felt for him too. Disgust, not hatred."

"Do you think that's what his wife felt as well?"

"I couldn't fathom what she thought then. She's the sort you look at and feel you never can. Those eyes—they're almost frightening. I think the old phrase about still waters running deep very much applies there."

Charlie shifted in his chair.

"The emotions you feel towards Mills are pretty similar to the ones your mother feels towards him, aren't they?"

"I suppose so. I've come to toe the family line on the subject."

"Do you think your mother could ever have had a similar experience?"

Her eyes opened wide.

"*No*! No, I really don't. I never thought about it, but it's absolutely out of the question. Mother and father are completely faithful to each other."

"A lot of children feel that about their parents, quite wrongly. And there has been talk in the parish recently about your mother and the boy from the pizzeria."

"Oh, you're on to that, are you?"

"I haven't talked about it with your mother yet. Have you?"
Janet nodded.

"A little. She is fond of him, she is sorry for him, she wanted to help him. Anyone would feel the same, except for someone like that old battle-axe Florrie Harridance. That's *all* there was to it. No affair. And no affair with Stephen Mills either."

"You're very loyal. Do you think your brother feels the same?"

"Mark? Oh, he's training for the priesthood and knows nothing whatever about real life."

"He struck me as a pillock."

"He is. You wouldn't trust his opinion rather than mine, would you?"

"No, I wouldn't," said Charlie truthfully. Especially as on the whole Janet's agreed with his own.

Janet's boyfriend Kevin had little to tell. He admitted that he had spent most of the evening observing the wrong things—in his case Mark Sheffield and Florrie Harridance. He had been watching and listening to them with an inexorable author's interest, and anything else had passed him by.

When he had got rid of them both it was half past nine. Time to knock off for the day. Charlie made some notes to himself for the next day's work and then drove back to the flat. His plans for a cosy supper and an early night were shattered the moment he opened the door.

"Do you want him?" Felicity asked.

"Who?"

"The boy from Pizza Pronto—the other one. I could be mistaken because he was working at the back of a long, narrow takeaway place, but I think he's at Pizza Suprema, which is on the Crompton Road—number 45."

Charlie thought, looking round regretfully.

"If I don't get him now—" he said, and then turned and ran down the stairs again. Felicity knew better than to ask if she could come. She felt rather proud, however, of the participation she had been allowed thus far and knew that that wasn't something Charlie was going to mention to Mike Oddie.

Charlie spotted Pizza Suprema well before he got there, so he parked a good way away. It was on a corner, and the little yard at the back was open to the street. He sauntered towards the place. The back door was open, and the lid of a garbage bin was on the ground. The boy—*a* boy—was cleaning up for the night. When he reached the place Charlie nipped into the shadows of the yard and waited. It was only a couple of minutes before the young man came out with an armful of tins, packets and other debris and began piling them into the bin. When he banged the lid on it and turned to go in he found Charlie in the doorway.

"Before you do anything silly, like trying to run away," Charlie said, "let's get this straight: I am a policeman but I'm not in the least interested in seeing your papers. I don't care if you're on the run from the police of five continents and I certainly don't care if you're working here illegally."

The young man was coffee-cream-coloured, round-faced and curly-haired. He looked at Charlie uncertainly.

"*C'est Stanko, n'est-ce-pas?*" he said, then changed to a very Gallic English. "It is about Stanko, is it not?"

"If he's the one who's sometimes called Silvio, yes. Shall we go inside?"

He stood aside, and they went into a long, narrow kitchen still smelling irresistibly of tomatoes and garlic and basil and oregano. He was reminded that he had had nothing but a sandwich all day. The young man, with the instinct of the hotel trade, sensed his need.

"You 'ave 'unger? You like 'alf a pizza?"

170

Charlie nodded, just at the moment when his stomach let out a pathetic whine. The boy smiled, took a large pizza from a cooling oven and cut it in half. When he handed Charlie his section they both agreed to dispense with a knife and fork, biting into the gooey heart of the pie.

"You eat with me. You can't mean me 'arm," said the boy.

Charlie could think of colleagues who could share a pizza with a suspect and nick him while he was wiping his fingers, but he didn't mention them.

"What's your name?" he asked, and then amended that to "What shall I call you?"

"Call me Yussef," the young man replied.

"Right, Yussef. I'm not going to ask you anything about yourself. How long have you known—Stanko, is it?"

"Yes, Stanko. But I don't think that's 'is real name. 'E 'ave many names. 'E came about three weeks ago to Pizza Pronto."

"Did you get on well with him?"

"Yes, very well. 'E is a nice, gentle man, very *sympathique*. We talk a lot, 'ave a lot in common—you know?"

"I know. Where was he from?"

Yussef considered his loyalties before replying.

"'E is from Yugoslavia—what used to be Yugoslavia."

"Are you both Moslem?"

Yussef spread out his hands.

"We 'ave not discussed. I am Moslem, but not so much. If 'e is Moslem, I think 'e is even less."

"Right. Did he have any friends in Leeds?"

"Oh yes. 'E 'ave Mr and Mrs Sheffield, especially Mrs."

"Nobody else?" Yussef shook his head. "Or enemies?" Yussef shook his head again.

"Right, now about yesterday. Was it a normal day, or did anything stand out?"

171

The young man thought long before replying.

"The evening 'e was different. When 'e came down 'e was all shook."

"Shook?"

"Like 'e'd 'ad bad news, or 'ear something 'orrible."

"You say came down. You were in the takeaway?"

"Yes. One of us always prepare for the evening with Signor Gabrielli. The other came down when we opened at half past five. Stanko came down then, and 'e was all shook."

"Did he say why?"

"No. I asked and 'e shook 'is 'ead and said 'e didn't want to talk, but 'e would tell me later. Said it was *atroce*. We talk French and sometimes Italian together."

"What does it mean?"

"'Orrible. Like you say a-att-atro-cee-us."

"Was that all he said?"

"Yes. 'E made a phone call—quite short. I didn't 'ear nothing what was said. We was very busy with lots of pizzas for the party at the church."

"He took them, didn't he?"

"Yes. 'E drove our little van."

"What about when he came back?"

"Was shook. Still more shook."

"I see. And what happened as the evening went on?"

"We was not so busy. About five to ten Stanko asked if 'e could go. Said 'e 'ad to meet someone. Signor Gabrielli said 'fine,' and 'e went."

"But that wasn't the last you saw of him?"

Yussef seemed to consider his loyalties again, then realised his own peril and shook his head.

"No. 'E come in about eleven, when I was going to bed. Come

into my room, all very shook and upset. Said 'e 'ad to leave Leeds that night."

"Did he say why?"

"Said 'e 'ad been in a fight. 'E 'ad some martial hearts—said they was very useful in Yugoslavia, with lots of troubles even before the war start. 'E said 'e'd done awful damages to this man. 'E didn't think the man—'e didn't say 'is name—would go to the police, but 'e couldn't risk it. Someone might find 'im before 'e come round, and call the police. So 'e 'ad to go."

"I see. And next day you heard of the murder?"

Yussef looked at him challengingly.

"'E is not a murderer. Is not possible. 'E is a *gentle* boy. But Signor Gabrielli, 'e think: better if neither of us is there, in case the police come, so 'e arrange a swap for me."

"With someone who has got his papers? Right. Stanko had already taken off, I suppose. Was there anything else—anything you know about Stanko?"

The young man shook his head.

"His surname?"

"We didn't ask. It was better."

"So you've nothing else to tell me?"

The boy came up close, wiping the tomato from his lips.

"Stanko is gentle. A good, gentle, peace-loving boy."

"A gentle boy with skills in martial arts?"

"*Yes.* That is the point of martial hearts. They protect you. Like they are taught to women who 'ave not great strength so they can protect themselves."

"And do you think Stanko was protecting himself last night?"

The boy looked down.

"I do not know. But if 'e attacked, 'e 'ad good cause. Terrible good cause."

CHAPTER FIFTEEN

Talking About Rosemary

"Fascinating evening?" Charlie asked Mike Oddie when they came in to work next morning.

"Wonderful," said his boss. "Now I know what it's like to be drowned in paper."

"So you know all about his cash flow, his assets and liabilities, his business plan and whatever."

"I have an idea," said Oddie cautiously. "That is if his papers are an honest record. It all seems above board, it all seems like a genuine service which fills a real need. Letters testify that he had expertise and contacts, used them intelligently . . ."

"But?"

"But why do I get the idea that I know everything about his business except the most important thing?" He paused to sort his ideas out. "The only obvious 'but' is that I can't see from the records that it would have been all that profitable. Of course we don't know that Mills had a lavish life style, his wife probably has plenty of money, and yet—"

"And yet what we know of Mills doesn't suggest he'd be content with a modestly successful business."

"No, it doesn't," agreed Oddie enthusiastically. "That's not my picture, anyway."

"Was there anything to suggest other activities—any other source of income?"

"Well, only something very small, something I very nearly didn't pick up: there were a couple of references in business letters to 'number 94.' " He frowned, trying to be as exact as possible. "Quoting from memory they were: 'This is straying in the direction of number 94 matters' and 'I'll leave the unfinished number 94 business until I see you at Rotary.' Not a lot to go on."

"You don't want to ask the people who wrote the letters?"

"Certainly not now. I may have to as a last resort. If we assume it's an address, and if we start on the idea that it's in the Abbingley area of Leeds, there aren't a great many roads that go up as high as number 94."

"You could try a camera shop called Snaps," said Charlie reaching across the desk for the telephone directory.

"Why there?"

"It's to a flat above that he took Janet Sheffield. She saw it as a love nest, but it could have had a business side as well. Yes—here we are: Snaps, 94 Ilkley Road."

Oddie rubbed his hands.

"Right! Got it in one! Let's hear about your evening before we do anything more."

When he had heard Charlie's account of the two interviews, Oddie said: "What do you make of Stanko coming down at half past five in a foul mood?"

"I'm kicking myself I didn't ask Yussef what there was

upstairs," Charlie admitted. "Was there a telephone? A television? Somehow or other he'd heard something that enraged him. That's how I read it, anyway."

"Why not ring Gabrielli at Pizza Pronto?"

Charlie leafed through the book and did just that. Luckily he found him in, taking in supplies. He also found him terribly and earnestly anxious to help the police. Charlie managed the conversation without even mentioning Stanko, and when he put the phone down he said: "Television but not telephone. If they needed to ring anyone they had to use the phone in the takeaway."

"So this 'Yussef' had been downstairs preparing for the evening trade, while Stanko was upstairs. It's a fair bet he wasn't watching *Neighbours* or *Home and Away.*"

"It was Saturday, remember. The likely thing is the BBC news, which is generally just after five."

Oddie nodded.

"In his situation, coming from Yugoslavia, watching the news would be pretty obsessive, I'd guess. Get on to BBC North and see if you can get a video, and if not get on to Television Centre in London. I'll see about getting a warrant to search the flat above Snaps. Do you want to come along with me? Or have you got things to do on your own?"

As Oddie knew he would, Charlie said he had one or two things he'd like to do on his own, follow-up things. Charlie believed in hunting solo whenever possible. His first port of call was a shop called Flowers First. It was on University Road, and the name meant (as its proprietor Florrie Harridance would explain when asked or if unasked) that if couples had had a tiff they should buy flowers first and have the explanations afterwards. This certainly made commercial sense, and perhaps psychological sense as well. Whether the university people who largely lived in the Abbingley area were particularly liable to tiffs and makeups she did not say, but there were no signs of the shop being other than a viable financial concern when he dropped in there, other than the fact that there were no customers, which on a Monday morning was hardly surprising.

"We've not met, but we've spoken on the telephone," said Mrs Harridance, coming weightily forward like an aircraft carrier doing a manoeuvre in shallow water. "And I've caught a loook at you as you've gone past in the police car."

"I stand out," agreed Charlie.

"You do. Footballers you expect, and pop stars and newsreaders and drug traffickers, but black policemen you notice, and you're the first that's come my way. Not that I have a lot to do with the police, though I've supplied flowers to funerals you've had an interest in, that's for sure."

Charlie murmured his interest.

"Well, it's the Mills murder you'll be wanting to talk about, won't you? Well, like I say, I'm not one to get involved with the police, and at St Saviour's—"

"Questions," said Charlie forcefully. "And answers."

"I beg your pardon, young man?"

"Questions and answers. I don't want to *talk about* anything. I want to ask questions, and get answers from you. Short and direct answers, please. Right?"

Florrie looked daggers, but nodded.

"Why was there all this fuss about Mrs Sheffield and the Mothers' Union?"

Florrie swallowed. Her answer, when it came, was more a protest against his demand for brevity than compliance with it.

"She lost her faith. The Mothers' Union is a church organisation. Everyone felt it wasn't right her holding office."

"I see," said Charlie carefully. "I can see that loss of faith would be fatal for a clergyman, but for his wife? You say 'every-one,' but I haven't come across a great deal of opposition to Mrs Sheffield as yet."

"Well of course it's not *personal*. It's a matter of principle. I mean we're all sorry for her (though I think she could make an *effort* to get it back) but when she's one of the officials of the organisation, and it's the main women's group in the parish—"

"Short," said Charlie. "Short answers. I get your point. But I'm not convinced it hasn't been a question of other people wanting to take over her job."

"You're trying to make it sound unpleasant, young man, but you'll not rile me. I'm made of sterner stuff. People who do jobs like chairing the Mothers' Union get no thanks for it, and no financial rewards either—not like the Masons and Rotarians. All you get is hard work from morning to night. So just because some people in the parish desperately wanted me to take over the chair, I'll not have you saying—"

"Right, well let's change the subject a bit. I gather that at some stage the matter developed into gossip about Mrs Sheffield's private life. Were you responsible for that?"

"I was *not*. Quite the reverse, young man, if you did but know. Not that I need to justify myself to you, but when Selena came to me with what she'd heard people saying in that guesthouse in Scarborough, I said 'Hold on,' I said. 'It's all very flimsy,' I said, 'and the last thing we'd want people saying about us is that we'd been spreading malicious gossip, and it could rebound on us,' I said—"

"Us?"

"Well—" She was caught up short. Charlie was sorry he had tried to insist on short answers, because she obviously gave more away when given her rein. "Well, I meant those of us who thought it was time for a change, and time for those who'd been

179

occupying all these positions for years to step aside and let others have the chance."

Charlie was a mite puzzled by this, because there was a ring of truth about what she said, and an atom of shrewdness. There had always been, he suspected, a good chance that sexual scandal about the vicar's wife, if ill-substantiated, would rebound on the scandalmonger. Apparently Mrs Harridance had recognised this.

"And yet the scandal did get around," he pointed out.

"Well eventually it did, yes. Don't ask me how. People only started gossiping later, more than a week after Selena got home from Scarborough, and it wasn't with my agreement, because I'd told her right away I thought it was wrong and silly. But then maybe she'd been talking to someone else, getting other advice—"

"Such as?"

A cunning look came into her bulging eyes.

"You'd better ask her that. I wouldn't know anything about Selena's private life. We're different generations. Manners are different these days, to say nothing of morals. Any road, she found she had to go round afterwards and take it all back, so it rebounded on us, like I said it would. I'm disappointed in Selena. Whoever gave her the advice, you couldn't say it was *good* advice, could you? Now what you'd best do, young man, and I'm sure you don't want my advice but you could do worse than take it, is go round to Selena's and ask her what and who—"

"That's exactly what I'll do," said Charlie and turned and got out of the shop.

As he drove to Selena Meadowes's house he was turning over in his mind two thoughts: if Florrie Harridance was to be believed, she and Selena had rejected using the Rosemary–Stanko story against her, believing it might do them harm rather than good. But later something had changed Selena's mind and she had gone ahead and used it. Secondly, Florrie knew, or had a good idea, what or who that was, but she wanted it to come from her lieutenant, especially since she felt let down by her. If these propositions were correct, they could be useful.

Selena Meadowes's reception of him was very different from Florrie Harridance's. The moment she opened the door to him her manner was winsomely welcoming to the point of flirtatiousness. She made no bones about the fact that she knew who he was, though Charlie had no idea which of his various activities of the day before she had watched him at. Perhaps the mere fact that he was black made her land on the right assumption. In any case she led him through to the sitting room and prepared—or so it seemed, and Charlie reserved judgment on that—almost enthusiastically to be grilled.

"Though to be honest I can't tell you much," she said, turning her full face and and smiling a Doris Day smile, "because I wasn't that close to the Encounter."

"Encounter?"

"Between the boy from the pizza place and Stephen Mills of course!" she said, as if talking to a child. "That's what everyone is talking about, isn't it? I could see there was *some*thing—I mean, I could feel the tension, almost *see* the electricity in the air—but I was too far away to know what was going on. Luckily Derek was near."

"Is that your husband? I'll have to talk to him."

"Oh, he'll be *thrilled*. He says the moment Silvio saw Mills—he was on his way round to help dish out the pizzas—he was thunderstruck. Flabbergasted. Obviously there was *some*thing in that boy's past—something criminal Derek thought—that he had thought was hidden forever, and there was Stephen Mills who knew all about it."

"That's how it struck him, did it?"

"Oh, I think it struck everyone like that."

181

Charlie raised his eyebrows.

"Because it could be exactly the other way round, couldn't it? Something criminal or disgraceful in Mills's past that the boy knew about."

She screwed up her English rose forehead.

"But why would he be thunderstruck?"

"Because he, or people close to him, had been affected by whatever criminal or disgraceful thing it was."

"Oh, I don't think that's very convincing. I don't want to teach you your job, but I mean, we've known Stephen at St Saviour's for *yonks*. And the boy is quite young."

"What about something disgraceful in his *present* life?"

"I don't think so," she said obstinately. "We know him."

She tried to give it a Lady Bracknell–like imprimatur of respectability.

"So what does your husband say happened then?"

"Silvio—if that is his name—turned, muttered something, some lame excuse or other, and fled. End of episode."

"I see," said Charlie neutrally. "Well, as I say, I'll have to talk to your husband if that episode does turn out to be significant. But that wasn't what I came to ask you about."

"Oh?" Slight access of tension, Charlie thought.

"It's the matter of Rosemary Sheffield I wanted to talk about."

She smiled forgivingly.

"Rosemary? Oh, the whole parish knows about that. Rosemary lost her faith—quite suddenly, like mislaying your spectacles, or so it seems. Odd, isn't it? Everyone thought it so sad in a vicar's wife. *Aw*fully embarrassing for both of them of course. But I can't see why you'd want to talk to me about *that*."

"Can't you? Well, let's just go through what happened after she lost her faith, can we? There was some trouble over the positions she holds, wasn't there?"

She bridled, very prettily.

"Well, where they were *church* positions there was bound to be, wasn't there? I mean, in a way she had signed herself *out* of the Church. So naturally people felt she shouldn't go on holding the positions she had had."

Charlie nodded, still very friendly. Those who knew him could have told Selena to beware.

"As I understand it, someone was retiring as chair of the Mothers' Union, and people—or rather *some* people, some parish members—didn't want Mrs Sheffield to move up from vice-chair and didn't want her to stay in that position. Is that a fair summary?"

"I suppose so, though you make it sound so nasty."

"I'm sorry. And Mrs Harridance would have liked to take over, is that right? And perhaps have you as her deputy?"

"Certainly there were some that wanted that—quite a *lot*, actually. But there was no row. I remember talking it over quite happily with Rosemary in the train when she was on her way back from Scarborough."

"Ah—I hadn't heard about that. Was that when you decided to go to Scarborough yourself?"

A shade came over her vapid prettiness.

"Well, no . . . No, I think that was later. I remember meeting Rosemary by chance in the street and asking her where she'd stayed, and thinking that was just the place to take my old mum, who needed a tonic."

"She must have recommended it powerfully. And while you were there, you met the boy who later came to work at Pizza Pronto and who confronted Stephen Mills at the church party?"

She pouted, not very prettily.

"You say 'met,' as if it was a social thing. Actually he was the waiter there."

"I know he was. And while you were there you heard a juicy

story: that he had been seen coming out of Mrs Sheffield's bedroom at night."

"Of course I never imagined—"

"And the day you left you heard he'd been sacked."

"We met the boy at the station, checking ticket prices, and that's what he told us. We were so sad."

"Right. Now we get to the interesting bit. You didn't use any of this when you got back to Leeds because you and Mrs Harridance thought that it might boomerang."

"That's most unfair!" said Selena, getting hot and flustered. "I would *never* have hurt Rosemary, who's the *sweetest* person. Who have you been talking to?"

"That's neither here nor there."

"I'll never speak to Florrie again!"

"What interests me is that something changed your mind. When you'd been home a week or so, the rumours started getting around. What was it made you switch tactics?"

"Nothing! I never spread those stories. If Florrie has told you so, she's lying."

Charlie leaned forward so his face was close to hers.

"I'm not sure you should try to pin blame on Mrs Harridance. I think you changed tactic because of someone else—someone you told the story to." Suddenly he saw a purple blush spreading up from her neck, and he added softly, just as speculation: "Pillow talk, perhaps?"

She broke down at once, taking out a delicate little hankie and a bundle of paper tissues and sobbing into the clumsy, absorbent ball, murmuring things like "You won't tell?" and "Derek would never forgive me." Charlie wished he could rid himself of the idea that he was being watched out of the corner of her eye and his reactions estimated. He congratulated himself on the success

184

of his long shot, but he was in no mood to let Selena Meadowes off the hook. He said briskly:

"There's no reason why anyone should know if you are totally honest. How did Stephen Mills get to hear about this?"

"Well, I don't *know*—because we haven't talked about it, how could we?—but I gave my husband some little . . . well, *hints* about Rosemary and the waiter, and that evening he was going to Rotary, and I think—"

"I get the message. Coy little jokes about the vicar's wife having been a naughty girl. I was once told that men make the best gossips, and my experience is that it's true. What makes you think that was how it was?"

"The next day we met—Stephen happened to be around when I dropped the children at school. He'd never been there at that time before. And he was very . . . par*tic*ular. Very warm. And he'd never done more than freeze me before, or sneer, even though I'd . . . well, sort of . . ."

"You'd sent out signals and he hadn't responded?"

"That's a horrible way of putting it," she protested. "You . . . people are so crude."

Charlie grinned, his teeth glinting terrifyingly.

"Well then, you'd sent out tiny, ever-so-subtle hints indicating interest, and he pretended he hadn't registered them."

"No. He indicated he had registered them but wasn't interested. I've known him do that to others too."

"Whereas now, suddenly, he was all over you. *Where* was he all over you?"

"Oh really—you are so . . . He rang that evening, when he knew Derek would be watching the European Cup. Said he'd be at the Quality Inn in Leeds all day the next day, under the name of Cameron Winchell. If I'd care to come along to do secretarial

work I'd be very welcome. I could use the name Beryl Bates. . . .
I should have been outraged, or pretended to be, but . . ."

"You went along."

Her voice took on a whining tone.

"I was flattered, and . . . it's a terribly expensive hotel. Way
outside our range. I told the receptionist I was there for secretarial work, like he'd said. . . . We were there from half past ten
to when I had to pick the kiddies up from school. He gave me a
wonderful time. He had a suite, and we ate lunch there, and we
. . . But after lunch he started asking about Rosemary Sheffield."

"And you told him all you'd learnt at Scarborough?"

"Yes. It didn't seem to matter, somehow, him being a man. And
we were in bed, and it was just—well, like you said, pillow talk.
But then, when he'd got it all out of me, I was about to swear him
to silence—"

"A bit late, though I don't suppose earlier would have made any
difference."

There was silence, then she said in a tiny voice:

"I don't think it would. Because before I could say anything, he
lay there and said, 'Very interesting. I owe Rosemary one.' And I
got panicky and said, 'What do you mean? You're not to say anything,' and I went on a bit, and he turned to me and smiled and
said, 'I never let a debt go unpaid. You should remember that. If
someone's done me an injury, I do them one back. That's
nature's law.' Then he got up and dressed and told me to do the
same."

"End of perfect romance."

The unlovely pout returned to her lips.

"You're horrible . . . but so was *it*, really. The experience. He
made it so clear that he'd got what he wanted, which wasn't even
me, and that was the end of it. He really liked turning the knife,
you know. As we were leaving the hotel, in the foyer and before

we got to the door, he said, 'Good-bye Selena, see you around,' and waved—he did it then so the receptionist would hear. I felt about two feet tall."

"If he liked turning the knife," said Charlie, getting up, "and we've other evidence that he did, maybe it's not surprising that someone took a knife to him."

"It wasn't me!" said Selena eagerly. "I wouldn't have—I mean it was just an episode. But I was terrified Derek would find out. He would have—"

She stopped, a horrified expression on her face.

"Don't worry," said Charlie. "Regularly in a murder investigation we hear someone say that someone else would have killed if they'd known. It's just an expression."

Selena nodded. Encouraged, she made a last attempt to make a better impression.

"I wish you'd understand about . . . what happened—my side of it, anyway. I *did* find him terribly attractive, had done for ages. I knew I was being unfaithful to Derek, of *course* I did, but somehow his showing interest was like a fairy tale, an Audrey Hepburn film come true, and it didn't seem sordid, or mean, but somehow . . . beautiful. I wish I could make you see that."

"I'll try," said Charlie. "But we blacks are so crude."

CHAPTER SIXTEEN

Scenarios

"You've got a nice new room for your little business," said the desk sergeant when Charlie arrived back at headquarters. "Very cosy—I think you'll like it. It's a sort of miniature United Nations in there."

Charlie saw what he meant when he'd been told where the room was and opened the door. Oddie had managed to get six small desks into a medium-sized room, and at them sat six people of various ages and types dictating translations of documents on to tape recorders in a variety of accents.

"And even so we've got two languages we haven't found translators for yet," said Oddie. "Azeri and Albanian. I'm not too worried. I'm getting the general picture."

"I'm glad about that," said Charlie, sitting on the edge of a desk. "And what is the general picture?"

"Settle down and I'll give it to you. . . . Number 94 was the centre of the other side of Mills's European activities—as well as a love nest, as we know. It's a two-bedroom flat, and most of this stuff was tucked away in filing cabinets in the second bedroom. He was good and methodical, thank heavens, so that's made the job easier. It's clear that the whole business grew into illegality, so to speak—left the track gradually before taking off into rough country. What started as a perfectly legitimate part of European Opportunities Ltd. began wobbling over during the eighties into something slightly off-colour, first, and then to something absolutely out of order."

"During the eighties . . . Was this because of some of the Balkan countries breaking free of the Soviet Union?" Charlie asked.

"Partly. But the biggest single factor was the rise of gangsterism in the Soviet Union itself. This started with bootlegging when Gorbachev tried to curb vodka consumption—a pretty futile endeavour, by the sound of it. Really it was very much like America during prohibition. Soon the bootlegging snowballed into large-scale crime and profiteering, with rival gangs, hit squads, politicians in the pay of the different groups, and so on. By all accounts that's the situation today. The gangs have more power than the politicians in some parts of the old Soviet Union."

"I was reading somewhere the other day that Cyprus is the place they all want to go to," said Charlie thoughtfully. "Sun and sand and unlimited vodka."

"And no questions asked. Yes, I read that too. Apparently they tip better than the Brits too, which is a bit humiliating. But they've been interested in London as well. They've been cut off for so long that they probably imagine it's still swinging—upbeat instead of deadbeat like it actually is. Quite clearly Mills was going way over the line in providing false documentation for them, setting up connections with all sorts of people in organised crime and specialised crime in this country. By the time he died this was one of the main planks in his business, presumably bringing in most of his money. But I don't think that's what we're interested in."

"What I'm interested in is: who was Stephen Mills?" said Charlie.

Oddie mimed a conjuror drawing a rabbit from a hat.

"And here is your answer: Stojan Milosevic."

"That's a surname you hear rather a lot of these days."

"Yes—I don't think they're related. I don't have a lot of details yet, but what I have says that he had an English mother, who came back to this country when her marriage to a Yugoslav broke down sometime in the early seventies, and he came with her—then in his late teens."

"Hence the perfect but rather precise English," said Charlie.

"Exactly. And the impression we've been getting that he's risen without trace."

"If we're not interested in the Russian Mafia side of his operations—"

"Not just Russian: Polish, Bulgarian, you name it."

"Then what are we interested in?"

"The business of arranging the illegal entry of anyone from Eastern Europe who could afford the hefty sums involved."

Charlie nodded. The thought that that was the connection with Stanko had crossed his mind.

"Ah . . . Does that mean that Stanko, Silvio—oh, I've just thought: we never had a surname for him—"

"Nor a Christian name either. I think I've found an identity for him. If I'm right he's Milan Vico, a Bosnian Serb, who was a student at Zagreb but was desperate to get out to avoid being drawn into the civil war. His family had Moslem connections, but he had—sorry, has—an uncle who is prominent in the struggle on the Serb side: a fearsome fanatic, by the sound of it. Somehow or other his family scraped together the money to get him out. Naturally a lot of Mills's business was done with Yugoslavia, and his name was known in an underground sort of way—particularly in

191

business and student circles. Contact was made, and he managed to get Vico into this country in late ninety-two."

"How?"

"Details are never given in these papers, or almost never. They're revealing in every other way, but not that one. Probably the arrangements were all made by phone. The reason I think this man is Stanko is that he's been in contact with him recently—about six weeks ago—when he was then said to be in Scarborough."

"Promising. What was the contact about?"

"About getting three of his cousins into the country."

"Ah. Again no details given, I suppose?"

"Not about method, not even about the sums of money involved, though there is something about the method of payment. Mills and Vico had met to sort out the details of the operation, but payment was to be handed to someone outside the Scarborough Town Hall. The description fits Brian Ferrett."

Charlie nodded, instinct confirmed.

"Good to have him tied to this side of the business. There might have been difficulties otherwise. I'm beginning to get a picture here. If I'm right, this boy's grievance against Mills could be not some long-ago crime or double-cross, but something very recent indeed."

"Yes—it's beginning to sound rather horrible. But of course it could be just what you call a double-cross: Mills taking the money and then not delivering the goods on the cousins."

"That doesn't sound like the way Mills built up his business. Delivering the goods is precisely what you would have to do to be as successful as he was. And the description of Stanko's reaction to him doesn't really square with that."

The door opened and a uniformed constable came in and handed Charlie a package.

"That came for you from BBC North. Are they giving you the token black part in *The Bill*?"

"That's ITV, you ignorant sod. The best I can hope for is a thirty-second slot on *Crimewatch UK*."

He took out a tape, slotted it into the video, and the two men drew up chairs and began watching. By judicious use of the fast forward button Charlie avoided stories about the dire economic statistics just announced and the government's latest U-turns on education and crime. The item they were waiting for came sixth on the BBC's order of priorities.

"Customs officials and police were called to Southampton this morning when suspicious sounds were heard from a freight container being unloaded from a Liberian-registered merchant ship. When the container was opened they found two men dead from dehydration and starvation, and a third in a very weak state. He has since died in hospital. Police say they believe the men were from Eastern Europe, possibly Yugoslavia. In the fourth round of the F.A. Cup . . ."

Charlie pushed the rewind, and for a moment the men looked at the stark picture of the reddish-brown container on the wharf in Southampton.

"Poor buggers," said Charlie. "What a way to go."

"There we have it," said Oddie sombrely. "The motive."

There was silence as they both considered this.

"Yes," said Charlie at last. "But the motive for what? For the beating-up or the murder?"

Oddie shifted in irritation in his seat.

"Both, surely. You're not saying it's insufficient motive for murder, are you? It doesn't look that way to me. The fight becomes nasty and it leads to murder."

"Maybe. What do the forensic people say?"

Mike Oddie shuffled through his papers.

"Blah, blah . . . There's not much more than in the preliminary report we had earlier. . . . Cutting through the jargon we come to . . . Oh here it is. Evidence of a fight of some duration, leading to bruising and cuts. The cuts were the source of the bleeding we found some distance away from the body, so the fight had gone on over a considerable area, as Mills tried desperately to get away. Just as we thought."

"Who needs forensics? Exactly. What then?"

"At some stage Mills collapsed, probably unconscious. Then at some subsequent point of time his throat was cut—source of the considerable amount of blood found under the upper part of his body—surprise, surprise."

"Any indication of the time difference between the end of the attack and the murder?"

"Not directly. To be fair, how could they know? But they do seem to think there could well be one—I think from the bleeding from the *other* wounds under the body."

"Nothing to indicate, then, that the attacker was the murderer?"

"No," said Oddie, irritation in his voice. "Why should we look elsewhere? You enjoy playing devil's advocate I know, but you seem to be placing an awful lot of weight on Yussef's statement that Stanko—Vico—wasn't the type to be a murderer. But he was his friend. He would say that."

"I don't like the idea of his going away from the body—or even just standing there thinking—then suddenly deciding to murder him."

"But that could be *exactly* how it happened," said Oddie, banging a fist on the desk. "He waited for him to come out from the church party, then attacked him in his rage at what he had done to his cousins. When he went away and thought about it he

194

realised that Mills was likely to shop him and that it would be better if he finished him off."

"So he went back, having conveniently a knife in his pocket, and slit his throat? I suspect that when you think about it, Mike, you're not going to like that any more than I do. For a start, it's almost inconceivable Mills would shop him, because it would draw attention to why he was attacked. Stanko said precisely that to Yussef when he went back to Pizza Pronto. If he left him alive, one option would have been to lie low for a few days to see if the police were brought in. By killing him he would make sure he had to disappear, because the police were in with a vengeance. It's a case a defence lawyer could find any number of holes in."

"Either way, we've got to get our hands on the boy. You'd agree about that?"

"Of course."

"We've got some descriptions, but we need a more detailed one. And it would be good if we could find someone who'd co-operate with an artist on an Identi-Kit picture. Would your Mrs Sheffield, do you think?"

"She's not mine, and I don't know her all that well, but no—I don't think she would."

"Then maybe our best bet is the woman who runs the guest-house in Scarborough. There's every reason for her to be helpful. Or Gabrielli at Pizza Pronto."

Charlie said thoughtfully: "We keep coming back to Mrs Sheffield. I wonder if Stanko has communicated with her. If only we could have put a bug on her telephone."

"You know damned well we couldn't. Do you think they were so close that he would have?"

"I got the impression that they feel very affectionately towards each other, in a nonsexual sort of way. That's how the daughter saw it too. Yes, I think he might have contacted her. And if she felt pretty confident he'd got away, there's a chance she might open up a bit on the subject."

Oddie looked dubious.

"Not to incriminate him, surely?"

"I'm not wanting to incriminate him. I just want to get at the truth."

"Christ, you sound a prig. Like someone in a very old-fashioned TV police series."

Charlie smiled wryly.

"Thanks. I'll remember you said that the next time you get on your moral high horse. Getting back to Mrs Sheffield. We've got to remember that she has other connections with Mills. She'd always disliked him and distrusted him, and according to Selena Meadowes she'd done something that Mills took so seriously that he wanted to get back at her. She's been very quiet about that."

"Well, I suppose she would, wouldn't she? But she's not going to be able to stay quiet about it."

"I wouldn't bet on that. I think she'd be very good at staying quiet if she dug her heels in. Anyway, it's probably nothing to do with the murder."

"You are on her side, aren't you? You've got no grounds for saying that. At the very least it's one little piece in the puzzle. And it could be a very important piece indeed. She left the party early, didn't she?"

"Yes."

"On her own?"

Charlie tried to remember her words.

"I don't think she said so specifically, but I think all the rest of her family stayed till later."

"There you are then. Now, before we go, let's review the evidence, and let's go by your scenario. At some stage towards the end of the party Mills leaves and walks home, as he was likely to do, living close and having been drinking. Stanko (let's call him that) is waiting for him, probably surprises him, and beats him up—the beating going on for some time, Mills trying to get away, but eventually being left unconscious. After Stanko goes back to Pizza Pronto and prepares to disappear again, someone comes along, sees who it is lying there, and, having the wherewithal to do it, cuts his throat. Is that it?"

"Pretty much so," admitted Charlie.

"Well, if you don't like my scenario, I sure as hell don't like yours."

They split up again, Charlie to pressure Rosemary Sheffield on the question of her past relationship with Stephen Mills, Oddie to prepare a detailed description and if possible an Identi-Kit portrait of Milan Vico.

"But press Mrs Sheffield for a good description too," he said to Charlie.

"I'll come the heavy," said Charlie, with no intention of doing so.

When he got to the vicarage it was Rosemary who answered the door. But as he stepped into the shabby hall her son appeared from the kitchen.

"*Again?*" he said, in his prematurely plummy voice. "You're not persecuting my mother, are you?"

"I wasn't intending to," said Charlie amiably. "Are you?"

"Oh Mark, don't be absurd," said Rosemary. The young man opened his mouth, stood there with it open for a second, then thought better of it and turned back to the kitchen.

"I've been perfectly beastly to poor Mark," Rosemary said, leading Charlie into the sitting room. "The other day I called him a pompous little prat."

"He *is* a pompous little prat, isn't he?"

Rosemary giggled, then obviously felt bad about giggling.

"Oh yes, he is. But whether calling him that is the best way of curing him is another matter."

"If it doesn't work I can't think what will."

"Anyway, he's now very wary of me. I'm glad you've called, as a matter of fact. I've heard from Stanko, you see."

"I thought you might have."

"Now that I know he's got right away I can talk about him more freely."

"Does that include giving me a good description of him?"

She looked at him steadily.

"No it doesn't," she said, without hesitation.

"You're determined to hinder the police in their investigations?"

"Now *you* sound like a pompous prat. I'm simply not going to help them."

"Even if I tell you that he beat up Mills very severely and left him for dead?"

"I know he did—though actually he was far from dead when he left him. I also know the reason for the fight."

"Three dead or dying illegal immigrants in Southampton."

"Ah—you've got there. I suppose you were bound to. . . . It's too horrible. I hadn't looked at the Sunday papers, and I've only just read the story."

"Nevertheless—"

Rosemary shook her head vigorously.

"As far as I'm concerned there is no 'nevertheless.' What he did is quite understandable."

"I suppose it was Stanko himself who told you he didn't kill him?"

"Yes, it was. And I believe him."

Charlie thought for a moment, then said: "I don't know that I disbelieve him myself."

"Good. But I suppose you'll be going after him and trying to send him back to Yugoslavia?"

"Yes."

"Doesn't that worry you?"

Charlie nodded.

"Some aspects of my job worry me. I expect some aspects of your husband's job worry him. I'd guess it's true of most people who do difficult work."

"That's sophistry. Sending him back would be cruel and wrong. Anyway, you'll do it without any help from me."

"I guessed I would. But you're willing to talk about him? I heard a bit from your daughter, but I'd rather hear it from you. How did the relationship develop in Scarborough?"

"I've thought about that." She looked down, trying to find words, then straight at him again. "You've seen Mark—poor Mark. I'm afraid I've got to the point, without realising it, where I thoroughly dislike my own son. Awful, isn't it? I can only hope it passes, but that will probably happen only if Mark gets out of the phase he's going through. Anyway I think that Stanko—such a nice boy, so quiet and pleasant, and such a sad background—I think he was suddenly there as some sort of substitute son. Certainly I felt motherly towards him."

"Did he tell you about his background?"

"A little, yes. He showed me photographs of his wife and their baby. It seemed so sad, so pathetic, so unnecessary in this day and age. He said that his family was all intermarried, and it was like fighting against a part of yourself. One night he broke down and was sobbing on my shoulder. That sounds like a May–October romance, doesn't it? That's what they tried to spread around the parish, but it wasn't true. It was me in need of a son, if anything, not me in need of a lover."

"Then what happened? He suddenly turned up here?"

"Yes—literally on the doorstep."

"You had no doubts about helping him?"

"No. Why should I?"

"You knew he had no papers?"

"Yes, he told us that on the first evening."

"It made no difference?"

"No," said Rosemary. "Not for either of us."

"Either of you," said Charlie, taking this in. "So you and your husband found him the job at Pizza Pronto. You didn't know of any connection between him and Mills then?"

"Not the slightest idea. His name never came up. At least, now I think about it, when we were looking for a job for him Gi—someone did mention Dark Satanic. We should have twigged, maybe, but we didn't. Of course I got inklings, or rather stronger indications than that, at the party, but the first hard information I had was when Stanko telephoned this morning."

"Did Mills's activities surprise you?"

"*No.*" She thought, trying to put her instincts into words. "You know, calling him Dark Satanic Mills was a joke, but like a lot of jokes there was a serious judgment behind it. There always seemed about him a total lack of moral sense—that in addition to the fact that I just found him, well, *yucky.*"

"But he was a member of your husband's congregation."

Rosemary laughed.

"I don't see what that's got to do with anything. There are a lot of thoroughly dislikable people in my husband's congregation."

"OK, OK—point taken."

"Though I have to say I did find him the *most* dislikable."

200

"You didn't have to . . . fend him off at any time?"

"Good Lord, no. I think he knew perfectly well how I felt about him. If he didn't, then I wasted a lot of body language and facial language."

"Never even had to slap him down?"

"No."

"What do you know about his home life?"

She gave a moue of distaste at the thought.

"Not very much. I suspect he didn't *have* very much. There's a rather sad little woman sitting there, but mostly he was out and about, making contacts and money. She had had very little to do with us at church in recent years. But her father—old 'Onions' Unwin—was a faithful member. A roaring hot gospeller in his time, and nonconformist, but more respectable with old age. Mills had a lot to do with him and ran his business for a while. They'd usually come to church together."

"Not recently?"

"I believe he's pretty infirm at the moment, and a little bit senile. That was the impression I got the last time I saw him."

"When was that?"

"Oh maybe a year or so ago. He and Dorothy were walking in Herrick Park. He looked so lost and uncertain. I tried to be sympathetic, said he must have a lot of time on his hands now the business was sold, but he just said, 'What? what?' like the mad George III and seemed—well, like him, gaga."

"And what about her? As a person."

"As I said, I very seldom see her, but if you were to press me I'd say she's a woman—was a woman—locked in an unhappy marriage and for some reason seeing no way out for herself. Maybe all I'm saying is that that's how I'd feel if I was married to him, but I don't think so. That said, I don't get the impression that she is a woman who is naturally happy or hopeful. Before she was married she went with her father to the Baptist Church which has closed down now. The impression she gave was that she was a bit put-upon—by him then, later by her husband."

"She didn't have a wide circle of friends?"

"Hardly any, that I know of."

"Why do you think Mills—by the way, his real name was Milosevic—"

"Milosevic! So there was a Yugoslav connection, was there? How interesting."

"Why do you think he was a regular churchgoer?"

"I don't know. I often wondered. It wasn't as though he was likely to meet an enormous number of business contacts there. He had the Rotary for that. One thing it could give him, though, was respectability. Perhaps with his lack of background—English background, anyway—that was what made it worthwhile for him: something to belong to, something to be said to belong to by people who mattered. Instead of being the Balkan on-the-make adventurer that he was, people mentioned him as a churchgoer— a sober, respectable English type. Though the other side always shone through, as far as I was concerned."

"Did the Church also give him a wife?"

"I don't really remember the sequence of events. We talked about this before. It seems to me he was always thick with Dorothy's father right from the first, but whether he met Dorothy through him or earlier I just don't know. You'd have to ask her."

"Was his grudge against you something to do with the church?"

"We just didn't like each other," said Rosemary, unfazed. "He didn't have a grudge against me."

"He told someone he did."

She looked at him with a blankness that he could have sworn was genuine.

"A *grudge*?"

"The burden of his remark was that you'd done him an injury, and he wasn't going to forget it."

"Done him an injury?" She shook her head, frowning. "I'm sure that can't be right. I'm not conscious of ever doing that. *Who* says he said that?"

"I can't tell you. But part of the paying back was spreading the story about you and Stanko in Scarborough."

"Really? I thought . . . Never mind. He was always very supportive to my face about the parish rows. Told me to fight the old cats—that sort of thing."

"Maybe that was part of the working out of the grudge—keeping the pot boiling."

"Maybe. Maybe it was part of the two-facedness that amused him. But the question is: what was the grudge to start with? I can't think of anything."

"Will you go on thinking?" asked Charlie, getting up to go. "It's probably quite marginal, but then again—"

"Of course . . ." She looked at him closely. "You are telling the truth about Stanko, aren't you? That you haven't made up your mind about his guilt or innocence?"

"Oh yes, I'm telling the truth. I feel we still haven't come to grips with the question of the knife. If Stanko had a knife on him, why did he have a long and vicious fight with Mills without thinking of using it? Apparently he had him unconscious on the ground before the idea occurred to him."

"I agree, that doesn't make sense. And by the way he told me he certainly wasn't carrying one."

"I'll report that, for what it's worth," said Charlie equably. "I think you're a bit biassed. I'm not, but I'm trying to fit the pieces into a sensible pattern. Equally difficult: who could have come along fully prepared to cut somebody's throat."

"Any woman—say a student—could carry a knife, after all the attacks on women in this area. A woman walking across Herrick Park at night could well feel the need for one as protection."

"She'd be a lot better advised *not* to walk across Herrick Park at night, but to stick to the lighted streets."

"People don't always do the sensible thing," said Rosemary, "particularly young people."

"It's something we'll look into. Certainly there may be a lot of women—women of all ages—who might have a grievance against Stephen Mills."

"I can well imagine," said Rosemary grimly.

"On the other hand, in spite of all the scare stories about crime in the press, this country is still a place where the ordinary, law-abiding citizen does not go around carrying a knife."

"Have you thought that Stephen Mills might have been carrying it himself?" asked Rosemary, then looked as if she wished she hadn't.

PART III

DOROTHY

CHAPTER SEVENTEEN

Getting at the Truth

When she opened the door she was wearing the same sort of nondescript clothing she had had on the day before: each garment could have been interchanged with no difference made to the overall effect. She seemed to be completely indifferent to the effect made, and this apparently was habitual. This time Charlie looked straight into her deep, dark eyes; but they were no more revealing than they had been the day before. It was like groping through underground caves that were close, stifling, part of an unending chain. There was certainly no sign that Mrs Mills felt fear, or even apprehension, on seeing them at her front door.

"Oh, do you have some news?" she asked, in a dry, low voice. "I'm so glad. There are so many people ringing or calling, and there's almost nothing I can tell them."

She led the way through to the sitting room. She had the curtains pulled in obedience to a largely dead custom—one which perhaps her father had insisted on. Again, they all sat down, none of them very sure of themselves, blinking in the dim light. She put on an expectant face, as if she thought she was about to hear that the case had been solved. Oddie started the questioning.

"Mrs Mills, did you know that your husband carried a knife?"

"Stephen? Oh no, he wouldn't do that. He didn't have any enemies." She caught a look in Oddie's eye and quickly amended her statement. "Of course he may have been carrying one on Saturday night."

Don't underestimate her, Oddie said to himself.

"Why should he carry one on Saturday night?"

"Because he'd be coming home across the park. There have been a lot of nasty incidents in the park at nighttime. Well, you'd both know about that. It would have been just elementary self-protection."

Oddie did not tell her that Forensics had said, on the basis of the fabric in the pocket of Mills's jacket, that the indentations were consistent with his habitually carrying a knife.

"You see, we think that was the murder weapon. One can imagine all sorts of possible scenarios. For example, your husband took out the knife during the fight, he was easily disarmed by his attacker who had martial arts expertise, and this man later picked up the knife and murdered him."

He did not mention the alternative possibility, that the knife was removed from his pocket by someone who knew it was there. Mrs Mills nodded seriously.

"Yes, I see." She dabbed at her eyes with her fist. "It seems so horribly *long,* doesn't it, the whole process. First the fight, and then—*that.*"

"Mrs Mills, how much did you know about your husband's business activities?"

She screwed up her face.

"Well, not very much, really, except roughly what he did. I told you all about that. I do remember his excitement when he set the business up. Ten or eleven years ago it must be now. Such a happy time! So much enthusiasm and drive!"

In his mind Oddie took a metaphorical pinch of salt.

"Did you know about the office in number 94 Ilkley Road?"

"Is that where it is? I knew he had some sort of overspill office. It was one of the consequences of success, I think. 'Just off to the second office,' Stephen would say."

"Did you know he was running a sort of sideline to the business from there that was, among other things, bringing illegal immigrants into the country?"

There was a silence. Mrs Mills had been maintaining a hard, bright tone, in keeping with her pretence that she was a recently widowed but loving wife, devoted to her husband and to his activities. She made a last shot at propping up the fiction.

"But that's quite impossible! Stephen was impeccably honest. He was a Rotarian." In spite of the tension Oddie and Charlie almost laughed. Again she saw their reaction and immediately backtracked. "Stephen was a man with a conscience. Ask any of his business associates, anyone in the parish. They all trusted him absolutely."

"Mrs Mills, we *know*. The question is, did you know?"

She tossed her head.

"I certainly did not, and I don't believe it. You're making a terrible mistake. . . . Maybe Brian Ferrett has been doing things Stephen knew nothing about."

"Did you know your husband took women to number 94 as well?" asked Charlie.

"You really have been digging for muck, haven't you?" Dorothy Mills asked bitterly, but looking down to shield her eyes. "Stephen often needed secretarial assistance. Naturally—they had only one girl at European Opportunities Ltd. I suppose policemen always believe the worst, don't they?"

Charlie had had enough of the pantomime.

"And did you accept that it was just secretarial assistance he was after when he brought girls back here and took them upstairs?" he asked.

"He didn't!" she cried, in a voice that was getting progressively more unconvincing. "What kind of filthy nonsense have you been listening to?"

"Janet Sheffield struck me as a very truthful young lady," Charlie said.

There was a long silence, then Dorothy Mills muttered feebly, "Stephen wasn't perfect. What man is these days?"

"Mrs Mills, bringing your girlfriend home, flaunting her at your wife, and then going upstairs and bedding her is not just 'not being perfect.' I think the time has come for you to be honest with us, don't you?"

Again she sat there, thinking, the ticking clock the only sound in the room. Then she turned to Oddie.

"Could you arrange for someone to be with my father? I should like to make a statement, and that had better be at the police station, hadn't it?"

Oddie slipped out into the hall to radio to headquarters. Charlie sat impassive, but even he was surprised when Mrs Mills turned to him and said almost conversationally: "I think it will be best to tell the truth about him, don't you?"

"It will, much the best. I think you'll find we know a lot of it already."

"I don't think so. Most of it only I can know."

Then she stayed quiet until a car came with the inevitable policewoman to look after the old man. Charlie offered Mrs Mills his arm; she got up from the chair and walked out ahead of them to the car.

When they got to police headquarters in the centre of Leeds, Mrs Mills waited quietly in the outer office, a nondescript lady who could have come in about a lost dog. When Oddie had arranged an interview room she followed him obediently as if she were one. But when all three had sat down and Oddie was getting out a tape, she showed that she had a mind of her own.

"Would you mind if I just told you—told you about me and Stephen and . . . everybody, right from the beginning? Of course you realise that much of what I told you before wasn't true. It will come out much more easily if I tell it my way than questions and answers."

"There may have to be questions if you forget to tell us something we need to know," said Oddie.

"Yes, of course. But otherwise will you let me tell it in my own way?"

"Yes. Certainly we can try it like that." He spoke into the microphone. "Interview with Dorothy Mills, seventeenth of May 1994. Detective Superintendent Oddie and DC Peace present."

She was sitting opposite him, still and collected, apparently perfectly calm. When he had recorded the necessary documentation he gestured to her to go ahead. She thought for a little, swallowed, and then began.

"I lied about how I met Stephen. It was something I liked to put out of my mind—it was so like his usual pickups. I met him in 1978 on a train from London. I was finishing my second term at teachers college, and already I'd decided I wasn't cut out to be a teacher. I was one of those many who aren't, but go on with it because they can't think of anything else to do. I had already more or less decided to get out. Stephen sat opposite me, across the table, and the moment I saw him I thought he was the handsomest man, the most exciting man, I'd seen in my life. A lot of people have thought that, before and since. When he started to talk to me my heart started to thump like a hammer on an anvil, and I know I blushed scarlet. Stephen was used to having that

211

effect, but he didn't let that show, then. Later he became sort of complacent, and put a lot of women off. He kept the conversation low-key, and before long I calmed down. He got me a cup of tea and a sandwich, and quite soon we weren't talking about the weather or the places we were passing in the train, but about me. Stephen was always very good at getting women to talk about themselves—at least, the sort of women who were attracted to the sort of man he was."

"Tell us something about yourself," said Oddie quietly. She looked surprised.

"Me? Somehow I don't seem to matter in all this. . . . All right, I'll try. I was brought up in what I suppose was a dull, middle-class household. My mother died when I was ten, so I was very close to my father, or perhaps I should say that I thought I was. What Dad had always wanted was a son. He owned a good furniture shop in Abbingley, and was—is—a very committed Christian. Our lives then revolved around the church, which was an evangelical Baptist one. It's gone now. The congregation got older and older, and then died. . . . I was a timid, repressed, not at all charming young woman."

With unfathomably deep eyes, thought Charlie.

"All this I told Stephen, that first meeting, and much more. When he wanted to—when he wanted to learn something—he could just sit quietly, listen intelligently, and hear everything he wanted to hear. By the end of the journey he knew me through and through. I would have felt naked before him, if I had thought like that. As it was, I remembered my manners enough to ask him about himself, though that was not before we drew out of Wake-field. He told me he was from London and was coming to Leeds to start a new job. That was fairly typical of Stephen: he was economical with the facts about himself. There are still large areas of his life about which I know nothing, though that's partly because for a long time I haven't wanted to know, preferred not to. That time he diverted me from the subject by asking for my address. I couldn't believe my ears. It was the first time I'd been asked for my address—and by *such* a man! As I was writing it down, eyes glued to the table to hide disappointment if he refused, I asked him if he'd like to come to supper the next night. He said at once, 'That would be wonderful. You'll be the first people I know in Leeds.' I just felt . . . elated, on a cloud, on a drug trip, if I'd thought like that. Like Cinderella suddenly confronted for the first time with Prince Charming."

She sat there for a moment, lost in memory.

"How did your father take to him?" Charlie asked.

"When I told him, he was suspicious. It was the first time I'd ever asked anyone home, anyone male, anyone young at all, and he said he didn't like his daughter asking to the house a young man she'd just met—he didn't say 'picked up,' but he probably thought it—on a train. But when Stephen came round everything changed. . . . Stephen was very good with men too, you know. Maybe better. He was good at drawing out women, but basically he despised them and thought they were good for only one thing. With men he was in his element: he could talk business, the economic situation, export possibilities, the trade unions—it was all grist to him, and he was very good, very convincing. I should have been bored, I had been a hundred times with that sort of conversation, but I sat there gazing at him fascinated, thinking I understood."

"I suppose they talked about religion too," said Oddie.

"Oh yes. With my father you always got on to religion. Stephen said he was an Anglican. I'm sure he'd thought about it, after our conversation on the train, and he was prepared to be a Christian but he was damned if he was going to be an evangelical nonconformist. After we were married he would go along now and then to the Baptist Church, and he'd ask father along to St Saviour's. Eventually Dad made the changeover completely."

"Why do you think your husband continued going to church?" asked Charlie.

"It was part of his respectable image. He half-realised there was something of the adventurer and gigolo about him, but the Anglican Church built up another side to him in people's minds. He did meet the odd influential person there, but after Dad nominated him for Rotary Club he used that mostly to get contacts. But Rotary Club is not respectable as the Church of England is respectable. People laugh at it a bit, as they do the Masons, and they think it's full of back scratchers."

She paused, having allowed herself to be sidetracked. She tried to get back to those early days.

"It was the happiest time of my life. Stephen was working with a building society, but he was anxious to start his own business. Dad was captivated by him and willing to do everything in the way of helping him and introducing him to people. In the little spare time he had we went places together—plays, concerts, church do's of one sort or another. After a respectable amount of time—after the middle-class, English amount of time—we got engaged. Dad was over the moon. So was I. We didn't sleep together. It seems funny to think of now. Stephen was acting his part well, but perhaps overacting a little. Did you realize he was only uncertainly English? He lived in Yugoslavia till he was seventeen. Of course now I know he must have been getting what he wanted from someone, perhaps many, but at the time I knew or suspected nothing. Dad gave me away at St Saviour's, and I think it was the happiest moment of his life as well as mine." She paused, then suddenly spat out: "I burnt the wedding pictures later. I couldn't bear to look at them. I couldn't even say I'd been sold. I'd sold myself."

There was silence in the room for a moment.

"How soon did things start going wrong?" Oddie asked gently. She answered him only indirectly.

"I once read about Lord Byron, and how he told his wife on their wedding night that he'd only married her for revenge. In my case it wasn't revenge, it was because of all Dad could offer, but he did make things pretty clear right from the start. . . . I wasn't very good in bed. Not at all what he had been used to. He wasn't gentle or understanding—he was contemptuous. He just gave up on me as soon as he'd had me. By the end of the honeymoon he wasn't bothering to hide his impatience to get home and get down to what really interested him in life: making money. He felt sure that, now we were married, Dad would be willing to make a big investment in him, and he was right. By the end of the honeymoon I knew I was an irrelevance in his life, a means, a stepping-stone. It hurt."

"Did you both put up a front for your father's benefit?" Charlie asked.

"Oh yes—at first. Later on Stephen stopped bothering, because Dad didn't notice. I'd been around all his life, and though he'd been forced to make do with what he'd got he'd never thought much to daughters. It was Stephen who fascinated him, and before long I stopped interesting him at all. He set Stephen up in business and was taken with the whole idea of European Opportunities Ltd. He'd come round to our house, Stephen would be round at his. Meanwhile the marriage became nothing more than a facade, a shell, a charade—call it what you will."

"But you didn't think of leaving him?"

"I *thought*. . . . But what would I do? Go back to live with Dad? I'd have seen more of Stephen there than if I'd stayed married to him. Get a job? But what could I do? I had no training, no experience, no confidence. And after a time Dad began to fail with very bad arthritis. I could see it happening, and in the end we moved into his house, our old home, and built a little flat on the back for him, and that seemed about as satisfactory a solution as I could hope for. I wasn't *happy*, but it worked."

She stopped. The men thought they'd asked too many questions, and they let her continue in her own fashion.

"I said the marriage was a shell. That was true for a long time. We would have the odd meal together, almost by accident, and that was it. Otherwise a meal was always there when he came in, and some days we hardly saw each other, hardly exchanged a word. That was perfectly satisfactory as far as I was concerned. Of course we didn't sleep together—the mere thought of it nauseated me—and I knew he had plenty of substitutes: paid, casual, sometimes a bit more than that, but never anything involving real feeling. Stephen was incapable of real feeling. Mostly what was involved was humiliation. I know because . . . There was a change, you see. For a time he was so busy running two businesses, Dad's and his own, that our marriage more or less ceased to exist. Eventually even Dad would have noticed that, but he was becoming more inward-looking, not noticing anything except his immediate comforts. Then Stephen got rid of the furniture business, and I think around that time he started getting into all sorts of dodgy businesses—organised crime in the East European countries, and so on. That was much more exciting than any boring old furniture firm, and more profitable too. It gave spice to his life, he began to relish living on the edge of danger. It brought out the buccaneer in him."

She looked up and straight at them.

"It spilled over into the marriage. Indifference, living our own lives separately, wasn't enough any more. It was as if he resented the fact that he'd trapped himself in a loveless, unexciting marriage when all the time there were these more thrilling ways of making money and getting on that he hadn't thought about when he used me to do that." She paused, and her mouth involuntarily went into a little moue. "He began to be around more, to torment me. He would sit at the breakfast table and read aloud from love letters begging him to leave his boring wife and go off with whoever it was. 'Why don't you?' I'd say. He began bringing girls home—all sorts of girls—and flaunting them in front of me before taking them upstairs to make love. . . . What a phrase: 'make love'! . . . I hated that, I have to admit. I couldn't cope with that, and I couldn't tell you why to this day. Some of them were tarts, but some of them were really nice girls like Janet Sheffield, and that was worse. I was sorry for them. . . . One day he raped me. I don't want to go into that. I told him that if it ever happened again I'd murder him."

"Did it?"

"No. He knew I meant it."

"Why didn't you turn him out of the house?"

"His own house? Dad had made it over to him the same time as he'd handed over the business to him. . . . Oh, I know there are ways, but I've never been a strong person. Not determined or single-minded. I felt trapped. If Dad had died I'd have done something, but he's still well apart from the arthritis, though his mind has been going for some time. Stephen found that mightily amusing, of course. Now and again he'd tell people at church about silly things Dad had said or done, exaggerating, to show what he'd sunk to. . . . I'd almost stopped going to church myself soon after we were married."

"Why?"

"I don't know. I don't think I'd lost my faith, at least not then, but I didn't want to be part of Stephen's *using* religion. It demeaned it. Stephen didn't have a faith! He didn't even have a moral code, not even the faintest ethical barrier beyond which he wouldn't go. . . . Stephen would do *any*thing. . . . Shall I tell you about Saturday evening?"

"Please."

She paused, collecting her thoughts.

"I had no intention of going to the church party. I never went to any function with Stephen unless he forced me, which he did now and then when the whim took him, mainly to establish respectable-married-man credentials. But it was true that the cat was missing. I'm very fond of Moggs. Sometimes he just sits there *looking* at Stephen, as if judging him, deciding he's lower than an insect he wouldn't waste his time catching. I like that. . . . Stephen came in to change about seven. There'd been a phone call earlier—a foreign man, sounding very upset. He didn't leave a message, but I told Stephen about it. He just shrugged. He went out shouting good-bye to Dad: ''Bye, Dad—have a good time.' His idea of humour." She frowned in thought. "That was the last time I'll ever hear his voice."

She paused, as if trying to order events in her own mind.

"During the evening I watched a bit of television, listened to Radio Three. I kept going out into the garden and calling for Moggs, then along the road too. He's a neutered tom, but he's a real prowler when the mood takes him. I always worry when he goes missing because we're so close to the Ilkley Road. I lied about his never crossing that. Once we found him in Herrick Park. Anyway I got Dad his nightcap. He always has Ovaltine around half past nine. Then I went out again, back home, out again. Eventually, after the ITV news, I decided to go across to Herrick Park. It was silly, I know: the only sensible thing when a cat is lost is to wait for him to come home. But when it's the only thing you've got, almost . . ."

"And that was—when?"

"Getting on for half past ten. The evening news had been at ten past ten, and I'd heard the item about the illegal immigrants who had died. It was quite horrible. I'd wondered whether Stephen was involved. He was, wasn't he?"

"Yes, he was."

"I knew that much about what he was up to, you see. Anyway, I walked down to the Ilkley Road, crossed it, keeping my eye skimmed all the time for Moggs, dreading to see him hit by a car or already lying dead in the road. It's a horrible sight, isn't it, a dead cat in the middle of the road? They're so fragile. . . . The edge of the park is only five or six minutes from our house, and as soon as I got there I started calling for Moggs. It was dark, of course, and I was rather afraid. It's not a place most people would willingly go on to at night, particularly women. First I kept near the road, close to the lights, but then I thought that defeated the purpose of looking for him because Moggs certainly didn't need street lights. . . . Anyway, I'd gone away from the road and was over towards the tennis courts when I jumped with fear. I'd thought I heard shouts."

"Where from?"

"From the other end of the park—from the edge of the clump of trees on the rise. It was the fight, of course. I was terrified. All those nasty incidents on the park—you know about them, of course—came flooding into my mind. I started to hurry to the road, but the quickest route to it didn't take me away from the fight but towards it. And the fight seemed to be coming in that direction. They were coming away from the trees and towards the road, one running, the other following. And as I looked and began to hurry away in the other direction I thought that one of the men looked like Stephen."

She stopped, remembering. Oddie and Charlie left her a moment or two to collect her thoughts. In those moments Charlie suddenly asked himself: why is she telling us this? He could not find an answer.

"What did you do?" Oddie asked at last, gently.

"I hid behind a tree. I thought, you see, that I probably wasn't in any danger. I thought it was most likely a husband or a boyfriend of someone that Stephen had . . . To tell you the truth I was pleased he was getting what he deserved. I wanted to watch it." She looked at them, not pleading, but to see if they understood. "I'm sorry, it sounds disgusting but that's the truth of it. . . . The other man was doing all sorts of things with his out-stretched hands and arms—like men I've seen on television slicing bricks in half and that kind of thing. He was using his feet too—like a modern ballet. Stephen was crying out. I knew it was him by now. Then suddenly there was a blow to the head and it was all over. Stephen was lying stretched out on the ground, and the other man was running away in the direction of the Ilkley Road."

"What did you do?"

"I stood there under a tree for a moment or two, uncertain what to do. The sensible thing would have been to go straight home. I don't know why I didn't, or why . . . I walked over to where Stephen was lying. He was quite unconscious, and I could see blood on him. But he was breathing. I stood there looking down on him. A great wash of feeling came over me, as if I was drowning, and everything he had ever done, to me, to Dad, to others, came over me like a big wave. . . . I can't explain the feeling, but it seemed somehow too little. . . . After *all* he'd done: the hateful things, the criminal things, the humiliating things. I think it must have been what the victims feel when a judge imposes a very light sentence on someone who has done really dreadful things to them. It was how he'd treated *everyone* that I was thinking of, not just me. The heartlessness, the hypocrisy, the double-dealing. It seemed too little. . . . I can't explain what I did, *why* I did it. I don't think I thought. But somewhere in the back of my mind there may have been the idea that if I didn't do it *now*, then so good an opportunity would never come again. . . . I bent down and took from his pocket the little knife I knew he always carried. It's small but very sharp—deadly. I pressed the catch and the blade sprung forward. He stirred. I knew if I was going to do it, it had to be then. I bent down and slit his throat."

There was utter silence in the little room. Oddie said, at last, "Just like that?"

"Just like that. Without any emotion."

"What did you do then?"

"I stood for a moment watching him die. Only that way could it seem *enough*." She looked at them to see if she had shocked them, but they remained impassive. "Then I walked back across the park on my way home, calling to Moggs all the time. I slipped the knife down a drain when I got to the road, and I held a scarf in my hand to hide the fact that my hands were bloody. Moggs was on the front doorstep when I got home—it's always the way, isn't it? I ran water into an old plastic bowl and washed the blood off myself. I've seen all those police things on television, you know, and I knew they can trace the tiniest bit of blood left in a sink. Then I went out again and disposed of the bowl in a skip, and the scarf too. Then I went home and began to prepare for all the pretence that would be necessary the next day. I decided I had to at least pretend to be the devoted wife. If I'd told the truth about him and me I'd be the first to be suspected. And what would Dad do if I was sent to prison? So I thought hard about what I'd say to you when you came. But I slept—I slept very well. I didn't have any doubts or pricks of conscience, and I haven't had since either. That's odd, isn't it? Someone who used to be a regular churchgoer. I suppose it's a measure of the sort of man Stephen was. . . . Is that enough? Will your tape have all that?"

"Yes, that's enough," said Oddie. He moved to switch off the tape, but Charlie put out his hand to stop him. He still hadn't found the answer to his question. He looked at the woman opposite, at her only good feature—her deep eyes, almost black: eyes that looked at him and told him nothing, except that what they probably concealed was pain, loneliness and the emptiness of being unloved. It seemed almost an act of cruelty to ask her anything more, but Charlie felt he had to chance his arm.

"Why did they call your father 'Onions'?" he asked.

She looked at him, quickly and sharply.

"What? What do you mean? Why on earth are you asking me about that?"

"His nickname in Abbingley. 'Onions.' Was it because he could cry at will at those revivalist meetings he went in for? Real, wet tears like he turned on for us?"

"I don't understand. Why are you saying those nasty things about him?"

"When did he find out that Stephen had sold his beloved business, and when did he start hating him as much as you did?"

"He didn't! He loved him!"

"Oh no, he didn't. Because it wasn't your cat you went to look for on Herrick Park, was it? It was your father. And by the time you found him he'd killed your husband."

The great eyes suddenly filled with tears and she fell forward on to the table, racked with sobs. They waited, listening to her barely distinguishable words. The only ones Charlie thought he could make out were, "Why did you let me go on? How did you know?"

CHAPTER EIGHTEEN

Envoi

It was several weeks before Charlie had any conversation about the case with Rosemary Sheffield. When he did he said rather more than, strictly, he ought to have done, mainly because in the course of the case he had come not only to like her but to trust her too. And it was not as though there was any prospect of the case coming to court.

It happened one Sunday, when he was jogging around Herrick Park, as he generally did on days off, though in no fanatical spirit. Running down the gentle incline from the small wooded area, very near the place where Stephen Mills's body had lain, he saw the Reverend Sheffield making pedantic little dabs at the door handle of his car with a cloth; and he saw Rosemary come out, a puppy in her arms. She kissed her husband and raised her hand as he drove off on his way to morning service. Charlie in turn raised his hand to her, then turned aside from his usual route and ran over to her. They both knew perfectly well what they were going to talk about, and when Rosemary had set the puppy down safely in the front garden they sat against the garden wall of the vicarage that abutted the road, Charlie panting slightly.

"They say the old man has been institutionalised—is that true?" Rosemary asked. Charlie nodded.

"Yes. It was the devil's own job to get a place for him at a secure establishment, but in the end, one had to be found. These days it's no good being mentally ill—you have to have cut someone's throat as well."

"Dorothy's had a lot of well-wishers from the congregation."

Charlie laughed cynically.

"I *bet* she has! They left her pretty well alone when she was the neglected and mistreated wife."

"Yes, we all did. To be fair, I was as guilty as anyone."

"And to be fair on the other side, she didn't want to have much to do with a church that could have Stephen as an honoured member."

Rosemary nodded.

"Yes, that always worried me too, but what could you do? He was, to all intents and purposes, an upright citizen. . . . She told one of the well-wishers that she had confessed to the murder. Is that true?"

"Yes, it is."

"I believe a lot of people do that during murder enquiries. Is that why you didn't just accept her confession?"

"We always look closely at confessions. They have to stand up in court. . . ." Charlie pulled himself up. He was starting to sound like a PR man. "But, well, the fact is that we very nearly did accept it, at least for a time. The fact is that most of what she told us the first time we talked to her was lies. The devoted husband and son-in-law stuff was the only thing she could think of to shield her father—and herself, by then his accomplice. Most of what she told us during the second interview was true. But not all. And there were significant gaps. You know, you sit there listening to someone confess, and if everything fits neatly with the facts—and it did in her confession, mainly because it was very *nearly* the truth—then your mind doesn't make the leap away from the facts to ask itself the bigger questions."

"Such as?"

"Such as: why is she making this confession at all? We had nothing on her, beyond her lying about her relationship with her husband—perfectly easily explained, when her husband had just been murdered. But we no sooner confronted her with those lies than she upped and confessed."

"She's such a depressed and depressing little thing that I think I'd have decided that she just didn't have the gumption to go on lying any more."

"I'm not sure I agree with the assessment," said Charlie thoughtfully. "Maybe you don't know her very well."

Rosemary nodded.

"I don't. I admit it."

"There's more *there* than you allow for. Though what exactly it *is* I'm not sure I could say. But however you assess her character, I would have expected her to go on protesting her innocence to protect the position of her father, who depended on her. That's one person she loves, even if that love isn't returned with any great enthusiasm. As they always say: he's all she's got. Her thought, her solicitude, were all for him. And yet her confession, her arrest, would leave him alone. So at one point I asked myself: why?"

"And the answer?"

"The only convincing answer I could come up with was that the alternative was worse."

"His arrest and trial?"

"Yes. Of course it hasn't come to that because he's been found unfit to plead."

There was a hesitancy in Charlie's manner that made Rosemary ask, "And are you happy with that?"

"Happy? Oh yes, happy we don't have to put an eighty-year-old on trial and imprison him for the few years he has left in a thoroughly unsuitable institution."

"Well, to put it another way: do you think it was the right decision?"

Charlie sat in the dim sunlight, pondering.

"The psychiatrist was the best of the bunch we have to call on: sensible, down to earth, not one of those who's crazier than the patient. He examined Unwin over a two-month period. At the end he was willing to declare him unfit to plead. Everyone breathed a sigh of relief."

"But it wasn't an open-and-shut matter?"

"No, it wasn't. He had several reservations which he put in his report, no doubt to satisfy his professional conscience. There were aspects of Unwin's behaviour that were not in accordance with the usual progress of Alzheimer's disease or senile dementia. But he was the first to admit that you can't be dogmatic about such things. And the fact is that the idea that Unwin is senile depends on his behaviour since the murder, his daughter's testimony—one of the places where she was lying, I suspect—and a few stories Mills told about him to the St Saviour's congregation. How often had you seen him in the last six or seven years?"

"Just the once—the time I told you about."

"I should think that was true of everyone. His contemporaries had either died off or were in a similar situation to his own. Old people do get forgetful, confuse names, muddle up past and present. Mills could no doubt have told true stories about the old man that suggested he was far gone mentally."

"But what makes you think he wasn't?"

226

"The tears when he heard about Mills's death. First I thought they were genuine grief. But later I heard from you about his nickname, 'Onions.' And I wondered whether this wasn't a satirical commentary on his being able to produce tears at will."

"It was," said Rosemary with relish. "The real waterworks. 'Oh Lord, I have been a great sinner!' with abundant liquid evidence of repentance."

"I thought that might be it."

"Oh, how nice it is to be able to laugh at things like that."

"Anyway, when I thought about the tears when Mills died, I realized that they were turned on in the old, practised way, and they fooled me, for one. I thought it was the most genuine grief I'd seen so far."

"But they *had* been fond of each other. Or rather, old Unwin had been fond of Stephen."

"That's right. But I think things had gone downhill in recent years—probably ever since Unwin stopped being useful to Mills. He'd begun flaunting his women in front of him—we learnt this from . . . one of his girlfriends."

"From Janet. Don't worry—I've guessed about that."

"Well, anyway . . . Unwin was a puritan of the old breed—possibly a fearsome old hypocrite to boot, but he would have been shocked and disgusted. Mills made satirical remarks about his physical and mental condition—we know that from Dorothy. And then he'd learned that his beloved furniture business had been sold off."

"Oh dear. Was that me?"

"I think it might have been. I think that was the grudge he had against you."

"I seem to have had fatal effects in this business."

"If it hadn't been you it could have been anyone. The fact is he only got out when the arthritis was in remission, when he tended to go off on his own. The likelihood was he wouldn't see anyone he knew on those wanderings."

"But the business had been sold without his knowing?"

"Yes. He'd made it over to Mills for tax reasons. When he took it over Mills stipulated that Unwin shouldn't interfere—he shouldn't even go back to his old shop. Actually it was a perfectly sensible condition. It's everyone's nightmare, the chap who had the job before you coming back and sticking his oar in. Unwin was a businessman himself, saw the point, and agreed without a qualm."

"But the business didn't prosper under Stephen?"

"I think it was the recession rather than Mills that sent it into a tailspin. You see all these rather desperate ads, don't you, on television: no interest for the first two years—that kind of thing. Heavy, traditional English furniture is not what people buy when times are hard. When Mills found the shop was making very little money for him, he sold it for what he could get and ploughed the money into his dubious East European activities."

"Bringing in illegal immigrants?"

"That and much, much more."

"But it's hardly a motive for murder, is it?"

"Not by itself. It was cumulative, I think. The old man had loved his business, lived for it and for his religion. He'd welcomed Mills as a son-in-law because he recognised him as a superb businessman who would take over after him. I think when he realised that the firm had been sold when things were difficult, when he realised his son was a common womaniser who had just used religion as a way of sucking up, when he became the butt of his cruel jokes, I think he realised that Mills had been using him for years, had made a complete fool of him. I think for the last few months, maybe years, he'd hated him. Probably it brought him and his daughter closer together than they'd ever been."

"I see. And I suppose the hatred and resentment would have gone on smouldering until the old man died without Stephen being murdered if the opportunity hadn't presented itself."

"Exactly. What *really* happened that night was not that Dorothy Mills came to Herrick Park looking for her cat. In fact, she was on her way up to bed when she saw through a crack in the door that the light was still on in her father's flat. She'd taken him his nightcap more than an hour earlier, and usually he'd have been well in bed by then. When she went in she found he'd gone wandering, as he had more than once before."

"I suppose he could have done that when I saw them on the park, and she'd come and got him."

"Exactly. The park was where he most often came. Now, what Dorothy said had happened to *her* was probably what happened to *him*. He probably told her about it later. He walked over to the park, then wandered around it, and eventually heard and saw the fight from a distance. Whether he recognised his son-in-law we can't say, but when it was over he went to where the man lay, saw it was Stephen . . ."

"Then cut his throat?"

"Yes."

"Just like that?"

"Well, we don't know how long he thought about it or what sort of thought he was capable of. I'm not denying he was old and confused, just that he was senile. Dorothy had by this time come on to the park. She saw the figure of her father in the distance and ran over to him. By then it was already done, and his jacket sleeve was covered with blood. . . . That was another thing that worried me with her account."

"What?"

"Not enough blood. You cut someone's throat and it really spurts blood."

"That must have made getting him home difficult."

"Difficult and dangerous. There's a stretch of well-lighted road between the park and the Ilkley Road, as you know, and she could avoid it only by taking a very long way round, which he probably couldn't manage. She solved it by making her headscarf into a sort of sling, which hid most of the blood. When she got home she washed him clean in a plastic bowl—she knew from those television crime series (isn't television wonderful?) that it is very difficult to get rid of all traces of blood in a modern plumbing system—then went out and disposed of the bowl and the bloody scarf in a skip. Unwin's jacket was the most dangerous thing: she put it in a plastic bag and dumped it in a large bin on the Ilkley Road which she knew was emptied every day. Then all she had to fear was her father giving things away, so she really had to tutor him in how he should behave when the murder came out. He was sharp enough to take her point and follow her direction—a practised old hypocrite, I suspect."

"She seems to have been rather clever."

"Yes. I said I didn't go along with your assessment of her. Granted the situation she was presented with, she showed great presence of mind."

"How *do* you rate her? What kind of person is she?"

Charlie shook his head.

"I don't know. I just can't fathom her. Unloved, neglected by both husband and father, seething with humiliation and resentment. But I don't *feel* her character. Anything I know, I've been *told* by her, which is different. I feel I know what kind of man Mills was by now, but I don't feel I have the same knowledge of his wife."

"People say she's going to move."

"I don't blame her. Though there's always the danger that she'll simply be even more lonely in strange surroundings. Still, there's nothing to keep her here. And she's used to loneliness—probably prefers it."

"Will she have any money?"

"Sure. The house will bring in plenty, even in the current state of the market; and the legitimate side of the business is saleable: it was a good idea, and there will be people who can carry it on. Personally I hope they don't continue to employ Brian Ferrett, but we can't do anything about that."

"Was that Mills's assistant?"

"Yes. In it up to his ears, but we can't charge him."

"Why not?"

"You've probably heard about the Crown Prosecution Service. These days they don't let us charge anyone unless it's almost one hundred per cent sure we'll get a conviction. It's very frustrating. On Ferrett we had no more than fingerprints in number 94—that's the place where all the dubious business was transacted—and a description in a letter. We might have had a hope if we'd managed to get hold of Stanko—of Milan Vico."

"Well, I'm very glad you haven't."

"Have you heard from him recently?"

"Just a one-minute phone call to say he's all right. I don't need anything else. I wasn't in love with him, you know."

"I know."

"I was just so sad for him—running away from the fighting, having to leave his wife and baby behind."

Charlie hesitated, shuffled his feet, and then said, "Actually, we know quite a bit about Milan Vico now. Nothing criminal or to his discredit. But we've never had the slightest hint that he was married."

"Oh." For a moment Rosemary was nonplussed. "You mean they were just sympathy getters?"

"Something like that. I expect they were relatives—a sister or

231

a cousin and her child, say—whose photographs he had brought with him."

Rosemary thought and then said, "It doesn't make any difference, you know, not to how I see him. I expect if I were alone in a foreign, hostile country (because that's what this is), I'd make a play for all the sympathy I could get from anyone who seemed kind or well disposed. I didn't befriend him because he was brave and truthful or the soul of honour."

"You befriended him because he was a nice boy and slightly pathetic."

"That's probably true. And as a son substitute."

"How is young Mark?"

"Hmmm. There's been a *slight* improvement. He sometimes stops himself before he makes a horribly pompous remark (I always know what the remark would have been). Or he says, 'I know you'll say I'm being pompous, but—.' I suppose you could say there's been a slight increase in self-knowledge. But I still feel very remote from him."

"Well," said Charlie, sliding off the wall and dusting the seat of his track suit, "I won't apply for the vacant post of son substitute."

"Please don't. I don't see you as one at all. You may be nice, but there's nothing of the pathetic about you."

"Oh, I'm not even nice. And I was—am—a lousy son."

"I don't believe that. Anyway, I certainly wouldn't want pathetic policemen, though a few more nice ones wouldn't go amiss. I'll try to make do with what I've got. Janet's a lovely daughter, I like her boyfriend, and Paul's come out of this best of all: loving and loyal and steadfast—everything a husband should be."

"I notice you don't put the final spit and polish to his car before service any longer."

"No, aren't I awful? One awakening leads to another, I suppose. It suddenly seemed too ridiculous to go on doing it."

"Anyway, I'll take my girlfriend along to St Saviour's to hear him sometime."

"Oh, I didn't say he was a splendid preacher," Rosemary laughed. "Workaday, but no more than that."

Charlie raised his hand. "See you," he said, and crossed the road and started jogging round the perimeter of the park.

There was a watery sun shining now, and Rosemary bent down to pick up her puppy, who had begun throwing himself against the wall. They crossed the road and walked under the trees, the puppy snuffling happily and independently. Rosemary's thoughts were far away. It was here that, for her, things had all started. Not for the main participants, of course. For them the thing had started long ago, probably when Dark Satanic and poor Dorothy had met. But for Rosemary life had changed suddenly here on Herrick Park; and as a consequence her life had become horribly, fatally involved with the affairs of a man she disliked and shrank from. Well, in that her instinct had been right.

How she had so suddenly lost her belief in God was still a mystery to her. The suddenness of its leaving her seemed almost, ridiculously, like an act of God itself. But she did feel, as she walked under the trees, her eye on her lovely new dog, with the everyday activities of the park going on around, that the very suddenness and out-of-the-blueness of its going was an indication that one day, possibly, it would return to her, descend, envelop her with the same odd unpredictability. Sometimes recently she had got as far as hoping that it would.

ROBERT BARNARD's most recent novel is *The Masters of the House*. His other books include *A Hovering of Vultures*, *A Fatal Attachment*, *A Scandal in Belgravia*, *A City of Strangers*, *At Death's Door*, *The Skeleton in the Grass*, and *Out of the Blackout*. A seven-time Edgar nominee and winner of the Anthony, Agatha, Macavity, and Nero Wolfe awards, he lives in Leeds, England.

The
Crocodile
Bird

Ruth Rendell

The Crocodile Bird

CROWN PUBLISHERS, INC.
New York

Originally published in Great Britain by Random House UK in 1993.

Published by Crown Publishers, Inc., 201 East 50th Street, New York, New York 10022. Member of the Crown Publishing Group.

Random House, Inc. New York, Toronto, London, Sydney, Auckland

Crown is a trademark of Crown Publishers, Inc.

Manufactured in the United States of America

Library of Congress Cataloging-in-Publication Data
Rendell, Ruth.
    The crocodile bird / Ruth Rendell.
    I. Title.
  PR6068.E63C76   1993
  823'.914—dc20   93-14734

ISBN 0-517-59576-1

10 9 8 7 6 5 4 3 2

To Don, Simon, Donna, and Phillip

THE world began to fall apart at nine in the evening. Not
at five when it happened, nor at half past six when the policemen
came and Eve said to go into the little castle and not show
herself, but at nine when all was quiet again and it was dark
outside.

Liza hoped it was all over. She watched the car go down the
lane toward the bridge and then she went back to the gatehouse
and upstairs to watch it from her bedroom window, the red lights
on its tail as it went over the bridge and its white lights when it
faced her again as the road climbed and twisted among the hills.
Only when she could see its lights no longer, could see no lights

anywhere but a red moon and a handful of stars, did she feel they were saved.

Downstairs she found Eve, calmly waiting for her. They would talk now, but of course about other things, or read or listen to music. Eve smiled a very little, then composed her face. There was no book in her lap or piece of sewing in her hands. Liza saw that her hands were shaking and this frightened her. The first real fear she felt came from the sight of those small, normally steady hands, faintly trembling.

Eve said, "I have something very serious to say to you."

Liza knew what it was. It was Sean. Eve had found out about Sean and didn't like it. With a sense of shock she thought about what Eve did to men she didn't like or who interfered in her plans. An attempt would be made to separate her from Sean and if that failed, what would Eve do? She herself was safe, she always was, she was the bird who pecked at the jaws of death, but Sean was vulnerable and Sean, she saw quite clearly, might be the next candidate. She waited, tense.

It was about something quite different. "I know it'll be hard for you, Liza, but you're going to have to go away from here."

Again Liza got it wrong. She thought Eve meant both of them. After all, that particular threat had been hanging over them for days. This was a battle Eve hadn't been able to win, a conquest she couldn't make.

"When will we have to leave?"

"Not we. You. I've told the police you don't live here. They think you just come sometimes to visit me. I've given them your address." She stared hard at Liza. "Your address in London."

The falling apart of things started then, and the real fear. Liza understood that she had never really known what fear was until that moment, a minute or two after nine on an evening in late

August. She saw that Eve's hands had stopped shaking. They lay limp in her lap. She clenched her own.

"I haven't got an address in London."

"You have now."

Liza said in a jerky voice, "I don't understand."

"If they think you live here they'll ask you about what you saw and what you heard and perhaps—perhaps about the past. It's not only that I can't trust you"—Eve offered a grim little smile—"to tell lies as well as I can. It's for your own protection."

If Liza hadn't been so afraid she would have laughed. Hadn't Eve told her that saying things were for people's own protection was one way totalitarians justified secret police and lying propaganda? But she was too frightened, so frightened that she forgot she had been calling Eve by her first name for years and reverted to the childhood usage.

"I can't go away alone, Mother."

Eve noticed. She noticed everything. She winced as if that name had brought her a twinge of pain. "Yes, you can. You must. You'll be all right with Heather."

So that's whose address it was. "I can stay here. I can hide if they come back." Like a child, not someone of nearly seventeen. And then, "They won't come back." A sharp indrawing of breath, the voice not hers but a baby's. "Will they?"

"I think so. No, I know so. This time they will. In the morning probably."

Liza knew Eve wasn't going to explain anything, and she didn't want an explanation. She preferred her own knowledge to the horror of naked confession, admission, perhaps excuse. She said again, "I can't go."

"You must. And tonight, preferably." Eve looked at the dark out there. "Tomorrow morning, first thing." She closed her eyes for a moment, screwed them up, and made a face of agony. "I know I haven't brought you up for this, Lizzie. Perhaps I've been wrong. I can only say I had the best intentions."

Don't let her say that about my own protection again, Liza prayed. She whispered, "I'm scared to go."

"I know—oh, I know." A voice caressing yet wretched, a voice that somehow yearned, Eve's large dark eyes full of compassion. "But, listen, it won't be too hard if you do exactly what I say, and then you'll be with Heather. You always do what I say, don't you, Lizzie."

I don't. I used to once. Her fear held her rigid and silent.

"Heather lives in London. I've written the address down, this is the address. You must walk to where the bus stops. You know where that is, on the way to the village, between the bridge and the village, and when the bus comes—the first one comes at seven-thirty—you must get on it and tell the driver where you want to go. It's written down here. You must hold out your money and say, 'The station, please.' The bus will take you to the station, it stops outside the station, and you must go to the place where it says 'tickets' and buy a single ticket to London. 'A single to London,' is what you say. It's written down here: Paddington, London.

"I can't get in touch with Heather to say you're coming. If I go to the house to use the phone, Matt will see. Anyway, the police may be there. But Heather works at home, she'll be at home. At Paddington Station you must go to where it says 'taxis' and take a taxi to her house. You can show the taxi driver the piece of paper with her address. You can do all that, Lizzie, can't you?"

"Why can't you come with me?"

Eve was silent for a moment. She wasn't looking at Liza but at Bruno's painting on the wall, Shrove at sunset, purple and gold and dark bluish-green. "They told me not to go anywhere. You aren't planning on going anywhere, I hope, is what they said." She lifted her shoulders in that characteristic way, a tiny shrug. "You have to go alone, Liza. I'm going to give you some money."

Liza knew she would get it from the little castle. When Eve had gone she thought of the ordeal before her. It would be impossible. She saw herself lost as she sometimes was in dreams. Those were the kind of dreams she had, of wandering abandoned in a strange place, and weren't all places strange to her? She would be alone in some gray desolation of concrete and buildings, of empty tunnels and high windowless walls. Her imagination created it out of well-remembered Victorian fiction and half-forgotten monochrome television scenes, a rats' alley from Dickens or a film studio. But it was impossible. She would die first.

The money was a hundred pounds in notes and some more in coins. Eve put it into her hands, closing her fingers around it, thinking no doubt that Liza had never touched money before, not knowing that she had done so once when she found the iron box.

The coins were for the bus, the exact fare. What would she say to the driver? How would she ask? Eve began explaining. She sat beside Liza and went through the instructions she had written down.

Liza said, "What's going to happen to you?"

"Perhaps nothing, and then you can come back and everything will be like it used to be. But we must face it. The chances are they'll arrest me and I'll have to appear in the magistrates' court and then—and then a bigger court. Even then, it may not be too bad, it may only be a year or two. They aren't like they used to be about these things, not like"—even now she could be reassuring, joky—"in the history books. No torture, Lizzie, no dungeons, no shutting up in a cell forever. But we have to face it, it may be—for a while."

"You haven't taught me to face anything," Liza said.

It was as if she had slapped Eve's face. Eve winced, though Liza had spoken gently, had spoken despairingly.

"I know. I did it for the best. I never thought it would come to this."

"What did you think?" Liza asked, but she didn't wait for an answer. She went upstairs to her room.

$$\backsim$$

Eve came in to say good night.

She was cheerful, as if nothing had happened. She was smiling and at ease. These mood swings made Liza more frightened than ever. She thought it likely Eve would fall asleep at once and sleep soundly. Eve kissed her good night and said to be off in the morning early, to take a few things with her, but not to bother with too much, Heather had cupboards full of clothes. Smiling radiantly, she said it sounded terrible to say it, but in a strange way she felt free at last.

"The worst has happened, you see, Lizzie, it's rather liberating."

The last thing Liza noticed before her mother left the room was that she was wearing Bruno's gold earrings.

She had meant not to sleep at all, but she was young and sleep came. The sound of a train woke her. She sat up in the dark, understanding at once it had been a dream. No train had run along the valley for years, not since she was a child. Without the trains the silence had been deeper than ever.

Fear came back before the memory of what there was to be

afraid of. A vague unformulated terror loomed, a great black cloud, that split into the constituents of her dread, the initial departure, the bus—suppose it didn't come?—the terrible train, in her mind a hundred times the size of the valley train with its toy engine, and Heather, whom she recalled as tall, strange, remote, and full of secrets to be whispered to Eve behind a guarding hand.

In all of it Liza had forgotten Sean. How could she let Sean know? The load of bewilderment and despair cast her down among the bedclothes again and she lay there with her face buried and her ears covered. But the birds' singing wouldn't let her lie quiet. The birds were sometimes the only things down here to make a sound from morning till night. The dawn chorus broke with a whistling call, then came a single trill and soon a hundred birds were singing in as many trees.

She sat up fully this time. The gatehouse was silent. Outside all but the birds seemed quiet, for the wind had dropped. The curtains at the window were wide apart as they always were, since the only lights ever to be seen were those of Shrove. She knelt up on the bed in front of the window.

Some demarcation was visible between the brow of the high wooded hills and the dark but clear and glowing sky. There, in the east, a line of red would appear, a gleaming red sash of light unraveled. Meanwhile, something could be seen, the outline of the house, a single light in the stable block, a dense black shape-lessness of woodland.

Knowledge of what was out there began to give the prospect form, or else the cold glow that comes just before dawn had started to lift the countryside out of darkness into morning twilight. The water meadows showed themselves pale as clouds and the double line of alders on either side of the river seemed to step out of the surrounding dark. Now Liza could see the shape of the high hills beyond, though not yet their greenness, nor the road that banded them halfway up like a white belt.

She got off the bed, opened the door very quietly, and listened. Eve, who never rested by day, who was always alert, attentive, watchful, uncannily observant, slept by night like the dead. She was going to be arrested today but still she slept. The uneasy feeling came to Liza, as it had come before, that her mother was strange, was odd inside her head, but how would she really know? She had no standard of comparison.

If she didn't think about what she was going to do but kept her mind on practical things, if she didn't *think*, it wasn't so bad. These moments had to be lived through, not the future. She went downstairs to the bathroom, came back and dressed. She wasn't hungry, she thought she would never eat again. The thought of food, of eating a piece of bread, of drinking milk, made her feel sick. She put on the cotton trousers Eve had made, a T-shirt from the reject shop, her trainers, Eve's old brown parka, the hundred pounds divided between its two pockets.

Did Eve mean her to say good-bye?

Opening her mother's door, she thought how this was the first time she had done so without knocking while Eve was inside since Bruno came, or earlier even, since the first Jonathan days. Eve lay asleep on her back. She wore a decorous white nightdress, high at the neck, and her thick dark brown hair was spread all over the pillows. In her deep sleep she was smiling as if she dreamed of lovely pleasurable things. That smile made Liza shiver and she shut the door quickly.

It was no longer dark. Clouds were lifting away from the thin red girdle that lay along the tops of trees, dark blue feathers of cloud being drawn away up into a brightening sky. Birdsong filled up past silence with its loud yet strangely remote music. Liza was thinking again, she couldn't help it. Opening the front

door and going outside and closing it behind her was the hardest thing she had ever done. It exhausted her and she leaned on the gate for a moment. Perhaps nothing would seem so hard again. She had taken her key with her, why she couldn't tell.

The chill of daybreak touched her face like a cool damp hand. It brought back the feeling of sickness and she breathed deeply. Where would she be this time tomorrow? Better not think of it. She began to walk along the lane, slowly at first, then faster, trying to calculate the time. Neither she nor Eve had ever possessed a watch. It must be somewhere between six-thirty and seven.

Too light for cars to have their lights on, yet these had, the two of them that she could see in the far distance coming along the winding road toward the bridge. She sensed that they were together because both had lights, one following the other, aiming for a certain goal.

By now she was in that part of the lane that was the approach to the bridge and where no tall trees grew. She could see the flash the morning light made on the river and see too the tunnel mouth on the other side where once the train had plunged into the hillside. Suddenly the car lights were switched off, both sets. Liza couldn't even see the cars anymore, but she knew they were coming this way. There was nowhere else for them to go.

If she got onto the bridge they would have to pass her, only they wouldn't pass her, they would stop. She climbed up the bank and hid herself among the late-summer tangle of hawthorn and bramble and wayfarer's tree. The cars glided up silently. One of them had a blue lamp on its roof, but the lamp wasn't lit.

Liza had been holding her breath all the time and now she expelled it in a long sigh. They would come back—they would bring Eve back—and in doing so pass the bus stop. She scrambled down the bank and ran onto the bridge. The river was wide and deep and glassy, not gulping at boulders and rippling between them until much farther up. On the bridge Liza did what it was unwise to do, she stopped and turned and looked back.

It might be that she would never see it again, any of it. She would never return, so she stopped and looked back like the woman in the picture at Shrove had done, the tall sad woman in white draperies who Eve told her was Lot's wife and her forsaken home the Cities of the Plain. But instead of those desolate and wicked places, she saw between the trees that rose out of the misty water meadows, the alders and the balsams and the lombardy poplars, the gracious outlines of Shrove House.

The sun that had risen in a golden dazzlement shed a pale amber light on its stone facade, the central pediment that held a coat of arms of unknown provenance, its broad terrace approached by flights of steps on both sides, its narrow door below and wide, noble door above. This was the garden front, identical to the front that faced the gates in all but that aspect's gracious portico. All its windows were blanked by this light that lay on them like a skin. The house looked as immovable as the landscape in which it rested, as natural and as serene.

From nowhere else could you see Shrove as from here. Trees hid it from spectators on the high hills. They knew how to conceal their homes from view, those old builders of great houses, Eve had said. Liza said a silent good-bye to it, ran across the bridge and out onto the road. The place where the bus stopped was a couple of hundred yards up on the left. Whatever Eve might think, she knew it well, she had often walked this way, had seen the bus, a green bus that she had never once been tempted to board.

What time was it now? A quarter past seven? When would the next bus come if she missed this one? In an hour? Two hours? Insurmountable difficulties once more built themselves up before her. Ramparts of difficulties reared up in her path, impossible to scale. She couldn't wait for that bus out in the open and risk the police cars passing her.

For all that, she kept on walking toward the bus stop, shifting the bag onto her other shoulder, now wondering about the train. There might not be another train to London for a long time. The train that had once run along the valley had passed quite seldom, only four times a day in each direction. How would she know if the train she got into was the one for London?

The sound of a car made her turn, but it wasn't one of their cars. It was red with a top made of cloth and it rattled. As it passed it left behind a smell she wasn't used to, metallic, acrid, smoky.

One other person waited at the stop. An old woman. Liza had no idea who she was or where she came from. There were no houses until the village was reached. She felt vulnerable, exposed, the focus of invisible watching eyes as she came up to the stop. The woman looked at her and quickly looked away as if angry or disgusted.

It took only one more car to pass for Liza to know she couldn't wait there, she couldn't stand on the verge and wait for the bus. What was she to do there? Stand and stare? Think of what? She couldn't bear her thoughts and her fear was like a mouthful of something too hot to swallow. If she waited here by the old woman with the downcast eyes, she would fall down or scream or cast herself onto the grassy bank and weep.

An impulse to run came to her and she obeyed it. Without looking to see if anything was coming, she ran across the road and plunged in among the trees on the other side. The old woman stared after her. Liza hung on to the trunk of a tree. She hugged it, laying her face against the cool smooth bark. Why hadn't she thought of this before? It had come to her suddenly what she must do. If she had thought of this last evening, how happy the night would have been! Except that if she had, she would have left last night, gone when Eve first told her to go, fled in the darkness across the fields.

A footpath ran close by here and through the pass. You couldn't really call it a pass, a pass was for mountains, but she had read the word and liked it. First of all she had to scramble up a hundred yards of hillside. The rumble of the bus, whose engine made a different noise from a car's, made her look down. Somehow she guessed it had arrived exactly on time. The old woman got on it and the bus moved off. Liza went on climbing. She didn't want to be there still when the cars came by. The footpath signpost found, she climbed the stile and took the path that ran close under the hedge. The sun was up now and feeling warm.

It was a relief to be far from the road, to know that when they came back they would be down there below her. When the path came to an end she would find herself in a web of lanes, buried in banks, sheltered by hedges, far from thoroughfares that went anywhere. The nearest town was seven miles off. It ought not to take her more than half an hour from here and she would be with him soon after eight. She wouldn't let herself think he might have gone, he might have moved on, that, angry with her, he had abandoned her and fled.

The birds had stopped singing. All was still and silent, her own footfalls soundless on the sandy track. The white and gold faces of chamomile flowers had appeared everywhere amid the grass and the old man's beard that had been clematis clung to the hedges in cascades of curly gray hair. She encountered her first animals, half a dozen red cows and two gray donkeys cropping the lush grass. A ginger cat, going home from a night's hunting, gave her a suspicious look. She had seen few cats, most of them in pictures, and the sight of this one was as pleasing as that of some exotic wild creature might be.

With the bright morning and her marvelous decision, fear was fast ebbing away. She had only one isolated fear left, that he wouldn't be there. The path came to an end with another stile and she was out in a lane so narrow that if she had lain down and stretched her arms beyond her head, her hands might have touched one side and her feet the other. A small car could have got along it, tunneling between the steep, almost vertical banks, green ramparts hung with the long leaves of plants whose flowers had bloomed and faded. The tree branches met and closed overhead.

It was flat, even a little downhill, and she began to run. She ran from youth and an increasing sense of freedom but from hope and anxiety too. If he had gone, meaning to let her know tomorrow or the next day ... Her hands in her pockets closed over and crushed the notes, two thin fistfuls—a lot or a little?

She ran on through the green tunnel and a rabbit ran across ahead of her. A cock pheasant squawked and flapped, teetered across the lane, a poor walker and a worse flier, its two hens following it, scrabbling for the shelter of the bank. She knew about things like that, knew far better she suspected than most people, but would it suffice? Would it do until she could learn about the other things?

The lane met another and another at a fork with a tiny triangle of green in the midst of it. She took the right-hand branch where the land began to fall still farther, but she had to go past one bend and then another before she saw the caravan below her. Her heart leapt. It was all right. He was there.

It was parked, as it had been for the past few weeks, since midsummer, on a sandy space from which a bridlepath opened and followed the boundary between field and wood. Horses were supposed to use it, but Liza had never seen a horse or a rider on that path. She had never seen anyone there but Sean. His old Triumph Dolomite, like a car from a sixties film, was parked where it always was. The curtains were drawn at the caravan windows. He only got up early for work. She had been running, but she walked this last bit, she walked quite slowly up to the caravan, mounted the two steps, and taking her right hand from her pocket and the notes it had still been enclosing, brought it to the smooth surface of the door.

Her hand poised, she hesitated. She drew in her breath. Knowing nothing but natural history and scraps of information from Victorian books, she nevertheless knew that love is unreliable, love is chancy, love lets you down. It came to her, this knowledge, from romantic dramas and love poetry, the sighs of the forsaken, the bitterness of the rejected, but from instinct too. Innocence is never ignorant of this, except in those nineteenth-century novels, and then only sometimes. She thought of how he could kill her with the wrong word or the abstracted look, and then she expelled her breath and knocked on the door.

His voice came from in there. "Yes? Who is it?"

"Sean, it's me."

"Liza?"

Only amazed, only incredulous. He had the door open very quickly. He was naked, a blanket from the bed tied around him. Blinking at the light, he stared at her. If she saw a sign of dismay in his eyes, if he asked her what she was doing there, she would die, it would kill her.

He said nothing. He took hold of her and pulled her inside, into the stuffy warm interior that smelled of man, and put his arms around her. It wasn't an ordinary hug but an all-enveloping embrace. He folded himself around her and held her inside

14

himself as a hand might enfold a fruit or a cone, softly but intensely, sensuously appreciating.

She had been going to explain everything and had foreseen herself telling her long tale, culminating in what had happened yesterday. It was a justification she had had in mind and a defense. But he gave her no chance to speak. Somehow, without words, he had made plain to her his great happiness at her untoward unexpected arrival and that he wanted her without explanation. As his arms relaxed their hold she lifted up her face to him, to look at his beautiful face, the eyes that changed his whole appearance when they grew soft with desire. But she was deprived of that too by his kiss, by his bringing his mouth to hers, so sweet-tasting and warm, blinding and silencing her.

When the bed was pulled down out of the wall the caravan was all bed. Her face still joined to his, she wriggled out of her clothes, dropped them garment by garment onto the floor, stepped out of the tracksuit pants, kicked off her trainers. She put her arms up again to hold him as he had held her. He let her pull him down onto the bed. It was warm where he had left it. They lay side by side, her breasts soft and full against his chest, hip to hip, their legs entwined. He began to kiss her with the tip of his tongue, lightly, quickly. She laughed, turned her face.

"I've run away! I've come to you for good."

"You're a marvel," he said. "You're the greatest," and then, "What about her?"

"I don't know. The police came, they came in two cars, they'll have taken her away." She appreciated his look of amazement, his interest. "I'd gone by then. Are you pleased?"

"Am I *pleased?* I'm over the moon. But what d'you mean, the police? What police?"

"I don't know. The police from the town."

"What's she done?"

She put her lips close to his ear. "Shall I tell you about it?"
"Tell me the lot, but not now."

He ran his hands down her body, down her back in a long slow sweep, and drew it close to him in a delicate arch. Without looking, she sensed him viewing her, appreciating her smoothness, her whiteness, her warmth. His hip touched hers, his thigh pressed against hers, warmth to warmth and skin to skin.

"Don't talk now, sweetheart," he said. "Let's have this now."

SHE slept for a long time. She was very tired. Relief had come too and a reprieve. When she woke up, Sean was sitting on the bed, looking down at her. She put out her hand and took hold of his, clutching it tightly.

Sean was wonderful to look at. She hadn't much to judge by, the painted man at Shrove, grainy monochrome images of actors in old movies, the postman, the oilman, Jonathan and Bruno, Matt, and a few others. His face was pale, the shape of the features sharply cut, his nose straight, his mouth red and full for a man's, dark eyes where she fancied she saw dreams and hopes, and eyebrows like the strokes of a Chinese painter's brush. She had seen a painting in the drawing room at Shrove with willow leaves and pink-breasted birds, a strange flower Eve said was a lotus, and letters made up of black curves like Sean's eyebrows. His hair was black as coal. Liza had read that, for as far as she knew she had never seen coal.

"You've been asleep for six hours." He said it admiringly, as one acclaiming another for some particular prowess.

"For a minute, when I woke up, I didn't know where I was. I've never been to sleep anywhere but in the gatehouse."

"You're kidding," he said.

"No, why would I? I've never slept away from home." She marveled at it. "This is my home now."

"You're the greatest," he said. "I'm lucky to have you, don't think I don't know it. I never thought you'd come, I thought, she'll never come and stay and *be* with me, she'll go and I'll lose her. Don't laugh, I know I'm a fool."

"I wouldn't laugh, Sean. I love you. Do you love me?"

"You know I do."

"Say it, then."

"I love you. There, is that okay? Haven't I proved I love you? I'd like to prove it all the time. Let me come in there with you, love, let's do it again, shall we? D'you know what I'd like best? To do it to you all the time, we wouldn't eat or sleep or watch TV or any of those things, we'd just do it forever and ever till we died. Wouldn't that be a lovely death?"

For answer she jumped up, eluding his grasp, and shifted to the far corner of the bed. He had laid her clothes there, the garments shaken and carefully placed side by side, like Eve might. Quickly she pushed her legs into the tracksuit, pulled the top over her head.

She said gravely, "I don't want to die. Not that way or any other." A thought came that she had never considered before.

"You wouldn't ever do it to me without me wanting it, would you, Sean?"

He was angry for a moment. "Why d'you say things like that? Why did you ask me that? I don't understand you sometimes."

"Never mind. It was just an idea. Don't you ever have nasty ideas?"

He shrugged, the light and the desire gone out of his face. "I'm going to make us a cup of tea. Or d'you fancy a Coke? I've got Coke and that's about all I have got. I haven't got nothing to eat, we shall have to go down to the shop."

Anything, she thought. *I haven't got anything to eat.* She wouldn't tell him this time. "Sean," she said, up in the corner, her back to the wall. "Sean, we'll have to *go*. I mean, leave here. We ought to put a good many miles between us and her."

"Your mum?"

"Why do you think the police came? I told you they came." As she spoke she knew he hadn't thought, he hadn't listened. Probably he hadn't heard her say that about the police. He had been consumed by desire, mad for her, closed to everything else. She knew how that felt, to be nothing but a deaf, blind, senseless *thing*, swollen and thick with it, breathless and faint. "I told you the police came."

"Did you? I don't know. What did they come for?"

"Can I have that Coke?" She hesitated and made the hesitation long. "I'm supposed to have gone to her friend Heather. That's where she thought she'd sent me. But I came to you."

"Tell me what she's done."

His expression was a bit incredulous and a bit—well, indulgent, she thought the word was. He was going to get a surprise. It wasn't going to be what he thought—she searched her imagination—stealing something or doing things against the law with money. He sat down where he had sat before and became intent on her. That pleased her, his total absorption.

"She killed someone," she said. "The day before yesterday. That's why they came and took her away and I'm afraid they'll want me, they'll want me to be a witness or something. They'll want to ask me questions and then maybe they'll try to put me somewhere to have people look after me. I've heard about that. I'm so young, I won't be seventeen till January."

She had been wrong about his absorption. He hadn't been listening. Again he hadn't heard her, but for a different reason. He was staring at her with his mouth slightly open. As she noted this he curled his upper lip as people do when confronted by a horror.

"What did you say?"

"About what? My age? Being a witness?"

He hesitated, seemed to swallow. "About her killing someone."

"It was yesterday, after I came back from meeting you in the wood. Or I think so. I mean I didn't actually see it, but I know she killed him."

"Come on, love." An awkward grin. "I don't believe you."

It left her helpless, she had no idea how to respond to this. She drank a few mouthfuls out of the open triangle in the top of the can. Eve had once told her that when a cat is in doubt how to act, it waves the tip of its tail. She felt like a cat but with no tail to wave. He must make the next move, for she couldn't.

He got up and took a few steps away. The caravan was too small for more than a few steps to be taken. She drank some more of her Coke, watching him.

"Why did you say that," he said, "about her killing somebody? Was you kidding? Was you trying to be funny?"

"It's true."

"It *can't* be."

"Look, Sean, I didn't make it up. It's why I came away. I

didn't want them to take me and shut me up, make me live somewhere. I knew they'd come this time. This time they'd find out and it wouldn't take long. I was expecting them all night."

His naturally pale face had gone whiter. She noticed and wondered why. "You mean she killed someone by accident, don't you?"

"I don't understand what that means." It was a sentence she was often obliged to utter since she had been with him.

"She was shooting birds and she shot someone by mistake, is that it? You told me she wouldn't never kill birds or rabbits, you told me that when we first met."

Only the last four words really registered with her. They made her smile, remembering. She slithered down the bed, jumped off, and put her arms around him. "Wasn't it lovely that I met you and you met me? It was the best thing that ever happened to me."

This time it was he who pulled away from the embrace. "Yes, love, okay, it was great. But you've got to tell me. About this killing, this is serious, right? What happened? Was it some guy poaching?"

"No," she said, "no, you don't understand."

"Too bloody right I don't and I won't if you don't tell me."

"I'll try." She sat down and he sat down and she held his hand. "She murdered him, Sean. People do do that, you know." It seemed a wild and curious statement for her to be making. "She murdered him because she wanted to be rid of him. She wanted him out of the way, it doesn't matter why, it's not important now."

This time he didn't say he disbelieved her but, "I *can't* credit it."

What had Eve said? "Then you must just accept."

"Who did she murder?"

She could tell from his tone that he still thought she was lying. That made her impatient.

"It doesn't matter. A man. No one you know. Sean, it's the truth, you have to believe me." She was learning truths of her own. "I can't be with someone who thinks I'm telling him lies." From delighted laughter, she was near to tears. She sought for a way out. "I can't prove it. What can I do to make you believe it?"

He said in a low voice, "I sort of do believe you—now."

"I'll tell you all about it." She was eager. She took hold of his shoulders and brought her face close up to his. "I'll tell you everything, if you like, from when I was small, from when I can first remember."

He kissed her. When her face was as close to his as that, he couldn't resist kissing her. His tongue tasted of the caramel sweetness of Coke as she supposed hers must. They were on the bed, that was where you sat in the caravan, and her body grew soft, sliding backward, sinking into the mattress, she was wanting him as much as she had when she first arrived that morning. He pulled her up, grasping her hands.

"I want you to tell me, Liza. I want to know everything about you. But not now. Now tell me what your mum did."

Being frustrated made her sulky. "What's the good? You won't believe it."

"I will, I've said so."

"I think we ought to leave, we ought to be on our way, not sitting here talking."

"Don't you worry yourself about that, I'll see to all that. You tell me about your mum and this man." She saw it in his eyes as the idea came to him. "Did he try raping her, was that it?"

"He was teaching her to shoot pigeons with a shotgun. He was out there shooting and she said, show me how."

"You've got to be joking."

"It's the truth. If you're going to say that, I won't tell you."

"Right, then. Go on."

"I hate shooting birds. I hate people shooting anything, rabbits, squirrels, anything, it's *wrong*. And I thought Eve—my mother—I thought she did too. She said so, she taught me to think like that. But she told him the pigeons were eating her vegetables and she asked him to show her how and he said he would. You see, I think he'd have done anything she asked, Sean."

"She's an attractive woman."

"More attractive than I am?"

"Don't be bloody ridiculous. Was you watching all this?"

"I'd been in the wood with you," Liza said. "They didn't see me. I came up through the garden and they were on the grass where the new trees are. Sound carries terrific distances there, you know. Even when people are speaking softly you can hear them. I saw the two of them with just the one gun and I thought she must be telling him not to shoot the pigeons. He was allowed to, you know, because though pheasant shooting doesn't start till October you can shoot pigeons when you like. Poor things! What did it matter to him, he wasn't a farmer, they weren't his cabbages they were eating, and even if they were, the pigeons have got to live, haven't they?

"I thought, good for her, she's going to stop him, but she didn't. She was out there with him for a shooting lesson. I'd heard her talking about it with him, but I didn't think she was serious. When I saw them I asked myself, what on earth is she doing? He started showing her things about the gun and she was looking and then he handed it to her.

"I didn't want to see the birds killed. I started to go back toward the gatehouse. Then the shot came and immediately afterward this screaming choking noise. So I turned around and ran across the lawn and there she was looking at him where he lay. She wasn't holding the gun, she'd dropped it, she was looking down at him and all the blood on him."

Sean had put up his hand to cover his mouth. His eyes had grown very big. He took his hand away, pushing at his cheek in a curious wiping movement. "What did you do?" he said in a small voice.

"I didn't do anything. I went home. She didn't tell the police and I didn't, so I think Matt must have. You know Matt?"

"Of course I do."

"He was there, up by the house. Only I don't think he saw any more than I did. He guessed."

"But you said the police had only just come, they were coming when you left—when? A couple of hours ago?"

"They came last evening. They didn't see me. You see, they didn't come to the gatehouse, not then. First of all, cars came and a black van to take away the body. I watched it all from my bedroom window. Eve told me to stay there and not come out, not to let anyone see me. I didn't want them to see me. She went up to Shrove and I think the policemen talked to her there. They talked to her and they talked to Matt and Matt's wife.

"She knew they'd come back, so she said I must go. For my own protection, she said. I ran away to you. That's it."

"That's all of it?"

"Not *all*, Sean. It'll take me a long time to tell you all of it."

"I'll get the van fixed up to the tow bar," he said.

She went outside with him. The day was warm and sultry, two in the afternoon, and the sun a puddle of light in a white sky. Watching him, she picked blackberries off the hedge and ate them by the handful. She was enormously hungry.

The battered Dolomite shifted the caravan with the slow weary competence of an old carthorse. It groaned a bit and expelled a lot of black exhaust. Liza got into the passenger seat and banged the door. Car and caravan lurched off the grass verge onto the harder surface of the lane.

"Where shall we go?"

"We have to go where they'll let me park the van. Before you come I was thinking of trying Vanner's. They're wanting pickers for the Coxes. We could both of us do that."

"Coxes won't be ready till the third week of September," she said, always glad to show off something she knew and he might not. "Anyway, how far is it?"

"Twenty-five miles, thirty. Far enough for you?"

"I don't know. What else can you do?"

He laughed. "Electrical work, sort of, put washers on taps, grind knives, I'm halfway to a motor mechanic, wash your car, do your garden—as *you* should know—clean windows, most things, you name it."

"Why apples, then?"

"Apples make a change. I reckon I always do pick apples in September and cherries in July."

"I'm hungry," she said, "I'm so *bloody* hungry."

"Don't swear, Liza."

"You do. Who d'you think I got it from?"

"It's different for me. You're a woman. I don't like to hear a woman swear."

She lifted her shoulders, the way Eve did. "I'm tremendously hungry. Can we buy some food?"

"Yeah, we can get takeaway." He looked at her, remembered and explained, "Stuff they've cooked for you in a shop, right? Or we'll find a caff, maybe a Little Chef if there's one on the A road."

She was no longer afraid. Fear might not be canceled, but it was postponed. The prospect of going into a café excited her. And she'd be with Sean. Shops she had been in, one or two over the years, but a real restaurant, if that was the word, that was very different. She remembered what she had taken with her when she left the gatehouse.

"I've got money. I've got a hundred pounds."

"For Christ's sake," he said.

"It's in the van, in my coat."

"Did you nick it?" His tone was stern.

"Of course not. Eve gave it to me."

He said nothing. She looked out of the window at the passing countryside, all of it new, all uncharted for her. They drove through a village as the church clock struck three, and ten minutes later they were in a sizable town with parking in the marketplace.

On either side of the carpark the roads that enclosed it were lined with shops. She had seen something like this before, though not here, the dry cleaner's, the building society, the estate agent, the Chinese restaurant, the Oxfam shop, the sandwich bar, the building society, the insurance company, the Tandoori House, the bank, the pub, the card shop, the estate agent. An arch, in pink glass and gold metal, led into a deserted hall of shops. Perhaps all towns were like this, all the same inside, perhaps it was a rule.

Sean's practiced eye quickly summed up the situation. "The caffs are closed, it's too late. Pubs are meant to stay open till all hours, but they don't never seem to. I can go get us pie and chips or whatever."

Her hunger was greater than her disappointment. "Whatever you like. Do you want some money?"

She said it cheerfully, trying to strike the right note, having never said it before. Yet for some reason he was offended. "I hope I'll never see the day when I've got to live off my girlfriend."

Once he had gone she got out of the car. She stretched her arms above her head, tasting freedom. It was heady stuff, for something was making her shiver and it couldn't be the day, which was as warm as high summer. She had never felt like this before, dizzy, faint was perhaps the word, as if she might fall.

She opened the door of the caravan and clambered up inside. Five minutes' sitting down and a few deep breaths and she felt better. The bed was stowed away in the wall, the sheets and blankets folded, and the table down, ready for a meal by the time Sean came back. The packages he was carrying had grease seeping through the wrapping paper and gave off a pungent smell of deep frying.

She had been so hungry and the smell from the chips and Cornish pasties he unwrapped was so enticing, but she couldn't help herself. Without warning to herself or him she burst into violent tears. He held her in his arms close to him, stroking her hair while she sobbed. Her body shook and her heart was pounding.

"It's all right, it's all right, sweetheart. You've had a shock, it's delayed shock, you'll be okay. I'll look after you."

He soothed her. He stroked her hair and when she was just crying, not sobbing and shrieking anymore, wiped her eyes with his fingers, as gently as a woman, as gently as Eve when she was being gentle. As she quietened he did something she loved him to do, began combing her hair with his own comb, which had thick blunt teeth. The comb ran smoothly through the length of her long dark hair, from crown to tip, and as he paused she felt his fingers just touch and then linger on her neck and the lobe of her ear. She shivered, not this time from shock or strangeness.

"Give us a kiss," he said.

It was more enthusiastic than he had bargained for, a deep sensuous kiss full of controlled energy now released. He laughed at her. "Let's eat. I thought you was hungry."

"Oh, I am. I'm starving."

"You could've fooled me."

This was her first Cornish pasty. She had no means of know-ing whether it was a good one or passable or bad, but she liked it. In the past she had never been allowed to eat with her fingers. There had been many gently enforced rules and much benevo-lent constraint.

"When we get wherever we're going," she said, "I'll tell you the story of my life."

"Right."

"I don't *know,* but I don't think there've been many lives like mine."

"You've got a long way to go with it yet, like maybe seventy years."

"Can I have the last chip? I'll tell you from back as far as I can remember. That's when I was four and that's when she killed the first one."

She pulled a length from the toilet roll he kept by the bed to use as tissues and wiped her mouth. When she turned back to him to say she was ready, they could be off as soon as he liked, she saw that he was staring at her and the look on his face was aghast.

ONE of the first things she could remember was the train. It was summer and she and Mother had gone for a walk in the fields when they heard the train whistle. The single track ran down there in the valley between the river and lower slopes of the high hills. It was a small branch line and later on, when she was older, Mother told her it was the most beautiful train journey in the British Isles. Her eyes shone when she said it.

But on that afternoon when Liza was four there were not many passengers and those there were couldn't have been looking out to appreciate the view, or else they were all looking out the other side at the high hills, for when Mother waved and she waved no one waved back. The train jogged along not very fast and disappeared into the round black tunnel that pierced the hillside.

Liza suspected that she and Mother hadn't been there very long the day she saw her first train. If they had been, she would have seen a train before. It was possible they had been at the gatehouse for only a few days. Where they had come from before that she had had no idea then nor for a long time to come. She could remember nothing from before that day, not a face nor a place, a voice nor a touch.

There was only Mother.

There was only the gatehouse where they lived and the arched gateway with the tiny one-roomed house on the other side and Shrove House in the distance. It was half-concealed by tall and beautiful trees, its walls glimpsed mysteriously and enticingly between their trunks. When Mother read stories to her and there was a palace in them, as there often was, she would say, "Like Shrove, that's what a palace is, a house like Shrove." But all Liza had seen of the real Shrove until she was nearly five and the leaves had turned brown and blown off the trees, were a dreamy grayness, a sheet of glittering glass, a gleam of sun-touched slate.

Later on she saw it in its entirety, the stone baluster that crowned it, broken by a crest-filled pediment, the many windows, the soaring steps, and the statues that stood in its alcoves. She was aware even then of the way it seemed to bask, to sit and smile as if pleased with itself, to recline smiling in the sun.

Nearly every day Mother went up to the house that was like a palace in a fairy tale, sometimes for several hours, sometimes for no more than ten minutes, and when she went she locked Liza up in her bedroom.

The gatehouse was the lodge of Shrove House. Later on,

when Liza was older, Mother told her it was built in the Gothic style and not nearly so old as the house itself. It was supposed to look as if it dated from the Middle Ages and had a turret with crenellations around its top and a tall peaked gable. Out of the side of the gable came the arch, which went over the top of a pair of gates and came down on the other side to join up with the little house that looked like a miniature castle with its slit windows and studded door.

The gates were of iron, were always kept open, and had SHROVE HOUSE written on them in curly letters. The gatehouse and the arch and the little castle were made of small red bricks, the dark russet color of rosehips. Liza and Mother had two bedrooms upstairs, a living room and a kitchen downstairs, and an outside lavatory. That was all. Liza's was the bedroom in the turret with a view over their garden and the wood and Shrove park and everything beyond. She disliked being locked in her bedroom, but she wasn't frightened, and as far as she could remember she didn't protest.

Mother gave her things to do. She had started teaching Liza to read, so she gave her rag books with big letters printed on the cloth pages. She also gave her paper and two pencils and a book to rest on. Liza had a baby bottle with orange juice in it because if she had had a glass or a cup she would have spilled the juice on the floor. Sometimes she had two biscuits, just two, or an apple.

Liza didn't know then what Mother did in Shrove House, but later on she found out because Mother began taking her too and she was no longer locked in her bedroom—or only when Mother went shopping. But that was more than six months later, after it had all happened and the winter had come, when snow covered the hillsides and the only trees to keep their leaves were the huge blue cedars and the tall black firs.

Before that, in the summertime, the dogs came. Except in pictures Liza had never seen a dog or a cat or a horse or any animals but wild ones. She thought these two came the day after she and Mother had walked in the fields and seen the first train, but it may have been some other day, a week or even a month later. It wasn't easy to remember time spans from so far back.

The dogs belonged to Mr. Tobias. It wasn't he who brought them but another man. Liza had never seen Mr. Tobias but only heard about him, and she wasn't to see him for a long, long time. The man who brought the dogs came in a kind of small truck with a barrier like a white wire fence across the back inside to keep the dogs off the front seats. His name was Matt. He was a short, squarish man with big shoulders who looked very strong and his hair grew up from his broad red forehead like the bristles on a brush.

"They are Doberman pinschers," Mother said. She always explained everything slowly and carefully. "In Germany, which is another country a long way away, they used to be trained as police dogs. But these are pets." She said to Matt, who was staring at her in a strange way, "What are their names?"

"This one's Heidi and he's Rudi."

"Are they nice, friendly dogs?"

"They'll be okay with you and the kiddy. They'll never attack women, they've been trained that way. I'd be up the nearest tree myself if someone called out 'Kill!' when they're around."

"Really? Mr. Tobias didn't say."

"Thought you might say no to looking after them, I daresay." He gazed around him, stared at the high hills beyond the valley as if they were the Himalayas. "Bit isolated down here, aren't you? Not what you'd call much life going on."

"It's what I like."

"It takes all sorts, I suppose, though I'd have thought a smashing-looking girl like yourself'd want something a bit more lively. Bright lights, eh, bit of dancing and the movies? You wouldn't have such a thing as a cup of tea going, I daresay?"

"No, I wouldn't," said Mother and she took the dog leashes in one hand and Liza's hand in the other, went into the gatehouse, and shut the door. The man outside on the step said something Liza couldn't catch but which Mother said was a dirty word and never to say it. They heard his van start up with a roar as if it was angry.

The dogs started licking Liza, they licked her hands, and when she stroked them, they licked her face. Their coats felt like nothing she had ever touched before, shiny as leather, soft as fur, smooth as the crown of her own head when Mother had just washed her hair.

She said to Mother, "Heidi and Rudi are black lined with brown," and Mother had laughed and said that was right, that was just how they looked.

"You can't remember all those things your mum and him said word for word, can you?" said Sean.

"Not really. But it was *like* that. I know all the kinds of things she says and ever could say. I know her so well, you see, it's as if I know her perfectly because I don't know anyone else."

"How about me? You know me."

She could tell she had hurt him and tried to make amends. "I know you *now*. I didn't then."

"Go on, then. What happened with the dogs?"

"Eve was looking after them for Mr. Tobias. He had to go away, he went to see his mother in France, and he couldn't take the dogs for some reason."

"Quarantine."

"What?"

"When he come back in he'd have to put the pair of them in quarantine for six months. That means they'd be in like kennels. It's the law."

"I expect that was it."

"Why couldn't this Matt look after them wherever it was he lived?"

"In the Lake District. He had a job, he was working all day. He couldn't take them out for exercise—or wouldn't. Anyway, Eve wanted to do this for Mr. Tobias, she wanted to please him.

"We were supposed to have them for two or three weeks, I can't exactly remember. I loved them, I wanted us to have a dog after they'd gone back, but Eve wouldn't. She said Mr. Tobias wouldn't like it."

"So it wasn't them she killed?"

"I told you, it was a person, a man."

Liza never knew who he was or what it was he had tried to do. Now that twelve years had passed and she was grown up, doing the thing that grown-ups did herself, she could guess.

It was she who saw him first. Mother was down at Shrove and she was locked up in her bedroom. Where the dogs were she didn't know. Probably in the little castle where they slept at night or even at Shrove, for in a sort of way it was *their* house. It belonged to Mr. Tobias, who owned them.

Mother had been gone a long time. Who could say now how long those long times actually were? It's different when you're four. Half an hour? An hour? Or only ten minutes? She had read the letters in the rag book and made them into words, "dog," "cat," "bed," "cot." The baby bottle had been sucked dry and the pencil had scribbled over every single sheet of paper.

She climbed upon the bed and crawled on all fours over to the window. The room had six sides and three windows but was too small for the bed to be anywhere but pushed against the wall with the window that had the best view. The sun was shining, sparkling on the river, and the wind was blowing the clouds and making their shadows run across the slopes of the high hills. A train whistled from somewhere out of sight and came into her view from out of the tunnel. She climbed onto a chair to look out of the window that overlooked the gateway and the little castle.

There was never anyone there. There was never anyone to be seen but Mother, the milkman and the postman in the morning, and Mr. Frost on his tractor on certain afternoons. Sometimes a car came down on its way to the bridge. Mostly the lane was empty and all that showed its face in the barn on the other side was the white owl, so seeing the man made her jump. He was holding on to one of the gates and looking toward Shrove, a tall man in blue jeans and a pullover and brown leather jacket and with a canvas bag on his back.

Suddenly he looked up in the direction of her window and saw her there between the curtains. She knew he saw her and it frightened her. She couldn't have said why it did, but it was something to do with his face, not a nice face, not the kind she had ever seen before. It was masked in yellow-brown hair all over it, great bushes of curly hair from which eyes stared and the nose poked out. Later she wondered if she had thought the face not nice because of the beard, which was new to her. She never saw another until the day Bruno and Mother took her shopping in the town.

She was afraid he was coming to the gatehouse and would get in and come to get her. Ducking down from the window and wriggling across the floor and hiding under the bed couldn't stop that and she knew it. She knew it even then. Under the bed she didn't feel safe, only a bit saf*er*, and she thought it might be a little while before he found her. Mother had locked the door of her room and the front door of the gatehouse, but that didn't make Liza think the man wouldn't be able to find her.

A long time went by and Mother came back. She pulled Liza out and hugged her and said she hadn't seen any man and if there was one he was probably harmless. If he wasn't she'd set Heidi and Rudi on him.

"How will you know?" Liza said.

"I know everything."

Liza believed that was true.

Late that afternoon there was a knock at the front door and when Mother went to answer it the man with the beard was on the step, asking for a glass of water. Liza thought Mother would say no, she hung on to Mother's skirt, peering around her until Mother said to let go, not to be so stupid. The man said he hoped he wasn't a nuisance.

"Go and fetch some water, please, Liza," Mother said. "Not a glass, a mug. You know how to do it."

Liza knew. In some ways Mother had brought her up to be independent. Only in some, of course. For a long while she had fetched her own water when she wanted a drink, climbing up onto the chair by the sink, taking a mug from the shelf, turning on the tap, and filling the mug and then being very careful to turn the tap off again. She did this now, filling the mug that had a picture on it of a lady in a crown, and carrying it back to the front door. Some of it spilled on the way, but she couldn't help that.

The man drank the water. She saw so few people she noticed everything about the ones she did see. He held the mug in his left hand, not his right like Liza and Mother did, and on the third finger of that hand was a wide gold ring. That was the first time she had ever seen a ring on anyone's hand, for Mother wore none.

He said to Liza, "Thank you, darling," and gave her back the mug. "Is there anywhere around here doing B and B?" he said to Mother.

"Doing what?"

"B and B. Bed and breakfast."

"There's nowhere around here doing anything," Mother said, sounding glad to say it. She took a step outside, making him step backward, and spread out her arms. "What you see is what you get."

"Best press on, then."

Mother made no answer. She did what Liza didn't like her doing to *her*. It was a way she had of lifting her shoulders and dropping them again while looking hard into the other person's eyes, but not smiling or showing anything. Until then Liza hadn't seen Eve do it to anyone but herself.

From an upstairs window, the one in Mother's room in the gable which overlooked the lane this time, they watched the man go. It was only from here that you could see where the lane ran along past the wood on its way to the bridge in one direction, and in the other to peter out into first a track and then a footpath. The man walked slowly, as if his pack felt heavier with each step he took. At the point where the lane wound and narrowed he paused and looked back in the direction of Shrove or perhaps just at the high hills.

They lost him among the trees, but they went on watching and after a little while saw him again, by now a small figure plodding along the footpath under the maple hedge. After that it became a game between the two of them, each claiming to be able to see him still. But when Liza got excited, Mother lifted her down from the window and they went downstairs to get on with Liza's reading lesson. An hour every afternoon was spent on teaching her to read and an hour every morning teaching her writing. The lessons were soon to get much longer, with sums as well and drawing, but at the time the man with the beard came they lasted just two hours each day.

Every morning very early, long before the writing lesson, they took the dogs out. Heidi and Rudi had been used to living indoors, so couldn't have kennels outside, which Mother would have thought best, but slept in the little castle. Liza had never been in there before the dogs came, but Mother had a key and took her in with her and she saw a room shaped like her bedroom with six sides and narrow windows with arched tops, only these had no glass in them. The floor was of stone with straw on it and two old blankets and two old cushions for the dogs. Rudi and Heidi bounded about and nuzzled her and licked her face, making noises of relief and bliss at being released.

Liza had thought how horrible it would be if they met the man with the beard while they were out in the water meadows. But they met no one, they hardly ever did, only a vixen going home with a rabbit in her mouth. Mother ordered the dogs to sit, to be still, and they obeyed her. She told Liza about foxes, how they lived and raised their young in earths, how people hunted them, and that this was wrong.

That might have been the morning she saw her first kingfisher. It was about that time, she couldn't be sure. Mother said kingfishers were not common and when you saw one you should phone up and tell the County Kingfisher Trust. So it must have been that morning, for after they got home and the dogs were back in the house next door, Mother locked her in her bedroom and went over to Shrove to phone.

Liza read the words in the rag book and drew a picture of

Mother on one of the sheets of paper. It might have been another day she did that, but she thought it was the Day of the Kingfisher. From about that time she got it into her head that all men had fair hair and all women dark. The man who delivered the oil was fair and so were the postman and Matt and the man with the beard, but Mother and she were dark. She drew a picture of Mother with her long dark hair down her back and her long colored skirt and her sandals.

It was just finished when Mother unlocked the door and let her out. There was something different in the living room, Liza spotted it at once. It was hanging up on the wall over the fireplace, a long dark brown tube with a wooden handle. She had never seen anything like it before, but she knew Mother must have brought it back from Shrove.

"It was a gun," said Sean.

"A shotgun. There were a lot of guns at Shrove. I began thinking about it later—I mean years later—and I think that man had really frightened her. Frightened is probably not the word, she doesn't get frightened. Let's say, alerted her to danger."

"Yeah, maybe she reckoned she should never have said that about what you see is what you get. I mean, like, you know, not being no one else around for miles."

"I expect so."

"But he'd gone, hadn't he?"

"He came back."

It stayed light in the evenings until nearly ten, but Liza was put to bed at seven. She had her tea, always wholemeal bread with an egg or a piece of cheese. Cake and sweets were not allowed, and years passed before she found out what they were. After the bread she had fruit, as much as she wanted, and a glass of milk. The milkman came three times a week, another man with fair hair.

Mother read her a story when tea was over: Hans Andersen or Charles Kingsley, books borrowed from the library at Shrove. Then came her bath. They had a bath in the kitchen with a wooden lid on it. She wasn't locked in her bedroom at night, she was never locked in except when Mother went to Shrove or shopping in the town. When Liza couldn't get to sleep she knew it was useless calling out or crying, for Mother took no notice, and if she came downstairs Mother would shrug at her and give her one of those wordless looks before taking her back up again.

So all she could do was wander about upstairs, looking out of the windows, hoping to see something, though she hardly ever did. If Mother knew Liza went into her room and played with her things, she gave no sign of it. Mother read books in the evenings, Liza knew that, or listened to music coming into her ears through wires from a little square black box.

In Mother's room she opened the cupboard door and examined all the long bright-colored skirts that Mother wore and the other things she never wore, long scarves, a couple of big straw hats, a yellow gown with a flounce around the hem. She looked in her jewel case, which was kept in the dressing table drawer, and could have told anyone precisely what the case held: a long string of green beads, two pairs of earrings, a hair comb made of brown mottled stuff with brilliant shiny bits set in it, a brooch of carved wood and another of mother-of-pearl. Mother had told her that was what it was when she wore the brooch just as she told her the beads were jade and the two pairs of earrings made of gold.

That evening the green beads and one pair of earrings were missing because Mother was wearing them. Liza closed the box, went back to her own room, and knelt upon the bed, looking out of the window. The gatehouse garden, in which Mother later on grew peas and beans and lettuces, soft fruit on bushes and strawberries under nets, was mostly bare earth at that time. Mother had been working on it that day, digging it over with a fork. There was just one tree, a single cherry tree, growing out of the soft red-brown soil, and two long grass paths.

Liza shifted her gaze upward, waiting for the last southbound train, which would go through a bit after eight-thirty. She hadn't known about north and south and eight-thirty then, though Mother was teaching her to tell the time and to understand a map, but she knew the last train would come out from the tunnel while it was still light but after sunset. The sky was red all over, though you couldn't see where the sun went down from her room. Once it had set, the high hills went gray and the woods changed from green to a soft dark blue.

The train whistled at the tunnel mouth and came chugging down. Lights were on inside, though there was a lot of light outside still. It would stop at the station, at Ring Valley Halt, but you couldn't see the station from here. In the distance, the train grew very small, long and wriggling like one of the millipedes that lived near the back door. After it was gone there would be nothing more to be seen from this window. Liza scrambled off the bed and went on tiptoe back across the landing to Mother's room.

From here, you could see the bats that lived in the barn roof on the other side of the lane and swooped after moths and gnats. Sometimes she saw the great cream-colored owl with a face like a cat's in a book. She had never seen a real cat. It was a little too early for owls this evening. Down below her, in the little patch of front garden, as twilight came, the color began to fade from the red and pink geraniums and the tobacco flowers began to gleam more whitely. If the window had been open she could have smelled them, for their scent came out at dusk.

Just as Liza was thinking nothing would happen, it would get dark without anything happening, the front door opened and

Mother came out in her green and purple and blue skirt and purple top, her green beads and gold earrings, with a black shawl wrapped around her. She opened the gate in the wall that ran around the garden, unlocked the door of the little castle, and the dogs came rushing out. Mother said, "Quiet. Sit," and they sat, though trembling and quivering, Liza could see, hating this enforced stillness.

Mother said, "Off you go," and the pair of them began gamboling about, jumping up and trying to lick her, leaving off when she didn't respond. She walked around the side of the gatehouse out of sight, the dogs following, but Liza knew she wouldn't go far because she never did in the evenings.

Liza ran back into her own bedroom, climbed onto the bed, and pressed her face against the window. Outside a bat swooped, so close that she jerked her face back, though she knew the glass was there. Rudi and Heidi were in the back garden playing, grappling with each other and making mock growling noises and rolling over and over. Mother wasn't with them, Mother must have come back into the house.

Back on the landing, Liza listened, but she couldn't hear Mother down there. She ran into Mother's room and up to the window. Mother was sitting on the wall, listening to the music coming out of the band around her head and holding the little black box in her hands.

Where were the dogs? No longer in the back garden, she discovered as she bounced back onto her own bed. They must have gone out through the opening in the fence and into the wood, as they sometimes did. But they were well-trained, they always came back at a call.

It would get dull now if nothing more happened than Mother sitting on the wall, waiting for the dogs to finish their play. Liza never considered getting back into bed and trying to sleep as an alternative to this roving from room to room. Either she fell asleep when she happened to be on her own bed or Mother found her asleep on the landing floor or in the chair by the front bedroom window. She always woke in her own bed in the mornings. But she didn't want to be there now, she wasn't tired.

Perhaps Mother had decided to do something different. Liza ran back to check. Mother was still there, still listening. It was nearly dark but not too dark to see the man with the beard come along the lane from the bridge direction. The man looked just the same except that this time he hadn't got his backpack with him.

His footsteps made no sound on the sandy floor. Mother wouldn't have heard them if they had with that thing on her head and the music that was called Wagner flowing into her ears. Liza began to be frightened. Mother had said the dogs would protect them but the dogs weren't there, the dogs were a long way away in the wood.

Liza couldn't look.

Why hadn't she banged on the window to warn Mother? She hadn't thought of that till afterward. The first time the man came she had got under the bed, the second time she had fetched him a drink of water. This time she put her hands over her eyes. They were talking, she could hear their voices but not what they said. Very cautiously she parted her fingers and peeped through them, but they had gone, Mother and the man, they had come too near the gatehouse for her to see or else they had walked around the back. She ran to the back and as she jumped on her bed, Mother screamed.

"What was he doing to her?" Sean said.

"She never told me, she never said a word about it, not then and not later. I know now, of course I do. When she screamed I was so frightened I covered up my ears, but I could still hear, the window was open. I thought the man would catch her and—oh, make her his prisoner or something—and then come and get me."

"You were only a little kid."

"And there was no one else for miles and miles. You know that. There never was. If there had been it couldn't have happened, none of it could."

It wasn't dark but the beginning of the long midsummer twilight. When Mother's scream died away she heard the man laugh but she couldn't hear what it was he whispered. She looked out of the window, she had to look, and Mother was on the grass path and the man was on top of her. He was trying to hold her there with one hand and with the other he was undoing his jeans.

Liza was so frightened she couldn't make a sound or do anything. But Mother could. Mother twisted her head around under the man's arm that pinned her neck and bit his hand. He jumped and pulled up his hand, shouting that word Matt had used on the doorstep, and Mother screamed out, "Heidi, Rudi! Kill! Kill!"

The dogs came out of the wood. They came running as if they had been waiting for the summons, as if they had been sitting among the trees listening for just that command. In the half-dark they no longer looked like nice friendly dogs that licked your face but hounds of hell, though that was before Liza had ever heard of hounds of hell.

They didn't jump at the man, they flew at him. All eight powerful black legs took off and they were airborne. Their mouths gaped open and Liza could see their white shining teeth. The man had started to get to his feet, but he fell over on his back when the dogs came at him. He covered his face with his hands and rolled this way and that. Heidi had half his great yellow beard in her jaws and Rudi was on him biting his neck. The dogs made a noise, a rough, grumbling, snorting sound.

Mother jumped up lightly as if nothing had happened and dusted down her skirt with her hands. She stood in that way she had, with her hands on her hips, the shawl hanging loose from her shoulders, and she watched them calmly, the dogs savaging the man and the man screaming and cursing.

Then, after a little while, she said, "All right, dogs, that'll do. Quiet now. Still."

They obeyed her at once. It was clever the way they stopped the moment she spoke. Rudi had some of the man's blood on his face and Heidi a mouthful of beard. The man rolled over again, his head on his arms, but he had stopped screaming, he didn't make a sound. Mother bent over him, looking closely, she didn't touch him with her hands but prodded him with one small, delicate foot.

Liza made a little sound to herself up in her bedroom, a whimper like a dog whining behind a closed door.

Sean said hoarsely, "Was he dead?"

"Oh, no, he wasn't *dead*."

"What did she do?"

"Nothing. She just looked at him."

"Didn't she get help? There was a phone in Shrove House, you said."

"Of course she didn't get help," Liza said impatiently.

Mother took hold of the dogs by their collars and put them in the little castle for the night. Liza saw her do that from the other window and heard her come into their own house and shut the front door after her. She went out onto the landing and listened. In the sitting room Mother was moving a chair about and it sounded as if she had climbed on the chair and jumped off it. Liza scrambled across the bed to have another look at the man on the grass. He was still there but not lying face-downward anymore.

It was really dark now, too dark to see much but the shape of the man sitting there with his head on his knees and his arms up around his head. Soon he would get up and go away and leave them and they'd be safe. She peered out through the dark, hoping for that to happen.

Suddenly she could see the man very clearly in a big oblong of light. The back door was open and light was coming from the kitchen. She wrinkled up her nose and made a face because the man's face and beard were a mass of blood. Her knees had looked like that when she fell over and hurt herself on the gravel.

Mother walked out into the light and pointed something she had in her arms and there was a tremendous explosion. The man tumbled over backward and jerked a bit and shuddered and lay still. In the little castle the dogs set up a wild barking. Mother came back into the house and shut the door and the light went out.

IN the late afternoon, going by the lanes instead of the A road, Sean and Liza reached Vanner's fruit farm. This was orchard country, acre after acre of close-pruned stubby apple trees in long lines and then acre after acre of Comice pears and Louise Bonnes. The big wooden crates that would take the apples were stacked on top of one another in the corners of orchards. Liza saw women mounted on steps picking the big green Comice. Very few of the pears had been left to fall, but the apple crop, Discovery and Jonagold, had been a heavy one, and under the trees the ground was scarlet with abandoned fruit.

Sean took the left-hand turn into Vanner's land. He had been there before and knew where to go. The long straight macadam-ized roadway was bounded on either side by lines of alders, neat quick-growing trees to make high hedges. He had to pull in to let a car with its soft top down go past in the other direction, coming from the farm shop. A woman was driving. She had shiny blond hair and red lipstick on, gold earrings and red varnish on her nails, and Liza stared at her, fascinated.

"You're not still thinking women are all dark and men are all fair, are you, love?"

"Of course I'm not. I was only *four*."

"Because there's other ways of telling the difference." He put his hand in her lap and moved the fingers into her crotch. "Bet you can't talk while I'm doing that. Go on, try. I bet you can't."

"I can do that too," said Liza, reaching for him. "It'll be worse for you, you won't be able to drive."

He laughed and gasped and grabbed her hand. "Better leave off till we get there or I'll have to stop the van and we'll cause an obstruction."

The parking place for caravans was in a remote spot where the orchards ended and the strawberry fields began. The straw-berries were long over, the people who came to pick their own departed, and the fields a desolate waste of brown tendrils and dying leaves. A line of extremely tall Lombardy poplars on a high bank divided these fields from the Discovery orchard, and under the shadow of the poplars, on a rutted area of dried mud and scrubby grass, stood a sign that said: PICKERS' VANS PARK HERE. Beside the sign was a water tap, and an arrow spraypainted on cardboard pointed to the waste disposal.

Other pickers there might be, but there was only one caravan. It was parked at the far end up against the bank and looked as if no one was living in it or had lived in it for a long time. Its door and windows were shut and its blinds down. Just the same, Sean parked his car and van as far away from it as he could.

He didn't uncouple the van from the car or get the generator going or fill the water tanks. He and Liza, without a word, with scarcely an exchanged glance, got out of the car, went into the van, and made love. They delayed for just the time it took to pull the bed down.

"I tell you what," said Sean, when it was finished and she was lying in his arms, warm and damp and sighing with pleasure. "Now we're here and got a base, you can get yourself to the family planning or whatever and go on the Pill. Then I won't have to keep on using these things, I hate them."

She looked up at him, uncomprehending. When he had explained she said, "You'll have to come with me, then. I won't know what to do."

"Haven't you never been to the doctor's?"

He would be hurt if she said, "Haven't you *ever* been," so she didn't say it. "Eve took me a couple of times. It's lucky I'm healthy. She said I had my injections when I was a baby."

"Yeah, okay, but injections won't stop you getting yourself pregnant."

"*You* getting me pregnant," she said.

He laughed. He liked her being a bit sharp with him. Hugging her tight, he said, "D'you mind talking about it or is this the wrong time? I mean, you know, what happened after your mum shot the guy with the beard."

"Why would I mind?"

She couldn't see why she would. Eve said people liked talking about themselves better than anything and now, savoring the pleasure of it for the first time, she understood this was right. Thinking about it, going over it all, picking the bits to

49

tell him and the bits not to, she enjoyed very much. It was her life and she was beginning to see what an extraordinary one it had so far been.

"I started crying, I couldn't help it. I lay on the bed sobbing and screaming."

"I'm not surprised."

"No, well, Eve came up and hugged me. She got me a drink of water and told me not to cry, not to worry, everything was going to be all right. The man had gone away, she'd blown him away."

"Christ."

"She didn't mean me to think she'd killed him. She didn't know I'd been watching. I didn't tell her. I was only four but somehow I knew not to tell her. All she knew was that I'd seen the man come and heard the shot. She got into bed with me and I liked that. I was always wanting to sleep in the same bed with her but she'd never let me. She was so nice and warm and *young.* D'you know how old she is now?"

"About thirty-five?"

"She's thirty-eight. But that's young, isn't it? I mean, it's not young to us but people would call it young, wouldn't they?"

"I reckon," said Sean, who was twenty-one. "How did she come to have a funny name like Eve?"

"It's Eva, really. It's German. Her father was German. I didn't know what her name was till I heard Mr. Tobias call her Eve. She was just Mother. And then when Bruno was always calling her Eve I started doing it too and she didn't mind."

"Who's Bruno?"

"Just a man. He doesn't come into it for years and years. I'll tell you about him when we get there. We'd got this other man lying dead on our grass, or Eve had, it wasn't really much to do with me. The thing was no one ever came near us then, no one at all but the milkman and the oilman and the man who read the electric meter at the cottage and at Shrove. And they didn't go in the back garden or ask any questions.

"The milkman was strange. I noticed more when I was older. I never knew any children so I don't know if he talked like a child but Eve said he had a mental age of eight. He used to say things about the weather and the trains and that was all he ever said. 'Here comes the train,' he'd say and, 'We're in for a cloudburst.' He never noticed things. That man's dead body could have been lying on our doorstep and he'd have just stepped over it."

"What about it, then?" said Sean. "The dead body."

She didn't know exactly. Real events got mixed up with dreams at this point. She'd had awful dreams that night, had woken screaming and found Eve gone, back to her own bed. But she had come and comforted her and stayed, as far as Liza knew, for the rest of the night.

But she couldn't have, Liza realized that later, for in the morning when she looked out of the window, the man was gone. What does death mean to a child of four? It hadn't really registered with her the night before, that the man wouldn't ever get up again, wouldn't ever speak again or laugh or walk about. She had just been terribly frightened. When he was gone she thought he had gone of his own volition. He had mended and got well and walked away.

It was years afterward when she was much older, piecing memories together and comparing them with similar contemporary events, that she understood he was dead and Eve had killed him with Mr. Tobias's shotgun. Not only had Eve killed him but had taken his body away.

Eve was a small woman with a tiny waist and slender elegant legs. She had small hands with long tapering fingers. Her face was wide at the cheekbones and narrow at the chin, her forehead high, her upper lip short, and her mouth full and lovely. Slightly tilted, her pretty nose was a little too small for her face. She had large hazel-green eyes and black eyebrows like Chinese brush-strokes, not unlike Sean's, and her thick, shiny dark hair reached to the middle of her back. But she was very small, no more than five feet or five feet one at best. Liza didn't know her weight, they had no scales, but when she was sixteen Eve estimated seven and a half stone for herself and eight stone and a bit for Liza and that was probably right. Yet this tiny woman had somehow moved a man one and a half times her weight and nearly six feet tall.

And put him where? Somewhere in the wood, Liza decided when she thought about it around that sixteenth birthday. She put the body in the wheelbarrow and took it through the gap in the fence and buried it in the wood. During the night while Liza slept and before she woke up screaming. Or after she had held her and soothed her and she had slept again, Mother had gone down and worked silently in the dark.

The first thing she saw from the window that morning—even before she saw the man was gone—was Matt opening the door of the little castle and letting the dogs out. He wasn't due till mid-morning, Mother said, running into the room. She sounded cross and upset. Liza went to the other window. The dogs had made straight for the place where the man had lain and ran about sniffing the grass in a frenzied way and pushing their noses into the earth.

"There's something fascinating them," Matt said when Liza and Mother went outside. "They been burying bones?"

"Do you know what time it is?" Mother said. "It's six-thirty in the morning."

"So it is. Dear, oh, dear. I'd some business down this way yesterday, so I stopped the night and come over here first thing. Not got you girls out of bed, I hope."

Mother ignored this. "Has Mr. Tobias come back from France?"

"Coming back tonight. He wants his dogs there when he gets home. They're all the company he's got, I reckon. It wouldn't suit me, I like a bit of action myself, but it takes all sorts to make a world."

"It certainly does," said Mother, not very pleasantly.

"You'd think he'd get himself a girl—well, he does, but nothing permanent." Matt spoke as if Mother didn't know it all already. "Of course he's loaded, got his own place and this here and the London one and there's girls falling over themselves to get him, but to be perfectly honest with you he's just not interested." He winked incomprehensibly at Liza. "Not in settling down, I mean."

In spite of what had happened, Liza wasn't afraid to put her arms around each dog's neck and place a tender kiss on each glossy black skull. She cried a bit when they had gone. She asked Mother if they could have a dog of their own.

"No, absolutely not. Don't ask me."

"Why couldn't we, Mother, why couldn't we? I do want a dog, I love Heidi and Rudi, I do want one of my own."

"Then you must want." Mother smiled when she said it, she wasn't angry, and she called Liza Lizzie, which she sometimes did when she was pleased with her or not too disappointed in her. "Listen, Lizzie, suppose Mr. Tobias came to live at Shrove? He might, it's his house—one of his houses. Then Heidi and Rudi would come with him and what would happen to our dog? They don't like other dogs, they'd attack it. They'd hurt it."

Like they hurt the man, Liza felt like saying but she didn't say it. Instead, she said, "Is he going to come? I'd like him to come because then we'd have *his* dogs and we wouldn't have to have our own. Is he going to come?"

Mother said nothing for a moment. Then she put her arm around Liza and pulled her close against her skirts and said, "I hope so, Lizzie, I hope he will," but she wasn't smiling and she gave a heavy sigh.

Next day was Mother's day for going shopping. She went once a fortnight to get the things the milkman wouldn't bring. He brought butter and eggs and porridge oats and orange juice and bread and yogurt as well as milk, but he never brought meat or fish. Until they grew their own, Mother had to buy vegetables. She had to buy fruit and cheese. The bus that went to the shops—to town, that is—ran four times a day and Mother had to walk down the lane and go over the river bridge and a hundred yards along the road to the bus stop. When Mother went to town she never took Liza with her. Liza was locked up in her bedroom.

She was used to it and she accepted, but not this time. At first she gave in, sat on the bed with the rag book and the pencils, sucked at her orange juice bottle. Mother had given her an apple as well for a treat, a Golden Delicious because there were no English ones in July. She knelt on the bed and watched Mother go along the lane toward the main road. Then she shifted her gaze from the distance to the foreground and saw where the man had been and the dogs and the explosion had happened. She began to scream.

Probably she couldn't have screamed for the whole hour and a half Mother was away. Halfway through she may have fallen asleep. But she was screaming when Mother came back. Mother said, "I won't leave you again," and she didn't for a long while but of course she did again one day.

It might have been that evening or an evening days or weeks later, at any rate it was after the dogs had gone, that Liza was playing her roving-between-the-bedrooms game after bedtime. She tried on Mother's straw hats, the golden one with the white band and the brown one with the cream scarf tied around it, and she stroked Mother's suede shoes, that had things inexplicably called trees thrust into them. When she was tired of that she looked inside the jewel case.

Mother was wearing one set of earrings and the mother-of-pearl brooch, so of course those things weren't in there. Liza hung the jade beads around her own neck, put the comb with the shiny bits on it into her hair, and admired the result in the mirror. She picked up the wooden brooch and found lying underneath it a gold ring.

Whose could it be? She had never seen it before, she had never seen any ring on Mother's hand. Examining it with great interest, she saw that there was some writing on the inside of the ring, but she was only four then and she couldn't read very well. Nor did she at that time connect the ring with the man with the beard.

⌒

"It was his ring?" said Sean.

"It must have been. I looked at it again later, when I could read. The writing said: TMH AND EHH, MARCH 3, 1974. I didn't know what it meant then, but now I think it was his wedding ring. Victoria had a wedding ring. Do men have them?"

"I reckon there's some as do."

"Those were his initials and his wife's and that was the date they got married, don't you think?"

"She must have took it off him, off his hand," said Sean, making a face.

"I don't know why she did unless she thought she might sell it one day. Or maybe she thought if she buried it with him someone might dig it up."

"Why did she do it?"

"Do what? Shoot that man?"

"Why didn't she get an ambulance, have him taken to the hospital? You said he could sit up, he'd have got all right. It wasn't her fault, no one'd have put the blame on her, not if she said he'd been going to rape her."

"I never knew quite why," Liza said, "but it might have been something like this. Later on someone told me a story about a child being attacked by dogs and I put two and two together. It was Bruno, as a matter of fact, he told me. You see, the man would have told them at the hospital and they'd have told the police. About the dogs, I mean. And the dogs would have been killed."

"Destroyed."

"Yes, I expect that's the word. The dogs would have been destroyed like the ones in Bruno's story. Mr. Tobias loved his dogs and he'd have blamed Eve and given her the sack and turned us out of the gatehouse. Or that's what she thought. Maybe he would and maybe he wouldn't, but she thought he would and that was the important thing. She couldn't leave Shrove, you see, she couldn't, that was the most important thing in the world to her, Shrove, more important even than me. Well, Mr. Tobias was important to her too but only in a special sort of way."

Sean was looking bewildered. "You've lost me."

"Never mind. That's really all there was to it. If the dogs had killed the man she wouldn't have had to kill him. I expect that's the way she thought. But they hadn't killed him, so she had to, or else he'd have told the police. She shut the dogs up and went into the house and got the gun and shot him."

"Just for that? Just so Tobias wouldn't get mad at her?"

Liza looked at him doubtfully. "I don't know. Now you put it like that, I really don't know. Perhaps there was more to it. Perhaps she had some other reason, something to make her hate him, but we're never going to know that, are we?"

She watched Sean as he got up and washed at the sink. He put his jeans back on again and found himself a clean T-shirt. It occurred to her that she hadn't any clothes except the ones lying in a heap on the floor. She'd have to wear his, or those of his that would fit her, and when she'd made some money picking apples . . . The hundred pounds, she had forgotten the hundred pounds.

"I want to drive into town, wherever that is," she said, "and go and eat in a real restaurant. Can we?"

" 'Course we can. Why not? We can go and have a Chinese."

Liza washed her knickers and her socks at the sink. She had to put her jeans on over nothing but that didn't much matter. Her jeans were a cause of great pride, not least because it had been such a struggle getting Eve to let her have them. She'd managed to get two pairs, these and a pair she'd left behind. Eve hated trousers and had never worn jeans in all her life. Liza borrowed a long-sleeved check shirt with a collar from Sean and thought a little about Eve, wondering where she was now and what was happening to her.

Sean had been thinking the same thing. "We ought to get a paper tomorrow. You haven't never seen a paper, I suppose? A newspaper, I mean."

"Oh, yes, I have." She was a bit huffy. Once, in a magazine rack at Shrove, she had found a newspaper called *The Times* and the date on it was the year before she was born. Eve had taken it away before she could read much of it. "What we ought to get is television."

"Now there's something you've never seen, telly, I bet."

She answered him in quite a lofty way. "I used to watch it at Shrove every single day. Eve never knew, she'd have stopped it but I didn't tell her. It was a secret thing I did."

"Like me," said Sean.

"Not really like you. You're much better. But I didn't know you then. I watched it for *years* till the set broke and Jonathan wouldn't have it mended." The expression on his face made her laugh. "Could we have one in here? Would your generator work it?"

"Hopefully," he said. " 'Course it would."

"Then I'm going to buy one." A thought struck her. "Only, I don't know—is a hundred pounds a lot of money, Sean?"

He said rather bitterly, "It's a lot for us, love," and then, "Hopefully it'd buy a little portable telly but I don't know about color."

Her eyes grew wide. "Does it come in color? Does it really?"

When they went outside to the car they saw that the other van, the camper, wasn't unoccupied as they had at first thought. A light was on inside it and the blind was raised in the window nearest to the roadway. They had to pass it to get out. Inside, a fiercer, bluer glow than the overhead lamp indicated the presence of a television screen, and as they passed within a few feet Liza saw the little rectangle filled with dazzling color, emerald-green grass, yellow-spotted leaves, and an orange-and-black tiger prowling.

"What a lot I've got to catch up with," she said.

Life at the gatehouse had been of the simplest. Much of it would seem dull to Sean, incredible. There was a good deal she wouldn't tell him but keep locked in her memory. For instance, how, because Eve wouldn't leave her alone in the cottage anymore even with the doors locked, couldn't bring herself to do that when she screamed so piteously, she had been obliged to take Liza with her.

And that was how she came to enter Shrove House for the first time. The palace, the house of pictures and secrets, dolls and keys, books and shadows. Sean would never see it quite like that, no one would but herself and Eve. Most of all Eve.

f i v e

THEY walked up the drive between the trees, the horn-beams that were nearly round in shape and the larches that were pointed, the silver birches whose leaves trembled in the breeze and the swamp cypresses that came from Louisiana but grew happily here because it was damp by the river. There were giant cedars and even taller Douglas firs and Wellingtonias taller than that, black trees you saw as dark green only when you were close up underneath them. The trees parted and she saw the house for the first time and to her then it was no more than a big house with an enormous lot of windows.

A man was mowing the grass, sitting up in a high chair on

wheels. She had seen him once or twice before and was often to see him again. His name was Mr. Frost, he wasn't a young man, but had wrinkles and white hair, and he came on his bicycle from the village on the other side of the river. White hair was only another kind of fair hair and his confirmed Liza's belief. He raised one hand to Mother and Mother nodded but they didn't speak.

Steps went up one side to the front door of Shrove and then there was a kind of platform before the stairs ran down the other side. The stairs had railings like theirs at the gatehouse but the rails here were made of stone with a broad stone shelf running along the tops of them. On the shelf were stone vases from which ivy hung and between the vases stone people stood looking toward the trees.

Liza and Mother went up the flight on the left and Liza held on to the stone railings. Everything was very large and this made her feel smaller than usual. She looked up, as Mother told her, to see the coat of arms, the sword, the shield, the lions. The house towered, its windows shiny sheets, its roof lost in the sky. Mother unlocked the front door and they went in.

"You will not rush about, Liza," Mother said, "and you will not climb on the furniture. Do you understand? Let me see your hands."

Liza held them out. They were very clean because Mother had made her wash them before they came out and she had held Mother's hand all the way.

"All right. You can't get them dirty in here. Now, remember, *walk*, don't run."

The carpets were soft and thick underfoot and the ceilings were very high. None of the ceilings was white but done in gold and black squares or painted like a blue sky with white clouds and people with wings flying across it, trailing scarves and ribbons and bunches of flowers. The lamps were like raindrops when it is raining very hard and some of the walls had things like thin carpets hanging on them. A huge painting covered one entire wall. Mother called it *The Birthday of Achilles* and it showed a lot of men in helmets and women in white robes all rushing to pick up a golden apple while a woman in green with flowers stood by holding a fat naked baby.

Mother took her through the drawing room and showed her the fireplace with the lady's face on it, the screen painted with flowers, and the tables that were of shiny wood with shiny metal bits on it and some with mother-of-pearl like mother's brooch. The tall glass doors were framed in mahogany, Mother said, and they were more than two hundred years old but as good as new. Liza and Mother went through the doorway out onto the terrace at the back, and when Liza ran down the steps and stood on the lawn and looked up at Mother, she was frightened for a moment because the back of the house was the same as the front, the same coat of arms, sword, shield, and lion, the same railing around the roof and up the stairs, the same windows and the same statues standing in the alcoves.

Mother called out to her that it was all right, it was supposed to be that way, but that if she looked closely she would see it wasn't quite the same. The statues were women, not men, there was no front door, and instead of ivy, small dark pointed trees grew in the stone urns on the terrace.

So Liza ran up again and she and Mother made their way to the kitchen. Mother unhooked an apron from behind a cupboard door, a big ugly brown apron, and wrapped it around herself, covering up her white cotton blouse and and long, full green-and-blue skirt. She took a clean yellow duster from a pile and tied her head up so that you couldn't see her hair, she trundled out a vacuum cleaner and found a large, deep tin of mauve polish that smelled of lavender.

For the next three hours they remained in Shrove House while Mother cleaned the carpets with the vacuum cleaner, dusted the surfaces and the ornaments, and polished the tables. She couldn't get it all done today, she said, and she explained to Liza how she did a bit one day and another bit two days later and so on, but she hadn't been in there for two weeks because, as she put it, of one thing and another. She had been afraid of Liza being a nuisance or of breaking something, but Liza had been as good as gold.

Remembering not to run, she had walked through all the rooms, looking at everything, at a table with a glass top and little oval pictures in frames inside, at a small green statue of a man on a horse, at a green jar with black birds and pink flowers on it that was taller than she was. One room was full of books, they were all over the walls where other rooms had paint or paneling. Another, instead of books, had those things hanging up like the one Mother had that made the explosion. She didn't stay in there for long.

A cabinet in one room was full of dolls in different dresses and she would have loved to touch, to get them out, she *longed* to, but she did what Mother told her, or if she didn't she made sure Mother couldn't find out. But mostly she did as she was told because as well as loving Mother so much, she was afraid of her.

The door to a room opening out of that one was shut. Liza tried the handle and it turned, but the door wouldn't open. It was locked, as her bedroom door used to be locked when Mother went out, and the key gone. Of course she very much wanted to get into that room, as much as anything because the door was locked. She rattled the handle, which did no good.

There were three staircases. By this time she had learned to count up to three—well, to six, in fact. She went up the biggest staircase and down the smallest, having been in every bedroom, and climbed onto one of the window seats—Mother wouldn't find out, the vacuum cleaner could be heard howling downstairs—and looked across the flat green valley floor to watch a train go by.

If not, then, conscious of beauty, she was aware of light, of how radiantly light the house was everywhere inside. There wasn't a dark corner or a dim passage. Even when the sun wasn't shining, as it wasn't that day, a clear pearly light lit every room and the things inside the rooms gleamed, the glass and the porcelain, the silver and brass and the gilt on the moldings and cornices. The biggest staircase had flowers and fruit carved on the wood on each side of it and the carving gleamed with a deep rich glow, but all she could think of then was how much she would like to slide down the polished banister.

They left at four o'clock, in time to get home for Liza's reading lesson.

"Doesn't Mr. Tobias ever live there?" she asked, taking Mother's hand.

"He never has. His mother did for a while and his grandfather lived there all the time, it was his only home." She gave Liza a thoughtful glance, as if she was pondering whether the time had come to tell her. "My mother, who was your grandmother, was his housekeeper. And then his nurse. We lived in the gatehouse ourselves, my mother, my father, and I." Mother squeezed Liza's hand. "You're too young for this, Lizzie. Look up in the ash tree, see the green woodpecker? On the trunk, picking insects out with his beak?"

So if the day the man with the beard came was called the Day of the Kingfisher, this was the Day of the Woodpecker, the day of the first visit to Shrove.

After that Liza always went with Mother to Shrove and now, when Mother went to town on the bus, instead of locking Liza in her bedroom in the cottage, she put her in one of the Shrove bedrooms. Mostly it was the one called the Venetian Room because the four-poster bed had its posts made out of the poles used by gondoliers in Venice, Mother said. Liza could read quite well by the time she was five and had a real book in the room with her. She wasn't in the least frightened of being shut up in the Venetian Room at Shrove, she wouldn't have been frightened of being in her own room anymore, but she did ask Mother why Shrove and not at home.

"Because Shrove has central heating and we don't. I can be sure you're warm enough. They have to keep the heating on all winter because of the damp, even though no one lives there. If it was allowed to get damp the furniture might be spoiled."

"Why is the little room next to the morning room always locked up?"

"Is it?" said Mother. "I seem to have mislaid the key."

Shrove was to become her library and her picture gallery. More than that, for the paintings were a guide to her and a catalog of people's faces. To them she ran when she needed to identify a new person or when confirmation was required. They were her standard of comparison and her secondhand portrait of the outside world. This was how other people looked, this what they wore, these the chairs they sat on, the other countries they lived in, the things their eyes saw.

⌒

In the cold depths of winter, a very cold one when the river froze over and the water meadows disappeared under snow for a whole month, a black car with chains on its tires slid slowly down the lane and parked in the deep snow outside the gatehouse. There were two men inside. One stayed in the car and the other one came to the front door and rang the bell. He was a fat man with no hair at all but for a fairish fringe surrounding the great shiny pale egg that was his head.

By chance, Liza and Mother had been sitting side by side at Mother's bedroom window, watching the birds feeding from the nut feeders they had hung on the branches of the balsam tree. They saw the car come and the man come to the door.

"If he talks to you you are not to say anything but 'I don't know,' " said Mother, "and you can cry a bit if you like. You might like that, it might amuse you."

Liza never found out who the man was. Of course she guessed later on. He said he was looking for a missing person, a man called Hugh something. She had forgotten his other name but Hugh she remembered.

Hugh came from Swansea, was around these parts last July on a walking holiday, but left the B and B he was stopping at without paying for his two nights. The fat man talked a lot more about Hugh and why they were looking for him and what was making them look six months later, but Liza didn't understand any of it. He described Hugh, which she did understand, she remembered his fair beard, she remembered tufts of it in Rudi's mouth.

"We are very quiet down here, Inspector," Mother said. "We see hardly anyone."

"A lonely life."

"It depends what suits you."

"And you never saw this man?" He showed Mother something in the palm of his hand and Mother looked at it, shaking her head. "You didn't see him in the lane or walking the footpath?"

"I'm afraid not."

Mother lifted her face and looked deep into the fat man's

eyes when she said this. Although it meant nothing at the time, when she was older, thinking back and comparing her own personal experience, Liza understood how Mother's look must have affected him. Her full red lips were slightly parted, her eyes large and lustrous, her skin creamy and her expression oh so winsome and trusting. About her shoulders her glorious hair, a rich, dark shining brown, hung like a silk cape. She had one small white finger pressed against her lower lip.

"It was just a possibility," the fat man said, unable to take his eyes off her, but having to, having to drag his eyes away and speak to Liza. "I don't suppose this young lady saw him."

She was shown the photograph. Apart from prints on the fronts of Mother's books, it was the first she had ever seen, but she didn't say so. She looked at the face which had frightened her and which Heidi and Rudi had ruined with their teeth, looked at it and said, "I don't know."

This made him eager. "So you might have?"

"I don't know."

"Have another look, my love, look closely and try to remember."

Liza was growing frightened. She was letting Mother down, she was obeying Mother but letting her down just the same. The man's face was horrible, the bearded man called Hugh, cruel and sneering, and who knew what he would have done if Mother hadn't . . .

She didn't have to pretend to cry. "I don't know, I don't know, I don't know," she screamed and burst into tears.

The fat man went away, apologizing to Mother, shaking hands with her and holding her hand a long time, and when he had gone Mother roared with laughter. She said Liza had been excellent, quite excellent, and she hugged her, laughing into her hair. For all that she loved Liza and cared for her, she hadn't understood that she had been really frightened, really shy of people, really bewildered.

It took the driver a long time to get the car started and an even longer time to pull it out of the snow without its wheels spinning. Liza calmed down and began to enjoy herself. She and Mother watched the driver's struggles from the bedroom window with great interest.

The snow went away and the spring came. Most of the trees that were coniferous looked just the same, always the same greenish black or light smoky blue, but the larches and the swamp cypresses grew new leaves like clumps of fur of an exquisite pale and delicate green. Mother explained that larches too were deciduous conifers and the only ones native to the British Isles.

Primroses with sunny round faces appeared under the hedges and clusters of velvety purple violets close by the boles of trees. Wood anemones, that were also called windflowers and had petals like tissue paper, grew in the clearings of the wood. Mother told Liza to be careful never to pronounce them an-enomies, as so many people did who ought to know better. Liza hardly talked to anyone but Mother, so was unlikely to hear the wrong pronunciation.

Except the postman, though they didn't discuss botany. And the milkman, who noticed nothing but the trains and the signs of changes in the weather, and the oilman who came to fill Shrove's heating tank in March, and Mr. Frost, the gardener who mowed the grass and trimmed the hedges and sometimes pulled out the weeds.

Mr. Frost went on never speaking. They saw him ride past the gatehouse on his bicycle and if he saw them he waved. He waved from his mowing machine if he happened to be there when they walked up the drive to Shrove. The oilman only came twice a year, in September and again in March. Liza had never talked to him, though Mother did for about five minutes, or listened rather, and listened impatiently, while he told her about his flat in Spain and how he had found a cut-rate flight to Malaga that was so reasonable you wouldn't believe. Liza didn't know what that meant, so Mother explained how he went across the sea in one of those things that flew overhead sometimes and made a buzzing noise about it, unlike birds.

The milkman said, "It feels like spring," which was silly because it *was* spring, and "Here comes the train," that he needn't have bothered to say because anyone could see and hear it.

They got very few letters. Liza never got any. Letters came for Mother sometimes, from someone called her aunt, though she never explained what an aunt was, from her friend Heather in London, and one regularly once a month from Mr. Tobias. This one had a piece of pink paper in it, which Mother said was a check. When next she went to the shops she took the pink paper with her and took it to a bank and they turned it into money. Like a good fairy waving a wand, suggested Liza, who was much into fairy tales at that time, but Mother said, no, not like that, and explained that this was money which she had earned for cleaning Mr. Tobias's house and looking after it and seeing it came to no harm.

In April the dogs came again to stay. Matt brought them and told Mother that Mr. Tobias had gone to somewhere called the Caribbean this time, not France. Liza hugged Heidi and Rudi, who knew her at once and were overjoyed to see her. Had they forgotten the man with the beard called Hugh? Had they forgotten how they attacked him? Liza wondered if they would attack Matt if she called out, "Kill!"

"Why doesn't Mr. Tobias ever come himself?" Liza asked Mother while they were out in the meadows with the dogs.

"I don't know, Lizzie," Mother said and she sighed.

"Doesn't he like it here?"

"He seems to like it better in the Dordogne and Moçambique and Montagu Square and the horrible old Lake District," said Mother incomprehensibly. "But perhaps he will come one day. Of course he'll come one day, you'll see."

Instead of coming himself, he sent a postcard. It had a picture on it of silver sand and palm trees and a blue, blue sea. On the back Mr. Tobias had written: *This is a wonderful place. It's good to get away from cold, gray England in the cruelest month, though I hardly suppose you would agree. Say hallo to Heidi and Rudi for me and to your daughter, of course. Ever, J.T.*

Liza couldn't read joined-up writing, even the beautiful curvy large kind like Mr. Tobias's, so Mother read it to her. Mother made a face and said she didn't like him putting his dogs before her daughter but Liza didn't mind.

"I know what T's for," she said, "but what's his name that starts with J?"

"Jonathan," said Mother.

By the time the summer came, Liza could read Beatrix Potter and the Andrew Lang fairy books if the print was large enough. She could write her name and address and simple sentences, printing of course, and she could tell the time and count to twenty and add up easy sums. Mother took her into the library at Shrove and said that when she was older she would be welcome to read all the books in there she wanted. Mr. Tobias had told *her* to help herself to any books she fancied reading, he knew she loved reading, and of course that invitation extended to her daughter.

"Jonathan," said Liza.

"Yes, Jonathan, but you must call him Mr. Tobias."

There were history books and geography books and books about languages and philosophy and religion. Liza noted the words without understanding their meaning. Mother said there were also a great many books that were stories, which meant made-up things, not things that had really happened, they were novels. Most of them had been written a long time ago, more than a hundred years ago, which wasn't surprising since they had belonged to Mr. Tobias's grandfather's father, who had bought the house when he got rich in 1862. The books were rather old-fashioned now, Mother said, but perhaps that was no bad thing, and she looked at Liza with her head to one side.

It grew hot that summer and one day Liza went with Mother to a part of the river that was very deep, a pool below the rapids that came rushing over the stones, and Mother began teaching her to swim. Mother was a good strong swimmer and Liza felt safe with her, even where the water was so deep that even Mother's feet couldn't touch the bottom. The second or third time they had been down there they were coming back up the lane—Mother said afterward she wished they'd come through the Shrove grounds as they usually did—when they had to flatten themselves against the hedge to let a car go by. It didn't go by, it stopped, and a lady put her head out of the window.

That was when Liza had to revise her ideas on her hair-color–sex-linkage theory, for the lady's hair was blond. It was not otherwise much like hair at all but seemed to be carved out of some pale yellow translucent substance, a kind of lemon jelly perhaps, and then varnished. The lady had a face like the monkey in the illustrations to Liza's *Jungle Book* and hands with ropes under the skin on the backs of them and a brown paper dress Mother said afterward was called linen and made from a plant with blue flowers that grew in the fields like grass.

The lady said, "Oh, my dear, I haven't seen you for an age. Don't you ever come down to the village anymore? I must say I've expected to see you in church. Your mother was such a regular at St. Philip's."

"I am not my mother," said Mother, very coldly.

"No, of *course* not. And this is your little girl?"

"This is Eliza, yes."

"She will be going to school soon, I suppose. I don't know how you're going to get her there with no car, but I suppose the school bus will come. At least it will come to where the lane joins the main road."

Mother said in the voice that frightened Liza when it was used to her, which was seldom, "Eliza will be educated privately," and she walked away without waiting for the lady to put her head in and her window up.

That was the first time Liza heard school mentioned. She didn't know what it was. At that time no school or schoolchildren figured in the books she read. But she didn't ask Mother, only what the name of the lady was and Mother said Mrs. Hayden, Diana Hayden, whom Liza would probably never have to see again.

They had the dogs back for a fortnight in October and again six months later. When the time came for Matt to come with the van to collect them he didn't turn up. Something must have gone wrong, Mother said. There was no means of letting her know, as they had no phone and it was impossible to send telegrams anymore.

But when he didn't come on the following day she got it into her head this was because Mr. Tobias would come himself. He had told the man to leave it to him this time, he would collect the dogs when he got back. But he wasn't due back till today. After he had had a good night's sleep and got over his jet lag he would get in his car, or more likely the estate car, and drive down here from Ullswater, where he lived but had no one willing to look after his dogs. Mother was sure he would come. She and Liza went over to Shrove early in the morning and Mother gave it a special clean.

At home she had a bath in their kitchen bath and washed her hair. That was the next day, in the morning. She put on one of her long bright-colored skirts and her tight black top, the green beads around her neck and the gold hoops in her ears. It took her half an hour to plait her hair in the special way she had and pin it to the back of her head. And she did all this because Mr. Tobias was coming.

He didn't come. Matt did. He drove up in the afternoon and pushed past Mother into the gatehouse before she could stop him.

"I've been down with one of them viruses that's going about," he said, "or I'd have been here before."

"Where is Mr. Tobias?"

"He rung up from Mozam-whatsit, said he'd be home today. Didn't he never let you know? Dear, oh, dear. Never mind, there's no harm done, is there?"

No harm done! Mother went up to her bedroom after Matt had gone and lay on her bed and cried. Liza heard her crying and went up and got into bed with her and hugged her and said to stop, not to cry, it was going to be all right.

And so it was. In the month of June, when all the wild roses were out and flowers were on the elder trees and the nightingales sang in the wood, Mr. Tobias came to Shrove in his dark green shiny Range Rover and, with the dogs at his heels, ran up the cottage garden path and banged on their door, calling, "Eve, Eve, where are you?"

That was how Liza learned what Mother's first name was.

She called the day gone by the Day of the Nightingale because the nightingales had sung from morning till night and beyond. People who didn't know, Mother said, believed nightingales only sang by night but that was false, for they sang all around the clock.

M Y real name's Eliza. I've sometimes thought she called me after Eliza Doolittle in *Pygmalion*."

"Come again?" said Sean.

"Because ⎯ intended to do the same thing with me as ⎯ Galatea and as Professor Higgins did with ⎯ ade her to be the way he wanted her, or ⎯ l and he tried to turn her into that."

⎯ he concentrated. "Sounds like *My Fair*

⎯ an."

⎯ anyway, when I asked her. She jus ⎯ ished her strawberry milkshake a wiped her mouth. "Sean, can I have a burger? D'you know I've never had one."

" 'Course you can. We'll both have a burger and chips."

"Isn't it funny? I was so afraid to leave the gatehouse and *her*, I thought I'd die of fright."

"You're always dying of something, you are."

"Only I never do really, do I? I was so frightened and now I'm out in the world—that's how I see it, out in the world—I really like it. Or perhaps it's just you I like. I wouldn't have liked Heather."

"You might've. You don't know her."

"Oh, yes, I do. I *did.* She came to stay. But not then, not till after Mr. Tobias had been."

They were in the town, Liza wary of the crowded pavements but liking the shops and the big green with a few old people sitting on wooden seats and children feeding ducks on a pond. Sean wouldn't take her money, he had a bit saved up, and when they had had lunch he bought two bottles of wine and sixty cigarettes, something else she had never tried before. Sean lit a cigarette as soon as he was in the car.

"Eve said they kill you."

"She's not the only one says that. But I reckon it's just the same old thing, them trying to stop you having a bit of pleasure. I mean, look at it this way, my grandad, he's eighty-seven, he's smoked forty a day since he went out to work at fourteen and there's not a thing wrong with him, spry as a cricket he is."

"What's a cricket, Sean?"

"There's the game cricket, you know, test matches and whatever, there's that, but it's not that, is it? I reckon I don't know what it is, to tell you the honest truth."

"You shouldn't use words if you don't know what they m

Sean laughed. "Sorry, teacher."

M<small>Y</small> real name's Eliza. I've sometimes thought she called me after Eliza Doolittle in *Pygmalion.*"

"Come again?" said Sean.

"Because she intended to do the same thing with me as Pygmalion did with Galatea and as Professor Higgins did with Eliza Doolittle, he remade her to be the way he wanted her, or let's say he had an ideal and he tried to turn her into that."

Sean frowned while he concentrated. "Sounds like *My Fair Lady* to me."

"She said she didn't, anyway, when I asked her. She just liked the name." Liza finished her strawberry milkshake and wiped her mouth. "Sean, can I have a burger? D'you know I've never had one."

" 'Course you can. We'll both have a burger and chips."

"Isn't it funny? I was so afraid to leave the gatehouse and *her*, I thought I'd die of fright."

"You're always dying of something, you are."

"Only I never do really, do I? I was so frightened and now I'm out in the world—that's how I see it, out in the world—I really like it. Or perhaps it's just you I like. I wouldn't have liked Heather."

"You might've. You don't know her."

"Oh, yes, I do. I *did*. She came to stay. But not then, not till after Mr. Tobias had been."

They were in the town, Liza wary of the crowded pavements but liking the shops and the big green with a few old people sitting on wooden seats and children feeding ducks on a pond. Sean wouldn't take her money, he had a bit saved up, and when they had had lunch he bought two bottles of wine and sixty cigarettes, something else she had never tried before. Sean lit a cigarette as soon as he was in the car.

"Eve said they kill you."

"She's not the only one says that. But I reckon it's just the same old thing, them trying to stop you having a bit of pleasure. I mean, look at it this way, my grandad, he's eighty-seven, he's smoked forty a day since he went out to work at fourteen and there's not a thing wrong with him, spry as a cricket he is."

"What's a cricket, Sean?"

"There's the game cricket, you know, test matches and whatever, there's that, but it's not that, is it? I reckon I don't know what it is, to tell you the honest truth."

"You shouldn't use words if you don't know what they mean."

Sean laughed. "Sorry, teacher."

He wanted her to try a cigarette, so she did. It made her cough and then it made her feel sick, but Sean said it was always like that the first time and you had to persist.

They called in at the farm shop on the way back to the caravan and saw Mr. Vanner in the office. He was short of pickers for the Emile pears and took them both on to start next day. On the way out Liza helped herself to a James Grieve from the basket with the notice that said: *Help yourself and enjoy a great taste.*

She'd taken a big bite out of it when Mrs. Vanner behind the counter said in a nasty tone, "Those apples are intended for our paying customers, if you don't mind."

No one had ever spoken to her in that rude way before. Sean squeezed her arm to stop her answering back, though she wouldn't have done that, she was too shocked.

"What a horrible woman," she said the moment the door closed behind them.

"Mean old bitch," said Sean.

Another camper had arrived at the caravan park. Whoever owned it had already put up a washing line with washing on it and tied a black terrier up to the steps. Liza glanced at the other camper, the one who was there before they came, and saw the blue glow of the screen under the raised blind.

"D'you know what we forgot, Sean? We forgot to buy the television set."

"I can think of better things to do than watch telly," said Sean, putting his arm on her shoulders and stroking her neck with his fingertips.

"And something to read," she said as if he hadn't spoken. "I'll need books to read. How can I get books?"

"I don't know." He wasn't interested.

"I can't exist without books."

But she went into his arms very willingly when they were inside the caravan and the door was shut. She was soon pulling off her clothes and climbing across the bed to where he waited for her. They hadn't bothered to put the bed back in the wall that morning, knowing they would be sure to need it again soon.

Mother said, "This is Mr. Tobias, Lizzie, that you've heard so much about," and to Mr. Tobias she said, "I'd like you to meet my daughter Eliza, Jonathan."

It was a new experience for Liza to shake hands with someone. Mr. Tobias's hand was warm and dry and his handshake very firm. He got down on his haunches so that their eyes were on a level. His were dark brown and his hair light brown, lighter than his skin, which was very deeply tanned. Of all the men that Liza had ever seen—the milkman, the postman, and the oilman, Mr. Frost, Mr. Tobias's man who brought the dogs, and that other one who had a beard—of all of them, Mr. Tobias had the nicest hands. They were thin and brown with long fingers and square nails.

And he had a lovely voice. Instead of sounding like Matt or the oilman or the man with the beard or the milkman, who all sounded different from each other, his voice was more like Mother's but deeper of course and somehow softer. It was the sort of voice you'd like to read you a story before you went to sleep.

"She's very like you, Eve," he said. "She is you in little. A clone, perhaps?"

"I'm afraid not," Mother said. "But I'm glad she looks like me."

Liza was very surprised to see a bottle produced and two glasses, a bottle with brown liquid in it, and orange juice for her.

Mr. Tobias was very tall and had to bend his head to get under the doorway into their living room. He wasn't wearing jeans like most of the other men she had seen or the bottom part of a suit like Mr. Frost, but trousers in pale fawn stuff like the ribbing on a sweater and a white shirt with an open neck and a brown velvet jacket. Eve told her afterward that it was velvet. It looked, and she imagined felt, like the mole she had seen come out of an earth mountain on the Shrove lawn.

She was very shy of him. While he talked to her in his bedtime-story voice, she could only stare at him with her eyes very wide open. He asked her what she did all day long and if she could read and would she draw something for him. While she was drawing a picture of Shrove with the river behind and the high hills and Heidi and Rudi running about on the grass, he said he expected she would be going to school soon. Mother said briskly that there was time enough for that and changed the subject. She wished he had let her know he was coming, she would have got some food in and given the house a special clean.

"*You* would? You're supposed to get a woman in from the village to do that."

"I know, but they aren't reliable and they'd have to have a car. It's easier to do it myself. I prefer to do it myself, Jonathan."

"I thought it was odd when I went through the accounts with Matt and there was no provision made for a daily."

Mother said again, "I prefer to do it myself." She looked down in rather a meek way, her long eyelashes brushing her cheek. "You pay me so generously that, really, I feel it's my duty."

"My idea when you came here was that you would be a kind of estate manager. You had the cottage and a—well, a salary, to run the place."

"Dear Jonathan, there's nothing to run but Mr. Frost and the oilman," said Mother and they both laughed.

Liza finished her drawing and showed it to Mr. Tobias, who pronounced it very good and said she must sign it. So she wrote Eliza Beck in the bottom right-hand corner and wondered why Mr. Tobias gave her signature such a strange long look before turning to Mother with one eyebrow up and a funny little crooked smile.

The dogs were not to sleep in the little castle this time but over at Shrove with Mr. Tobias. Liza played with them until it was her suppertime, and then she and Mother took them halfway up the Shrove drive and released them. She stood under the tallest Wellingtonia and called to them to run home, to run and find the master. Mr. Tobias came to the front door of Shrove and down the steps and waved to them.

He had something hanging around his neck on a strap. Liza couldn't see very well from that distance, but as they came closer she thought it looked rather like the thing Mother had that made music. He beckoned and put the thing up to his face, holding it in both hands. Mother went on walking toward him, telling her not to be shy, Mr. Tobias was only taking a photograph of them. But Liza *was* shy, she hid behind a tree, so Mother got into the picture by herself.

By this time she had almost grown out of that baby game she used to play after she was put to bed, running from one room and one window to the other, but that night, for some reason, she felt like playing it again. Perhaps the reason was that Mother had come upstairs to check that she was asleep. Liza dived under the covers and lay with her eyes shut, breathing steadily.

She half opened an eye as Mother tiptoed out and saw that she had changed into her best skirt, the one she made herself from a piece of blue and purple and red material she had bought when she went to town. Mother wore the new skirt, which was very full and long, nearly to her ankles, a tight black top, and a shiny black belt around her little waist. Her hair was done in the way Liza loved and which took half an hour to do, drawn back from her face and done in a fat plait that started at the crown of her head and was tucked under at the nape of her neck.

Liza thought she heard the front door close. She jumped out of bed and ran across to Mother's room and the window. Mother was letting herself out by the front gate. It was a warm evening, still daylight, but the sun was low in the faded blue sky. Mother hadn't a coat or a shawl. She was going toward the gateway. Liza ran back into her own room, the turret room, stood on the chair, and watched Mother passing through the open gateway and starting up the drive to Shrove.

Liza had never been left alone before, unless she was locked in and safe. Mother was walking under the trees, through the park and up to the house; she had never gone so far before. Fear sprang within her and, as it does when one is a small child, touched off immediate tears. In a moment she would have screamed and sobbed but in that moment, while her breath was held, Mr. Tobias came strolling out from the back of Shrove House. He stopped and held out both hands and he and Mother looked at each other.

Somehow, Mr. Tobias being there, knowing that all Mother was doing was meeting him, made everything all right. Mother took both his hands in her hands and said something and laughed. He walked around her, looking her up and down, nodded, touched the beautiful shiny plait with one finger. Then he took her hand and hooked it over his arm and they went on toward the house, walking very closely side by side. Liza no longer much minded Mother going because they were together and would only be at Shrove.

She minded a very little bit because she wasn't there with them, she felt left out. But not afraid anymore. She ran back into Mother's room to see if anything was going on at the front, even if it was only rabbits feeding on the grass verges. There were always rabbits in the evening, that wasn't exciting. They couldn't get at Mother's vegetables because most things were covered in nets, the lettuces, the cabbages, the peas, and the carrots, but not the beans and the strawberries because rabbits never ate them.

The sun was setting behind the woods, turning the trees black and the sky almost too dazzling a gold to look at. She watched it dip and sink until all the gold was drained away and the sky turned from yellow to pink to red. Once the sun went the bats came out. Mother had explained how they can hunt for insects in the dark, by their squeaks, which humans can't hear, bouncing off flying objects and echoing back at them.

A moth flew up to the window and Liza identified it as a privet hawk, though its body was yellow and brown instead of pink and brown and its lower wings were yellowish. Perhaps it was just a common yellow underwing. Mother had brought her a moth book from the library at Shrove as well as *Frohawk's Complete British Butterflies*. She ran downstairs and fetched the book. Perhaps she would have an apple too, but there were no apples at this time of the year. Instead she ate some of the strawberries she and Mother had picked before Mr. Tobias came.

She couldn't find the moth, or a picture she could be sure was of the one outside the window, and she must have fallen asleep when she got back into bed, for she remembered nothing else from that night and it was the following evening or the next that she looked out of Mother's room much later, in the dusk, and saw them at the gateway of Shrove, standing close up against the wall of the little castle. Mr. Tobias had his arms around Mother and he was kissing her in a way Liza had never seen anyone kiss anyone before, on the mouth.

The truth was that she had never *seen* anyone kiss anyone ever except Mother kissing her, which wasn't the same thing. Mr. Tobias let Mother go and Mother came into the house. Liza crept very quietly across the landing on her way back to her own room and as she passed the top of the stairs she heard Mother singing down there. Not very loudly but as if she was enjoying singing. And Liza knew the song and that it was something called Mozart, for she had often heard Mother play the record where the lady sang how she would make her lover better with the medicine she kept in her heart.

When the weekend came, so did a lot of visitors to Shrove. They were all friends of Mr. Tobias, Mother said, two men and three ladies, and they came along the lane and past the gatehouse and right in through the gates of Shrove up to the house. Liza said, could they go up there, she and Mother, and see the people, but Mother said, no, she wouldn't be going there again till Monday and Liza certainly would not.

"Why?" said Liza.

"Because I said no," said Mother. "Mr. Tobias invited us but I said no, not this time."

"Why?"

"I think it best, Liza."

On the Saturday evening she saw all the people coming back from a walk. She was at Mother's window and she saw them all very clearly, passing the gatehouse garden. One of the ladies had stopped to admire Mother's big stone tub that was full of geraniums and fuchsias and abutilon in full bloom.

The men were just men, nothing special, though one of them had bare skin instead of hair on top of his head, and the ladies were nice-looking but not one of them as pretty as Mother. Perhaps Mr. Tobias thought so too, for he turned his head as they passed and gave the gatehouse a long look. Liza didn't think he was looking at the flowers. But still, there was something special about the ladies, they looked different from anyone Liza had ever seen before, smoother somehow and cleaner, their hair cut as trimly and evenly as Mr. Frost cut the edge of the lawn where the flower border began. All three wore jeans like the milkman and Hugh, but one had a jacket like Mother's best shoes, the suede ones with the trees in them that Liza liked to stroke, and a silk scarf with a rope and shield pattern, one a wondrous sweater with flowers knitted into the pattern and her face painted like Diana Hayden's and the third a shirt like a man's but long and made of bright green silk.

Half an hour later one of their cars came down the drive from Shrove House—well, from the stable block, really, where cars were kept—with Mr. Tobias's Range Rover ahead of it to show the way, and in the morning Mother told her they had all gone out to dinner in a hotel somewhere. By Monday they had gone away and she and Mother went up to Shrove to change the beds and clear up the mess. Or Mother did. Liza talked to Mr. Tobias and he showed her his holiday pictures. He took her into the library and said she must have any book from it she wanted to read. They took the dogs down to the river and waved to the train and when they got back Mother had finished.

"I'm not at all happy about you doing this, Eve," Mr. Tobias said and he didn't *look* happy.

"Perhaps I will try to get someone," Mother said.

Liza thought she seemed quite weary and no wonder, the house had been an awful mess, Mother had said nothing when they first arrived, but Liza had stared wide-eyed at the sticky glasses, the cups and plates standing about everywhere, the powdery gray stuff mixed up with burned paper tubes in the little glass trays, and the big brown stain on the drawing room carpet.

"I should have cleared up myself," said Mr. Tobias, which, for some reason, made Mother laugh. "Come out with me tonight? We'll go somewhere for dinner."

"I can't do that, Jonathan. I have Eliza, remember?"

"Bring her too."

Mother just laughed again, but in a way that somehow made it clear they weren't going out for dinner and that it was an absurd suggestion.

"Then you can cook my dinner. At the gatehouse. It's a poky little place and I'm going to have it done up for you from top to bottom, but if we haven't a choice, the gatehouse it must be. Needs must when the devil drives. You're a bit of a devil, you know, Eve, and you know how to drive a man, but you shall cook my dinner. If you're not too tired, that is?"

"I'm not too tired," said Mother.

Liza didn't expect to be allowed to stay up with them. It was a nice surprise when Mother said she could, though she must go to bed straight after. Mr. Tobias came at seven with a bottle of something that looked like fizzy lemonade but had its top wired on and a bottle of something the color of Mother's homemade raspberry vinegar. The top came out of the lemonade bottle with a loud pop and a lot of foam. They had a salad and a roast chicken and strawberries, and when Liza had eaten up the last strawberry she had to go to bed. Oddly enough, she went straight to sleep.

Next morning she did what she always did in the mornings, ran into Mother's room for her cuddle. Mother had always been alone in her big bed but she wasn't alone this time. Mr. Tobias was in the bed with her, lying on the side nearest to the window.

Liza stood and stared.

"Go outside a moment, please, Liza," Mother said.

A moment always meant counting to twenty. Liza counted to twenty and went back into the room. Mr. Tobias had got up and done his best to get his broad shoulders and long body inside Mother's brown wool dressing gown. He muttered something, grabbed his clothes from the chair, and went downstairs to the kitchen. Liza got into bed with Mother and hugged her, she hugged her so tight that Mother had to say to let go, she was hurting. The bed smelled different than usual, it didn't smell of clean sheets and Mother and her soap, but a bit like the river in a season of drought, a bit like the dead fishes washed up on the sand, and like water with a lot of salt in it for cooking.

Mr. Tobias came back, washed and dressed, saying it was terrible they hadn't got a bathroom, he would have a bathroom put in as a priority. And why on earth didn't Eve have a phone? Everyone had a phone. He went away after breakfast but came back in the afternoon with a present for Liza. It was a doll. Liza had very few toys and what she had had been Eve's—a rag doll, a celluloid one, a dog on wheels you pulled along with a piece of string, a box of wooden bricks.

The doll that Mr. Tobias had bought her wasn't a baby but a little girl with dark hair like her own that you could wash and legs and arms and face that felt like real skin and a wardrobe of clothes for her to put on when the dress she was wearing had to be washed.

Unable to speak, Liza stared mutely.

"Say thank you to Mr. Tobias, Lizzie," said Mother, but she didn't seem very pleased and she said, "You really shouldn't, Jonathan. She will get all sorts of ideas."

"Why not? Harmless ideas, I'm sure."

"Well, I'm not. I don't wish her to have those ideas. But you are very kind, you are very generous."

"What shall you call her, Liza?" Mr. Tobias said in his softest sweetest voice.

"Jonathan," said Liza.

That made them both laugh.

"Jonathan is a man's name, Lizzie, and she's a girl. Think again."

"I don't know any girls' names. What were the ladies called who stayed with you?"

"Last weekend? They were called Annabel and Victoria and Claire."

"I shall call her Annabel," said Liza.

After that Mr. Tobias slept in Mother's bed most nights. Liza slept with Annabel and brought her into Mother's bed in the morning, knocking on the door first as instructed to give Mr. Tobias a chance to get up. He stayed at Shrove for three weeks, then four, and the dogs with him, but no more people were invited for the weekends.

Mother was very happy. She was quite different and she sang a lot. She washed her hair every day and made herself another new skirt. Every day they were either up at Shrove or Mr. Tobias was with them at the gatehouse, and if anything was wrong it was only that when Mr. Tobias wanted to take them out in the Range Rover, Mother always said no. Liza very much wanted to go to the seaside and the suggestion was made, but Mother said no. All right, said Mr. Tobias, come to London with me for the weekend, come to Montagu Place, but Mother said that would be worse than the seaside.

"You like it here, Jonathan, don't you? It's the most wonderful place in the world, nowhere is more beautiful."

"I like a change sometimes."

"Have a change, then. That's probably the best thing. Have a change and then come back here to us. I can't believe the Ullswater house is more beautiful than this."

"Come and see. We'll all go up for the weekend and you shall judge."

"I don't want to go from here ever and Liza doesn't. I thought"—Mother turned her face away and spoke quietly— "I thought it might be attractive to you now because I am here."

"It is. You know it is, Eve. But I'm young and, frankly, I'm rich. You know my father left me very well-off. I don't want to settle down in one place for the rest of my life and see nothing of the world. That doesn't mean I don't want you to see the world with me."

Mother said she didn't want to see the world. She had seen enough of it for a lifetime, enough forever, it was all horrible. Nor did she want the gatehouse done up and a bathroom put in. She didn't want him wasting his money on her. Luxuries of that kind meant nothing to her and Liza. If he must go away and she could tell he wanted to, he must leave the dogs with her and that way he would come back.

"I don't need a reason to come back. Matt can look after the dogs."

"Leave them with me and then I'll know you have to come. You must always leave them with me."

He slept in Mother's bed that last night and went back to Shrove in the morning. Later on he came to the cottage in the Range Rover and said good-bye. He hugged Mother and kissed her and kissed Liza, and Liza said Annabel would miss him. They waved after the Range Rover as it went down the lane and Liza ran upstairs to watch it go over the bridge. When it was out of sight she and Mother put the dogs in the little castle and Mother said they might as well go up to Shrove to tidy up and put things to rights.

Mr. Tobias had left a lot of mess, though for the past three weeks he hadn't been there much. While Mother was running the vacuum cleaner over the bedroom carpets, Liza went into the morning room and looked at the door that was always locked. She tried the handle just in case it was, for once, unlocked. It wasn't. Squatting down because she was quite tall by then, she put one eye to the keyhole and closed the other. She was surprised to find she could see quite a lot, a piece of the red upholstery of a chair and the braid on its arm, the corner of a kind of table with drawers in it, the bright-colored spines, blue and green and orange, of books on a shelf. What could there be in there she wasn't allowed to see?

Liza now wished she had told Mr. Tobias about the locked room on the several occasions he and she had been together in the house while Mother was cleaning upstairs or in the kitchen. But of course they had never been in the morning room, it wasn't much used and there was no reason why it should be when there were a drawing room, a dining room, and a library as well. Liza was convinced that if she had asked Mr. Tobias he would have fetched the key and opened the door at once.

Next time he came she would ask him. When he came back to fetch the dogs. But the weeks went by and he didn't come. He didn't write, not even a postcard, and after nearly a month Matt came in the Range Rover and took the dogs away. Mother happened to see the Range Rover coming across the bridge. It was the right color, though she couldn't see the number, she was sure it was Mr. Tobias himself coming and even more sure when she saw it in the lane. Mr. Tobias had never before sent Matt in the Range Rover but he had this time, and when Matt had gone and Heidi and Rudi with him, Mother went into her bedroom and cried.

Liza had never told anyone about that. Well, she had had no one to tell until now, but she didn't tell Sean, she kept it locked up and secret inside her head. And when Sean said, this guy Tobias, the one that Shrove House belongs to, did he ever come, she said only, yes, he did, but he didn't stay long.

"And didn't you never go to school?"

"No, I never did. Mother taught me herself at home."

"It's against the law, that."

"I expect it is. But you know where Shrove is, the back of beyond, far away from just about everywhere. Who would know? Eve told lies about it. She was very open with me. She said it was important not to tell lies unless you had to, but if you had to the important thing was to know they were lies. She told some of the people that asked that I went to the village school and the other people that I went to a private school. We met Diana Hayden in the lane and Eve told her we were in a hurry because she was taking me to catch the bus for school. You have to remember there weren't many people. I mean, basically, there were just the milkman, the postman, the man who read the meter, Mr. Frost, and the oilman, and they weren't going to ask. None of them was there for more than five minutes except for Mr. Frost and he never spoke."

"Didn't you want to go to school? I mean, you know, kids want friends."

"I had Eve," Liza said simply, and then, "I didn't want anyone else. Well, I had Annabel, my doll. She was my imaginary friend and I used to talk to her and discuss things with her. I used to ask her advice and I don't think I minded when she didn't answer. I didn't *know*, you see. I didn't know life could be different.

"When I could read, I mean really read, Eve started teaching me French. I *think* I speak quite good French. We did history and geography on Mondays and Wednesdays and arithmetic on Tuesdays. She started me on Latin when I was nine and that was on Fridays, but before that we did poetry reading on Thursdays and Fridays and music appreciation."

Sean was staring at her aghast. "What a life!"

"I really didn't need to go to school. We talked all day long, Eve and me. We walked all over the countryside. In the evenings we played cards or did jigsaws or read."

"You poor kid. Bloody awful childhood you had."

Liza wasn't having that. She said hotly, "I had a wonderful childhood. You mustn't think anything else. I collected things, the gatehouse was full of my pressed flowers and pine cones and bowls with tadpoles in and caddises and water beetles. I never had to dress up. I never ate food that was bad for me. I never quarreled with other children or fought or got hurt."

He interrupted her and said perspicaciously, "But you know about those things."

"Yes, I know about them. I'll tell you how, but not now, not this minute. Now I just want you to know my childhood was all right, it was fine. She's not to blame for anything that happened to *me,* she was a wonderful mother to me."

Again his face wore that incredulous expression and he shook his head faintly. She was silent and gently she took his hand. She wasn't going to tell him—or not yet—that things had changed, that the happiness was not perpetual.

Eve told her the myth of Adam and Eve, insisting as she did so that it was only that, a myth. They read the passage on the creation in Genesis, and then the expulsion from the Garden in Milton, so she knew about the serpent in paradise and later imagined it was Eve and herself who hand in hand through Eden took their solitary way.

But all she told Sean of the months before her seventh birthday was that Mr. Tobias came back once, for a day and a night, a night he didn't spend at the gatehouse with Eve but in his own bed at Shrove. Then he went away, if not forever, for a very long time.

AT first Sean was better at picking pears than she was. He knew how to lift each fruit from the twig on which it grew and bend it gently backward until it came away in his hand. Liza just pulled. The pears got bruised and sometimes her fingernail went through the mottled green skin, wounding the white flesh beneath. Mr. Vanner would dock her pay, Sean said, if she damaged his fruit, so she tried to be more careful. She was used to being told, it wasn't something she had learned to resent.

They picked the pears before they were ripe, before the outside turned yellow with a red blush and while the inside was still firm and waxy. Since they came to Vanner's, the sun was always shining. Each morning they woke to a pale blue sky, a stillness and a white mist lying on the fields. Over the farm buildings the Russian vine spread snowy clouds of blossom and Mrs. Vanner's garden was overgrown with yellow and orange nasturtiums. They began picking before it grew hot and took a couple of hours off from noon till two. At that time they had lunch, packets of crisps and a pork pie, cans of Coke and Mars bars, sticky from being kept in a hot pocket.

The pear fields were a long way from the caravan, so mostly they didn't bother to go back but ate their food sitting on the bank under the quickthorn hedge. At first they were nervous about being seen by the other pickers, but no one was interested in them, no one came their way, and on the second day they slipped into the little sheltered place where the elders made a tent of branches and made love on the warm dry grass. Both knew they would make love that evening and when they went to bed but it seemed too long to wait.

Afterward Sean fell asleep, stretched out full-length, his head buried in his arms. Liza lay awake beside him, her cheek resting on his shoulder and her arm around his waist. She liked looking at the way his dark hair grew on the nape of his neck, in two points like the legs of an M, and she thought for the first time that it was also the way Mr. Tobias's hair grew.

Mother hadn't told her the history of *her* mother and the Tobiases until she was older. She must have been about ten when she learned about her grandmother Gracie Beck and old Mr. Tobias, also called Jonathan, and the will; old Mr. Tobias's daughter, Caroline, who was Mr. Tobias's (that is, Jonathan's) mother, and her enormously rich husband, who left her because she was so awful. When she was seven all Liza knew was that Mother and Mr. Tobias had known each other since he was a big child and she a small one and that somehow or other Shrove House ought to have belonged to Mother and not been Mr. Tobias's at all.

Oh, and that Mother loved Mr. Tobias and he loved her. Mother told her that one evening in the winter when they were sitting by the big log fire and Liza had the doll called Annabel on her lap. Liza had noticed that Annabel often brought Mr. Tobias into Mother's mind.

"The difficulty is," Mother said, "that Mr. Tobias is a restless man and wants to see the world, while I intend to remain here for the whole of my life *and never go away."* She said that last bit quite fiercely, looking into Liza's eyes. "Because there is nowhere in the world like this place. This place is the nearest thing to heaven there is. If you have found heaven, why should you want to see anywhere else?"

"Have you seen everywhere in the world?" Liza asked, carefully combing Annabel's hair.

"Near enough," Mother said mysteriously. "I have seen more than enough of people. Most people are bad. The world would be a better place if half the population were to perish in a huge earthquake. I have seen more than enough places. Most places are horrible, I can tell you. You have no idea how horrible and I'm glad you haven't. That is the way I want it to be. One day, when you have grown up the way I want you to, you can go out and have a peep at the world. I guarantee you'll come running back here, thankful to be restored to heaven."

Liza was uninterested in any of that, she didn't know what it meant. "Mr. Tobias doesn't think other places are horrible."

"He'll learn. It's only a matter of time, you'll see. When he has traveled about for long enough and seen enough, he'll come back here. It just takes him longer than it took me."

"Why does it?"

"Perhaps because I have seen more dreadful things than he has or just that I'm wiser."

In the spring of that year Heather came to stay. Mother said nothing about it until the day before she arrived, and then all she said was, "You'll be sleeping in my room with me for the next week, Liza. Miss Sawyer is coming and will have your room."

Liza knew who Miss Sawyer was from the letters Mother got. She was the same person as Heather.

"For heaven's sake don't call me that, child," said Heather five minutes after she got there. "My name is Heather. 'Miss Sawyer' sounds like a headmistress. What's your headmistress called?"

Liza, who had understood almost nothing of what was said, simply gazed at her, her extreme thinness, her height, her small head and sleek red hair.

"Head teacher, then? I can't keep pace with all these new terms."

Mother changed the subject. She explained to Liza that she and Heather had met while they were at college and Heather knew Mr. Tobias.

"Is he still around?"

"Shrove is *his* house, Heather. Surely you remember that?"

That was when Heather first began whispering to Mother behind her hand. She gave Liza a glance, then quickly turned, put up her hand, and began the whispering. "Wishy, wishy, wishy," was how it sounded to Liza.

After she had been upstairs and seen her room, Heather said she had never before stayed in a house without a bathroom. She didn't know houses without bathrooms existed anymore. But no, of course she wasn't going to allow Mother to carry hot water upstairs for her, which Mother had offered to do. She would use the bath in the kitchen like they did, only it was going to be very awkward.

Another awkwardness was what she called "lack of TV." Liza didn't understand that either and wasn't very interested. The weather was fine, so they went out for many long walks and Heather went for a ride in the train from Ring Valley Halt. She had to go alone. Mother said she had been too many times to want to go again, so Liza couldn't go either.

There was no car to go out in—Heather had come by taxi from some distant station—no record player, hardly any books published later than 1890, no phone, and no restaurants nearer than eight miles away. The village where Mr. Frost came from had something called a pub, Mother said, but they couldn't go there because pubs didn't like children and wouldn't let them in.

"Wishy, wishy, wishy," whispered Heather behind her hand.

"Oh, do speak out, Heather," said Mother. "You are creating mysteries where none need exist."

So Heather stopped whispering and said boldly, the night before she was due to go, "You'll go mad here, Eve."

"No, I shall go sane," said Mother.

"Oh, dear, how epigrammatic!"

"All right. I mean I shall become normal again. I might even be happy. I shall recapture the old-fashioned values and bring up a daughter who has been kept clean of the hideous pressures of our world."

"It all sounds very high-flown and unnatural to me. Anyway, you won't be able to. Her contemporaries will see to that. When you get tired of being a noble savage, remember I've always got a couple of spare rooms."

Eve must have remembered those words when she was finding somewhere for Liza to seek sanctuary. Or else Heather wrote it in a letter, for she never came back and that was the only time Liza ever saw her.

Mother left Liza to her own devices while she swept the bed-room carpets at Shrove with the vacuum cleaner ("You must never say 'hoovered,' Lizzie") and at those times Liza explored the library. One of the books she found was of fairy stories and the tale of Bluebeard was in it. After she had read it she began to associate the locked room with Bluebeard and wondered fear-fully if it might contain dead brides. She thought perhaps old Mr. Tobias had married several women, killed them all, and left them to molder behind that locked door.

Even when Mother showed her old Mr. Tobias's portrait, a big painting that hung in the upstairs hall of a man with a proud expression and gray hair but no beard, blue or otherwise, she still wondered. She wanted to know what that thing was sticking out of his mouth, a stick with a little pot on the end of it. Mother said it was called a pipe, something you put ground-up leaves in and lit with a match, but Liza, remembering that Mother claimed to be a good liar, for the first time disbelieved her.

In a much more prideful place, where the light was bright and no eye could fail to be drawn to it, hung a portrait of the lady called Caroline. She wore the kind of dress Liza had never seen on an actual woman, ankle-length, flowing, low-cut, and of silk the same red as her mouth. Her hair was chestnut-colored, her skin like the petals of the magnolia even now blooming in the Shrove gardens, and her eyes fierce. Liza spent a long time looking at all the pictures in the house that were of real people, alive or long dead. There was no portrait of Mr. Tobias and none of the rich man who had run away from Caroline.

Heather wrote Mother a thank-you letter and after that weeks went by without the postman ever coming to their door. The milkman came and said, "The ten-thirty is late" and "This sunshine is a real treat," but they never saw the postman until one day he brought an envelope with a little paper book in it. Liza managed to get a fascinated look at this book, which was full of pictures of irons and hair dryers and towels and sheets and dresses and shoes, before Mother came and took it away from her. A log fire was burning in the grate and Mother got rid of the book by tearing it into pieces and putting the pieces on the fire.

After that there was no post for weeks, nothing from Mr. Tobias until a postcard came, a plain one, not even a picture, with just a few lines on the back asking them to have the dogs.

"Not if it's a nuisance," he wrote. "Matt will willingly have them. It is only for two weeks while I go to France to see my mother."

"Caroline," Liza said.

Mother said nothing.

"Does she live in the house in the place called Dordogne?" Liza had spent a long time studying the large maps of France in the library atlas. "Does she live there by herself? Is she called Mrs. Tobias?" She remembered the fierce eyes and the red, mouth-colored dress.

"She is now. She is called Caroline Tobias. When she was married she was called Lady Ellison, but our Mr. Tobias was always called Jonathan Tobias because that was his grandfather's wish. She lives in a house in the Dordogne her husband gave her when they were divorced." Mother gave Liza a speculative look as if she was considering explaining something, but she must have thought better of it. "Mostly, she lives by herself. Mr. Tobias goes to see her."

"We can have the dogs, can't we?" said Liza. "Even if Matt really wants them, we can have them, can't we?"

"Of course we shall have the dogs."

So that Mr. Tobias would be sure to come. Liza knew that only in retrospect, not at the time.

It was the day of her first French lesson *("Voici la table, les livres, la plume, le cahier")* that Matt came with the dogs. She was pursing her lips, trying to make that funny sound which is halfway between an E and a U, when they heard the van coming and then the knock at the door. It was rather a cold day even for April, she remembered, and the old electric heater was switched on.

The dogs were pleased to see her, as they always were, jumping up and licking her face and wagging the bit at the end of their backs where their tails had been chopped off. But Rudi was less violent in his affections than in the past, his breath smelled, and his muzzle was going gray. Dogs had seven years to every year of ours, Matt said, and that made Rudi over seventy. Heidi, of course, was only six, or forty-two.

"Will he die?" Liza said.

Matt's hair was much longer than last time, hanging down in greasy hanks. "Don't you worry yourself about that," he said. "That's a long way off."

But Mother said, "Yes, he'll die this year or next. Dobermans don't live much past eleven."

Liza knew her tables. "Or seventy-seven."

It had the effect of making Matt ask her why she wasn't at school. Before she could reply Mother said coldly, "It's Easter. The schools have broken up for Easter."

Some years went by before Liza realized a vital fact about that statement, though she knew there was something odd about it at the time. Mother hadn't told a lie, it *was* the Easter holidays, but just the same the impression she had given Matt was a false one. Later on she observed other instances of Mother doing this and learned how to do it herself.

Mother asked Matt how long they were to have the dogs this time and he said two or three weeks, he couldn't be more precise. But they'd let her know.

"Still haven't got no phone, I see."

"And never shall have."

"It'll have to be a postcard, then."

"I think we can leave that to Mr. Tobias," Mother said in the very cold way she sometimes had, and then, less coldly, almost as if she was asking for something she didn't want to have to ask for, "Will he come for them himself?"

Liza didn't like the look Matt gave Mother. He wasn't smiling but it was as if he was laughing inside. "Like you said, we'll have to leave that to him." With one of his winks, he added, "It'll depend on what Miss Fastley has to say."

Liza had never heard of Miss Fastley, but Mother looked as if she had, though she said nothing.

"When him and her get back from France," Matt said.

As soon as he had gone, Liza thought they would return to the French lesson but Mother said that was enough for today and to take the dogs down to the river. They wrapped up warmly and went down through the Shrove garden. A couple of trains had very likely passed by, Liza couldn't remember details like that, but it was probable at that hour. Likely too that she had waved to the train and one or two passengers waved back. There were never more than a few to wave back.

Mother stood looking across the valley and up to the high hills where the white road ran around among the greening trees. The woods were white with cherry blossom and primroses grew under the hedges.

"It's so beautiful, it's so beautiful!" she cried, spreading out her arms. "Isn't it beautiful, Lizzie?"

Liza nodded, she never knew what to say. There was something about the way Mother looked and the breathy edge to her voice that made her feel awkward.

"I don't mind the trains, I think in a way the trains make it better, it's something to do with all the people being able to sit inside and see how beautiful it is."

And she told Liza a story about a man called George Borrow who sold Bibles, wrote books, and lived in Norfolk, and who moved away and lived away for years because he couldn't bear it when they built a railway through the countryside he loved.

"Who's Miss Fastley?" Liza said on the way back.

Mother can't have heard her that first time because she had to say it again.

"She is one of the ladies who came to stay at Shrove for the weekend last year. She is the one called Victoria."

"Annabel had the sweater with flowers on," said Liza, "and Claire had the jacket like your shoes, so Victoria must have been the one in the green silk shirt."

"Yes, I believe she was."

They didn't put the dogs straight into the little castle but had them in with them for the evening. Rudi lay in front of the electric heater and slept. He was tired after his walk, Mother said they had taken him too far. Liza sat on one side of the fireplace and Mother on the other side. Liza was reading *Winnie the Pooh* by A. A. Milne and Mother was reading *Eothen* by A. W. Kinglake. They sometimes read bits aloud to each other and *Winnie the Pooh* was so funny there were a lot of bits Liza would have liked to read aloud but when she looked up she saw that Mother wasn't reading but gazing sadly at the hearth rug and she had tears on her face.

Liza didn't offer to read aloud but went silently back to her book. She thought Mother was crying because Rudi was old and would soon die.

◇

The money they earned Liza wanted to save up. Eve had set her an example of thrift. There had been the bank account and the tin in the kitchen. And, of course, the secret box in the little castle. Strict accounts had been kept of what Eve earned and what they spent and these were consulted and referred back to before a length of material was bought to make a dress for Liza or a new skirt for Eve. The biggest expenditure Liza remembered was on the tape player Eve bought so that Liza could learn about music and get used to hearing the works of the great composers. She was nearly eight when that happened.

Sean appreciated her economies. He said that being sensible about money was one thing she *could* teach him. They might have Cornish pasties or pork pies and crisps for lunch with chocolate bars afterward, but it would be wiser not to go into town so much in the evenings for a meal at the Burger King or even Mr. Gupta's Tandoori. One evening Sean saw a notice in the window of the new supermarket that they wanted assistants. It would be only for sticking labels on packets and putting cans on shelves, but he said he was going to apply for it. The money would be at least twice what he earned at Vanner's, maybe three times as much.

"I will too, then."

"I don't reckon you can, love. They'll want your insurance number and you haven't got none."

"Can't I get one?"

"Not without giving your name you can't."

They found the family planning clinic too—Liza gave Sean's name and called herself Elizabeth Holford—and a notice board in a newsagent's window on which five people were advertising for domestic help. Liza studied it thoughtfully. Housework was something she could do.

When they got back, the man with the black dog put his head around the door of his camper, said hi and how about a cup of tea?

Liza could see Sean didn't want to, but it was rude to say no, so they went into the man's camper, the kitchen part, where the black dog was sitting on a counter, watching television. Instead of tea the man, who said his name was Kevin, produced a bottle of whiskey and three glasses, which Liza could see made Sean feel a lot better about going in there.

The little glowing screen fascinated her, the picture was so clear and the colors so bright. But at first she was half-afraid to look in case a policeman appeared describing her own appearance or even Eve herself. There was no need to worry. This was a program about small mammals in some distant part of the world, ratlike creatures and squirrellike creatures, which perhaps accounted for the dog's absorption.

He was much smaller than Rudi and Heidi, less sleek and with a real tail, which thumped on the counter when the squirrels jumped about, but just the same he reminded her of Mr. Tobias's dogs, now long dead. She and Mother had looked after them for three weeks, not two, on that occasion and at the end of that time, without warning, Matt appeared to take them away. When Mother saw his van stop outside and saw him get out of it, his hair longer than ever and tied back now, all the color went out of her face and she grew very white.

Liza thought she would be bound to ask him where Mr. Tobias was but she didn't, she hardly spoke to him. The dogs were handed over, Liza having hugged them both and kissed the tops of their heads, and somehow she knew as she watched the van depart that they would never come again, or not both of them, or not in the way they had before. She didn't know how she knew this, for Mother said not a word about it, didn't even look out of the window but set the French book in front of Liza and told her quite sharply to begin reading.

That evening Mother said they must go over to Shrove House, which surprised Liza because they never did. They never went there after about three in the afternoon. It was just after six when they walked across the parkland between the tall trees. There were cowslips in the grass and against the hedges cow parsley and yellow Alexanders. But this time Mother said nothing about how beautiful it was. They walked in silence, hand in hand.

Mother took her into the library and set her a task: to find the French books, to count them and then to see if she could find one called *Émile* by Jean-Jacques Rousseau. It took Liza no time at all. There weren't many French books, she could count only twenty-two, *Émile* among them. She took it down from the shelf, a very old book bound in blue with gilt letters, and went to look for Mother.

She was in the drawing room, talking into the telephone. Liza had never before seen anyone do that. Of course she had seen the telephone and more or less knew what it was, Mr. Tobias had told her, and on that occasion she remembered, while he was explaining, Mother had frowned and shaken her head. It was Mother using it now. Liza kept very still, listening.

She heard Mother say, "I've said I'm sorry, Jonathan. I've never phoned you before." Her voice went very low so that Liza could hardly hear. "I had to phone. I had to know."

Somehow Liza had expected to hear Mr. Tobias's voice

coming out of the other end of the receiver, but there was silence, though she could tell Mother could hear him.

"Why do you say there's nothing to know? If there was nothing, you would have come."

Liza had never heard Mother speak like that, in a ragged, pleading, almost frightened voice, and she didn't like it. Mother was always in control of things, all knowing, all powerful, but that wasn't how she sounded now.

"Then, will you come? Will you come, Jonathan, please? If I ask you, *please* to come."

Even Liza could tell he wasn't going to come, that he was saying, no, I can't, or, no, I won't. She saw Mother's shoulders hunch and her head dip down and heard her say in her cold voice, not unlike the one she used to Matt, "I'm sorry to have troubled you. I do hope I haven't interrupted anything. Good-bye."

Liza went up to her then and put out her hand. She showed her the blue book called *Émile* but Mother seemed to have forgotten what she had asked her to do and everything about it. Mother's face was as pale as a wax candle and as stiff. . . .

"You lost in a dream, love?" Sean said. "I offered you a penny for them and you never heard a word I said. Kevin wants to know if you'd like a glass of his Riseling?"

Liza said, yes, thanks, she'd love some, and when she saw the wine box and read the name she somehow managed to stop herself telling them it was pronounced "reesling," she thought their feelings might be hurt. Kevin was a small man with a nut-brown face and black hair, though not much of that was left. He might be thirty or he might be forty-five. Liza couldn't tell, she wasn't much good at guessing ages, and no wonder.

The men talked about football and then about the dog that Kevin said was a good little ratter. It had started to rain, Liza could hear it drumming on the roof of the camper. What would become of them if it rained? Mr. Vanner wouldn't pay them if they couldn't pick. She suddenly thought, with a fierce hunger, not altogether unlike the desire she often had for Sean, that if she didn't soon have a book in her hands, if she couldn't soon read a book, she'd die.

She asked Kevin how much his TV cost and could tell at once from Sean's expression that she shouldn't have. But Kevin didn't seem to mind. He said he didn't know, he hadn't a clue, because it was one of the things he'd brought with him from their household when he and his wife split up and he reckoned it was she who bought it in the first place.

"Not thinking of getting married, are you?" he said when she and Sean were going. "Only you want to think twice. Hang on to your freedom while you can."

"Of course we're not thinking of getting married," said Liza, and she laughed at the very idea, but Sean didn't laugh.

‿〰

She hadn't said much to Sean at all about Eve and Mr. Tobias, it had all been in her head, all memories. It was he who brought the subject up next day, he must have been thinking about it, she didn't know why. They were still in bed, though it was quite late in the morning, but there was no point in trying to go out and pick with the rain pouring down.

When she first woke she had been quite disorientated, not knowing where she was but imagining she must be in the gate-house. The rain made it unnaturally dark. Half-asleep still, she had looked for the book that should have been open and face-downward on the bedside cabinet. But there was no bedside cabinet and no book, and when she turned over she rolled into the warm eager arms of Sean. Instead of reading she cajoled and kissed him into making love to her—never a hard task—which he would have said was better any day, and often she would agree.

Suddenly he said, "This guy Tobias, he slept with your mum? I mean, they was in the same bed?"

"They were lovers, they were like us."

"That wasn't right," Sean said very seriously, "not with you in the house, not with a little kid."

"Why not?"

She didn't know what he meant and she could tell he found it hard to explain.

"Well, it's just not. Everyone knows that. They wasn't married. Your mum should have known better, an educated woman like her. It's one thing just the two of them, but not with a little kid in the house. You got to have principles, you know, love."

She said, no, she didn't know, but he took no notice. "D'you reckon she thought he'd marry her?"

"She hoped he would."

"Yeah, she must have been lonely. It wasn't right, him taking advantage of her like that."

Liza told him about the phone call and how Eve had been afterward, quiet and preoccupied and sometimes as if she was frightened.

"Well, she was in love, wasn't she?" Romantic Sean pressed his lips into her neck. He stroked her hair. "She loved him and she thought she'd lost him, you got to pity her."

"I don't know about being in love," Liza said. "Maybe a bit. She wanted Shrove House, that was what all that was about. She wanted Shrove House for herself, to make sure she'd never be parted from it. That was the only way. If she married Mr. Tobias it'd have been hers."

He was shocked. "That's not right."

"I can't help it. It's the way it was. It was always like that. She wanted that place, to be there all the time and to be sure she could be, more than anything in the world. It was all she wanted."

"It sounds crazy to me." She could feel him shaking his head as it lay on the pillow beside hers. "Whatever happened, then?"

"He married someone else," said Liza. "He married Victoria."

e i g h t

∽

LIZA was eight years old and for as long as she could remember she had never been away from Shrove. Once a week Mother went on the bus into town to do the shopping, but Liza had never asked if she could come. Now, when she thought about it, she couldn't imagine why she had never said, "Can I come?" Locked up in her bedroom or else locked up in one of the rooms at Shrove, she had been content or she had accepted.

"That was wrong." Sean was in censorious mood. "Suppose something had happened to you."

"It didn't."

"Maybe not. Just as well for her. You might have hurt yourself or the place caught on fire."

She thought but didn't say that the place burning down would have been a bigger tragedy for Eve. Shrove on fire would be worse than Liza dying in it.

"If they'd found out what was going on they could have took you away and put you in care."

"They didn't know, whoever they are."

"Wasn't you scared?"

"No, I don't think I was, not ever. Well, for a bit after the man with the beard, but I saw what she did about that, you see. It showed me she'd always look after me. I liked being locked up in the library at Shrove best, there or in the morning room. It was so warm."

"What d'you mean, warm? The place was empty, wasn't it?"

"The heating was always on from October to May."

"He must be rolling in it," Sean said disapprovingly. "Central heating blasting away when no one lived there and there's poor buggers sleeping rough on the streets."

She wasn't interested, she hardly knew what he meant. "I used to read the books. Of course there were lots I didn't begin to understand, they were years and years too old for me. Eve said to me once, I just wonder what people would say, the ones who think you ought to have gone to school, if they could have seen you trying to read Ruskin and Matthew Arnold at seven-and-a-half."

Sean had no comment to make on that.

"Anyway, I was never left for more than two hours. Then Eve would come for me and she'd always have something nice, some treat, colored pencils to draw with or a new pair of socks or a painted egg. I remember once she came home with a pineapple,

I'd never seen one before. Then one day she brought a picture."

It was a painting of Shrove House. Mother had to tell her what it was or she might not have known, the painting was so strange, the colors so strong and the house not looking the way she had ever seen it. But when Mother explained that this was just one man's, the painter's, view of it, that he had chosen to paint it at sunset and after a storm, that he saw it as a symbol of wealth and power and had therefore accentuated all the yellows to express gold and the dark purples to reveal strength, then she began to understand. Mother had seen the painting in the window of a place she called a gallery and had bought it "on an impulse." It was cheap, she said, for what it was.

"Besides, we've got quite a lot of money," Mother said, and proudly, "We don't fritter money away."

She hung the painting on the wall in their living room where the gun had once been. When Liza climbed up on a stool to look more closely at it she saw that the words Bruno Drummond were written in red in the bottom right-hand corner with the date 1982.

It was the next morning, or perhaps the morning after next, that the postman came and brought with him the letter from Mr. Tobias. Mother tore open the envelope and read it. She threw the envelope into the rubbish bin, read the letter a second time, and folded it up. She said a strange thing, she said it in an intense concentrated way while she stared at the folded letter in her hand.

"In ancient times they used to kill a messenger who was a bearer of bad news. It's fortunate for that postman that things have changed."

Liza could hear his van going back up the lane. She waited for Mother to tell her what Mr. Tobias had written, but Mother didn't tell her and there was something in her face that stopped her asking. There were more lessons than usual that week and sometimes they went on into the evening. That was one of the signs that something had happened to upset Mother, an increase in lessons.

On the Saturday morning, while Liza was eating her breakfast, Mother said, "Mr. Tobias is getting married today. This is his wedding day."

"What's wedding?" said Liza.

So Mother explained about getting married. She turned it into a lesson. She talked about marriage customs in different parts of the world, how in some countries, for instance, a man could have several wives, but not here, here people could be married only one at a time. It was called monogamy. She told Liza about Islam and about the Mormons, about Christian brides in white dresses being married in churches and Jewish people under canopies stamping on glass. Then she read out something from the Book of Common Prayer about marriage being forever until the two people were parted by death. Mr. Tobias wouldn't be married like that, however, but in an office by a registrar.

"Were you ever married?" Liza asked.

"No, I never was," said Mother.

At a quarter past twelve she said it must all be over now and they were man and wife. Liza said, wasn't he a man before, and Mother said she was quite right, it was just an expression and not a very good one. They were *husband* and wife.

"Will they come and live here?" said Liza.

Mother didn't answer and Liza was going to repeat the question, but she didn't because Mother had gone a dark red color and clenched her fists. Liza thought it best to say no more about it. She married Annabel to the rag doll in a ceremony of her own invention but she did it upstairs in the privacy of her bedroom.

And of course Mr. and Mrs. Tobias never did come to live

at Shrove, though they stayed there from time to time, the first time being a fortnight after the wedding. Another letter came first. Mother read it, screwed it up, and looked cross.

"What does he mean, get a woman in to get the place ready? He knows I'll never do that. He knows I clean it and that I'll clean it ready for his wife." And she said those final two words again. "His wife."

She and Liza spent the afternoon at Shrove. Mr. Tobias would no longer be sleeping in his old bedroom but in the one that had been Caroline Ellison's in the four-poster with yellow silk curtains. With Victoria, Liza thought, though Mother hadn't said so. The four-poster was quite different from the Venetian one and made of dark brown carved wood with a carved wood roof Mother called a tester. She said that in olden times before there was glass in windows and when ceilings were very high, birds used to fly in and roost in the rafters on cold nights. You needed a roof on your bed to protect you from owl and hawk droppings.

While Mother put clean white sheets on the four-poster and mats of yellow silk and white lace out on the dressing table, Liza tried the handle of the door to the locked room on the off-chance of its not being locked for once. But it was, it always was.

Mother had said she must start writing compositions—well, stories really—and asked her to do one about getting married. Liza was already working it out in her head. She was going to have a girl called Annabel get married to a man called Bruno who brought her home to his big house in the country by a river. Annabel found the locked room while Bruno was out riding on his horse and then she found the key to the door in the pocket of his dressing gown. Next time he went out she unlocked the door and inside she found the dead bodies of three women that he'd killed before he married her because only Moslems could have more than one wife. Liza didn't know what would happen next but she'd think of something.

She expected Mr. Tobias to come running to their door as he had in the past, the dogs at his heels. Mother was busy sewing, her back to the window, her feet working the treadle on the machine faster than usual and her hands guiding the cloth, but Liza sat on the step outside, waiting for him. It was October but warm and sunny, the leaves on the balsam tree still green, the blackberries and the elderberries over and the holly berries turning from green to gold. The morning had been misty but now the air was clear, the sky blue, and everything very still.

They were late. Liza was almost at the point of giving up and going indoors when at last the car came, not the Range Rover but the Mercedes. Later on Liza was to learn to identify many makes of cars, but at that time she only knew a Range Rover, a Ford Transit van, a Mercedes, and whatever kind it was the police used. The Mercedes was going quite fast, it was going to sweep straight in through the open gates, but Mr. Tobias did see Liza, and he stuck his arm out of the window and waved. Of course he was on the near side of the car, the side nearest to her. On the other side sat the lady who had worn the green shirt. Victoria. Mrs. Tobias.

It was a pity because Liza couldn't see her very well. She wasn't wearing a green shirt this time but a fawn sweater with a neck that came right up to her chin and then folded over. Her hair was fair, a pale blond, it was exactly the same color as the jumper but silky instead of woolly and rough. Her face wasn't visible. Liza supposed the dogs must be in the back, though she couldn't see them. She waved and waved until they were out of sight and then she went in to give Mother all the details. That evening she expected them to come or him to come, best of all she would have liked him to come alone, and she sat in the window with Annabel, as if Annabel would draw him in some magic way.

"It must have been like turning a knife in the wound," she said to Sean, "the way I went on and on about him. When was he coming? Could we go up there? Poor Eve! But I didn't know any better. I was only a child."

"I shouldn't worry. You said yourself, she only wanted him for that place of his."

"Things aren't so simple," said Liza. "Anyway, they came next day, both of them."

Mrs. Tobias was tall and slim. ("Quite elegant, I suppose," Mother said.) Her fair hair, the color of newly sawn wood, was cut very short like a man's, but her face was painted in a way Liza had never seen before, not in the least like Diana Hayden's. The effect was more like a wonderful picture or a piece of jewelry. Her mouth reminded Liza of a fuchsia bud and her eyelids were crocus purple. She had fuchsia bud nails and on one finger were Mr. Tobias's rings, gold and diamonds flashing brilliantly.

She was very nice and polite to Mother, thanking her for making the house so clean and beautiful and telling her what Mr. Tobias was always saying, how she must, she just must, get a woman in to do all this cleaning. Either she found someone or she, Mrs. Tobias, would absolutely have to find someone herself.

All the while Mr. Tobias was looking rather strange, rubbing his hands together, walking up and down, then studying their old chromium electric heater as if he was passionately interested in things like that.

Liza said, "Where are Rudi and Heidi?"

"I'm afraid Rudi's dead," he said.

He looked more awkward than ever and tried to explain it away, as if it wasn't important, a dog dying. Rudi was old, he lost his appetite, he'd got a thing called a tumor growing inside him, and the kindest thing was for him to die a peaceful death.

"Did you shoot him with a gun?" Liza asked.

Mrs. Tobias screamed out when she said that. "Oh, my God, where does the child get these ideas!"

"I took him to the vet," Mr. Tobias said, "and he was very quiet and peaceful and happy. The vet gave him an injection and he went to sleep with his head on my lap."

"He never woke up again, he died," said Mother, getting a very strange look from Mrs. Tobias, who curled back her upper lip and showed her little white top teeth. "What about Heidi?"

Mr. Tobias said Matt had her with him in Cumbria. Heidi lived with him now, in his council house. "Victoria's allergic to dogs."

"It isn't something I can help," Mrs. Tobias said. "Of course I adore them but just having one near me can bring on these horrendous attacks of asthma."

After that they saw Mr. and Mrs. Tobias only in the distance. From her bedroom window, one evening, Liza saw them come walking out of the wood with their arms around each other. She heard the car go past several times and when they had been there nearly a week she heard shots.

"Mr. Tobias never used to shoot things," she said to Mother. "Why's he doing it now?"

"I expect it's his wife's influence."

"What is he shooting?"

Mother shrugged. "Pheasants, partridges—rabbits, perhaps."

Mr. Tobias called on them and brought a couple of dead pheasants. A brace, he called it. He came alone. Mrs. Tobias had a pain in her back and wasn't feeling well. Liza didn't think she would be able to eat things she had seen in the meadows, such beautiful birds, as beautiful as the peacocks she had seen in pictures, but when it came to it and Mother had roasted them she found that she could. When she ate the soft brown meat that seemed to melt in her mouth, she forgot about the shining blue and gold feathers and the bright beady eyes.

The Day of the Pheasant, she called it. She wrote the composition about marriage for Mother and had it given back with just a red tick on the bottom but otherwise no comment. That was the week Mother smacked her, the first and the last time this happened. Mother found her playing with the husband and wife dolls and came upon her just as the rag doll was killing Annabel with a gun made from a twig.

It was as if she didn't stop to think but lifted up her hand and smacked Liza on the bottom. Afterward she said she was sorry and that she shouldn't have done that.

The weather got cold very suddenly, the night frosts so heavy that in the morning it looked as if snow had fallen. The frost drove the Tobiases away. They called at the gatehouse as they were leaving, and Mrs. Tobias, who was wearing a wonderful coat of white sheepskin, said it was shocking having no bathroom at the gatehouse and one must be put in as a matter of priority. Mr. Tobias had used those very words himself but done nothing about it, Liza remembered. His wife urged Mother once more to get a cleaner. After all, if she knew Mother was doing it on her own she would have to tidy up herself, her conscience would make her.

"Please, Eve," said Mr. Tobias, looking more uncomfortable than ever. "And we'll see about that bathroom."

The car had disappeared up the lane for no more than ten minutes before Mother and she were on their way to Shrove House to clear up the mess.

But there was no mess. Everything was clean and tidy and someone had washed the dishes and done the dusting. Liza couldn't tell how she knew this but she sensed that Mother, curiously, would have preferred a mess. While Mother was stripping the bed and putting the sheets in the washing machine, Liza made another attempt on the locked door. This time, for the first time ever, it wasn't locked. She turned the handle and the door came open.

There were no bodies, no dead brides. She found herself in a small sitting room in which was a writing desk, a pair of occasional tables, three armchairs, and a sofa. On the walls, in frames of polished wood, were the kind of dull gray pictures Mother said were called etchings and a pair of vases with Chinese people on them that held bunches of dried red roses. Facing the sofa and the chairs, on a cabinet made of a rather bright golden wood with a complicated curly grain, stood a large brown, box-shaped thing with a kind of mirror on the front of it. She could see herself in the mirror, but not very clearly, rather in the way she could in a window with dark curtains drawn behind the glass.

"What was it?" Sean asked. "A TV?"

"Yes, but I didn't know that then. I couldn't think what it was. The extraordinary thing was that I wasn't very interested in it. I was *disappointed*. You see I'd given that room such a terrific buildup in my mind, I thought there'd be at least some amazing wild animal in there or a box of jewels, treasure, really, or even a skeleton. I'd seen a picture of a skeleton in one of the books in the library. And all there was was this box thing with a mirror that didn't even work like mirrors are supposed to."

"But you switched it on."

"No, I didn't. Not then, not for ages. I wouldn't have given it another thought, I'd probably never have gone back there, if Mother hadn't come in. It was her coming in and being so obviously, well, taken aback that I'd got in there and found the thing that made me so anxious to know what it was."

"Kids are like that," said Sean sagely.

"Are they? I don't know. I only knew me. She wasn't cross. It was more as if she was worried. It's hard to describe, I have to find an expression, sort of knocked sideways, the wind taken out of her sails. She took my hand and led me out of there and got the key and locked the door again."

"But why?"

"That was the point of the whole thing, wasn't it? The whole way I was being brought up. The world had treated her so badly, it was so awful out there, that I wasn't to be allowed to go through any of that. I was to be sheltered from the world, hence no school and no visits to the town, no meeting other people, other people kept down to the minimum, a totally protected childhood and youth."

"She taught you to express yourself all right, didn't she?" he said admiringly and he lit a cigarette as if he needed it.

Liza wished he wouldn't. The caravan quickly filled with smoke, it was so small, and it made her cough. She sighed a little before going on. "Television would have undone a lot of her work. Once I'd seen that, I'd know about the world out there, I wouldn't only want to see it, I'd start talking like the people on TV and learning the sort of ways she thought were bad."

"You said the world had treated her bad. I mean, like what? What had it done to her?"

"You won't believe this, but I don't know. That is, I don't know the details. She'd had me without a husband, there was that, she hadn't got Shrove when she thought she was going to, she told me a lot more about that later, but she never told me what made her, well, bury herself and me down there. When she took me out of that room and locked the door again I hadn't any idea why and she didn't explain. I only knew it had something to do with the box with the glass front."

"You said she got the key. Where did she get it from?"

That had been the most interesting thing. Mother had looked around her for the key and clicked her tongue when she saw it lying on top of the glass-fronted cabinet that was full of dolls. She locked the door and then, in Liza's presence, not bothering to hide from her what she was doing, she climbed onto a chair and from the chair onto the top of a dresser in which was kept breakfast china and cutlery. The top of the dresser was on a level with Liza's head.

On the wall above hung a large picture Liza was to learn was called a still life. This one was by Johann Baptist Drechsler and was of a bunch of roses with dew on them and fritillaries and morning glory. The painter had put a Painted Lady butterfly on a blade of grass and on the top left-hand side a moth with brown forewings and yellow underwings and a strange pattern on its back. The picture was in a thick gilt frame that stuck out six inches from the wall. Mother put the key on top of the frame, over to the right-hand side, and while she did so she explained to Liza that the moth was called the death's-head hawk moth because the pattern on its back looked like a skull, or the bones inside a person's head. If this was designed to distract Liza's attention from the key and the locked room, it failed to do so.

Liza knew she had about as much chance of getting up there as she had of owning a dog. But she wanted to get up there. Soon it became the thing she most wanted to do in all the world. She thought about it a lot and she thought that in that little book that had once come in the post and she had managed to study for five minutes before it was taken away and torn up, in there had been a picture of just such a box as was in the locked room at Shrove House.

When it was winter and Mother went shopping she was always locked up at Shrove because of the warmth there. Sometimes in the morning room, sometimes in the library, sometimes in one of the bedrooms. When it was the morning room she had been in the habit of spending a lot of the time just gazing at the dolls in the cabinet. The dolls were of historical personages, Mother had said and had named some of them, Queen Elizabeth I, Mary Queen of Scots, a man called Beau Brummel and another called Louis Quatorze, Florence Nightingale and Lord Nelson. But now instead she stood staring at the picture of the flowers, the butterfly, and the moth with the skull on its back, knowing the key was lying there on the top of the frame, though she couldn't see it even if she stood on a chair.

Her ninth birthday came and went. It was very cold and the grounds of Shrove lay under six inches of snow. A partial thaw came but the half-melted snow froze again, and the house, the stables and coachhouse, the gatehouse, the little castle, and the owl barn were hung with icicles. Hoar frost turned all the trees into pyramids and cascades and towers of silver lace. The lane was blocked with snow drifts and Mother couldn't get out to catch the bus for town. When she did, at last, she left Liza in the library.

Reading books, playing with the terrestrial globe, looking out of one window after another at the birds in the snow, Liza came to the far end where it was always rather dark, the darkest place in that light house, and saw, resting against the wall, something long-familiar yet forgotten, the library steps.

There were eight steps, enough to get even a small person up to the topmost bookshelf. But Liza was locked in the library. Anyway, she thought the steps would be too heavy for her, they looked heavy, they were made of dull gray metal. She touched them, she put both hands to them and clasped the rails that enclosed the treads. She tried to raise them as if they would be heavy and they flew up in her hands. The steps were light, they were nearly as light as if made of cardboard, a little child could lift them, she could lift them with one hand.

But she was locked in. Mother came for her soon afterward and they went back to the gatehouse through the snow. It snowed even more heavily that night and they spent next morning digging themselves out and the afternoon making cakes of dripping and bread for the bird feeders. Two weeks, three, went by before Mother could go to town again. It was soon after that, in March probably, when the snow had gone but for patches of it left in shady places, that the postman brought the letter that was to change their lives.

"Tobias again?" said Sean.

"No, we never heard from him. Well, Eve got her money all right and Mrs. Tobias sent a postcard from Aspen in America that they went skiing, but there was never a thing from him. This letter was from Bruno Drummond."

"The artist guy."

"Yes. The Phoenix Gallery had told him about Eve buying his painting, I don't think he sold many paintings—well, I know he didn't. He said he'd wanted to phone her but he couldn't find her number in the book. Not surprising, was it, since she'd no more have a phone than she would a television. He said the painting ought to be varnished and if she'd bring it to him he'd do it. He told her where he lived and said it was easy to park her car outside!

"Of course she didn't answer. She said if the painting needed varnishing she was capable of doing that herself. And she was very annoyed with the gallery for giving him her address. She kept saying, 'Is nothing sacred? Is there no privacy?' "

In February the Latin lessons began. *Puella, puella, puellam, puellae, puellae, puella.* And *Puella pulchra est.*

"The girl is beautiful," said Mother, but it was herself that she looked at in the mirror.

Liza enjoyed learning Latin because it was like doing a hard jigsaw puzzle. Mother said it would stretch her brain and she read aloud from Caesar's *Invasion of Britain* for Liza to get accustomed to the sound of it.

In March she began her collection of pressed wildflowers. Mother bought her a big album to keep them in. To the left-hand page she attached the pressed flower and on the right-hand one she painted a picture of it in watercolor. A snowdrop was the first one she put in and next a coltsfoot. Mother let her borrow *Wild Flowers* by Gilmour and Walters from the library at Shrove so that she could identify the flowers and find their Latin names.

The weather grew warmer and in April Mr. and Mrs. Tobias came down to Shrove to stay, bringing four other people with them. Claire and Annabel and a man Liza had never seen before and Mr. Tobias's mother, Lady Ellison.

"Caroline," said Liza.

"Yes," said Mother, "but you mustn't call her that."

As it turned out, Liza didn't get the chance to call her anything.

Before they came, Mrs. (not Mr.) Tobias had written to Mother and said some more about a cleaning woman.

"Can you imagine having such a person here?" Mother was calm but Liza could tell she was angry. "She would come in a car and we should have that noise and dirt. I would have to let her in, I couldn't trust anyone with a key, and then teach her what to do and, just as important, what *not* to do. Why can't Victoria Tobias leave it alone? Why can't she just leave me to do it?"

Liza couldn't answer that. Mother thought about it all day, she *worried* about it, she kept saying she didn't want any more intruders, Mr. Frost was bad enough, not to mention the postman *and* the milkman *and* the man who read the meters *and* the one who serviced the Shrove central heating, there was no end to it.

"You could do it yourself and pretend you'd got a lady to do it."

At first Mother said, no, she couldn't, and, how about the money, and then she said, why not? It wouldn't be dishonest to take the money so long as the work was done, so Mother invented a woman and she and Liza thought up a name for her. They laughed until they almost cried at some of the names Liza thought up. She got them from the wildflower book, Sweet Cicely Pearlwort and Mrs. Sowthistle and Fritillaria Twayblade. But Mother said it mustn't be funny, it must sound like a real name, so in the end they called her Mrs. Cooper, Dorothy Cooper.

Mother wrote to Mr. (not Mrs.) Tobias and said she'd found a cleaning woman called Dorothy Cooper who would come once a week and if he sent the money to her she would pay her. In the week before Easter, Mother gave Shrove House a tremendous spring clean while Liza sat in the library reading *Jane Eyre*. That is, for most of the time she read *Jane Eyre*. She also carried the steps out of the library and into the morning room.

At the morning room windows hung long heavy curtains of slate-gray velvet. Even when you pulled the cords that drew them across the windows they still covered about two feet of the gray-and-white wall on either side. Liza put the steps up against the wall on the right-hand side of the right-hand window. The curtains covered them, you couldn't see they were there.

It was just as well she hadn't used them to get the key down and open the door because, when she had finished upstairs, Mother came into the morning room, climbed onto a chair and then onto the sideboard, and reached up for the key on top of the picture frame. Liza crept out of the library and watched her from the morning room doorway. Mother unlocked the door and went into the secret room, pulling the vacuum cleaner behind her.

She was in there for half an hour. Liza kept dodging from the library to the morning room door to check on her. When she heard the howl of the vacuum cleaner from the morning room she went to the door and said she was hungry and could they go home and have lunch?

The key was in the lock of the door to the secret room. It had to be, of course it did, because Mr. and Mrs. Tobias and their friends were coming. Liza and Mother had their lunch in the Shrove kitchen and all the time Liza was thinking, perhaps the key will still be in that lock after they have gone away again.

It wasn't. Liza thought Mother had probably gone over there and put it back on the picture before she was even up. She had seen very little of Mr. and Mrs. Tobias and their friends, just the Mercedes going by once or twice with the other car following behind and once caught a glimpse of Claire and a tall old woman in a tweed skirt down on the Shrove lawn with golf clubs. Could it be Caroline? Could *that* be the Caroline of the plump white shoulders and the lipstick-colored dress? But one evening, after she had gone to bed, she heard someone come to their front door. There was a low murmur of voices, a man's and Mother's.

She was almost but not quite sure the other voice was Mr. Tobias's. They were downstairs in the living room, talking, and she crept out of bed to listen at the top of the stairs. But Mother must have heard her because she came out and called up to Liza to go back to bed at once.

The murmur went on and on, then she heard the front door close and Mother come up to bed. If Mother had been crying it wouldn't have surprised her, she didn't know why, but instead Mother was talking out loud to herself. It was uncanny and rather frightening.

"It's all over," Mother was saying. "You have to get it into your head that it's all over. You have to start again. Tomorrow to fresh woods and pastures new."

Did that mean they were going away?

"Tomorrow to fresh woods and pastures new," Mother murmured and closed her bedroom door.

"No, of course we're not leaving," Mother said in the morning. "What on earth gave you that idea? Mr. and Mrs. Tobias are leaving and goodness knows when they'll come back again."

Liza saw the cars come down the drive from Shrove House, the Mercedes with Mr. Tobias driving and Mrs. Tobias beside him and Claire in the back. A minute later along came the other car with the man driving and Caroline Ellison beside him. It stopped outside the gatehouse and the man sounded his horn. Liza didn't know what he meant by it but Mother did. Mother was furious. I'm not going out there, I'm not being summoned in that way, she was fuming, it's like the Royal Family stopping outside some keeper's house. But she did go out and talked to Lady Ellison.

This enabled Liza to get a good look at Mr. Tobias's mother, who had actually got out of the car. She was so tall she made Mother look child-sized. And Mother made her look like a giantess as well as uglier than ever. Liza thought her hands were like a hawk's claws that had been dipped in some poor small animal's blood.

Mother came back into the house making terrible faces of rage and disgust, which the people in the cars couldn't see because her back was to them. The cars were hardly out of sight before she and Liza were up at Shrove House, where there was an awful mess to be cleared up. No doubt, Mrs. Tobias thought Dorothy Cooper would be clearing it up. That was when Liza found the secret room door locked and the key, so far as she knew, back on top of the picture.

It was May now but not very warm, though beautiful to look at, as Mother kept saying. The new leaves were a sharp fresh green and the cream and red flowers on the broom were out, sweet smelling and covered with bees. Last autumn Mr. Frost had planted hundreds of wallflowers. Like folds of multicolored velvet they were, red and amber and gold and chestnut brown, spread across a whole sweep of land with not a blade of green to be seen between them. Liza picked speedwell for her wildflower collection and Mother said she could take one, but just one, cowslip.

They had lunch at home. The afternoon was for Latin, arithmetic, and geography. Liza was doing long division when the doorbell rang. Because the doorbell hardly ever rang it was always a shock when it did.

"That will be Mr. Frost wanting something," Mother said, though he hardly ever did want anything.

She opened the door. A man was standing there. His car, which was the orange color of a satsuma and looked as if made of painted cardboard, was parked outside their gate. He was quite a young man with curly brown hair long enough to reach his shoulders and very big blue eyes with long lashes like a girl's. Well, like hers or Mother's. There were little brown dots, which Mother later explained were freckles, sprinkled on his small straight nose. His lips were red and his small teeth very white. He wore blue jeans and a denim jacket over a check shirt and a gold ornament hanging from a chain around his neck. Liza stared fascinated at the earrings he wore, two gold rings both in the same ear. He was carrying a bag made out of a carpet. It looked as if it was made from one of the Persian rugs at Shrove.

"Oh, hi," he said. "This really is the end of the world, isn't it? I'm amazed that I've found you. Let me introduce myself. My name is Bruno Drummond."

Liza said she was like Scheherazade, telling her man stories every night. Only Sean wouldn't chop her head off in the morning, would he, if one night she was so worn out she couldn't collect her thoughts? Sean said, who was that then, that She-whatever, but Liza was too tired to explain.

They were both exhausted, picking Coxes. The crop was a particularly big one this year. They picked from first thing in the morning until sunset, which was as long as Mr. Vanner would let them. He said he'd have to take on extra labor to cope with the crop and they wanted to stop him, they wanted to earn all the money that was going, but it was a losing battle. On the third morning a troop of women moved in to help, housewives from the village that was a mile away.

Sean wanted to hear more about Bruno, but Liza was too tired to tell him, too tired to watch the little colored television set she'd finally bought with the hundred pounds and some apple money, too tired for everything but making love, and they only managed that because it happened in bed and they fell asleep straight afterward.

The news was something Liza had seldom been able to watch on television even if she had wanted to. It is rarely transmitted between two and five in the afternoon. Now she learned it was for mornings and evenings, so she watched it at breakfast time and, once the women had come and there was no point in working so hard, at six o'clock and nine. She was looking for something about Eve. But there never was anything.

"That's because they've had her in court," Sean said, "and now she's on what-d-you-call-it, remand, that's it, remand, and the papers and the telly can't have anything on about her until she comes up in court again."

This was very much what Eve herself had told her. She admired him for knowing it. Feeling very pleased that he knew about this legal matter, she realized she had begun accepting that she knew much more than he did about almost everything but the absolutely practical things. Of course he *thought* he knew more than she, but she could tell that mostly he didn't. When it was books and music and nature and art and history, she knew it all and he knew nothing, so she was pleasantly surprised.

"When will that happen, Eve coming up in court?" she asked him.

"Not for weeks, maybe months."

She was disappointed. "Where do they do it, this remand?"

"In prison."

Her knowledge of that had its base on her reading of fiction, *A Tale of Two Cities* and *The Count of Monte Cristo*. She saw Victorian hellholes, she saw dungeons with a tiny barred window up in the wall.

"What do you care?" he said. "You ran away, you got out of that and quite right too."

"I'm tired, Sean. I've got to go to sleep."

She crept into his arms, her naked body close up against his. The nights were starting to get cold. He slid his mouth over hers and entered her smoothly as if it were the natural next step. They were like that, locked together, when she woke up in the deep night and moved her body gently to arouse him again. He said sleepily that he loved her and she said, I love you too, Sean.

Next day wasn't the last one for picking the Coxes but Friday would be. Kevin said he was moving on before the end of the week and why didn't they follow him? They were advertising for unskilled hands at the Styrofoam packings works on an industrial estate ten miles away. Kevin thought he'd give it a go.

But Sean wasn't interested. He knocked off early, spruced himself up, put on a clean shirt and jeans, and went into town to apply for the supermarket job. Liza wasn't a bit surprised to hear he'd got it. They asked Kevin in to share a couple of bottles of wine. Kevin said his telly wasn't a patch on hers, it was wonderful, really, the way the colors came up so bright and the picture so sharp on a screen that size.

Liza said good-bye to the dog. She put her arms around it and its cold nose nuzzled her neck. It was a gentle mild creature. The feel of the fine skull and sleek black pelt under her lips reminded her once more of Heidi. It still made her indignant, thinking of how Mr. Tobias had simply ditched Heidi when he married Victoria, handed her over to Matt as if she were a piece of furniture he didn't need anymore.

She had still liked Mr. Tobias, but her affection for him had been shaken by his treatment of Heidi. To handle that she had blamed the changes in him on Victoria, as she guessed her mother did. It was Victoria who made him shoot things and Victoria who kept him away from Shrove.

Perhaps Victoria would die. Dogs died, so why not people? It was about this time that she began fantasizing how life would be if Mr. Tobias married Eve and they both went to live at Shrove House. Like children in books, she would have a father as well as a mother.

Sean was to start his job on Monday. They'd have to find somewhere else to put the caravan but before that he was going to take advantage of being on Vanner's land.

He often called her Teacher when she imparted information. This time, he said, he was going to teach her something. He'd teach her to drive.

She wouldn't be old enough to get a license till she was seventeen, which would be in January, but she could drive on the tracks around the orchards, that was private land. They picked the last row of trees on Friday morning and collected the last pay they would get. Then Sean got her up in the driving seat of the Dolomite and taught her how to start it and use the gears. It wasn't difficult.

"Like a duck to water," Sean said, very pleased.

She wanted to drive out onto the road and take them to wherever the new place they were going to park would be, but Sean said no. It wasn't worth the risk. They couldn't afford to pay fines. Reluctantly, Liza agreed.

"I suppose I can't risk the police getting hold of me."

"Anyway, it's against the law," Sean said very seriously.

She sat in the passenger seat next to him, eating Coxes. She'd filled a cardboard box with apples she'd picked up. Vanner was so mean he didn't even like the pickers taking home windfalls.

"You mind he don't put the fuzz on you," Sean said, but he laughed and she knew he was joking. Then he said, out of the blue, "Your mum, she ever try to get this Tobias away from his wife?"

"What made you suddenly ask that?"

"I reckon I was thinking about the cops and about them catching her and remembering you never said if he come back again after he had all them people there for the weekend."

"Well, she never did, no. At least, so far as I know she didn't. She didn't get a chance, did she, with him so far away and then we hadn't a phone or a car, we were trapped down there in a way."

"But wasn't that what she wanted?"

"Oh, yes, it was what she wanted. She wanted to be at Shrove and be undisturbed and isolated, but what she'd wanted most was to *own* Shrove. I think she gave up that idea when he got married. I mean, she gave it up for a while. It was very hard for her, she'd counted on it for so long, but she had to give it up. Of course, I don't know what went on in her mind, I was only a child, but I think she regretted a lot of things, she had bitter recriminations."

"Come again?"

"I mean she was sorry she hadn't behaved differently. You see, maybe if we'd gone to London with him when he first asked or gone traveling with him, he'd have got so close to her he'd have thought he couldn't live without her. It might only have been for a year or two and then we could have all come back to Shrove together. He and she were mad about each other then, I'm sure they were, like you and I are."

"That's true anyway," said Sean with a smile, looking pleased that she'd said it.

"But she wouldn't because of me. She was determined to bring me up without—well, the contamination of the world. I wasn't to be allowed to suffer as she'd suffered. If she'd gone to London with Mr. Tobias she'd have had to send me to school there and I'd have met other children and seen all sorts of things, I suppose. You could say she put me first or perhaps she just put Shrove first. The irony was that she lost Mr. Tobias because she put his house first. As for me, I'd have loved to live at Shrove House and have Jonathan Tobias for my father. You'll laugh but I used to think that if I lived there and it was mine I could get into that room."

Sean did laugh. "But he married someone else and that was the end of her love life."

"Oh, no, you could say it was the beginning of it. That was when Bruno came. Now that I'm grown up, I think I know what went through her mind. She thought, I've lost Jonathan, I can't waste my whole life mooning over him, so I might as well cut my losses and have a new lover. She was only a bit over thirty, Sean, she was young. She couldn't give up everything."

"How about that bathroom? Did he have it done?"

"In the end. Not for years. He forgot about it the minute Shrove was out of sight. He meant to do it but he just forgot, he was very thoughtless. When I think about it all now I really believe that when Shrove was out of sight he forgot about Eve too. She'd come into his mind once or twice a year and then he'd send her a postcard."

～

The place they found to park the caravan was a piece of waste ground at the point where a bridle path turned off a lane. No one used it much. People on horseback might notice they were there, but it could be weeks before whoever owned the land did. Law-abiding Sean had tried to find out who that was but had failed. The difficulty was that there was no water supply apart from the stream that tumbled over rocks under the stone bridge a little way up the lane. That was all right to drink, Liza told the dubious Sean. Mostly they'd boil it, anyway. They could get washed in the public swimming pool next to the supermarket he'd be working at. She was full of plans. Of much of the world she might be ignorant, but she knew how to *manage*.

The day he started she was left alone. Winter was coming and it had started to get cold. They heated the caravan with bottled gas and an oil heater, so that was all right, but for the first time in her life she had nothing to do.

It was rainy and cold out there, but she went out and walked along the public footpath down to the stream and over the bridge close by the ford. The leaves were falling now, gently and sadly dropping from the boughs because there was no wind. They floated down to make another layer on the wet slippery mass underfoot. Leaves coated the surface of the sluggish stream. The sky was gray and of a uniform unbroken cloudiness. She walked for miles along woodland paths and meadow edges, keeping the church tower always in sight so that she would know how to find her way back.

Once or twice she crossed a road, but she saw no one and no traffic passed her. A muntjac stag appeared under the trees, showed her his top-heavy antlers, and fled through the bracken. Jays called to one another to warn of her approach. She gathered all kinds of fungus but, in spite of her knowledge, feared to cook them and shed a trail of agarics and lepiotas as she walked. When it was about noon, according to her haphazard but usually accurate calculations, she made for home.

There, with no prospect of Sean coming home for four hours,

she was at a loss. Never before had she been without something to read. There was no paper in the caravan and nothing to write with, no means of playing music, no collections to pore over, no needles or thread to sew with. At last she turned on the television. An old Powell and Pressburger film with Wendy Hiller in it mystified her as such films had when the Shrove House set was available to her. Had such people ever existed, talked like that, dressed in those clothes? Or was it as much a fairy tale as Sheherezade?

When Sean came back she had fallen asleep. The television was still on and he got cross, saying she was wasting power. Next day she went with him into the town and applied for the job with Mrs. Spurdell.

✍

Liza said she was eighteen. She had no references because she had never worked for anyone before, but she knew all about housework. She had watched Eve and later on helped Eve.

The house in Aspen Close was a little like the house Bruno had wanted them all to live in. But inside was different. She had never before seen anything like this large, dull, ugly room carpeted and curtained in beige, with no pictures on the walls and no mirrors and, as far as she could see, no books. Flowers that could not be real, artificial white peonies and blue delphiniums and pink crysanthemums filled beige pottery bowls. Across the middle of a table and along the top of a cabinet lay pale green lace runners.

Mrs. Spurdell was the same color, except that her hair was white. Her fat body was squeezed into a pale green wool dress and underneath that, Liza thought, must be some kind of controlling rubber garment that made her shape so smooth, yet segmented and undulant. Like a plump caterpillar shortly to become a crysalis. The shoes she wore, shiny beige with high heels, looked as if they hurt her ankles, which bulged over the sides of them.

Liza was shy at first. If Mrs. Spurdell had been kind and friendly she might have found things easier, but this fat old woman with the surly expression made her speak abruptly and perhaps too precisely.

"You don't sound the sort of person I was looking for," Mrs. Spurdell was moved to say. "Frankly, you sound more as if you'd be off to university than looking for a daily's job."

Liza thought about that one. It gave her ideas but of course she didn't voice them. She said, "If I can work for you I'd do it properly."

Mrs. Spurdell sighed. "You'd better see the rest of the house. It might be too much for you."

"No, it wouldn't."

But Liza went upstairs with Mrs. Spurdell, walking behind her. The caterpillar waist and hips and the wobbly fat legs threatened to made her giggle, so she made herself think about sad things. The saddest thing she could contemplate was Eve in prison. Her thoughts flew to Eve and she experienced a moment or two of sharp fear.

Mrs. Spurdell's bedroom was all in pink. A white fluffy rabbit sat in the middle of the pink satin bed. Another bedroom was blue and a third a kind of peach color. Liza began to hope and hope she would get the job because there were so many things here she longed to look at more closely, to study and speculate about. Then Mrs. Spurdell took her into a room she said was Mr. Spurdell's study and Liza saw the books. There was a whole bookcase full of them. There was a box full of white paper on the

you early in the day and then later the same information comes up again in quite another context—Miami was on the television that evening. Not Miami, L.A., said Sean, but it looked the same to her. Probably, then, such places existed just as, in another program, the great castle called Caernarvon and the place called Oxford.

"Eve was there," she said, answering the bell that rang in her head.

"What was she doing there?"

"She was at a school. It's called a university. Mrs. Spurdell thought I was going to one, she said so."

"Your mum was at Oxford University?"

She was genuinely puzzled. "Why not?"

"Come on, love, she was having you on."

"No, I don't think so. She had to leave it, I don't know why, something to do with me being born."

Sean didn't say anymore, but she had the impression he wanted to, that he was struggling to say something but didn't know how to put it. At last he said, "I don't want to upset you."

"You won't."

"Well, then, d'you know who your dad was?"

Liza shook her head.

"Okay, sorry I asked."

"No, it's all right. It's just that she doesn't know, Eve doesn't know."

She could see that she had shocked him. The spraying bullets on the screen and the spurting blood didn't affect him, nor did the violated women or the bombs that flattened a city, but that Eve was ignorant of the identity of her child's father, that shook him to the core. He was bereft of speech. She put her arm around him and held him close.

"That's what she said, anyway." She tried to reassure him. "I've got my own ideas, though. I think I know who it was, whatever she said."

"Not that Bruno?"

"Oh, Sean. She didn't know Bruno till I was nine. Shall I go on telling you about him?"

"If you want." He said it gruffly.

"Well, then. He stayed and varnished the picture. He'd brought all the stuff with him in his bag. I didn't think Eve would let him do it but she did. I didn't think she'd speak to him but I was wrong there too. She asked him how he'd ever come to paint Shrove House and he said he'd seen it from the train.

"Not with the sun setting behind it you didn't, she said, you must have been looking eastward. Ah, but I could tell how wonderful it would be from the other side, he said, so I came down here one summer evening and made a start. I was here a good many summer evenings. I didn't see you, Eve said, and he said, I didn't see *you*. If I had I'd have been back sooner."

It was as if Sean hadn't heard a word since she said that about not knowing who her father was. "She must have had one bloke after another," he said, "one one night and another the next or even the same day. That's really disgusting. That's a terrible what-d'you-call-it to bring a child up in, especially a girl."

"Environment," she said. "Why especially a girl?"

"Oh, come on, Liza, it's obvious."

"Not to me," she said, and then, "Don't you want to hear about Bruno Drummond?"

THE second time he came, the important time, was the day Liza saw the death's-head moth. It was June.

He was thirty-one and lived in the town, in rooms over Mullins the greengrocer's. His father was dead but his mother was still alive up in Cheshire. Once he had had a wife but she had left him and was living in somewhere called Gateshead with a dentist.

Liza, who was listening to this, said, "What's a dentist?"

Bruno Drummond gave her the sort of look that meant he thought she was teasing him and said something about expecting she'd been to one of those a few times. But Mother said, "A kind of doctor who looks after your teeth."

The reason for his visit, he said, was to paint the valley with the train, and perhaps he had done some painting earlier, but he called at the gatehouse soon after ten in the morning, stayed to lunch, and was still there in the evening. Instead of a chair he sat on the floor. He related the story of his life.

"I should never have married," he said. "I don't believe in marriage but I allowed myself to be persuaded. Marriage is really the first step in getting swallowed up in the killing machine."

"What do you mean, the killing machine?" said Mother.

"Society, slavery, conformity, the poor ox that treads out the corn, walking round and round all day long, and muzzled too, most likely. I'm an anarchist. Now you'll say, what sort of an anarchist is it that marries and gets a civil service job to pay the mortgage? Not exactly a card-carrying one. My defense is that I got out of it after three years of hell."

"Were you really a civil servant?"

"On a low rung. Of course I'd been to art school. As a matter of fact, I was at the Royal College. When I was married I worked in the DSS benefit office in Shrewsbury."

"So how do you live now?"

"I paint, that's what I always wanted to do, but it's not lucrative. Then I paint houses too, rooms, that is. I'll tell you how I got into that. Someone, a woman, asked me what I did and I said, I paint, so she said, would you come and paint my dining room? I'd like to have spat in her face, the fool. But then I thought, well, why not? Beggars can't be choosers. And I've been doing it on a regular basis ever since—more or less, I'm opposed to regularity of any kind. I don't pay tax, I don't pay National Insurance. I suppose somewhere someone's got a record of me and keeps sending me demands to my old address. But they don't know where I am, no one does but my mother, even my ex-wife doesn't. That's freedom and the price I pay is relatively small."

"What price is that?" said Mother.

"Never having any money."

"Yes, that's freedom," said Mother. "Some would call it a very high price."

"Not me. I'm different."

Bruno played his guitar after that and sang the Johnny Cash song about finding freedom on the open road and men refusing to do what they were told. Liza could tell Mother liked him, she was looking at him the way she had sometimes looked at Mr. Tobias. Perhaps she liked his voice and the way he pronounced words, unlike the way anyone else did. Liza remembered Hugh with the beard, his fuzzy cheeks and upper lips. Bruno looked as if no hair had ever or could ever grow on his smooth girlish face.

In the summer the solanum plant that climbed over the back of the gatehouse showed its blue flowers at Liza's window. Mother called it the flowering potato because it and potatoes and tomatoes all belonged to the same family. When she came up to bed that evening Liza knelt on the bed up at the window and saw, a few inches from her eyes, the death's-head moth, immobile and with its wings spread flat, on one of the solanum leaves.

The moth book had told her *Acherontia atropos* likes to feed on potato leaves. It also told her how rare a visitor to the British Isles this moth is. But she was in no doubt about it, this was no Privet Hawk. No other moth had that clear picture of a skull on its back between its forewings, a pale yellowish death's-head with black eyeholes and a domed forehead. This was the moth Drechsler had put into his painting, the one at Shrove on whose frame the key was kept.

She knew Mother would want to see it too. Mother might be quite cross, at the very least disappointed, if she didn't tell her about *Acherontia* outside the window. She went down and opened the door. Bruno was softly twanging his guitar and they each had a glass of red wine. They didn't look very busy, but Mother said she couldn't come now, Liza ought to be in bed, and if it really was a death's-head moth it would no doubt reappear the next day.

But the next morning it was gone, never to be seen again. Because she had found Mr. Tobias in Mother's bed after just such an evening, with wine and food and enjoyment, she expected to see Bruno there in the morning. She was older now, she approached the door more tentatively and pushed it open with care. Mother was alone and when Liza went to the window she saw that the little orange car was gone.

The day gone by, the first time Mother had been indifferent to the things she cared for, she called the Day of the Death's-head.

It was over a week before they saw Bruno again and that was the day Mother went into the town on the bus. She had a list with her, and most of the items on it were the kind of things you bought at a fruit and vegetable shop. Liza had seen pictures in a baby's book when she was little. A greengrocer's was the correct word, Mother said.

"Can I come?"

Mother shook her head.

"All right, but I don't want to be left here in my bedroom. It's boring."

"You can go in the library or the morning room at Shrove if you prefer that. It's up to you."

"The morning room."

Because it was much lighter and from the windows you could see the trains go by, Mother must have thought. Or because the famous people from history were there in their glass case. Perhaps, though, she was thinking about Bruno Drummond, and not about Liza at all.

After Mother had gone and she had seen a train going south and had studied once more the wedding photograph of Mr. Tobias in a sleek dark suit and Mrs. Tobias in a large hat and spotted dress, she drew aside the curtain to reveal the stepladder. It was just as she had left it.

She carried it across the room and set it up close beside the picture of the flowers and the death's-head moth. She took great care to press down the top step, which would lock the ladder and make it safe. It was possible, of course, that the key was no longer there. Mother had been in this room many times since Liza had seen her place it on top of the picture frame and it was a wonder she had never come upon the hidden steps. Climb up and find out.

The key was there. Liza jumped down, unlocked the door, and opened it. She stood in front of the box thing with the window on the front and studied it. There were knobs and switches underneath the window, rather like the knobs and switches on Mother's electric stove. Liza pressed or turned them one after another but nothing happened.

She understood about electricity. Their old heater wouldn't work unless it was plugged into the point and the switch pressed down. Here the plug was in but the point not switched on. She pressed the switch down. Still nothing. Try the routine of pressing or turning all those knobs and switches.

When she turned the largest knob nothing happened but

when she pushed it in a buzzing sound came out of the box and, to her extreme astonishment, a point of light appeared in the window. The light expanded, shivering, and gradually a picture began to form, gray and white and dark gray, the colors of the etchings on the morning room walls, but recognizably a picture.

And not a still picture, as an etching was, but moving and happening, like life. There were people, of about her own age, not speaking but dancing to music. Liza had heard the music before, she could even have said what it was, something called *Swan Lake* by Tchaikovsky.

Briefly, she was afraid. The people moved, they danced, they threw their legs high in the air, they were manifestly real, yet not real. She had taken a step backward, then another, but now she came closer. The children continued to dance. One girl came to the center of the stage and danced alone, spinning around with one leg held out high behind her. Liza looked around the back of the box. It was just a box, black with ridges and holes and more switches.

A lot of print, white on black and gray, came up on the window, then a face, then—most alarming of all—a voice. The first words Liza ever heard come out of a television set she could never remember. She was too overawed by the very idea of a person being in there and speaking. She was very nearly stunned.

But that feeling gradually passed. She was afraid, she was shocked, she was filled with wonder, then she was pleased, gratified, she began to *enjoy* it. She sat down cross-legged on the floor and gazed, enraptured. An old man and a dog were going for a walk in a countryside very like the one she knew. Sometimes the old man stopped and talked and his face got very large so that she could see all the furrows in his face and his white whiskers. Next there was a woman teaching another woman to cook something. They mixed things up in a bowl, eggs and sugar and flour and butter, and no more than two minutes later, when the first woman opened the oven door, she lifted out the baked cake, all dark and shiny and risen high. It was magic. It was the magic Liza had read about in fairy stories.

She watched for an hour. After the cooking came a dog driving sheep about on a hillside, then a man with a lot of glass bottles and tubes and a chart on the wall, not one word of which she could understand. She went into the morning room to look at the clock. Mother couldn't get back before five and it was ten past four now. Liza sat down on the floor again and watched a lot of drawings like book illustrations moving about, a cat and a mouse and a bear in the woods. She watched a man telling people the names of the stars in the sky and another one talking to a boy who had built a train engine. If it had been possible, she could have watched all night. But if Mother came back and caught her she would never be able to watch it again, for she had intuited that the door was kept locked because Mother didn't want her to watch it at all.

At five minutes to five, most reluctantly, she turned off the set by pulling toward her the knob she had pushed in and switched off the plug at the point. She locked the door and climbed up the steps to put the key back on the top of the picture frame. It was just as well she started when she did. Carrying the steps back to hide them behind the curtains, she saw through the first window Mother coming up the drive toward the house and Bruno Drummond with her.

～

They were early because he had brought Mother back in his car. Liza wasn't much interested in him that evening. Her head was full of what she had seen on, or through or by means of, the window on that box. She wondered what it was, how it did what it did, and if there was only one like it in the world, the one at Shrove, or if there were others. For instance, did Mr. and Mrs. Tobias have one in London? Did Caroline have one in France and Claire have one wherever it was she lived? Did Matt and Heidi, Mr. Frost and the builders? Did *everyone?*

There was nobody to ask. Why was it bad for her to see? Would it hurt her? Her eyes, her ears? They felt all right. It was strange to think of Mother knowing all about this magic and never saying, to think of Bruno Drummond knowing too, very probably having one of his own at home over the green-grocer's shop.

Why didn't they have one in the gatehouse? There was no one she could ask. She was so quiet that evening, hardly saying a word throughout the meal—which Bruno stayed for—that Mother asked her if she was feeling all right.

After she had gone to bed, she heard them go out of the front door. She got up and looked out of the window she used only to be able to reach by standing on a chair. She didn't need the chair now. They were going into the little castle. Mother unlocked the front door and they went inside. It reminded her of the dogs and when they used to live in there and she was suddenly sad. She would much rather have had Heidi and Rudi in there than Bruno Drummond. Without knowing why, she didn't like him much.

They didn't stay long in the little castle and soon she heard Bruno's car depart, but he was back next day with paints and canvas and brushes and a thing he called an easel. The easel he set up on the edge of the water meadow and began painting a picture of the bridge. Liza stood watching him while Mother did her cleaning at Shrove.

He disliked her being there, she could sense that, she could sense waves of coldness coming at her. Bruno looked sweet and gentle, he looked kind, but she guessed he wasn't really like that. People might not always be the way their faces proclaimed them to be.

Mother was watching her from the window, "keeping an eye on you," and she smiled and waved, so Liza didn't see why she shouldn't watch *him* as he mixed up his colors from those interesting tubes of paint and then laid thick white and blue all over the canvas. She came quite close till she was nearly touching his arm. The cold waves got very strong. Bruno stirred his brush round and round in swirls through the whitish-blue mixture and said, "Don't you have anything to play with?"

"I'm too old to play," said Liza.

"That's a matter of opinion. You can't be more than nine. Don't you have a doll?" His voice was like the voices that came out of the box in the locked room.

"If you don't want me looking at you I'll go and read my French book."

She went into Shrove House but, instead of reading her book, made her way upstairs to the Venetian Room, where there was a picture she thought might look like Bruno. Or he look like it. And she had been right. It was a pious saint in the painting, kneeling in some rocky desert place, his hands clasped in prayer, a gold halo around his head. Liza sat on the gondolier's bed and stared at the picture. Bruno was just like that saint, even to his long silky brown hair, his eyelashes, and his folded lips that had a holy look. The saint's rapt eyes were fixed on something invisible in the clouds above his head.

Bruno wore two gold earrings in one ear and the saint none. That was the only difference between them as far as appearance went. Liza took her book of fairy tales onto the terrace on the garden front and sat reading it in the sunshine.

He was much nicer to her when Mother was there. She soon noticed that. They all had lunch together and he said it was amazing, seeing her reading French fairy tales. "Like a native," he said. "You've got a bright one there, Mother. What do they say about her at school?"

Mother passed over that one and said nothing about Bruno calling her "Mother." They talked about the possibility of Bruno having his studio in the little castle and Mother explained what a studio was. Liza wasn't sure she liked the idea of Bruno being next door all day long.

"It belongs to Mr. Tobias," she said.

"I shall write to Mr. Tobias," Mother said, "and ask if Bruno can become his tenant."

But whether Mr. Tobias said yes or no, Liza never discovered, for it was into their house, the gatehouse, that Bruno moved. It happened no more than a fortnight later. He moved into the gatehouse and went to sleep in Mother's bedroom.

Unlike Heather, he never complained about the lack of a bathroom. Washing, he said, was bourgeois. Liza looked up the word in Dr. Johnson's dictionary, which was the only dictionary in the Shrove library, but there was nothing between "bounce" and "to bouse," which meant to drink too much. Guesswork told her that "bourgeois" was probably the opposite of "anarchist."

The little castle had a north light, which Bruno said was good for artists. Good or not, he never seemed to go in there very much, though he filled it up with his things, stacks and stacks of canvases and frames as well as brushes and jars and dirty paint rags. And he never went to town, painting people's houses.

It was at this time that Liza stopped going into Mother's

bedroom in the morning. Once she had gone in, having first knocked on the door, but even so had found Bruno on top of Mother, kissing her mouth, his long brown curly hair hiding her face. Liza felt heat run up into her face and burn her cheeks, she didn't know why. She retreated in silence.

Her life had changed. She was never again to be quite as happy as she had been in those early years. A cloud had come halfway across her sun and partially eclipsed it. Until Bruno came she had sometimes been alone and enjoyed aloneness, but now she knew what it was to be lonely.

Her consolation was the television set at Shrove. She found out what it was called from Bruno. Not that she told him what she watched up at the house whenever she got the chance. It was he who asked Mother why they hadn't got one.

"I can bring mine over from the flat," he said. "The flat" meant his rooms over the greengrocer's.

Mother said, no thank you very much, that was something they could happily do without. He could go home and watch his own, if that was what he wanted. You know what I want, he said, looking at Mother as the saint looked at the clouds.

More often alone and often lonely, Liza found it easy to go to Shrove more or less when she liked. She grew adept at climbing up for the key and hiding the steps. But—and she had no idea why—Mother had grown reluctant to lock her in anywhere since Bruno came. She had the run of the house now and carried the steps back and forth between the library and the morning room. Aged ten, she discovered to her astonishment and pleasure that she no longer needed the steps. She had grown. Like Mother, she could reach the key by mounting a chair and standing on the cabinet.

When Mother sat by Bruno while he painted, she watched

television. On the rare occasions that Bruno took Mother out in the car, she watched television. From the television she began to learn about the world out there.

It was Bruno who put into her head the idea that it was time she saw the reality for herself.

She sat in the back of the little orange car. Mother was in the passenger seat next to Bruno, and Liza could tell by the rigidity of her shoulders and the stiffness of her neck how deeply opposed to this outing she still was. She had allowed Bruno and Liza herself to win her over.

Bruno had said, "I'm being quite selfish about this, Mother. Maybe you'll think I'm being brutally honest but the fact is I want to take you out and about and to do that we have to take the kid with us." He always called her "the kid" just as he always called Mother "Mother" when Liza was being discussed. "Taking her into town'll be a start. Get her into that and next we can all have a day out." He whispered the next bit but Liza heard. "I'm not saying I wouldn't rather be on our own if there's any option."

"I can't keep going out, anyway," Mother said. "I haven't got time. For one thing, Liza has to have her lessons."

"That kid ought to go to school."

"I thought you were an anarchist," said Mother.

"Anarchists aren't against education. They're all in favor of the right sort of education."

"Liza is getting the right sort. If you set her beside other children of her age, she'd be so far ahead, she would be years in advance of them, it would be laughable."

"She ought to be in school for social reasons. How's she going to learn to interact with other people?"

"My mother interacted with other people and she died a miserable disappointed woman in a rented room in her sister's house. I interacted with other people and look what happened to me. I want Liza kept pure, I want her untouched, and most of all I want her *happy*. 'A violet by a mossy stone, half-hidden from the eye.' "

Bruno made a face. "I ask myself what's going to happen to that kid. How's she going to earn her living? Who's she going to have relationships with?"

"I earn my living," said Mother. "*I* have what you call 'relationships,' horrid word. She will be me, but without the pain and the damage. She will be me as I might have been, happy and innocent and good, if I had been allowed to stay here."

"All that aside," said Bruno, who liked arguments only when he was winning them, "I still think she ought to come into town with us, Mother, for her own good."

And eventually Mother had agreed. Just for this once. She could come for once.

Nothing happened for a while that Liza hadn't expected. There was the lane and then the bridge, the village, and at last the bigger road. Cars passed them and once they overtook a car, a very slow one because Bruno's orange cardboard car couldn't go fast. Most of the things Liza saw she had seen before or else seen them on television, if not in color. It was different in the town, mainly because there were so many people. The number of people staggered her so, she was afraid.

Bruno put the car in a car park where hundreds were already parked. Liza couldn't believe there were so many cars in the world. She walked along in silence between Mother and Bruno and, to her own surprise, scarcely aware of doing it, she took Mother's hand. The people clogged the pavement, they were everywhere: walking fast, dawdling, chatting to each other, standing still in conversation, running, dragging along small children or pushing them in chairs on wheels. You had to take care not to bump into them. Some smoked cigarettes, like on the television, and you smelled them as they passed. Quite a lot were eating things out of bags.

Liza stared. She would have liked to sit on the low wall outside that building Mother said was a church and just watch the people. Most of them in her eyes were ugly and awkward, fat or crooked, grotesque or semisavage. They compelled her gaze, but as a toad might or a frightening picture in a book, with horrified fascination.

"How beauteous mankind is!" said Mother in the special voice she put on when she was saying something from a book. "O, brave new world that has such people in it." The laugh she gave was a nasty one as if she hadn't meant those words seriously.

As for a brave new world, Liza thought most of the shops nasty and boring. There were clothes in one window, magazines in another. The flowers in the flower shop weren't as nice as those at Shrove. The places that interested her most were the shop with four boxes like the one in the locked room at Shrove in its window, four blank screens, and the one that was full of books, but new ones with bright pictures on their covers.

She wanted to go in that shop but Mother wouldn't let her, nor was she allowed inside the one that sold newspapers, though Bruno was sent in there to buy a tape of Mozart's horn concertos. They went to the greengrocer's and bought fruit, then through a side door and upstairs to where Bruno used to live. It smelled so nasty in there, like the kitchen at Shrove after the Tobiases and their guests had gone and as if things had been left to go bad, that Liza started to cough.

Mother opened the windows. They collected some stuff of Bruno's, which he packed into a case, and then he picked up off the doormat the heap of letters that had come for him while he was away. For a man whose whereabouts no one knew he got a lot of letters.

Looking about her, Liza began to understand what Mother had meant when she said those things about most places being horrible. She wrinkled up her nose. Bruno's flat was very horrible, dirty and uncomfortable, with nothing in it that looked as if it had been cared for, every piece of furniture bruised or broken, the windows blue-filmed and with dead flies squashed against the panes. The only books were on the floor, in disorderly heaps.

She was glad to get out again, and said so, even though being out meant once more avoiding bumping into people. There seemed more of them than ever and a good many were of her own age or a bit older. They had come out of school, said Bruno with a meaningful look at Mother, school stopped each day at three-thirty.

Liza had never seen children before. Well, except on the television, that is. She had never seen a real person who was less than in his or her twenties. She took back what she had thought about all mankind being ugly. These people weren't. There was a boy with a black face and a girl she thought might be Indian with deep-set dark eyes and a long black pigtail. She wondered how it would be to talk to them.

Then a boy walking along in front of her stuck out his leg and tripped up the boy beside him so that the second one staggered and nearly fell into the road in front of an oncoming car and a girl screamed and another one started shouting. Liza felt herself shrink back against Mother and hold on to her hand more tightly. She had realized what was making her feel dizzy: the noise.

Once she had turned up the sound on the television by mistake. It was like that here, a continuous meaningless roar of sound, interspersed with the squeals of brakes, music that wasn't real music strumming out of car windows, the peep-peep-peep of the pedestrian signal at a traffic light crossing, the revving up of engines. As they made their way back to the car park, a siren started up. Bruno told her it was the siren on a police car and he said the sound it made was supposed to imitate a woman screaming.

"Oh, it can't be, Bruno," Mother said. "Where on earth did you get that from?"

"It's a fact. You ask anyone. They invented it in the States and we copied it. That's supposed to be the sound that most gets under people's skins, a woman screaming."

"Well, don't talk about it to me, please," Mother said, so loudly and sharply, that one of the ugly people turned to stare at her. "I don't want to hear. It just expresses the worst side of men."

"All right, all right," said Bruno. "Sorry I spoke. Please excuse me for living. Will madam condescend to accept a lift home, her and her charming, courteous offspring?"

As soon as she was in the car Liza fell asleep. She was exhausted. The people and the noise and the newness of it all had worn her out. At home she lay on the sofa and slept, though not so deeply that she failed to hear Mother tell Bruno she had told him so, Liza hadn't liked it, it had been too much for her and no wonder. Wasn't it a horrible place, a travesty of what a country town should be and once had been, noisy, dirty, and tawdry?

"She wouldn't feel that way if you hadn't sheltered her from everything the way you have."

"I feel it and God knows I haven't been sheltered."

"You know what you'll do, don't you, Mother? You'll turn the kid psychotic. Or maybe schizophrenic, one of those what-d'you-call-its."

"Talk about what you understand, Bruno, why don't you?"

With half an eye open, she thought they would start quarreling again. They were always quarreling. But instead they did what often impeded or ended their quarrels. Their eyes met, they reached for each other and began kissing, the kind of kissing that soon got out of hand, so that they were grappling and climbing all over each other, grunting and moaning. Liza turned over and squeezed her eyes tightly shut.

In the days that followed she felt unwell, what Bruno called "under the weather," something unusual for her. She remembered the town and its people not with longing or nostalgia, but with revulsion. The peace of Shrove and its lands was more than usually pleasurable. She lay in the long grass and the cow parsley, watching the insect life moving among the mysterious green stems and the nodding seed heads, saw a raspberry-winged cinnabar moth climbing a ragwort stalk. There was no sound but the occasional heavy hum of a bumble bee passing overhead.

A week after their day out in the town she became ill with chicken pox.

H ADN'T you had any of those things, measles and what-ever?"

"I'd had some immunizations when I was a baby. I got chicken pox because I hadn't built up any natural immunity. I'd never been with people."

"Did the doctor come?"

"Eve phoned him from Shrove. He said he'd come if I got worse but otherwise there was nothing to be done but let it take its course. I wasn't very bad. Eve was strict about scratching. She said if I scratched my face she'd tie my hands up, so I didn't except for one awful big spot on my forehead."

Liza pulled back a lock of dark hair and showed him the small round hole on her left temple. "She was afraid of me getting those all over."

"I know you didn't," said Sean, giving her a sidelong sexy look.

"No, nothing like that. All that happened was that I gave Bruno shingles."

"You what?"

"The virus or whatever you call it, it makes chicken pox in children and shingles in grown-ups. It's the same thing. Eve didn't catch anything, but Bruno caught shingles."

"My grandma had that. She had it around her middle and she was dead scared because if it meets around your waist you die. That's a fact."

Liza doubted it but she didn't say so. "He got it on the side of his face and down the back of his neck. He was quite ill and he looked quite ugly with all that red on his face. I thought he disliked me because I gave him shingles, that was the way I reasoned when I was ten. But if he hadn't made me go into town with them I wouldn't have caught chicken pox and couldn't have given him shingles, so it was his fault, really. That was how I saw it. Of course now I know it wasn't that at all. I was in the way, I was a nuisance, I came between him and Eve."

Now she was more or less grown-up herself and sexually involved, Liza could understand what had held Eve and Bruno together. She hadn't understood at the time. It puzzled her and made her increasingly uneasy that two people could quarrel so much, could behave as if they hated each other, but still seem to need each other's company in a hungry way.

She was aware too of something else. There was something Bruno wanted to do with her mother that he couldn't do unless Liza wasn't there. It was to do with the kissing and struggling and lying on top of Mother. Liza knew and had known for some time the facts of human and animal reproduction, Eve had taken care to educate her in these matters, but for some reason she never connected them with what Bruno wanted to do with Mother. And what, though less urgently, Mother wanted to do with Bruno. She didn't understand and she shied away from understanding. All she knew was that Bruno wanted her out of the house as much as she could feasibly be out of it and that Mother to some lesser extent went along with this.

Without saying a word as to her destination, she went up to Shrove and watched the television in the once-locked room. It was always in late mornings and early afternoons that she watched it. Old films were what she saw and nature programs, productions for schools and the Open University, chat shows and quiz games. Some of the programs came from America. They taught her that Bruno was an Englishman who for some reason put on a half-American voice.

When he was well again things got worse. It was late summer and fine weather and he took Mother out in the car every day. Liza could have gone with them, Mother was always suggesting it now as enthusiastically as she had once vetoed it, but Liza wouldn't. She remembered the day in town with a kind of horror, as if the experience had been inextricably entangled with police sirens and scratching and chicken pox. So Mother and Bruno went and she stayed behind alone, often doing no more than sitting outside on the gatehouse wall or lying in the grass wondering what would happen to her if Bruno prevailed and she was sent away.

More than once he had mentioned sending her to something called boarding school. Mother said she had a lot of money when she bought his picture but now, she said, she had none and boarding schools cost a lot. Liza clung to this. Mother had no money and Bruno had no money and no prospect of getting any. Bruno himself would never go, she was sure of that with the pessimism of a ten-year-old who believes that good things never last and bad things go on forever. He was a bad thing that would never change, he was the hated third in their household, with as permanent a place in their lives as the balsam tree and the train.

Two things happened that autumn. Bruno's mother fell ill, very ill, and Mother heard on her radio that British Rail intended to stop running the train through the valley.

The first time Mrs. Spurdell went out, Liza took the opportunity to have a bath. It was ten o'clock in the morning. The bath was a muddy beige color and the bathroom carpet grass-green and beige in little squares, but the water was hot. The soap smelled of sweet peas. When she had finished she cleaned the bathroom thoroughly, washing down and polishing all the tilework.

Mrs. Spurdell had been rather reluctant to leave the house. Liza hadn't much experience of human behavior, but even she could tell Mrs. Spurdell thought she would come back and find her cleaner gone and the video, microwave, and silver with her. She nearly laughed out loud at Mrs. Spurdell's face when her employer came in the back door to find her sitting at the kitchen table polishing that same silver. That was the first occasion on which Liza got a cup of coffee in the house in Aspen Close.

While they were together Mrs. Spurdell talked most of the time. Her conversation was primarily concerned with demonstrating her superiority and that of her husband and grown-up daughters to almost everyone else, but particularly to her employee. This was an ascendancy in the areas of social distinction, intellect, wordly success, and money, but principally of material possessions. Mrs. Spurdell's possessions were more expensive and of better quality than those of other people, more had been paid for them initially, and they lasted longer. This applied to her engagement ring, a massive stack of diamonds, the allegedly Georgian silver, the Wilton carpets, the Colefax and Fowler curtains, and the Parker-Knoll armchairs, among many other things. Liza had to be taught these names, shown these objects, and instructed in how to examine them for evidence of their worth. She was adjured to be very careful of all of them, with the exception of the engagement ring, which never left Mrs. Spurdell's finger. The finger was so grossly swollen above and below the ring that Liza doubted if it would come off.

The husband and the children couldn't be demonstrated, but they could be talked about and photographs produced. After that first cup of coffee, reward for not decamping with the precious artifacts, a mid-morning refreshment session became the regular thing. Liza was told about Jane, who was an educationalist after having got several degrees, and about Philippa, a solicitor married to a solicitor, and erstwhile top law student of her year, now mother of twins so beautiful that she was constantly approached by companies making television commercials for the chance of using their faces in advertising, offers which she indignantly refused. Liza listened, memorizing the unfamiliar expressions.

Mr. Spurdell, said his wife, was a schoolmaster. Liza thought they were called teachers, that was what Bruno had called them and Sean called them, but Mrs. Spurdell said her husband was a schoolmaster and a head of department, whatever that was.

"At an independent school," she explained, "not one of these comprehensives, I wouldn't want you to think that."

Liza, who was incapable of thinking anything about schools, merely smiled. She never said much. She was learning.

"He could have been a headmaster many times over but he

isn't one for the limelight. Of course there is family money, otherwise he might have been forced to take a higher position."

A fresh set of photographs came out, Jane in gown and mortarboard, Philippa with the twins. The impression was subtly conveyed that their mother was prouder—and fonder—of Philippa because she had a husband and children. Liza preferred Jane, who hadn't any lipstick on and wasn't simpering. She was longing for Mrs. Spurdell to get up and say she was going out so that she could have another bath. It wasn't easy managing in the caravan, and the swimming pool was expensive besides leaving you smelling of chlorine.

At last Mrs. Spurdell put the photographs away and prepared to go out. The weather was colder today and it was a different coat she had put on, of a thick hairy stone-colored cloth with lapels and cuffs of glossy brown fur. Liza was told that this coat had been bought twenty years ago—"in the days when no one had these ridiculous ideas about not wearing fur"—and had cost the then-enormous sum of sixty pounds. She had to feel the quality of the cloth and stroke the fur. It simply refused to wear out, said Mrs. Spurdell with a little laugh, tying her white hair up in a scarf with "Hermès" written all over it. Liza wondered what a silk scarf had to do with the Messenger of the Gods.

She went without her bath. On her way to run it she paused at the doorway of Mr. Spurdell's study. This was a room she wasn't supposed to touch beyond vacuum cleaning the floor, for his books were sacred, never to be dusted, and the papers on his desk inviolate. But Liza was alone in the house now and Mrs. Spurdell would no more know she had been in there than she knew the purpose for which her hot water was often used.

Once or twice she had taken fleeting looks at the bookshelves while pushing the vacuum cleaner about, but she had never examined them thoroughly. Now she did. They were of a very different kind from those in the library at Shrove. Here were no eighteenth-century works on travel and exploration, no theology, philosophy, or history, no essays from the eighteen-hundreds, no poetry of a century before that, no tomes of Darwin and Lyell, and no Victorian literature. Mr. Spurdell's fiction came in the form of paperbacks.

These shelves carried the kind of books Liza had never seen before. Accounts of people's lives, they seemed to be, and she recognized the names of some of their subjects: Oscar Wilde, Tolstoy, Elizabeth Barrett Browning. But who was Virginia Woolf and who was Orwell? Apart from these, there were books about how writers wrote what they wrote, or as far as she could gather they were about that, one called *The Common Pursuit* and another *The Unquiet Grave*. Liza sat down at Mr. Spurdell's desk and leafed through his books, wondering how it was that she understood so little of what she read yet passionately wanted to understand.

Time passed quickly when she was occupied like this. It always went very fast while Mrs. Spurdell was out, but this time it seemed to fly by. Reluctantly, she had to stop reading because she needed at least ten minutes to look at the papers on the desk and there was no chance of Mrs. Spurdell being out for more than an hour and a half. It was lucky she could do the housework in half the time allowed for it.

The papers were essays. She could tell that much. They had names written along the tops of the first pages, of their authors presumably. It took the minimum of detective work to infer that these were pupils of Mr. Spurdell's. He had gone through the pages with a red pen, correcting the spelling and making acid comments. Some of these made Liza laugh. What interested her most, though, were the pieces of yellow paper he had stuck to the first page of each. These were small paper squares of a kind she had never seen before and which had a sticky area on them that you could nevertheless peel off. She tried this carefully and then to her satisfaction re-stuck it.

Each yellow square had something different written on it in Mr. Spurdell's writing. One said, "Should get at least an A and a B," another, "Doubtful university material," and a third, "Oxbridge?" Liza had heard of Oxford and of Cambridge but not of that place. She had to stop at this point, it would be awful to jeopardize her future chances by letting Mrs. Spurdell catch her snooping. The papers replaced exactly as she had found them, she grabbed the vacuum cleaner and was removing white hairs from the master bedroom carpet when the front door opened and closed.

In a little while Mrs. Spurdell came lumbering up the stairs and into the bedroom to hang up the precious coat. Liza moved along, back into the study, only to clean the carpet of course, but while she was there she wondered if she dared borrow a book. Would he know if one was missing? If one was missing for just two days? She would very much like to read the life of Elizabeth Barrett Browning. When she first met Sean she had read the "Sonnets from the Portuguese" and memorized several of them. ("How do I love thee? Let me count the ways.") Putting herself into Mr. Spurdell's shoes—a pair of them, slippers really, sat side by side under the desk—she decided that, yes, she would know if a book of hers was missing. If she had any books, if only she had.

Mrs. Spurdell paid her for her morning's work. She always did this grudgingly and very slowly, choosing from the wad in her handbag the oldest and most crumpled five-pound notes, never handing over a ten. The rest of the sum she made up in small change, twenty- and ten-pence coins and even twos. This time she was worse than ever, giving Liza a whole seven pounds in fifty pees and tens and fives and keeping her waiting while she went off somewhere to hunt for a fiver. Eventually she came back with it, a worn and withered note that had been torn in half and stuck together with tape.

The secondhand bookshop took it. Liza had been worried they wouldn't when she handed it over in payment for three shabby paperbacks she had found among a row of others on a trestle outside. The real bookshop, the proper one in which everything sold was new, was far beyond her means.

It was nearly five-thirty and Superway would be closing. She walked along the High Street and across the marketplace. Soon it would get dark, they would soon put the clocks back, and the chill of evening was already apparent. Was it cold in prison? She thought about Eve in the prison, she often did, she thought about her every day, but she never said any of this to Sean.

He was waiting for her outside the main entrance with a carrier bag full of food. Superway encouraged employees to buy the products that had reached their sell-by date and at a very reduced price. Liza and Sean walked together to the car. He told her what he'd got for their supper and then he wanted to know what was in her bag. She showed him *Middlemarch*, a *Life of Mary Wollstonecraft*, and Aubrey's *Brief Lives*, and saw at once the displeasure in his face.

"We can't afford to spend money on books."

"It's my money," she said. "I earned it."

"I wonder what you'd say, Liza, if I said that when you wanted me to get your food."

She was silent. He had spoken reproachfully and like a middle-aged person. Mr. Spurdell would talk like that, she thought.

"You've got telly," he said. "I don't know why you need books as well."

She got his supper and while he watched his favorite serial, she started reading *Middlemarch*. A good many Victorian girls must have lived very much as she had, being educated at home, knowing no one but the nearest neighbors, sheltered from everything. With Dorothea Brooke she could identify, though society wouldn't have allowed Dorothea a Sean.

Now that his program was over, she was aware that he kept glancing uneasily at her. He would have to get used to it, she thought. He would have to get used to her being more and more preoccupied with books. It came back to her, as her concentration weakened under his gaze, that Bruno had never much liked her mother reading. He had done all kinds of things to capture her attention, walking about, pacing the room, even whistling. Sometimes he had sat down beside her and taken her hand or stroked the side of her face. Liza remembered her mother jumping up on one of these occasions, shaking him off, and shouting at him to leave her alone.

It was soon after this that Bruno had gone away to be with his sick mother. He had gone on the day the last train ran through the valley.

Liza hadn't known it would be the last train. How could she? She never saw a newspaper and she could never watch television at the times the news was on. It was a fine warm day in October, just over six years ago and a year before the hurricane. The blackberries were over and the crabapples were ripe. Liza went down through the meadows and along the hedges looking for crabapples to make into jelly. You boiled the apples, then strained them through a cloth tied to the four legs of an upturned stool before adding the sugar. She had seen Mother do it many times and thought it was time she tried.

Before she had picked a single apple, before she had even found a tree, she saw the people lined up along the railway line. She thought she was dreaming, she closed her eyes and opened them again. Never in her life had she seen so many people all at once except on television and that didn't count. There must have been hundreds. They stood along the railway embankment, on both sides of the line, between the boundary of the Shrove land and the little station that was called Ring Valley Halt, and each one of them was holding a big placard.

From where she was Liza couldn't read what was on the placards. She forgot about crabapples and jelly, stuffed the big plastic bag she was carrying into her pocket, and ran down the field path toward the river.

Some of the placards said, SAVE OUR RAILWAY, and others, FOR BR READ USSR and LAST TRAIN TO CHAOS. On the far side a group of people were holding a long banner with WILL BR CARE WHEN WE MISS THE TRAIN? on it. Liza sensed something was going to happen, though she couldn't tell what. Besides, the sight of so many people fascinated her, there were more than on that day in town, there were more than in the film she'd seen about Ancient Rome.

Reserved by conditioning if not by nature, she considered concealing herself in the bushes to watch. She didn't want to talk to anyone, talking to strangers was something she was beginning to find hard, she met so few. It had been a dry autumn and the river was low, at this point just a broad sheet of shallow water trickling and splashing over boulders. While on this side she couldn't talk to anyone, but even as she thought that, she had her shoes and socks off and was wading across.

It was too late to hide. They all seemed to be looking at her. Before she could pretend to be merely taking a walk, a woman had grabbed her by the arm and, evidently mistaking her for some other child, asked where on earth she had been and to take hold of this banner at once.

It was a replica of the one on the other side and it took four

people to hold it up. Liza did as she was told and held on to the
bit above the letters BR. A man was to the left of her and a boy
to the right. Both of them said hi and the boy said, did she live
around here? Up in one of the cottages, Liza said, you couldn't
quite see from here, but only half a mile away.

"On your own doorstep, then," the man said. "Your family
use the train a lot, do they? Or should I say, did they?"

"Every day," Liza said.

It wasn't the first lie she had ever told. She'd been telling lies
regularly to Mother about where she'd been when she'd really
been watching television.

"They take it for granted everyone's got a car," the man said.
"Has your dad got a car?"

The woman on the other side of him said, "Sexist. Why not
ask if her mum's got one? Women are allowed to drive here, you
know. We're not talking about Saudi Arabia."

Liza was just saying they hadn't got a car—she didn't count
Bruno's—and thinking of saying she hadn't got a dad, when the
train whistle sounded on the far side of the tunnel. It always
whistled going into the tunnel and coming out of it, it was a
single-line track and maybe there was a remote possibility of
another train meeting it in the dark and going headlong into it.
There wouldn't be any more such possibilities, however.

"The last train ever," the man said. "The last poor bloody
train."

When it came out of the tunnel and whistled again some of
the people cheered. Liza could hardly believe her eyes when
the four people holding the banner on the other side and three
others with placards all began climbing down the embankment
toward the line. The seven, four men and three women, took
up their positions right across the line, in the path of the oncoming train, holding their banner and their placards aloft. The

train could now be seen in the distance, heading this way.

What if it didn't stop? What if it came right on, ploughing the people down, as Liza had seen in a television film about the Wild West? She held on tight to the banner, clenching her fists around the cloth, making white knuckles.

"Look at them," shouted the woman who had seized her arm. "The Magnificent Seven!"

As the train came on the crowd began to sing. They sang, "We Shall Overcome." Liza had never heard it before but the tune was easy, she soon caught on and began singing it too. "We shall overcome one da-a-a-ay. Deep in my heart, I do believe that we shall overcome one day!"

The engine driver saw them in plenty of time. You could hear him applying the brakes, a long, low howl like a dog baying. The train came slowly on and ground to a halt a good hundred yards from where the Magnificent Seven held their banner and placards aloft. The crowd started singing "Jerusalem." The engine driver and another man in the same kind of uniform got down from the train and came marching up the track to argue with the protestors. All the train doors and windows opened and passengers stuck their heads out. Then they too began getting out and pouring along the line.

It was more than ever like a Western film when the Indians came or the mob of robbers from Dodge City. Liza and her fellow banner-carriers moved closer to the line to get involved in the arguments. There was a lot of shouting and threatening and one man had to be restrained from punching the engine driver. It wasn't his fault, anyway. Liza thought it most unfair. But she enjoyed every minute of it, she hadn't enjoyed anything so much since before Bruno came. In fact, thinking about it afterward, she understood she hadn't enjoyed anything since the coming of Bruno.

She stayed with the protestors right over lunch and well into the afternoon. They gave her sandwiches and biscuits from their lunches, all of them believing her parents were down by the station and she had somehow got detached from them. The train people went on arguing. The Magnificent Seven stood firm. After a while some British Rail officials arrived, there was talk of the police, the protestors on the embankments sat on the grass, and a couple of people fell asleep. Liza listened to a discussion about nuclear power, destruction of the environment, and the betrayal of democracy. She noted all the words, stored them in her memory without understanding anything that was said, until at last, growing bored, she wandered away.

She was still barefoot, her shoes tied to her belt with the socks stuffed inside them. From the position of the sun and the feel of the air she calculated it must be at least three-thirty. She sat down on the grass to put her socks on. As she was tying her shoelaces, she heard the train start and turned around to watch it.

The protestors must have been persuaded, cajoled, or threatened into leaving the line. Gradually the train gathered speed, passed between the rows of the defeated demonstrators, and came to the station. Liza saw it leave again and finally disappear into the curve that the hills swallowed, the last train forever.

She went home by way of the Shrove garden, across the smooth lawn cut by Mr. Frost that morning. Mother was sitting on the wall in front of the cottage, eating an apple. The orange car wasn't there.

"Where have you been? I was worried when you didn't come home for lunch."

Lies were easier and safer. "I took my lunch with me. I made sandwiches."

Mother wouldn't have known. She'd been in bed with Bruno. Where was he, anyway?

Before she could ask, Mother said, "Bruno's gone up to Cheshire to be with his mother. His mother's very ill."

Nothing could have been better, more calculated to make her happy, nothing except to hear he wasn't coming back.

"He may be gone a long time," said Mother.

She took Liza into the house and when they were inside and the door was closed she put her arms around her and said, "I'm sorry, Liza. I've been neglecting you, I haven't been a good mother to you lately. I can't explain, but you'll understand one day. I promise things will be like they used to be now we're alone again. Will you forgive me?"

Mother had never apologized to her before. She hadn't had to until Bruno came. Liza would have forgiven her anything now Bruno was gone.

It had been the Day of the Last Train.

Sean said gruffly, "Did he ever do anything to you, this Bruno guy?"

"Hit me, d'you mean?"

Sean said, no, not that, and explained what he did mean.

"I never heard of that," Liza said. "Do men really do that?"

"Some do."

"Well, he didn't. I told you, he hated me. He wanted to be alone with Eve and I got in his way. It wasn't always like that, he quite liked me at first, he painted that portrait of me, the one I told you about. He was always painting pictures of Eve and then he said he'd do one of me. I sat on a chair inside the little castle and he painted me. He was very kind then. I had to sit still for a long time and he bought cranberry juice for me, I'd never had that before, and biscuits with icing on that Eve wouldn't let

174

me have. He used to buy lots of things for me when they went shopping. When I look back, I think he was just trying to ingratiate himself with Eve."

"Do what?"

"Ingratiate himself. Make her like him more. But then he must have realized he didn't have to do that, she liked him enough. And he changed. When he was ill and he realized he couldn't persuade Eve even to send me to a day school, that was when he changed. I can't tell you how relieved I was when I knew he'd gone, I was so happy."

Sean turned off the television. It was a concession, Liza realized that and closed her book. He put his arm around her.

"Who was that woman you were talking about, the one who told her husband stories?"

He'd remembered, Liza thought, pleased. "Scheherazade. She was an Eastern woman, an Arab, I suppose. Her husband was a king who used to marry women and have them executed the morning after their wedding nights. He'd have their heads chopped off."

"Why did he?"

"I don't know, I don't remember. Scheherazade was determined not to have hers chopped off. On their wedding night she started telling him a story, a very long one that she couldn't finish, but he longed to know the end so much that he said he'd keep her alive until the morning after the next night so that he could hear the end. But it didn't end or she started another, and so it went on until he got sort of addicted to her stories and couldn't have her killed, and in the end he fell in love with her and they lived happily ever after."

"What about all the other poor women he'd killed?"

"Too bad for them," said Liza. "I don't suppose that bothered her. Why did you ask about Scheherazade?"

"I don't know. I wanted you to tell me a bit more about what happened. You've stopped telling me."

"Lucky to be alive, then, am I?" She laughed but he didn't. "What happened next, after Bruno'd gone that is, is that Mr. and Mrs. Tobias came down. It was the first time for about a year. Mr. Tobias said he wanted to meet Bruno, and Eve had to tell him where Bruno had gone. Seeing his paintings was the next best thing, Mr. Tobias said, so Eve took him and Mrs. Tobias into the little castle and the first thing they saw was the portrait of me.

"Of course they saw other pictures, too, and Mrs. Tobias, Victoria, said she'd like to buy one. She wanted one he'd done of Shrove by moonlight. 'Oh, I adore it,' she said and she clapped her hands, and when Eve said four hundred pounds she didn't even flinch. Mr. Tobias—Jonathan, why do I keep on calling him that, like a child?—he wrote a check for it there and then and gave it to Eve."

"Didn't she wait to ask Bruno?"

"I suppose she knew he wanted to sell them. Anyway, she didn't wait. She was very pleased about getting money for him. Next day Jonathan started shooting and Victoria did too. There was a pair of partridges used to strut about, I'd got fond of them, red legs they were and a beautiful pattern on their backs. She shot them both. I wish I'd had a gun, I'd have shot *her*. When they'd shot all the birds they wanted they went back to London and as soon as they'd gone Eve sat down with me and told me the whole story of old Mr. Tobias and Caroline and *her* mother and why she never got Shrove for herself."

Eve's parents had gone to work for old Mr. Tobias and his wife when Eve was five and Jonathan was nine. Jonathan didn't live at Shrove at that time, but he came down for the holidays with his mother and father, Caroline, who was Lady Ellison, and her husband, Sir Nicholas Ellison. Then Sir Nicholas left Caroline and Caroline went back home to her parents.

Eve's father was a German called Rainer Beck, he'd been a prisoner of war in this country and after the war was over he didn't go back to Germany but stayed on and married Gracie, the daughter of the farmer he worked for. They were married for ages without having any children and Gracie had given up hope.

She couldn't believe it when, after ten years, she became pregnant. The baby was a girl and they called her Eva, after Rainer's mother in Hildesheim.

Agricultural laborers were nearly the worst paid of all workers and, in any case, as farms became mechanized and hundreds of acres could be run with only a couple of men, they weren't much needed. Gracie saw the housekeeper and handyman's jobs advertised in *The Lady* magazine while she was at the dentist's, so they applied for it and got it. One of the inducements was that a house went with the job.

Old Mr. and Mrs. Tobias interviewed Gracie and offered her the job at once. Rainer was too hard for them to pronounce, so they called him Ray.

The Tobiases liked making people change their names. Jonathan had been christened Jonathan Tobias Ellison but at his grandfather's suggestion he dropped the Ellison and became Jonathan Tobias. He went away to his public school but he was at Shrove during the holidays, and he and Eve grew up together. That was the way she put it, grew up together. They were inseparable, they were best friends.

Old Mrs. Tobias was ill. She died when Gracie and Rainer had been there a year, and soon after that Caroline went off with a man she'd met on holiday in Barbados. Jonathan remained at Shrove. Sometimes he went to stay with his father, but mostly he was at Shrove telling Eve he was going to marry her when he grew up. He and she would marry and live together at Shrove forever until death parted them.

Ray wasn't a gardener or a butler but a handyman. Mr. Frost, who was quite young then, came up from the village on his bicycle—the same bicycle, Eve said—to do the garden. There wasn't enough work for Ray to do full-time. By a great stroke of luck he got a job in the village working for a builder as a bricklayer, the job he'd been trained for all those years ago in Germany. Ray put in a few hours every week at Shrove, cleaning the windows and the cars. It was Gracie who was the important one. But for Gracie the place would have fallen apart. With Mr. Frost's daughter to help her three times a week, she kept Shrove clean and did all the cooking. She did the washing and ironing, ordered the groceries, made jam and pickles, acted as secretary to Mr. Tobias and, increasingly, as his nurse. She was indispensable.

Eve went first to the village school, then to the school in town where you had to pay fees. Mr. Tobias paid her fees. She was very bright, brighter than Jonathan, Mr. Tobias said, and he adored Jonathan. Gracie thought he was going soft in the head, maybe it was the onset of Alzheimer's, when he said Eve would very likely get to Oxford. Gracie's sister had had nine months at a secretarial college and she looked on that as the summit of academic ambition.

Mr. Tobias didn't have Alzheimer's but a very slow growing cancer. He was eighty and malignant growths proceed slowly in people of that age. He could get up and walk about, go out in the car with Ray to drive him, and lead quite a normal life. But sometimes he had to go into hospital for radiotherapy and then, when he came home, he was very ill for a while. There was plenty of money and he could easily have afforded private nursing, but he didn't want anyone near him but Gracie.

The doctors at the hospital—they were called oncologists, Eve explained—called him their longest surviving cancer patient. The primary cancer had been detected nine years before and still he lived on. It wasn't Mr. Tobias who died but Rainer Beck. The planning authority had given permission for some "in-filling" in the village and Ray's employer was putting up a house on the site between the row of cottages and the village hall.

While Ray was laying bricks for the front wall he keeled over and died of a heart attack with his trowel still in his hand.

"He was clutching on to it and the cement got hard," said Liza. "The cement stuck it onto his dead hand and they had to prise it open. They had to break his fingers. It was either that or burying him with that trowel in his hand."

Sean turned his mouth down. "Yuck. Do you mind?"

"I'm only telling you how it was."

"You don't have to go into details."

When Ray was dead Gracie began worrying about her future. One week she had a husband's income to depend on and the next week she hadn't. She never would have again. She had no home of her own, a sixteen-year-old daughter dependent on her, and an employer who might die and leave her jobless at any moment. Caroline occasionally reappeared at Shrove, beautifully dressed, arriving in a big new car, still not divorced, still married to Sir Nicholas and supported by him, but often with a man friend in tow. She had never liked Gracie, disapproved of the friendship between her son and "the housekeeper's girl," and made it plain Gracie wouldn't last there a week after her husband was dead.

Gracie laid her troubles before Mr. Tobias. She was young enough to get a job if she left now. Her sister was a travel agent with a small business in Coventry, from which her partner had just pulled out. If Gracie would join her, learn the business, and take the partner's place, she'd help her with a mortgage on a flat. But it would have to be now, not next year or in five years' time when Gracie would be well over fifty.

It happened that she said all this just at the time the doctors had discovered another lump on Mr. Tobias's spine. Once it was removed, he'd have more radiotherapy and be convalescent for weeks. He begged Gracie not to leave him. Caroline had gone off again. Not that she ever did a hand's turn in the house and moreover she was too squeamish, she said, to be a nurse. Jonathan was up at Oxford. If Gracie left he would have to resort to private nurses and that would kill him.

Gracie told her sister she would need awhile longer to make up her mind. Meanwhile Mr. Tobias went into hospital and the growth on his back was surgically removed. He became extremely ill.

"I expect she hoped he'd die," said Liza.

"Come on, Liza, the poor old fellow. He was all on his own with no one giving a bugger what happened to him. It's only natural he didn't want her to go."

"She had to think of her future. Rich people like him just use people like my grandmother, Eve said. It wasn't as if he couldn't afford to pay nurses."

"Money never brings happiness," said Sean with a sigh.

"How do you know? Have you ever known any rich people? I have. Jonathan was ever so rich all the time I knew him and he was happy for years and years."

Mr. Tobias came home and Gracie nursed him. She moved herself and Eve out of the gatehouse and up to Shrove. For a whole two weeks before he could get up she had to give him bed pans and dress the wound on his back, which started suppurating. The doctor came every day and said she was wonderful. Meanwhile Eve sat for her O-Levels and passed in eleven subjects. Mr. Tobias called her into his bedroom to congratulate her and gave her fifty pounds "to buy some dresses."

What about me, said Gracie when he was up and about again, what's going to become of me? My sister's starting to get impatient. Mr. Tobias had been thinking about it and he told her the decision he'd come to.

If she would guarantee to stay with him until he died, having sole care of him and nursing him—she could have any help in the house she wanted—if she'd do all that, he would leave her Shrove House in his will. He knew she loved it, he knew how she appreciated this beautiful place.

It's my daughter that loves it, said Gracie, so shocked by what he'd said that she couldn't think of any other answer to make. It's Eve who couldn't bear the thought of leaving. This had held her back from agreeing to her sister's proposition nearly as much as Mr. Tobias's dependency on her. Eve worked so hard and did so well at school, was such a happy girl, because she loved Shrove and its surroundings and the whole lovely valley. And being with Jonathan whenever he was at home, thought Gracie, though not saying this aloud. She hadn't dared tell Eve there was a chance they might leave and go up to Coventry.

So what do you think of my idea? Mr. Tobias had perhaps expected more enthusiasm. It came. Gracie was stunned, Gracie couldn't believe what he'd said. Did he really mean it? What about Caroline? Wasn't it Caroline's by right?

Caroline hates the place, said Mr. Tobias, confirming what Gracie had long known. She couldn't wait to get away. Besides, she may not have lived with Nicholas for the past ten years but he's still mad about her and he'll leave her everything he's got, you'll see. He's not a well man, poor Nicholas, he'll not last as long as I will, and when he goes Caroline will be a rich woman, even allowing for the bulk of his fortune going to Jonathan.

It took Gracie five minutes to say yes. Yes, she'd stay. Then you can phone my solicitor and ask him to pop in sometime next week, said Mr. Tobias.

The new will was made and Mr. Frost and Mr. Tobias's doctor witnessed it. In the presence of the testator and of each other, Eve explained. That was the law.

Mr. Tobias made a quick recovery after that. Making sure

that Gracie would stay spurred him on to get better. He was up and actually walking about the garden by the time Jonathan came home for the long vacation. Gracie's sister took a friend of hers into the travel agent's business, a woman who had been secretary to the managing director of a domestic airline.

Having no secrets from her daughter, Gracie told Eve about the will. It made Eve feel as if Shrove was already hers. She had always felt about Mr. Tobias as if he were her grandfather and now she saw herself inheriting the place as his natural heir. It was true what her mother said that she loved it. All she wanted, at age seventeen, was to live there forever. With Jonathan, of course. Jonathan could come and live there with her.

Eve got three A-Levels to A and went to Oxford. Jonathan was still there, though he had his degree, and they saw a lot of each other.

"What does that mean?" said Sean. "D'you mean they was lovers?"

"I suppose. Yes, I'm sure they were. Eve didn't actually say. Well, she wouldn't then. Not to me. I was only ten."

"Old enough to see her in bed with one man after another."

Liza shrugged. There was no answer to that. Eve and Jonathan must have been lovers. What was there to stop them? Besides, Liza had her own very personal reasons for knowing they were. Back at Shrove, Mr. Tobias lived on. He often had setbacks and once he had a bad fall trying to get down the steps from the terrace, his arm was broken, and while they X-rayed it they found cancer in the bone. Gracie nursed him through it all.

At the end of her first year at Oxford Eve came home for July and August and September and Jonathan with her. They spent all their time together. But when Eve went back Jonathan didn't go with her. He stayed behind to be with his grandfather, who everyone said was really dying now. There were no audio books in those days and Jonathan spent hours every day reading aloud to Mr. Tobias.

Jonathan was going to be "something in the City." That was what Eve had said. Liza didn't know what it meant and Sean had only a hazy idea.

"In a bank maybe," he said, "or a stockbroker."

"What's that?"

"Don't know really. It's like doing stuff with shares."

"Anyway, he didn't. He didn't have to because his father died and left him everything, all his money, which was millions—well, a million or two—and the house in London and the place in the Lake District. He got to be something called a 'name' at Lloyds, whatever that is, but it wasn't work. Caroline got the house in France and something called a life interest in a lot more money. Only no one knew."

"What d'you mean, no one knew?"

No one at Shrove knew. Gracie and old Mr. Tobias knew Sir Nicholas Ellison was dead, of course they did, Gracie sent a wreath from Mr. Tobias to the funeral, but they thought all the property had gone to Caroline. Eve knew. Jonathan had written to her at Oxford and told her, but it didn't occur to her to tell her mother, it didn't interest her much who got the money, Jonathan or Caroline, one of them was bound to have done.

Mr. Tobias must have assumed it was all Caroline's. After all, he had forecast it would be. There was so much money, you see, Liza, Eve said. These people, they don't know how much money they have got. People like us, we always know, down to the last pound, maybe the last fifty pee, but the Tobiases and the Ellisons of this world, they could have two million or three or something in between, they don't exactly know. It's all in different places, making more, accumulating, and they lose count of now much there is.

There was money slurping around, lots of it, more and more, some coming from here and some from there. Maybe Mr. Tobias didn't even care, didn't worry about it, didn't *think* about it. He was very old and very ill and very rich and the last thing he was going to get precisely sorted out in his mind was who had what when it came to money.

Something unexpected happened next. Eve had been two years at Oxford; Jonathan divided his time between visiting her and visiting his grandfather; Mr. Tobias at eighty-four was very feeble and needing constant attention but not in danger. It was autumn. Gracie, who had been fit all her life, suddenly had alarming symptoms. They did tests and told her she had cancer of the womb. She was rushed to hospital for a hysterectomy.

There was nothing for it but nurses, a nurse for the day and a nurse for the night. Jonathan couldn't manage the bedpans and the blanket baths. The nurses were there all the time, a rota of nurses coming and going. Jonathan sat with his grandfather, wrote letters to Eve, shot pheasants. What else happened while Gracie was in hospital became clear after Mr. Tobias was dead.

He bitterly resented her leaving him. It was impossible to make him understand that she had had no choice, that it was her life that was threatened. Perhaps she should have explained to him more carefully what was happening to her. But she was afraid. For once, she was thinking of no one but herself.

As for him, it was as if he refused to admit that anyone but himself could have a life-endangering disease. He spoke to her in the tone of a disappointed father whose daughter has let him down by behaving immorally or in some criminal way. He constantly alluded to "the time you left me on my own."

Gracie took over the care of him once more. The nurses left. Jonathan left for France and his mother. Gracie had been told not to lift heavy weights for six months, and Mr. Tobias, though so old and thin, was very heavy. When she couldn't lift him up in bed properly and prop him on pillows, he grumbled and reproached her.

Eve came home at Christmas, and returned to Oxford in January. She was expected to get a first.

"What's that?" said Sean.

"The best kind of degree. Like getting a first prize."

By the time the spring came, Mr. Tobias couldn't be at home anymore, he was too ill. He was taken to a nursing home, where he went into a coma, lingered for a few weeks, and died in May. Gracie was sad in a way, but he had been so unkind to her those past months that she had lost most of her affection for him. She knew Shrove was hers now, when she woke up on the morning after Mr. Tobias's death, she had gone outside and laid her hands on the brickwork of the wall, saying, "You're mine, you're mine." But she thought she should phone the solicitor to ask when she could legally take possession.

He told her his client had left everything to Jonathan Tobias Ellison, known as Jonathan Tobias. Well, not quite everything. There was a legacy for her of a thousand pounds.

"He had made a new will while she was in hospital," said Liza. "He got Jonathan to send for the solicitor and the nurses were witnesses. In the presence of the testator and of each other."

"You mean Jonathan fixed it."

"Eve says not. She says he told his grandfather he didn't need Shrove, he had what his father left him. But Mr. Tobias didn't understand or didn't want to. He told him he wouldn't leave it to 'that woman who's deserted me.'"

"What did your grandma do?"

"What could she do? Eve didn't mind too much, not then. It would be all the same to her in the end because she and Jonathan were going to get married."

Jonathan asked Gracie to stay on at the gatehouse. He might live at Shrove one day but not yet. All she would have to do would be a kind of caretaker. No nursing, no cooking, it would be almost the same as if it were actually hers. Gracie wouldn't, she was too humiliated. As for Eve, it made her furious. Where was she supposed to go on the holidays until she and Jonathan were married? Gracie was adamant. She went off to Coventry and rented her sister's spare bedroom.

That was nearly the end. Eve didn't come into the story for a while and when she reappeared she had no degree, first or otherwise, but she did have a baby.

"Me," said Liza.

"Is that all you know?"

"She said she'd tell me when I was older."

Eve knew Jonathan was going to South America. He had already started going to places "just to see what it was like." "Come too," he said, but of course she couldn't go to Brazil or Peru or wherever it was at the start of the university term. They quarreled a bit about that and didn't see each other for a fortnight, but the day he went to catch his plane for Rio, Eve went to Heathrow with him to see him off.

He was expected back after three months, after six months, but he didn't come back, he stayed and stayed. Eve had to leave Oxford because she was going to have a baby. In a Coventry hospital Gracie was dying. She hadn't had the hysterectomy soon enough.

After she was dead, Eve and Liza stayed with Eve's aunt. She made it plain she didn't want a niece and a great-niece in her little house, she didn't like babies, but she meant to do her duty. Eve had a hard time making ends meet. For one thing, she was in a bad psychological state. She'd never got over what happened before Liza was born, though she never wished she'd had an abortion. She'd never considered it, she wanted Liza to know that.

"Fine thing to tell a kid of ten," said Sean.

"Okay, I know what you think of her. You don't have to go on and on."

Heather got in touch with her and said, come and live with me. Eve was so unhappy with her aunt that she accepted, though Heather's flat in Birmingham was tiny with only one bedroom. They all three lived there as best they could. Heather found Eve a job teaching in a private school where they would take on staff who weren't qualified. She put Liza with a baby-minder, but that wasn't very satisfactory. When she went to pick her up in the afternoon she found the babies, all six of them, strapped into push-chairs that were stuck in front of the television.

"So I had seen television before, when I was one, but I couldn't remember."

It made Eve determined never to let her child watch television. And that started a train of other ideas about bringing up her child. If only she had somewhere to live, but there was only one place in the world she really wanted that to be.

Jonathan didn't know where she was. She'd changed her job twice and the baby-minder three times before he found her.

Liza was three and Eve had had a job handing out freebie magazines in the street, another trying to be a secretary and learning to type at the same time, and Liza had fallen over at the baby-minder's and cut her head. Jonathan had found a letter at Shrove with the aunt's address on it and, thinking it worth a try, came to find her. One evening he rang the bell at Heather's flat.

When he said he'd a proposal to put before her she thought

for one mad moment he was going to ask her to marry him, even now, even after all that had happened. He was friendly but cool. Would she like to live in the gatehouse at Shrove in exchange for keeping an eye on the house? That was the expression he used, "keeping an eye on." He would pay her a salary, a handsome one, as it turned out.

She accepted. She really had no choice.

"It got her back there, you see. It got her to the one place in the world she wanted to be, even though in the gatehouse she was like the Peri outside the gates of paradise."

"The *what?*"

"Peris were superhuman beings in Persian mythology, sometimes called Pairikas. They were bad spirits, though they hid their badness under a charming appearance, but of course they couldn't get into paradise."

"Of course not," Sean said sarcastically.

"And that was it, you see. That was how we came to live there and it all began."

B RUNO was gone and life went back to what it had once been. Lessons resumed. It was just as well Liza liked learning, because she seldom had a chance in his absence to get up to Shrove and watch television. Mother taught her relentlessly. Sometimes the way she instructed and lectured was almost ferocious in its intensity.

Winter came and with it the sunless days and long nights. Every morning the two of them went walking, but they were gone for only an hour and the rest of the day was spent with Liza's books. Occasionally Mother would insist that they spoke only French, so breakfast, lunch, and supper were eaten in

French and their discussions of other subjects were in French. She set Liza an examination in English, history, and Latin. Liza learned whole pages of poetry by heart and in the evenings she and Mother read plays aloud, Mother taking all the male parts and she the female. They read *Peter Pan* and *Where the Rainbow Ends* and *The Blue Bird*.

Bruno was never mentioned. If letters came from him, Mother never said so. Now that Liza was older she didn't get up so early, Mother was always up before her, so Liza wouldn't have known if letters had come. She knew Heather sometimes wrote, her letters were left about. The Tobiases sent a Christmas card, as did Heather and the aunt. Did we send them cards? Liza wanted to know. Mother said no, certainly not. It was absurd celebrating Christmas if you didn't believe in the Christian God, or indeed any god at all, but she gave Liza a lesson on the Christian religion just as she taught her about Judaism and Islam and Buddhism.

One day, shortly before Liza's eleventh birthday, she was looking through Mother's desk for a pad of lined paper Mother said was in the middle section, when she came upon a letter in Bruno's writing. She recognized the writing at once. Without ever having been told, she somehow knew that reading other people's private correspondence was wrong. It must have come from all the highly moral Victorian books she read from the Shrove library, the works among others of Charlotte M. Yonge and Frances Hodgson Burnett. She read it just the same.

Mother had gone upstairs. She could hear her moving about overhead. Liza read the address, which was somewhere called Cheadle, and the date, which was the previous week, and the first page of the letter. It started, "My darling lovely Eve." Liza wrinkled up her nose but read on. "I miss you a lot. I wish I could call you, it's crazy us not being able to call each other in this day and age. *Please* ring me. You can call me collect if you're afraid of J.T. getting his knickers in a twist. Now my ma is dead I'm not poor anymore, do you realize that? It won't be much longer now, I've just got all this stuff to see to, inevitable really, and I must grin and bear it. Just to hear your voice would—"

She had to stop there because she heard Mother's footsteps on the stairs. She didn't dare turn the page over. Much of what she had read about "calling" and "collect" was incomprehensible, but not "it won't be much longer now." He was coming back. For a moment she wondered why his mother's dying stopped him being poor, but then she remembered the tale of Shrove and old Mr. Tobias and understood.

It was a hard winter. A little snow fell before Christmas, but the first heavy fall came in early January. It lay in deep drifts, masking the demarcations between the road surface and the grass verge, then piling up to hide the ditch and spreading a thick concealing cloak over the hedgerow. And when it melted a little it froze again, more fiercely than ever, so that the thawed snow, falling in drops and trickles, turned into icicles, pointed as needles and sharp as knives.

Icicles hung around the eaves of the gatehouse like fringe on a canopy. A crust of ice lay on top of the thick snow. It had been two days since a car had been able to get down the lane. The council, Mother said, hadn't bothered to snowplow it because they were the only ones living there and they hadn't a car.

The postman stopped coming, which pleased Liza because it meant no more letters from Bruno. While the lane was blocked like this, Bruno couldn't come. The little orange car would never get through where the post van failed. And still the snow fell, day after day, adding more and more layers to the deep quilt of crisp whiteness that covered everything.

They fed the birds. They had a bird table for bread crumbs,

two bird feeders made of wire mesh to fill with nuts, and they hung up pieces of fat on string. One morning Liza saw a woodpecker at one of the wire feeders and a tree creeper hanging on its tail, both pecking at the nuts. Remembering Jonathan taking photographs, she said she wished they had a camera, but Mother said, no, your own mind is the best recording instrument, let your memory photograph it.

And then she said the bird was like Trochilus, a kind of hummingbird. So Liza looked Trochilus up in the encyclopedia and she thought she saw what Mother meant, for its other name was the crocodile bird, so called because it is the only creature that can enter with impunity the mouth of a crocodile and pick its teeth. It also cries out to warn the crocodile of an impending foe.

Liza loved the snow. She was too old to make snowmen, but she made them. She made herself an igloo. When it was finished she sat inside her igloo, eating a picnic of Marmite sandwiches and Nice biscuits and rejoicing in the snow that would keep Bruno away, wishing as hard as she could that more and more snow would fall, that it would lie heavy and impenetrable in the lane until March, until April. Mother had told her about a very bad winter when she was a little girl, even before she and Gracie and Ray came to Shrove, when the snow started in January and lasted for seven weeks and all the water pipes froze. It was a bad winter, but to herself Liza called it a "good" winter.

Mother had a cold that she must have caught in town the last time she went there before the snow came. Coughing kept her awake at night so she lay down to rest in the afternoons, and when she did Liza made her way up to Shrove for an hour or two of television. She had missed the old films and school programs and quiz shows. She was beginning to understand too, in a vague, puzzled way, that the small square screen was her window to a world of which she otherwise knew very little.

The second time she went up there she saw the snowplow as she came out of the cottage gate. It was clearing the lane. The big shovel on the front of it was heaving up piles of snow, spotted like currant pudding by the gravel lodged in it, and casting it up on the verges. Liza felt sure this would somehow open the way for Bruno. It was as if he had been waiting on the other side of the bridge in his orange car for the snowplow to come and make a smooth, clean road for him.

But when she returned there was no car and no Bruno. She should have asked Mother, she knew that, she should have said to Mother, "Is Bruno coming back?" but she couldn't bring herself to do this. She was afraid of being told yes and of being given a definite time. Doubt was better than knowing for sure.

The snow thawed and he hadn't come. All that was left of the snow were small piles of it lying in the coldest shady places, map-shaped patches of snow on the green grass. Mother's cold went when the snow did, so there was no more television but plenty of lessons. In February, on a freak warm day, Liza went up into the wood to see if the aconites were out, and when she got back a car was parked outside the cottage, a dark brown car of a shape and make she had never seen before. Instead of a letter of the alphabet at the start of the registration number there was one at the end. She had never seen that before either. The car was called a Lancia.

The Tobiases, she thought, having long dropped the respectful Mr. and Mrs. They were always getting new cars. She went warily into the house, preparing to say a cool hallo before going upstairs. The memory of the partridges remained with her and now the story of Gracie and the grandfather too.

She saw Bruno before he saw her, she moved so quietly. He was sitting on the sofa beside Mother, holding both her hands in his and looking into her eyes. Liza stood quite still. He was unchanged, except that his long, soft wavy hair was longer and his freckles had faded. He still wore denim jeans and a leather jacket and the two gold earrings in the lobe of one ear.

Perhaps there was some truth in the theory she had read that you can sense when someone is staring very intently at you, for although she hadn't moved or made a sound Bruno suddenly raised his head and met her eyes. For a moment, a very brief instant of time, there came into his face a look of such deep hatred and loathing that she felt a shiver run straight down her back. She had never seen such a look before, but she knew it at once for what it was. Bruno hated her.

Almost immediately the terrible expression had passed and a look of bland resignation replaced it. Mother also looked around, dropping Bruno's hands. Mother said, "Goodness, Lizzie, you're as quiet as a little mouse."

Bruno said, "Hi, Liza, how've you been?"

That was the way he talked. Not like an English person and not like an American person—she had heard plenty of them on television—but as if he lived midway between the two countries, which was impossible because it would have been the Atlantic Ocean. She noticed a red blush on Mother's face. Mother hadn't told her he was coming. She must have known. Why hadn't she told her?

"What d'you reckon to my new jalopy, then?"

"He means his car," said Mother.

"It's okay," Liza said, a television expression that made Mother frown. "I liked the orange one."

"The orange one, as you call it, has gone to where all bad old cars go when they die, the breakers' yard."

"Where do the good ones go, Bruno?" said Mother.

"They go to people like me, my sweet. The one outside's

what I mean by a good one. It was my ma's, still is, as a matter of fact, I've never transferred it. She had it for ten years and only did seven thousand miles on it."

Mother was laughing. Liza thought, she didn't tell me because she knows I hate him. I wonder if she knows he hates me? In that moment she lost some of her respect for Mother, though not her love. That was the evening when, as soon as she could get Mother alone, she asked if she could start calling her Eve.

"Why do you want to?"

"Everyone else does."

If Mother thought "everyone" a bit thin on the ground, she didn't say so. "You can if you like," she said, though not in a happy voice.

Liza had been wrong when she thought Bruno hadn't changed. She would have understood that he had even if Eve hadn't pointed it out, if Eve hadn't said while they were having their dinner, "You never used to care about money, you used to be indifferent to it."

He had been talking about all the things "they" could do now he had his mother's house to sell.

"You'd better wait till you've sold it," said Eve in the dry voice she sometimes used.

"I've practically done that small thing," Bruno said in his twangy tone. "I've got a buyer who's even keener to buy it than I am to sell."

That was in the boom time of five and a half years ago. Eve said she understood you could sell anything these days, a remark that went down less than well with Bruno, who started insisting on how lovely his mother's house was, how he *and* she would have been delighted to live in it if only it hadn't been in the north.

"You can leave me out of it," said Eve. "I live here and I'm going to live here for the rest of my life."

He wasn't an anarchist anymore. He had forgotten about money and property being unimportant. Having a big house to sell and a proper car and some thousands of pounds in the bank had gone to his head.

"I didn't even have a bank last time I was here, Eve."

"Aren't we going to talk about anything but money?" said Eve.

She was so rough with him, "scathing" was the word, that Liza really expected him to go off somewhere for the night. But the guitar music went on playing softly and persistently down-stairs, sometimes Bruno sang in his Johnny Cash or his Merle Haggard voices, and she wasn't really surprised when, hours later, their footfalls on the stairs woke her and she heard them go into Eve's bedroom together.

The only good that came of Bruno's return was free afternoons for watching television. Lessons didn't stop, but once more they became few and far between. Bruno was almost always there and when he was he sneered at Eve's teaching methods, picked on her for not being a qualified teacher, and went on and on about how "the kid" ought to be at school.

"Why ought she?" Mother said at last.

"Come on, Mother, she's not getting a proper education."

"Don't call me 'Mother,' you're only two years younger than I am. How many children of eleven have you come across that can read, write, and talk French, can do a Latin unseen, recite *Lycidas,* and give you a thoroughly good precis of at least four Shakespeare plays?"

"She doesn't know any science and she doesn't know any maths."

"Of course she doesn't. She's only eleven."

"That's the age they're supposed to start these things, re-member?"

"You teach her, then. You were good at maths, you're always saying."

"I'm not a teacher," Bruno said. "I'm not like you, I know my limitations. She needs real teachers. I bet that kid couldn't do a simple sum. I'm not talking about calculus and logarithms and all that, I'm talking about, say, long division. Come on, Liza, you've got a bit of paper there. Divide eight hundred and twenty-four by forty-two."

Eve snatched the paper away. "Nobody needs to divide eight hundred and twenty-four by forty-two on paper anymore. Even I know that, out of the world as I am. You have calculators to do that for you."

"Calculators can't do algebra," said Bruno.

And so it went on. Liza knew very well—though Eve didn't seem to—that Bruno only wanted her to go to school to be rid of her, to get her out of the way. He didn't care whether she learned algebra or got to know about biology. He just didn't want her there when he was there. She understood now, because Bruno had told her, that Eve was breaking the law in not sending her to school. Bruno made a lot of that, he was always saying how Eve broke the law, though he was breaking it himself not buying a new Road Fund license for his car.

But for all the fault he found with Eve, Bruno wanted to be with her, he wanted her to be with him. When his mother's house was sold, he wanted to buy a new one for him and Eve to live in. It could be near Shrove, only in the town, for instance, or in one of the villages on the other side of the valley. He liked it around here, he was happy enough to stay around here, knowing how Eve loved it.

"I thought you wanted to be free," Eve said. "That's what you always used to say, how you loved freedom, how you didn't want to be tied down."

"I've changed. Becoming a property owner changes you. You start to understand the meaning of responsibility."

"Oh, really, Bruno, you'll be asking me to marry you next."

"I can't. I'm already married, you know that. But I do want to live with you for the rest of my life."

"Really?" said Eve. "I don't know what I want to do for the rest of my life except stay here."

"But that's what I'm saying. We'll stay here. You *can* stay here. You'll only be four or five miles away."

"I mean here. *Here.* On this spot. You may as well make up your mind to it, Bruno. You can buy a house if you want, I'll even drop in sometimes if you ask me, but I'm staying here."

Bruno never said anything about Liza living in the house he was proposing to buy. She wanted to ask Eve what was really going to happen. Did she mean it when she said she wouldn't leave here in any circumstances? Was she definite about not living in Bruno's house? And what about Liza? Would Eve give in to Bruno and send her away to school? Liza longed to ask Eve for the truth, she desperately wanted to know, but she was never alone with Eve, Bruno was always there.

In March, when the weather got a bit warmer, he and Eve started going for a lot of drives in the brown car with the out-of-date Road Fund license that had been Bruno's mother's. Eve tried to get Liza to come with them, but Liza wouldn't. She went up to Shrove instead and watched television. Bruno had said, and Eve hadn't denied it, that they went on trips looking at houses that were for sale.

"If I did come with you," Eve said one evening when they were all sitting around the fire in the cottage, "if I did, which I wouldn't dream of, but if I did, what would we live on? Have you thought of that? Your mother's bit of money won't last forever. It won't last for *long*. While you're here, you live off me, in case you need reminding, but if I left here my money would stop. I get paid for being here, have you forgotten that?"

"I'm a painter. If I don't make much it's because I refuse to compromise, you know that. But things are looking up. You know what they say, nothing succeeds like success. Those To-biases bought my painting, didn't they? Or we could start up in business, you and me, we could be interior decorators, for instance." Something she had said seemed to strike him for the first time. "What d'you mean, you wouldn't dream of it? Why've you been coming to look at all these houses with me if you wouldn't dream of it?"

"I've told you," she said, "I've told you a hundred times. You buy a house, go on, if you want to, I'll go with you and look at it, but I'm not living in it. I'm living here in this house, at Shrove. Is that clear?"

They had this conversation every evening, or one very like it, until Liza didn't listen anymore. She sat reading her book or went up to bed while they argued. But one evening things took a different turn. It had been a bad day, a day on which a nasty, frightening thing happened, something quite unforeseen.

The weather was perfect, the kind of April day that might have been June, but clearer and fresher than June would be. Bruno was out painting somewhere. This meant that Liza could have her Latin lesson without fear of interruption, which might be a sarcastic comment or derive simply from his presence, silent, looming, his eyes sometimes cast upward.

If Liza had been able to express it in words, she would have said Bruno was taking them over, controling them, setting the pace, or calling the tune. But she knew none of these expressions, only that where Eve had ruled he was fast becoming the ruler. Eve was sharp with him or scathing but she resisted him less and less. She was gradually ceasing to give Liza lessons because of his disapproval.

They could have this one because he wasn't there. As if it was something wrong or against the law, they had to do it in secret. The French lesson had to be outside in the garden. This, Liza suspected, was because if he came back sooner than he had said, he would think they had gone out somewhere, he wouldn't look for them down there under the cherry tree.

The cherry blossoms were out everywhere and the woods were white, not sprinkled with white as when the blackthorn flowered in March, but a pure, clean white like a fallen cloud. When the lesson was over, Liza and Eve went out walking to look at all the cherry trees because Eve said, quoting a poet, you could see it only once a year, which meant that at her age she probably only had forty more chances. They went to the woods down by the bridge and to their own wood, and after that Eve went home in case Bruno was already there.

Liza wandered off on her own. She crossed the bridge and began walking along the old railway line, disused for six months now, but the rails and sleepers still there. If you followed the line, just walking along it and through the quarter mile of tunnel, out the other side into another valley, eventually you'd come to the town and then another town and at last to the big city. Not yet, but perhaps one day, she would do that.

It was six o'clock in the evening but not yet sunset. The warmth had lasted and there was no wind. She walked along the line the other way, toward the station at Ring Valley Halt. Would they have taken the station name away? And what had become of the building, red brick with a canopy and a ginger-bread trim, with windowboxes and tubs of flowers, which had also been the signalman's house?

She didn't see Bruno until she was no more than a few feet from him, until she couldn't avoid him or hide. The station house looked just the same from a distance, but as she came closer she saw that the curtains upstairs were gone and the door marked PRIVATE stood open. Instead of flowers in the windowboxes and the beds that ran along the backs of both platforms, weeds had sprung up. Where last year there had been daffodils and grape hyacinths grew dandelions. Liza climbed up onto the platform and made her way through the door marked EXIT into the room where people had bought tickets, through that room and, sus-pecting nothing, out of the main door onto the sandy lane that had been the station approach.

Bruno was sitting there, not on his camp stool but on the low wall with his easel in front of him. He was holding up a brush loaded with gamboge and he was staring straight at her.

Of course, what he had really been staring at was the station entrance from which she had come. She went closer, she went right up to him, because retreat was impossible. The picture he was painting was of what could be seen through those open doors, the empty line, the deserted platform, paint peeling off the gingerbread fringe on the canopy, the sunflower faces of the dandelions.

When Eve wasn't there he didn't bother with any of that "hi, and how are you?" He cast up his eyes, the way he often did when he saw her. She was at a loss, suddenly frightened with no real reason to feel fear. Could she just pass on? Was it possible to ignore him and go on up the sandy path until she was out of his sight?

The brush approached the canvas, touched it, painted in the

dandelion petals. His box of paints, the heap of paint-stained rags, the jar of sticky brushes were on the wall beside him. He drew the brush away and began wiping it on a strip of cloth, which she saw had been torn from an old skirt of Eve's, a skirt she remembered her wearing years before, when first they came to Shrove.

He spoke in a tone that was at first mild and conversational. "You're old enough to realize what's being done to you. She's denying you your birthright—well, what's the birthright of kids living in civilized countries. We're not talking about the Third World. This is the United Kingdom in the nineteen-eighties, in case she hasn't noticed."

Liza said nothing.

"She's crippling you. She might as well have chopped off one of your legs or arms. In another way she's buried you. You're not dead, but she's buried you just the same. In one of the remotest parts of England. She's cut you off. You're not much better than one of those poor devils that get lost as babies and bears or wolves raise them."

"Romulus and Remus," said Liza.

"There you are, you see. That's just it. You know all that stuff, that god-awful useless crap, but I bet you can't tell me who the president of the United States is."

Liza shrugged, the way Eve did.

"You're so like your goddamn mother you might be her clone, not her daughter. Maybe you are, eh? Only you don't know what a clone is, any more than you know what H_2O is or pi or anything that's not Shakespeare or fucking Virgil."

The word was new to her. Strange, then, that she sensed he shouldn't have used it, it shouldn't be uttered in her presence. A blush climbed up her neck and made her face hot.

"I'm gonna say just one more thing to you and then you can

go home to her and tell tales out of school. That's a laugh, isn't it? Out of school is right. I'm gonna say one more thing and it's this: If you don't get yourself sent to school right now, in the next six months at the very outside, if you don't you won't have a chance of life, you'll be lost forever. All that learning'll be wasted. It's all very well her saying education doesn't have a purpose, it's not *for* anything, it's all very well her quoting fucking Aristotle or Plato or whoever and saying it's for turning the soul's eye toward the light or some shit like that, but you try telling that tale when you want to go to college, when you want a job, when you haven't got any qualifications, not even O-Levels. Who's going to give a shit about your French and your Romulus and Remus then?"

"I hate you," Liza said softly.

"Big deal. I'm not surprised. I've been telling you this in your best interests and maybe you'll realize it one day. When it's too late. The best thing you can do is go home and tell her you want to go to school. The term starts next week. You go and tell her that."

Liza did go then. She walked until she was sure he could no longer see her and then she ran. She was shaking inside and something she called her heart felt as if it had swelled up until it was too big for her chest, until it must burst.

If she had met Eve at that moment, as she was running along the footpath by the maple hedge, if Eve had come out to look for her and they had met, she would have thrown herself into her mother's arms and told her everything he had said. But she didn't. Eve was at home making the dinner. And by the time Liza reached the gatehouse she had slowed her pace to catch her breath, she had collected her thoughts.

The awful knowledge had come to her that whatever she told Eve of the things Bruno had said, it would make no difference.

Eve was somehow conquered by him, in ways beyond Liza's understanding. It was as if she didn't really like Bruno any more than Liza did herself, but still she wanted him there and she wanted him to like her. Rude to him she might be, but she wanted him to look at her in that way he had, as if she were an angel in the clouds.

She even dressed in a different way to please him, with her hair loose down her back, the jade beads around her neck, and sashes and scarves and chains decorating her, things he'd bought her on their outings. The two of them clattered around in beads and chains, their hair shaggy, barefoot or wearing boots. He talked his mid-Atlantic language, and sometimes Eve, precise, pedantic Eve, echoed his expressions. Why then did Liza have this rooted idea that though Eve would never tell him to go, she would be just as happy as Liza if he were gone?

Calling out to Eve in the kitchen that she was back, she went upstairs and looked hard at her own face in the mirror. She had never noticed it before but now she could see that what he had said was true in at least one respect, she did look like Eve, she was exactly a younger version of Eve, same features, same golden-brown flushed skin, clear water-brown eyes, and golden-gleaming dark brown hair, exactly as curly and exactly as long.

That day, when she remembered the weeds' sun-shaped faces and the yellow paint on the brush tip, she thought of as the Day of the Dandelions but she was growing out of giving names to special days and she only ever named one more.

After a little while she heard Bruno come in. His arrival was followed by utter silence. She hoped for something, though she hardly knew what. Perhaps she hoped that Eve, without being told, would somehow guess her unhappiness and the reason for it. She would guess and make things right again, as she had used to do when Liza was miserable. Bruno being reprimanded over her, really reprimanded, was something she longed to see. She could bear Bruno if Bruno were changed, were made nicer.

As silent as they were themselves, she tiptoed down the stairs.

The two of them were on the sofa, embracing, wound around each other, devouring each other, so closely locked it looked as if it must hurt. At that sight, Liza's sense of isolation, even of rejection, was so great as to amount to panic. A sound escaped her, she couldn't help herself, a whimper of pain. They were too preoccupied with each other to hear her.

Or Mother was. Bruno's blue angelic eye appeared above Mother's curved cheek. It stared at Liza coldly, unblinking. The worst thing was that it went on staring while Bruno's mouth kept sucking Mother's mouth and Bruno's hands clutched and pummeled her back.

Liza turned and ran. She remembered the Andrew Lang fairy stories from long ago and thought he had put Mother under an evil spell.

f o u r t e e n

MAGIC spells," Sean said indulgently, "they don't happen in this day and age."

"This one did."

"What did you do, make a wax what-d'you-call-it and stick pins in him?"

She didn't understand. "I didn't have to do anything. He did it himself. I could have told him there were things meant more to her than he did. Well, two things."

"Shrove and you."

"Shrove, anyway. I mattered, but not as much." She hesitated. "I can't help wondering now how much I matter, Sean. I know she's in prison but it's as she said, it's not a dungeon, it's not the Tower of London. They'd let her try to get in touch, wouldn't they? She doesn't know where I am, she thinks I'm with Heather, but she can't have checked or she'd know I'm not. And then wouldn't they have the police look for me?"

"You can't have it both ways, love. You can't not want them to look for you and want them to."

"No, you're right. But still I think it's that she loved me when I was a child and she could sort of remake me, shape me the way she wanted, but when I grew up she lost interest. I could *feel* her losing interest."

"You've got me now."

"I know. I'll go on about Bruno and breaking the spell, shall I? He must have been very stupid to threaten her and not see it wouldn't work. I see that now but I didn't then, I was too young. I thought she'd send me away and leave the place and if that happened I thought I'd die."

Bruno kept on and on at Eve to come and live with him in this house he wanted to buy. He'd found somewhere he liked but he wouldn't make the vendor an offer until he got a promise out of Eve. His mother's house was sold by then and he'd got far more for it than it was worth, as often happened in the late eighties. The place he'd found was a big house built fifty years before on the edge of the village where Eve went to catch the bus for town.

Even Liza had been to see it. They took her with them in the car. She thought it very ugly with the dark wooden strips on the yellow plaster, done to look like houses she'd seen in pictures of when Elizabeth I was on the throne of England, the red roof and the windows made of hundreds of tiny diamond-shaped panes.

The garden was very big, which Bruno kept saying Eve would like, and surrounded on three sides by enormously tall hedges of the cypress Liza knew was called leylandii. The ugliest tree in the world, Eve had once said. They drove through the village and Eve pointed out the place where Rainer Beck had fallen down dead while building the wall of bricks. Someone else must have finished building the house between the row of cottages and the village hall, for there it stood, looking quite old, as if it had been there for a hundred years.

Almost into town, on the outskirts, they called at a supermarket that looked a bit like Bruno's new house, but fifteen times as big and only on one floor. It was another first time for Liza, going in there, and she enjoyed it tremendously. She walked slowly past the shelves, counting how many kinds of fruit juice there were, how many sorts of canned vegetables. The different varieties of biscuits numbered over a hundred. There were dozens of types of food she didn't recognize, that she wouldn't have known were food at all. The soaps and sprays and cleansers fascinated her. She could happily have spent the rest of the day there but Eve got fidgety and made her leave as soon as they had bought their fruit and cornflakes. Liza was being exposed to just the kind of thing Eve most dreaded.

It was that evening, when they were quarreling again about the house, when Liza was curled up in an armchair reading *Kim* in the crimson and gold Shrove library edition, that Bruno suddenly said, "Does Mr. Jonathan Tobias, your liege lord and master, by any chance know that kid doesn't go to school? That she's never been to school?"

The question distracted Liza from Kim Rishti Ke and the Eye of Beauty and she looked up. The truth was that Jonathan Tobias didn't know. Even she knew that, or guessed it. Of course she was always at home when the Tobiases came to Shrove, but they didn't come often and always came on the school holidays or at half-term. If Jonathan Tobias had ever asked Eve how she was getting on at school she no doubt lied to him. Liza hadn't actually heard her do so but she wouldn't have been surprised.

"He doesn't know, does he?"

"It's no business of his," Eve said.

"It's everyone's business in the community. If he knew, I doubt if he'd let you stay here. It's not just the not going to school, it's all the rest of it. Keeping her isolated here, not employing a woman to clean because you don't want any more prying eyes, keeping the money yourself you're supposed to pay to this nonexistent woman, not to mention letting the kid run wild at Shrove, taking what she wants out of the library. Look at her now. That's probably a first edition she's got there. A first edition in the hands of an eleven-year-old who's never even been to school!"

"I didn't keep her isolated enough," Eve said quietly. "I didn't keep myself isolated the way I promised myself I would. I've been weak, I've been a fool. The biggest mistake I made was letting you in."

He said to Liza, "Go to bed. It's nearly nine o'clock at night and you've no business down here."

"Don't you dare speak to her like that!" Eve stood up, facing him. "This is Liza's home, she can do as she likes. Do you really think threatening me is likely to make me come and live with you in that mock-Tudor monstrosity? Don't you know anything about human beings?"

He flinched from the flash of her eyes. "I thought you liked the house," he said sulkily. "I thought you did. You didn't say anything about it being a monstrosity."

"And you who called property-owners bourgeois! Truly money is the root of all evil if it changes people the way it's changed you."

Liza got up, took her book, and said she was going to bed. She got halfway up the stairs and stopped, listening. They were off again. Did she want to hear what was said or didn't she? She couldn't be sure. If he made Eve believe he'd tell the Tobiases, wouldn't she have to give in? Wouldn't she have to send Liza to school and go and live with him, whatever she said about not being forced by threats? Would school be like the school in *Jane Eyre*?

She crept down again and listened.

"I don't have to tell Tobias, Eve." Bruno had stopped calling Eve "Mother." "I only have to contact the County Education Authority. No, it's not spite, it's not revenge, it's my duty. It would be anyone's duty."

Eve said in a wheedling voice, the kind of tone Liza had never heard her use, "And if I agree, that is if I go and live in that house with you, you'll keep silent about this?"

"More or less. Hopefully, I'd persuade you that what you're doing is wrong, but I wouldn't take any direct action. Not for a while, anyway."

"I think you're right when you say they would take her into care. I also think it probable I should lose this house and my job. Without this place I really don't know what would become of us."

Liza came closer to the door.

"There's no point in being so goddamned sarcastic."

"I'm not being sarcastic. I mean it. I'm simply being frank about the facts. Without this place I don't know what would become of us. There's nowhere I could go and keep Liza."

"There is a place you can go. A real home. A far better home than this antiquated little dump. A hovel without a bathroom!"

Liza heard Eve's little laugh. "And you called yourself an anarchist. You were a free spirit."

"All right. I can be frank too. Have you ever heard of an

anarchist with money or a free spirit with a hefty bank balance? Can't you see it's for the best, Eve? Can't you face up to it and go the whole hog, come and live with me and give up this whole crazy project? Let the kid go to school and lead a normal life like other kids. I could afford fees for boarding school, you know, a good *co-ed* private school. She could come home at weekends."

There was silence. Liza held her breath. The door was suddenly flung open and Liza saw the wild face Bruno wasn't allowed to see, the dilated eyes and curled lip, the nostrils narrowed like a cat's.

"Go to bed at once! How dare you listen at doors! Perhaps you *should* go away to school, perhaps I've been wrong all these years. I haven't just sheltered you, I've spoiled you. Go to bed now."

Liza seldom cried but she did that night. She wept until she slept, woke again at the sound of Eve and Bruno coming up to bed together, whispering tenderly, no longer angry, reconciled, content with each other.

⌒

Years later, three or four years, she went back to look at the house Bruno had wanted to buy.

It was on the other side of the valley, about two miles away by road or one as the crow flies and as she walked, wading through the river where the water was low, and crossing the disused railway line. By this time the rails and sleepers had been taken away and the line was a grassy track between embankments overgrown with gorse and wildflowers. Climbing the slope, she looked back at the station house where on the frightening occasion she had encountered Bruno painting. The painting he had done Eve had liked and had hung it up in the cottage living room. Every time Liza looked at the dandelion faces in the foreground she remembered the gamboge on his raised brush as he spat out those harsh words to her.

She climbed the hillside, took the footpath, then went across the fields that were private land yet where no one ever came but the sheep that grazed there. It was scarcely a village, just a church, a meeting hall and a green with a few old houses and the four newer ones built around a half-moon-shaped road. The people who had bought the house she called Bruno's, though it never had been his, though he had never even made that offer for it, had cut down all the Leyland cypresses and painted the walls pink. A child's climbing frame stood in the middle of the lawn. Lying down asleep inside a wire enclosure was a big yellow dog with a feathery tail and long ears.

She might have lived there herself. But perhaps not, perhaps there had never really been a chance of that. She sat on the green for a while, then lay face-downward in the sun, the prickly scented grass pressing into her skin. When she got up she could feel with her fingertips the ridges the grass had made on her cheek, like wrinkles.

This time, for a change, she went back through the woods, though it was a longer way around. There were still great spaces in there where giant trees had fallen and no new ones yet been planted. Rocky outcrop appeared all over this hillside, among the trees as well as on the open heathland. It was very pale gray rock that sometimes looked white, like bones lying among the brown beech leaves and the gnarled dark tree roots. You might fancy you saw a skull, but when you approached more closely you could see it was only a bowl-shaped lump of rock, just as the bone-white strips among the brambles were limestone, not a weathered femur or humerus.

"Did she give in to him, then?" said Sean.

"I don't know. I don't exactly know what happened. I never saw him again."

Sean put up his eyebrows. "What, you mean you never saw him after that night?"

"I told you, I didn't get up very early. I came downstairs at about nine and Eve said he'd gone out painting. It was midsummer, you see, and sometimes the light was best for painting very early in the morning. He often went out early. Now he didn't need to, he painted all the time. We had our lessons. We'd got into the way of having them while he was out of the house. I can't remember but I think it was French that morning and maybe history. Yes, it was history because I remember Eve wanted me to read Carlyle's *French Revolution* and I couldn't, it was too hard for me, too many difficult words."

"Surprise, surprise," said Sean.

"She was cross. She grumbled at me and called me a coward for not trying harder. I mean, you have to understand she was hardly ever cross with me and never about things like that. But she was irritable and jumpy that morning. When it got to midday she said she'd made a picnic lunch for me, it was too nice a day to stay in, I should be out in the fresh air. That was unusual too, if there was to be a picnic she always came with me, but not this time. You may wonder how I remember all this, all the details, but the fact is I've thought about that day a lot ever since. I've turned it over and over in my mind."

Bruno's car was parked outside the cottage, where he always left it. That signified one thing to Liza, that he couldn't be far off. If he went to paint more than a mile away he always went in the car. Carrying her picnic, she made her way cautiously toward

Shrove House. This time she wasn't going to let herself come upon him by chance as she had when she went marching confidently through the station. He was nowhere to be seen, he must have gone northward through their wood or down the lane toward the river bridge.

The sun was too hot to walk or sit out in, and in the shade under the trees flies swarmed. She let herself into Shrove, into its silent rooms that were as cool in summer as they were warm in winter, replaced *Kim* on the library shelves and took down *Stalky and Co.* For the next four hours she sat watching television.

On those days when she had been out for a long time she always had to brace herself before going home and confronting him again. It had got worse as she knew him more thoroughly, not better, and on the way home she reflected how terrible the future was, filled with days of meeting and being with Bruno, or else—and she hardly knew if this would be worse—going away to the school of his choosing. And still she would see him, for her weekends and holidays would be spent in the "monstrosity," exiled from Shrove.

His car was gone. Her heart leapt up, then dipped again. Of course it most likely only meant he and Eve had driven off somewhere and would return in time for supper. She went despondently into the house. Eve was at home and alone, preparing a chicken to roast, mixing the stuffing, and setting the giblets on to boil.

"Where's he gone?" She no longer used his name when speaking of him.

Eve's face showed nothing, neither happiness nor sadness, it was blank, her large brown eyes empty. "He's gone. Gone for good. He's left us."

At once Liza was enormously happy, bubbling over with delight, with joy. Some precocious sense of what was fitting restrained her from crowing or cheering. She said nothing, she just looked at Eve. Her mother set down the spoon she was holding, rinsed her hands under the tap, dried them, and put her arms around Liza, hugging her tight.

That evening they read Shakespeare together. Liza took Macbeth's part and Eve Lady Macbeth. As Eve predicted, there was a lot of the scene where the wife urges the husband to murder the old king that Liza couldn't understand, but Eve didn't get cross when Liza spoke sentences wrong or put incorrect stresses on certain words. Afterward, they played a tape of Mozart's *Sinfonia Concertante* and then had a French conversation, all things they hadn't been able to do when Bruno was there.

Liza was so happy that she should have slept soundly that night but she didn't. She fancied she heard all sorts of sounds, creaking boards and thumps and something heavy being dragged down the stairs. It could all have been in dreams, it was impossible to know. For instance, she had no reason to believe Eve didn't come to bed until four or five in the morning, only a feeling or intuition that she hadn't. It wasn't as if she had been into the other bedroom to look. The car she thought she heard at one point was probably farther away than she believed, not passing the gatehouse door but a hundred yards away in the lane.

She said nothing about it in the morning, for she and Eve had never been in the habit of telling each other their dreams. Nothing could be more boring, Eve sometimes said, than other people's dreams. But later, while her mother was up at Shrove, cleaning the house in her role as Mrs. Cooper, Liza went into the little castle that Bruno had used as a studio.

His easel was there and his two boxes of paints as well as innumerable extra tubes of color, the names of which fascinated her, though she had never cared to show her interest in front of him. Rose madder tint, light viridian, Chinese white, burnt umber. How strange of him to have gone without his painting things. Even stranger that he hadn't cleaned the brushes he always complained were so expensive, but left them dipped in an inch of turpentine in a jam jar. Pictures, finished, half-finished, blank canvases, rested against the wall. Her own portrait was there.

It was not for a long time that she connected the paint rags in the little castle with Bruno's departure. Then, during that morning visit, they were just rags, a rather larger than usual pile of them filling up nearly half the floor space. A much larger than usual pile, in fact. Old skirts of Eve's torn into strips, a sheet that went on her own bed until she put her toe through a hole in it, a ragged towel.

Another odd thing about the paint rags, which didn't particularly register at the time but remained in her memory, was the color of the paint on them. One had a streak of sap green on the edge of it and another looked as if it had mopped up a spill of Prussian blue, but for the most part they were stained reddish-brown—and not just stained, coated in that color.

Liza tried to decide what color it might be. Not crimson or scarlet lake or vermilion, it wasn't bright enough for that. Too dark for rose madder tint and not dark or dull enough for Vandyke brown. Light sienna? Burnt sienna? Either was possible but that didn't explain why Bruno had used so much of it.

Did the mess in here and the stack of canvases mean he was coming back? She looked for his clothes in Eve's wardrobe, the leather jacket, the check shirts, the sweatshirt with UNIVERSITY OF CALIFORNIA, BERKELEY mysteriously printed on it. Everything was gone. Sometimes he had left his gold earrings on Eve's dressing table, but these too had gone with him. The awful possibility that, having gone, he might still tell tales of Eve to the Tobiases or to education authorities brought her down from euphoria into the depths again.

She had to ask.

"He won't be telling anyone anything," Eve said. "Believe me. I promise."

A letter came addressed to him and Eve opened it. He had asked her to do that, she said. Inside the envelope was a note from an estate agent who wrote that he would have phoned but it appeared that Mr. Drummond and Mrs. Beck were not in the directory. Was Mr. Drummond still interested in making an offer for The Conifers? The name, for some reason, made Eve laugh a lot.

She wrote a letter to the estate agent but Liza didn't see what she had said. They went out together to post it, up the lane to the main road where there was a little old post box with VR on it for Victoria Regina, which meant it had been there for a hundred years.

The month was July and Liza was eleven and a half. The good weather lasted for only a short time, it rained and grew cold and Eve and Liza stayed in, doing more lessons than they had for months. Liza could write French composition now and recite from memory Keats's "Ode to a Grecian Urn."

Because it was so wet, the Tobiases didn't come down as they had said they would, and in August Jonathan Tobias came alone. Liza noticed he had some gray in his hair. Perhaps because Victoria wasn't with him, he spent more time at their house than he had done for years. Liza couldn't help overhearing some of the things that were said, for Jonathan seemed to think that when a person was reading they were deaf to everything.

Victoria, he said, was in Greece with friends. To Liza, Greece was a place full of gray stone temples with colonnades and marble statues and where gods lived in the rivers and trees. It hardly accorded with her ideas to hear that Victoria and her friends found beaches there to sunbathe on and big hotels to stay in, the kind of thing, Jonathan said, that they preferred over Shrove or Ullswater.

Sometimes, aware that she had looked up from her book, he would lean closer to Eve and speak in a whisper. Wishy-wishy-wishy, the way she remembered Heather murmuring. And Eve nodded and looked sympathetic and whispered something back. It troubled Liza that Jonathan seemed to think Bruno was only temporarily away, for this made his departure seem less than permanent.

"I can't help being envious, Eve," he said one sunny afternoon.

The summer had come back and they were all having tea in the garden, under the cherry tree. The bird cherries were ripening to yellow and red and there was scarlet blossom on Eve's runner beans. The courgette plants had flowers shaped like yellow lilies and the gooseberries were dark red beads, but beads that grew hair on their crimson skins.

"Of *me?*" said Eve. "Envious of me?"

"You've got someone you can be happy with. You're in a good relationship."

Liza waited for Eve to deny it or even tell him not to say "relationship." She didn't. She gave Jonathan a mysterious sidelong glance, her eyes half-closed.

"I don't want you to envy me," she said. "I'd rather you were jealous."

There was silence. At last Jonathan said, "Of him?"

"Why not? How do you think I have felt about Victoria?"

Eve got up then and carried the tea things into the house. Instead of following her, Jonathan sat there on the grass, looking glum. He pulled a daisy out of the lawn and picked the petals off. Liza thought he was getting to look old. The freshness had gone out of his face and there were lines across his forehead. His eyes had once been of the most piercing clear blue, but the color was muddied like a blue china bowl with dirty water in it.

She expected him to stay to supper and perhaps for the night. Where Bruno had been, beside Eve in bed, he would be found in the morning. But he didn't even stay to eat with them and was gone by seven. The next day Liza thought Eve seemed particularly pleased and happy and she connected this with the appearance of Jonathan at their door at nine in the morning, calling in to say good-bye on his way back to London.

⌣

Sean said, "This is five years ago you're talking about, right?"

She nodded. They were in bed now, snuggled close together for warmth under the two quilts. Sean had bought a second one he'd seen in a closing-down sale. The caravan got bitterly cold at night, but if they kept a heater burning, the condensation was streaming down the walls by morning and their pillows felt damp. Liza, her head on his shoulder, his arms tightly around her, thought of those warm dry weeks, her bedroom with the windows wide open at night, lessons, lessons, lessons, every day in the garden, and Eve saying, "You see, if you went to a so-called proper school you'd be on holiday now, you wouldn't be learning anything but just running wild."

"Wasn't that around about the time of the big storm? What they called the hurricane? I remember because it was when I'd just got to be sixteen. I'd got my first job and I had to get up at five. I was in our kitchen at home, making myself a cup of tea, and the oak tree next door blew over and came through the roof.

It was only a lean-to, our kitchen, and the roof broke like an eggshell. Lucky I was quick off the mark, I got out just in time. It must have been like September."

"It was October. October the fifteenth."

"What a memory! I reckon you had a lot of trees come down at Shrove. Is that how you remember?"

The Day of the Hurricane, the last day she ever gave a name to.

"You're not to hurry me, Sean. I'll get to that soon. We got the hurricane very badly at Shrove. We were one of the worst-hit places, and you'll see why I remember it, the precise date and everything. But there was something else happened first."

〜

The outbuildings at Shrove House were seldom used. They had been stables once and there was a coach house. The stables were built in the same architectural style as the house, of small red bricks with white facings, a pediment over the central building, and above it a clock tower on which the clock face was blue and the clock hands gold. The weathervane on the tower was a running fox with brush extended.

Mr. Frost kept his lawnmowers, the big one he rode on and the small one with which he did around the flowerbeds, in the section of stable to the left of the coach house. Other garden tools were kept in there as well as a ladder and an industrial vacuum cleaner. As far as Liza knew, no one had ever kept cars in the stables. Perhaps they might have done so when old Mr. Tobias was alive, but Jonathan always left his car standing out in the courtyard in front of the stables, and visitors left their cars there too. The stables were really useless, no one went into them, and they remained standing, Liza had heard Jonathan say, only because they were pretty and also a listed building. That meant they were of historic value and must never be pulled down.

She had never been inside them, though she had once seen Mr. Frost come riding out of the section by the coach house on the little tractor that pulled the mower. She came to search them as a last resort.

It was years since she had needed the library steps to climb up to the picture frame for the key to the television room. At nearly twelve she was almost as tall as Eve, would be much taller by the time she was grown-up. Eve, in any case, had long ceased to bother to hide the key or even take it out of the lock. She must have decided Liza was too old now to be seduced by the charms of television, too mature to be intrigued by locked rooms, or thoroughly conditioned in the discipline of a sequestered life. These days she even pushed the vacuum cleaner about in that room in Liza's presence and seemed to take it as quite natural her daughter never asked what the box with the screen on it was.

When she needed the steps but couldn't find them it was for quite another purpose, their primary purpose. *The Confessions of an English Opium Eater* was on the top shelf, far out of reach. The book would have been out of Jonathan's reach and he was six feet three. Although she knew that it was all of two years since she had put the steps back in the library, that she had several times used them in the library since then, she still went to look behind the long curtains in the morning room.

Returning to the library, she saw why they had been replaced. The new ones were up in the dark corner, farthest from the windows, wooden ones this time, perhaps of dark oak, and almost invisible against the dark oak floor where the carpet ended. They were not really steps at all but more like a piece of a staircase consisting of three stairs. Jonathan must have brought them with him when he came in August. Liza could see without attempting to move them that even when she stood on the top stair she wasn't going to be high enough to reach that shelf.

She started to search the house for the missing steps. Eve said she wasn't old enough yet for De Quincey, she wouldn't understand the *Confessions,* there would be plenty of time for her to read it when she was older. And Liza hadn't even wanted it that much when she first came into the library. The title had drawn her to it, for it seemed to have something to do with those drugs she heard about on television. But she wanted it now. She wanted it because she couldn't have it, she couldn't reach it, it was up there in its faded blue binding with the faded gilt flowers on its spine, smugly sitting where it had sat undisturbed for years, for perhaps a hundred years.

The steps wouldn't be in any of the bedrooms but she searched them anyway. She found clothes that must be Victoria's in the wardrobe of what she had always thought the nicest bedroom, a big, light room that looked across the water meadows to the river. A skirt hung there and a pair of jeans and the green silk shirt she had been wearing the first time Liza ever saw her. There were also an embroidered white cotton nightdress and a matching dressing gown. It looked as if Victoria had been sleeping in that room while Jonathan slept in the big room at the front. The steps weren't in there either, or in any of the cupboards, or downstairs in any of the rooms that gathered around the kitchen, the boot room and the pantry, the washing room, the larder, and the storeroom.

Liza went outside to the stables. She could hear the drone of Mr. Frost's mower from the bit of lawn behind the shrubberies. The stables were never locked. There were no locks on the doors, though the coach house had a padlock fastening together the handles on each of its double doors. For some reason, she left looking in the section where the mower had been till last, which was strange because it was the obvious place. Except for the one where the tools were kept, the stables were all quite empty. She couldn't open the coach house doors, only peer through the cracks in them. They were old doors with quite a big split between two of the boards. She could just make out a car inside.

The steps were propped up against the wall between where the tractor had been and where the small mower stood. Liza took them into the house, carried them into the library, and climbed up to get *The Confessions of an English Opium Eater*. It was while she was coming down with the book in her hand that the significance of a car in the coach house where no car had been before fully struck her.

Mr. Frost was now in sight, wheeling around the big lawn on his tractor, wearing gloves and ear muffs. He didn't see her. She replaced the steps, then thought better of it, carried them out again and propped them up in front of the locked doors. High up under the pediment were two small windows.

Liza climbed the steps to the top. That brought her just high enough to see over one of the windowsills. The car stood in the middle of the coach house floor with plenty of space around it. Even so, she couldn't see the name of the make, but she could see the registration plates with the letter at the end of the number instead of the beginning. It wasn't too dark to make out the color, a deep brown, the burnt sienna of Bruno's paintbox. Bruno was gone, but this was Bruno's car, the Lancia car Bruno's mother had had for ten years and only driven seven thousand miles.

The sound of the mower approaching made her look around. Mr. Frost got off his tractor to open the stable. He never talked much, he wasn't the kind of grown-up to ask what she was doing.

"Mind you don't fall," he said.

Going home, carrying the book, she had thought of that night after Bruno had left, how she had slept so uneasily and dreamed so much she couldn't tell in the morning what had been dream and what real. The car she had heard—that had been Bruno's car. She had heard Eve driving Bruno's car up here to hide it in the coach house.

⌒

Sean was asleep.

Liza wondered how long he had been asleep, at what point in her narrative he had ceased to listen. Scheherazade. Did the king or sultan or whatever he was fall asleep while she told her stories? Was that in fact the reason she never reached the end of each tale? Because her husband fell asleep first?

Sean was snoring lightly. She pushed him over onto his side so that his back was toward her. Another thing she wondered about was if the sultan and Scheherazade made love before she started on the story or in the middle or what? They must have done that, that was the point of his marrying all those women, wasn't it? There was nothing about it in the book she had read. There wouldn't be, she thought, people cut things out of versions meant for children. Even for children who'd seen what she had seen.

Invisible in the dark, she smiled to herself at Sean's squeamishness. She hadn't told him about the smell of those stained rags or, to spare him, about the red paint fingerprints on the stone floor of the little castle. Up in the vaulted ceiling among the beams a spider had caught the death's-head moth in its dusty web. Sean wouldn't have wanted to hear about that, either, the rare moth long dead among the dusty threads, but the skull pattern on its back still palely gleaming.

A disused airfield near the place where the caravan was parked provided them with somewhere for Liza to have her driving lessons. With Sean in the suicide seat—his words—she drove up and down the old runways and learned how to do a three-point turn on the flat area outside a dilapidated hangar.

"You'll pass your test first go," Sean said.

As November began, Liza began to think more and more about Eve and about her trial, which was surely due. She regretted now that when she had the chance she hadn't learned more about crimes and justice and courts. Eve would have known, Eve could have told her.

For instance, would they have it here in the city, which had once been the place the train started from? Or would it be far away in London at what she thought might be called Newgate? I must go to London sometime, she thought to herself. It's absurd never having been to London, even Sean's been to London. She ought to start buying newspapers, but she didn't know which one would be best. Already she had seen enough of them to know that the little ones with the tall headlines would only print the most sensational or sexy parts of a trial while the big ones with pictures of politicians might not print it at all. Television might have it on only once and that maybe on the evening Sean was watching his football.

Life wasn't easy in the caravan. If you wanted to be warm you also got wet. Sean got hold of a tarpaulin from a farmer who had used it to protect a haystack from heavy rain and they spread it right over the caravan. That helped, but it also made it dark. All their water had to be fetched from the stream and boiled. It was impossible to wash clothes and bed linen, which had to be taken to the one launderette still remaining within a ten-mile radius. They used two inches of water in a bowl and tried to wash themselves all over in that.

Liza had got very good at sneaking baths at Mrs. Spurdell's, quite often managing to have one while Mrs. Spurdell was actually in the house, waiting till she was on the phone—she spent hours on the phone talking to her daughter or her friends—and taking two minutes in the tub before giving the bathroom a thorough clean. Even so, Mrs. Spurdell had once or twice remarked on the quantity of water she had heard gurgling down the plughole.

At the school half-term, when Mr. Spurdell had also been in

the house, bathing was impossible, the risk was too great. His study was upstairs next door to the bathroom and he was usually in the study, or liable to go in there. On that late October day, a Monday, she arrived at Aspen Close determined on having a bath. Mrs. Spurdell would be out for an hour, having her hair done. Liza had overheard her making the appointment. She was therefore dismayed to find Mr. Spurdell at home, apparently recovering from the flu, which had struck him down on the previous Friday afternoon while he was reading, according to his wife, Spenser's *Faerie Queene* with the A-Levels English form.

He wasn't up but she had no reason to believe he was asleep. Mrs. Spurdell said he would probably get up later and come down in his dressing gown. Then, if she was still at the hairdresser's, Liza could make him a cup of tea. Mrs. Spurdell put on her new Burberry. She tied a plastic rain hood around her head, not because it was raining, it wasn't, but to make sure she had it with her to protect her set on the way home.

Liza thought she would have to do what she had advised Sean to do. Knowing nothing of hotels, she just the same understood that they must have a great many bathrooms. The Duke's Head, which she passed on her way to Aspen Close, must have more bathrooms than any private house. If Sean didn't want to pay for the swimming pool or the showers, why didn't he just walk into the Duke's Head, march upstairs as if he was a guest there, find a bathroom, and have a bath? Who would know? He'd have to make sure to take a towel with him, of course. He could put a folded towel inside his jacket and take a plastic bag to put it in after it got damp.

It was stealing hot water, Sean said, it was dishonest. He was quite shocked. Stay dirty then, said Liza. She wouldn't think twice about doing it, in fact she'd probably do it on her way to meet him after work. Realizing that she couldn't because she had no towel made her feel cross and she thumped her way into the study, dragging the vacuum cleaner behind her.

Mr. Spurdell had acquired two new books since she was last in there. Liza cared very little about Mrs. Spurdell having a new Burberry or her hair done or unlimited hot water or Mr. Spurdell driving a six-month-old BMW, but she did envy them the books. She resented them for the books, it made her hate Mr. Spurdell especially, though in many ways he seemed nicer than his wife. She sometimes saw him on Friday afternoons returning home just before she was due to leave. The new books he had got were a *Life of Dickens* and *The Collected Short Stories of Saki.*

What wouldn't she give to read that *Life of Dickens*! She could never afford it, she wouldn't even be able to afford it when it came out in paperback. Quickly she forgot all about Mr. Spurdell. She ceased to listen for him. The Dickens in its brown-and-gold jacket was in her hands, she was sitting at the desk reading the introduction, when he came quietly into the room. It was only because of the little dry cough he gave that she knew he was there. She jumped up, clutching the book.

He was a small man, as thin as Mrs. Spurdell was fat. Liza had sometimes thought they were like Jack Sprat and his wife, he able to eat no fat and she no lean. He looked old, an old man who should have retired by now, his jowls melting into a withered neck, his head bald but for a white fringe around the back. Over striped pajamas he wore a brown tweed dressing gown with a cord around the waist tied in a neat bow.

His genial smile brought her immense relief. She wouldn't have to go back to Sean now and tell him she'd got the sack.

Relief became indignation when he said, still smiling, apologizing as if to an ignorant child, that it was a pity there were so few pictures in that book.

"I don't want pictures," Liza said and she knew her tone was surly.

Up went his white tufts of eyebrows. "How old are you?" he said.

After she had spoken the truth she remembered too late the lie she had told his wife. "I'm nearly seventeen."

"Yes, I would have guessed about that. Some of my pupils are your age, only they prefer to be called students." He held out his hand for the book and she gave it to him. "Thank you. I haven't read it yet." Without knowing in the least how she could tell, she fancied this was the way teachers behaved. Bossy. Commanding. Imparting information. As she thought this, he imparted some. "Dickens was a great English writer, some would say the greatest. Have you read any of his books at school?"

"I don't go to school," she said, and added, "anymore. I don't go anymore." What did he think, that she took days off school to come and work for his wife? "But I've read Dickens. I've read *Bleak House* and *David Copperfield* and *Oliver Twist* and *Nicholas Nickleby* and *A Tale of Two Cities.*"

His evident astonishment gave her a lot of pleasure. She thought he'd ask her why she left school so young, she was prepared for almost anything, but not for him to point to the several volumes of Dickens he had in paperback and ask her if she had read *Our Mutual Friend.*

"I told you the ones I've read," she said but not this time in the surly voice.

"Well, you're a surprising young lady. Not quite what you seem, is that right?"

Liza thought this was truer than he knew. She changed the

subject, asked him if he would like her to make him tea, and when he said he would, preceded him downstairs.

Mrs. Spurdell was back before the kettle had boiled, recounting to her husband some long tale of how the hairdresser had read their daughter's name in a magazine, as the author of a letter to the editor about family law. The hairdresser—"who was really quite an intelligent girl, considering"—had cut out the letter but forgotten to bring it. She would bring it next time. Philippa was so modest she hadn't said a word about it. She hadn't mentioned it to her father, had she?

While this was going on, Liza went back upstairs. She finished the study, she made the bed Mr. Spurdell had recently vacated, and ran the vacuum cleaner across the carpet. By then it was time to leave. Mrs. Spurdell was paying her, fishing about in a jar on the windowsill for a five-pound note and claiming to have mistaken a ten-pee piece for a fifty-pee, when her husband came back into the kitchen and handed Liza *Our Mutual Friend* and *The Old Curiosity Shop*.

"I should like them back sometime but there's no hurry."

"You'd better write your name on the flyleaf, dear," said Mrs. Spurdell. She laughed reminiscently. "Do you remember how Jane used to write inside *her* books: 'This book was stolen from Jane Spurdell'?"

It was extremely rude but Liza didn't care. Having something new to read was wonderful. She'd been spinning out the *Life of Mary Wollstonecraft*, making it last, which was an irritating way to have to read something. Mr. Spurdell giving her *Our Mutual Friend* was rather interesting, a sort of coincidence, because that was the book she'd tried to read when she gave up on *The Confessions of an English Opium Eater*. Eve had been right about that, she wasn't old enough for it, and she hadn't been old enough for *Our Mutual Friend*, either, but she would be now.

She'd started to read it that same evening, when she got back from finding Bruno's car in the Shrove coach house. It was a strange thing but she'd never really considered telling Eve what she'd found or asking her why the car was there. She thought she knew why and then she wasn't sure if she did or not. It might only mean that Bruno was coming back, that for some reason he had gone without his car and Eve was storing it for him, he hadn't gone for good. Eve had said he had, but Liza no longer entirely trusted her to tell the truth.

After concentrating on it for all of an hour, she had abandoned the De Quincey and attempted *Our Mutual Friend.* Perhaps she was tired because she hadn't been able to cope with more than the first page. She still lay awake a long time, wondering about the car and what might have happened to Bruno. Nobody had ever known where Bruno was except his mother and now she was dead. His wife hadn't known and neither had his wife's friend the dentist. The estate agent had but Eve had written to him.

That was the night she dreamed Bruno was with them still but about to leave. His silky brown hair was tied back with a piece of ribbon so that you could clearly see the two gold rings in his ear. And his face had even more than usual that angelic look, like a saint in a painting, that so belied the rough speech that sometimes came from that cherubic mouth. She didn't see him leave in the dream. Eve told her he had gone, and later she heard a gun being fired. She was walking in the wood and she heard shots behind her. But this was all in the dream, not in life. On the actual night after Eve said Bruno had gone she had heard no shots, she had heard nothing but a heavy object dragged downstairs and a car being driven away.

Where had the car been all day? Bruno couldn't have gone away in it or it wouldn't have been there for Eve to drive up to Shrove in the nighttime. But it wasn't there, it hadn't been outside when Liza came home. So had Eve hidden it somewhere? Liza realized she could have hidden it almost anywhere, behind the birch tree copse or under the overhanging branches of a hedge, she could have hidden it a few yards from the gatehouse and Liza wouldn't have seen.

Watching a football match that was coming from somewhere in Germany, Sean didn't for a while try to stop her reading. He no more expected her to watch football than she expected him to read Dickens. They had a bottle of wine the supermarket had on sale, the week's special offer.

Rain lashed the tarpaulin that covered the caravan. A howling gale blew the rain in savage spurts against the uncovered parts of the windows so hard it sounded as if they must break. The caravan rocked and shivered.

Liza and Sean sat close together with one of their quilts wrapped around their legs. While Liza read about Eugene Wrayburn, Sean watched the German team soundly beat the English one. He switched off with a sigh and, having first put his arm around her, began to comb her hair. It was a cunning move on his part, he knew the sensuous pleasure she took in it, stretching like a cat and extending her neck as the comb passed slowly through the curtain of smooth dark hair.

He said softly, "What had happened to him, Bruno, I mean?"

Liza closed her book. "I don't know. I mean, I didn't know then. I found out later." She considered. "You'll have to wait till I come to the hurricane."

"Okay, then what about those Tobiases? They split up, didn't they?"

"Not until the following year. But I never saw Victoria again. Jonathan wrote to Eve and told her he was living at Ullswater and Victoria was living in the London house, and soon after that Victoria left altogether. I think she went off with someone."

"So your mum started hoping again?"

"Yes. But that was a way off. I don't know what she felt about the divorce—they got divorced two years later—she never showed me her feelings about that. Somehow I think she understood she'd played it all wrong before."

"She should have made herself harder to get," said Sean.

"Or easier. If she'd gone with him to all those places he wanted her to go to, even to London sometimes, if she'd done that I don't think he'd have ever taken up with Victoria. Eve was prettier than Victoria and cleverer and he'd known her since forever. She had all the advantages. Except that she'd never go away from Shrove, not even for a weekend." She looked up at him. "Should I have made myself harder to get, Sean? I was easy, wasn't I? I just jumped into your arms."

"Oh, you." He laughed and, putting the comb down, hugged her in his arms. "You was a real little innocent, you didn't know no better."

"Was I? Shall I tell you about the hurricane?"

"Wait a minute, I'll fill up your glass. There's one thing I want to know first. Didn't no one come looking for Bruno?"

"Who was there to look? If his mother had still been alive it might have been different. If he'd said he wanted to buy that house. If he'd been to a lawyer or whatever it is you have to do when you buy a house. If the sale of his mother's house hadn't gone through and he'd still been waiting for the money. If he'd still been living in those rooms over the greengrocer's. But as it was, nobody knew where he'd lived and no one needed to get in touch with him."

"It gives you the creeps when you come to think of it."

"I went back into the little castle and everything of his was gone, the paintings, the canvases, the paints, and that pile of rags. It was all gone and the place had been scrubbed out. Even the ceiling, she'd cleaned the ceiling and got rid of the spider's web with the moth in it."

"Those rags, what was it you thought was on them?" Sean spoke in a low voice, tentatively. "You never thought that was paint, did you?"

"I did then. Now I think it was blood."

Sean was silent, his face grim. After a moment or two he said, "Tell about the hurricane, then."

"There's one other thing first. That picture Bruno painted of me, it turned up on our living room wall. One morning I came downstairs and there it was. Eve had taken away the Shrove at sunset picture and put the one of me there instead."

"What did she do that for?"

"I don't know. It didn't look like me, but I suppose she liked it. I'll come to the hurricane now."

As if to encourage her, the wind slapped another burst of rain against the window behind them. The caravan rattled. It hadn't rained that night, the Night of the Storm, the Hurricane, the Great Gale. The storm had been dry, an arid tempest that came up out of the Atlantic, bearing salt on its back. Salt lay in drifts on the windows of Shrove the next day, white as frost, dry crystals the wind had sucked off the sea.

"All the leaves were still on the trees," she said, "that was the worst of it. If the branches had been bare the gale wouldn't have been able to pull the trees over, but they were still in full leaf, leaves don't really fall till November, and they made the treetops like great sails."

"Was you at the gatehouse, you and your mum?"

"When weren't we there? We never went anywhere."

She would have slept through it, enormous though the noise of it was. A heavy sleeper, at the age of eleven she would have slept through bombs falling. Eve woke her up. Eve, who was frightened of nothing, was frightened of this. She woke her up for companionship, for someone to be with, not to be alone while the world was torn to pieces around her.

It was just after four in the morning. Pitch dark and the wind roaring up the valley like an invisible train, a ghost train. The real train that had once run along the valley had never sounded as loud as this. They still had electricity when she came downstairs, rubbing her eyes, peering about her, but the lights went out as she entered the living room. Somewhere out there the wind had brought the power lines down.

"What is it? What's happening?"

Eve said she didn't know, she'd never heard wind like this. Not in this country. We didn't have hurricanes.

"Perhaps it's not a hurricane," Liza said. "Perhaps it's the end of the world. The Apocalypse. Or a nuclear bomb. Someone's dropped a nuclear bomb."

Eve, putting candles into jam jars, said how did she know about things like that? How did she know about the Apocalypse? Who had told her about nuclear bombs? *The television,* thought Liza. She didn't answer.

"Of course it's not a bomb," said Eve.

The candle flames guttered as the windows rattled. Something of the wind penetrated even in here. The curtains bellied out and flattened again against the glass. Eve tried the radio before she remembered that electricity worked that too. For the same reason she couldn't make tea. The nearest gas was five miles away. Liza thought how isolated they were, the nearest house in that village where Bruno had nearly bought a house two miles distant. It was like being marooned on an island in the midst of a rough sea.

She looked out of the window, the glass shuddering against her face. It was still too dark to see much beyond the tendrils of creeper that cloaked the gatehouse till the leaves fell. These streamed out in the wind like blown hair, pulling a black curtain across the window. An enormous crash from somewhere not too far distant drove her back into the middle of the room.

"Come away," said Eve.

Roof tiles clattered off one by one, three of them, each making a sharp crack as it fell and smashed on the stones. The wind was both constant and sporadic. All the time it blew at a steady rate, but it came in gusts too, each one thunderous, tearing through trees and leafy branches, between tree trunks, among bushes, each gust blowing itself out on a howl and a final crash. The earth shook and the ground heaved.

"The trees," said Eve, and then, "the trees."

Her face was white. She put her hands over her ears, then brought them down and clasped them, wringing them. Dismayed, Liza watched her pace the room. This was Shrove where it was happening, Shrove which meant more to her than anything in this world or out of it. These were Shrove trees and at each nearby or distant crash Eve winced. Once she put her hand over her mouth as if to stop herself crying out.

At about six it started to get light. Dawn had been a yellow bar across the eastern horizon. Liza crept out into the kitchen to look at it, for Eve wouldn't let her go upstairs. The wind abated not at all with the pale spreading of light but seemed to take new

life from it, roaring and tossing and circling with a shrill whistling sound. A single leafy branch spun in the air and crashed to
the ground. The walls of the gatehouse shuddered. The windows
rattled. Liza watched the darkness recede from the sky, the livid
streak fade, the gray color whiten, and a mass of high, clotted,
scurrying cloud reveal itself.

The cherry tree lay across the garden, its branches and dense
foliage spread over the lawn, the flowerbeds, Eve's kitchen garden, its roots pointing dark brown, thready fingers into the air. As
she watched, the whistling wind, the invisible engine, struck the
ash that marked the edge of the lane and the giant tree shuddered. It seemed to hold itself suspended before a quivering
convulsed it and it toppled over out of Liza's sight, leaving a
sudden white space where all her life had stood this strong, stout,
leaf-crowned barrier. She gasped, putting her hand up to her lips.

"Come away," said Eve. "Don't look."

It wasn't until the afternoon that the gale blew itself out. Eve had
tried to go outside before that but the wind had beaten her back.
Broken branches and twigs, dying leaves, covered the front garden and the lane. One of the Shrove gates had come loose from
its fastenings and slammed shut, tendrils of solanum trapped
between its iron curlicues.

Liza had never seen her mother in such a tragic mood. She
was unhappier than she had been when she heard of Jonathan
Tobias's marriage. She was worse than unhappy, she was distraught. The sight of the fallen cherry tree made her weep and
she kept crying out that it wasn't real, it couldn't be true.

"I can't believe it, I can't believe it. What's happening?
What's happened to our climate? This is madness."

From the gatehouse they couldn't see much. The balsam still stood, though stripped of one of its limbs, but fallen trees blocked their view on all sides. It was as if the gatehouse had been surrounded by a barricade of broken tree trunks and branches, as if the wind, invested with purposefulness and malice, had built it up to hem them in. They were in the midst of a fortification of wind-hewn timber. Liza could see that they would have to climb over logs and scramble through leafy boughs to get out the front gate. Eventually they emerged together at three in the afternoon, clambering over the balsam's huge bough, which blocked their way.

Liza felt very small and alone but she would have considered herself too old to take Eve's hand if Eve hadn't taken hers first. Hand in hand, they stumbled toward the gateway of Shrove. Inside the park, devastation lay on both sides of them, ruined trees and shrubs in heaps where they had fallen, havoc as if man-made, Eve whispered, like pictures she had seen of country- side after battles. Tree stumps stood with shredded trunks point- ing skyward. A bird's nest, a huge structure of thick twigs and woven reeds, had been torn from some once-high treetop and lay in their path.

"Paradise destroyed," Eve said.

Two of the great cedars had gone. The limes were down, most of the ancient trees, only the slender supple birches and the little pyramidal hornbeams remaining. Laying waste the park, the wind had spared the house, which stood staring calmly at them, its glazed eyes all intact, its roof unscathed. All that was changed was that a stone vase had tumbled off a pillar at the foot of the steps.

A pale sun, weak and watery, though no rain had fallen, gleamed like a puddle of silver among the soft drifting clouds. Beyond the gardens, beyond the water meadows, a waste of

felled willows and splintered poplars, beyond the shining ribbon of the river, the high hills showed hollow places in their
woods, holes in the fabric of tree cover as if scissors had ripped
rents in cloth.

The air was scented with sap from the ripped leaves and salt
from the distant sea. All was silent, the birds silent, but for a
plover making its unearthly cry as it wheeled above them.

"Eve was in an awful state," Liza said to Sean. "She was like
someone bereaved. Well, like I imagine someone bereaved
would be. You know you read in books about people tearing out
their hair. She almost did that. I found her sitting in our living
room clutching handfuls of her hair. She moaned and cried and
threw herself about as if she was in pain. I didn't know what to
do, I'd never seen her like that.

"I wonder if she'd have been half as bad if it wasn't trees that
had been destroyed but me. That was when I began to get the
feeling Shrove was more important to her than I was. It frightened me and I didn't know what to do.

"There wasn't anyone I could turn to, you see. There wasn't
anyone. Well, the milkman came and he was useless. Now the
trains didn't run anymore he could only talk about the weather
and I'd had enough of weather for a lifetime. Mr. Frost came to
see if there was anything he could do. I said, you could get her
a doctor and I think he thought I was crazy. What's she got wrong
with her, then, he said, and I couldn't answer him, I knew he'd
think Eve was mad or I was. No one's phone was working, he
said, and it might be a week before we got our electricity back.
I was left alone with her and I felt helpless. I was only eleven.

"She calmed down a bit next day. She lay on the sofa. We
couldn't cook anything but we'd got bread and cheese and fruit.
I went up to Shrove and found a packet of a dozen candles. I
found a Calor gas burner we could boil a kettle and an egg on,

though it took hours. She fell asleep in the afternoon and I went up into the wood, the bit we called our wood.

"I don't know why I went really. It didn't upset me the way it had her, but I'd seen enough fallen trees and destruction to last me forever. But I still went up there. Maybe I thought that if somehow the wind hadn't done much damage there, if for some reason it had escaped, that would be something to tell her and cheer her up.

"Afterward I wished I hadn't gone. I wished I'd stayed at home with her. It caused me such a lot of worry."

"What d'you mean?" Sean asked.

"You'll see. It was what I found there," she said. "Of course it didn't matter in the end."

As soon as she came close to the wood, to what had been the wood, she knew her hope had been forlorn. From a distance you couldn't see what lay beyond the outer circle of trees, she and Eve hadn't been able to see when they walked up the lane on the previous day, for the oaks and chestnuts on the perimeter remained standing. Like a whirlwind the gale had bored its way in through the outer ring and once inside behaved like a maddened animal, spinning in circles and destroying every vulnerable thing in its orbit.

Not quite everything, she saw as she came carefully between the standing oaks. A few young trees still stood. Here and there a giant had resisted the onslaught while one or two mature trees leaned at an angle, their final collapse delayed. But between them lay devastation.

The leaves on the tumbled limbs and branches were still fresh. They were still as if growing from twigs that proceeded from branches that grew from a living, rooted trunk. A sea of leaves lay before her. There was no wind now, only a little breeze, a joke of nature playing with destruction, that fluttered all the leaves, scalloped oak and pointed cherry, five-fingered chestnut and oval beech. The leaf sea was a dark quivering green from which protruded here and there an upturned root like a fin, or a broken trunk like the funnel of a wrecked ship. It reminded her of the sea after a storm in a picture in the library at Shrove, for the real sea she had never seen.

For a while she stood there, just looking. Then she waded into the sea of green. Once she began, the image ceased to hold, the comparison was wrong. This was not a matter of striding through water, but of clambering across a rough terrain. Where once had been paths and clearings were broken wood and torn brambles, concealed stumps to trip her up and shattered logs to block her way.

Yesterday she would have been incredulous if anyone had told her she might not find her way through the wood. But so it was. Everything was different. The wind had laid it waste and made a nearly impenetrable wilderness where yesterday morning had stood the ranks of trees and between them, in the depths, had stretched aisles of mysterious green shade. All was havoc now and all was curiously the same. Was it here, for instance, that the great isolated beech had stood, spreading its branches in an arc so huge as to form a circle of deep shade with a radius of fifty yards in which no grass or plant could grow? Or was it here that the larches had been, conifers leafless in the winter but green with new needles in the spring? She couldn't tell, but when she found the beech, felled and prone, its vast trunk gray as a wet seal, its wrenched-out roots clotted with earth and stones, when she saw that she could have cried like Eve.

Struggling onward, climbing over fallen trunks and pushing

aside sheaths of thick foliage, she made her way aimlessly, hardly knowing what she was seeking. Somewhere it hadn't happened? A region of the wood miraculously untouched?

There was just one place. But this only because no trees had stood in the clearing she came to. She had an idea where she was now, in the very heart of the ruined wood, its center, where once a ring of cherry trees and field maples had encircled a grassy space. On the tree stump in the middle of that grass she had sometimes picnicked.

She moved toward it now and sat down on the broad, flat, smooth stump. She looked about her, aware for the first time of the silence. No birds sang. There had always been birds in the wood but at the hurricane's assault they had departed.

The maples and cherries were mostly fallen but some still stood, the biggest and oldest leaning at a steep angle. She wondered if it would be possible to save those half-fallen trees, if there was some way of hauling them up and holding them. Who would do it? Who was there to care? She got up and made her way to the half-toppled cherry, put her hands on its trunk. It felt firm, as steady as an upright, growing tree.

There was nothing to do now but go back, to try to find her way back through the welter of broken branches. She ducked under an overhanging limb of maple, looked down and recoiled, jumping backward and hitting her head. She scarcely felt the pain. Her breath indrawn sharply, she put her hand up over her mouth, though she had no inclination to cry out.

Almost at her feet, *at* her feet until she had retreated that step or two, lay a long bundle of sacking. She could see it was a sack, of the kind Eve said they used to put potatoes in and of which there was a pile in the stable at Shrove, though it was stiff with earth and gravel. And it wasn't just a sack, it was a bundle with something inside it. A length of string, now quite black, had been tied around the top and another length around the bottom.

No, not the top and the bottom, Liza found herself saying, not that but the head and the feet. She came a little closer, not frightened but awed. It had made her flinch and jump back at first; now she was curious. Whatever this was, the storm had unearthed it, tearing up a tree root and heaving it out of its burying place.

Its burying place . . . She was conscious of the smell now. It was a smell she had never smelled before. Strange, then, that she knew it was of something rotten, something that decayed, re-minding her—yes, she knew what it was—of long ago, when Heidi and Rudi used to come. One of them had buried a meaty bone and later, perhaps weeks later, Eve while gardening had dug it up, stinking, maggoty, as green as jade, a beautiful color really. . . .

She knelt down. She held her breath, somehow knowing she must hold her breath. There was a tear in the sacking at the top of the bundle just above the string. She picked at it, making the hole bigger. It split open quite suddenly and a flood of soft brown, silky hair spilled out. It spilled into her hands, thick and slippery. The hair came off in her hands and she was holding it. She stumbled away and was sick among the broken branches.

IT was Bruno?" Sean said.

She nodded.

"You poor kid. A kid might never get over something like that."

She wished he wouldn't say "somefink" but there was nothing to be done about it.

"Well, I did. I got over it. I didn't even dream about it. It's a funny thing, you know, but you can't help being sick. It's not what your mind does, it's your body. I was curious, I really wanted to know, I suppose you could say I was *interested*. I knew it was Bruno's hair, I knew it was Bruno dead in there, and I hadn't liked Bruno, I'd hated him, I was glad he was dead, but I threw up just the same. Weird, isn't it?"

He didn't understand. "You must have been shattered to bits. You didn't know what you was doing."

Useless to persist. She gave up trying. "I didn't know what to do next. There wasn't anything I could do but go back home and leave that thing lying there for anyone to find."

"Let's get this straight," said Sean. "She'd killed him, right? She's real bad news, your mum, isn't she? She'd killed him like she killed the man the dogs went for?"

"Oh, yes, she'd killed him. I don't know how. I never said anything about it to her. I was only eleven but I knew she'd killed him and—well, there didn't seem anything to say, if you know what I mean."

He didn't know. She could tell that. "She was in a state, anyway. She was depressed, in a real black depression, for quite a long time. I wasn't going to tell her a thing like that, not something that would worry her as well."

"There must have been someone you could tell. Tobias, like, or the old chap—Frost was his name? No one'd have expected you to get the police, not at your age, but hopefully they'd have done that for you. Didn't you never think of that?"

It was dark in the caravan. She looked at him in the dark and made out his puzzled expression. "She's my *mother,*" she said quietly. He didn't respond, and when she said how it had worked out for the best, how the body was concealed once more, he hardly reacted. "She killed him because he threatened everything," Liza said. "He was going to part her and me and make us leave Shrove."

"Okay. No need to get excited." Sean hesitated. "How did she do it?"

"I don't know. I didn't hear any shots that day he disappeared, but I wouldn't have so far away. You remember that blood on the rags in the little castle? I think she may have used a knife."

He had gone a little pale. "Wasn't you scared of being with her? I mean, she could have turned on you."

"Oh, no." Liza laughed. "I was like the bird that lived inside the crocodile's mouth, I was safe whoever else wasn't."

"I wish you hadn't told me, not that about the sack and the hair. I shan't get no sleep."

"I shall," said Liza, and she was asleep very quickly, her arm around his waist and her forehead pressed between his shoulder blades. If he lay awake, haunted by what she'd told him, she was oblivious of it.

⟿

Cautiousness made her rather quiet next morning. She boiled the water for their tea and her perfunctory face-washing in silence. It was perhaps unwise to go into too many details with him. She had told him rather too much on the previous night but now she would be more careful. That remark of his about the police she hadn't liked. Eve had been arrested, had no doubt appeared in one court, was somewhere in a prison, but still there must be many things they didn't know and need not know.

It wasn't one of her days at Mrs. Spurdell's, but still, "I'll come into town with you," she said. It was almost the first thing she'd said that morning. She took the spare set of car keys with her.

For the first time she went all the way into the Superway car park with him, noting where he put the car. He went off into the store and she, having bought a pair of bath towels at Marks and Spencer, wandered casually into the Duke's Head, where she encountered no one in the front hall or on the stairs.

There was no soap in the bathroom. She should have thought of that but how was she to know? She took a bath just the same, enjoying a prolonged soak in the hot water, free from any anxiety about Mrs. Spurdell returning unexpectedly, and dried herself on both of the thick fleecy towels. On her way out a man in a suit and tie asked her if she needed help. Liza said she was looking for Mrs. Cooper. She didn't know many names, having come across so few people, and had to fall back on those from fiction or, as in this case, the name of Eve's invented cleaner.

"Is she staying in the hotel?"

Liza said she was expected today or tomorrow. The man looked in his book and said she'd made a mistake but cast no suspicious glances at the Marks and Spencer's carrier full of wet towels. He didn't seem at all cross or anxious for her to go and as he talked to her about the fictitious Mrs. Cooper, speculating as to where this woman might be staying or how a member of his staff could have made an error, Liza was aware that the way he looked at her and the way he spoke were full of admiration. As Sean would put it, he fancied her.

From Sean alone had she experienced this, had accepted it without thinking others might share his feelings. Now she was beginning to understand desiring her wasn't some idiosyncracy of his but might even be common. She felt her power.

"Don't hesitate to come back if we can help you at all," the man said as she left.

At the rear of Superway she got into the car and started the engine. She drove around the town, teaching herself things Sean hadn't been able to teach her on the airfield. How to start on a hill, for instance, and how to stop in a hurry. He would have been cross because she hadn't got a license or insurance, but that didn't matter because she wasn't going to tell him.

After returning the car, she had to wait nearly an hour for the bus to get her back and then there was a mile-long walk from the bus stop in the rain.

The days that followed her discovery of Bruno's body remained very fresh in her mind. They were dark days, there was no electricity and they lit log fires to keep themselves warm. Because Eve did almost nothing, sat staring at the wall or hid herself in bed, Liza did her best to clear up the front garden, moving all but the biggest and heaviest branches. She went up to Shrove every day on her own, fetching back useful things from the kitchens, firelighters and nightlights, stone hot-water bottles, tinned food, coffee and sugar. It was stealing, she now supposed, though she hadn't thought of that at the time.

One afternoon she went up to watch television. She hadn't associated the television with the electricity supply but she did when she switched it on and nothing happened. It occurred to her to try the phone, though she had never used a phone, but that too seemed dead and stayed silent no matter how many of the buttons she pressed.

She and Eve had no idea of what might be happening in the outside world. That, she now understood, was what Eve had always wanted, to be isolated, to be cut off from all that lay beyond Shrove. But she had hardly wanted it to this extent. Liza suddenly thought of the radio in Bruno's car. That didn't work off the main electricity, somehow it worked off the car itself, perhaps by some means from the engine.

Bruno's radio would tell them what the hurricane had done, if the whole world was devastated, if the electricity had gone for good, if all the phones had been destroyed. But it was no good thinking of that. She wouldn't know how to start the engine or turn the radio on and, even if she could find out, the car was locked away in the stable and the key hidden somewhere.

The next day it no longer mattered, for the electricity men came to mend the lines. Their van went past the gatehouse, bumping over broken twigs and dead leaves. Later, when she went out, she came upon them up on the high poles, restringing cables, and one of them, thinking perhaps that she came from Shrove itself, called out to her that her TV antenna was broken. The storm had torn it from the roof and it was hanging over one of the chimneys.

Liza didn't know what he meant. She had never heard of a TV antenna. To her the complicated grid thing that looked like one of the shelves from their oven was just something you saw on roofs, probably a kind of weather vane. After the men had gone and the lights and heating came on again, she went up to Shrove to watch television.

This time it came on but not properly. The picture ran about all over the place, it rolled over as if someone were turning a handle inside it, lines formed, or the screen looked like a piece of coarsely woven gray material. You couldn't see the people's faces clearly and their voices sounded as if they all had colds.

It was a long time before Liza made the connection between the failure of the television and the broken oven shelf on the roof. She thought it had simply gone wrong. It was old and it had gone wrong. She felt helpless, knowing there was nothing she could do without telling Eve. Her viewing afternoons were over. Jonathan never watched television, this set had been his grandfather's and he certainly wouldn't get a new one or have the antenna mended.

She walked sadly back to the gatehouse. Watching Eve, who hardly spoke, who went through the motions of getting their supper while her thoughts were far away, Liza decided that her mother had no more cause for grief than she had, who had lost just as much, who had lost her only friend.

She had grown up a lot in the weeks that followed the hurricane. It was as if she aged three or four years. She began to know all sorts of things, she was sure, that people don't usually know at eleven. For instance, how to be alone with a woman nearly mad with misery and grief, while feeling—yes, she'd felt it even then—that somehow it was wrong to care so much about a *thing*, a place, a piece of land, a house. If she cared in the same way about the television set, she was only a child while Eve was grown up. It only made her pity her mother the more. She had to look after her, be kind, not trouble her, encourage her in the only thing that distracted her: giving lessons, imparting knowledge. Liza sometimes worked at her textbooks from early morning until late in the evening just to keep Eve's mind off the destruction and the mess out there.

The other thing that helped this fast growing up was her anxiety over Bruno's body. Eve had buried it in the first place because she wanted it hidden, because if it was found she might be in serious trouble. Liza had some inkling of the kind of trouble from reading the Victorian novelists. *Oliver Twist* was her handbook and so was *The Woman in White*. Did they still hang murderers? She couldn't ask Eve. And what did hanging actually mean? What bit of you was hung up? She knew a lot more about beheading. From reading about the French Revolution and Mary Queen of Scots and the wives of Henry VIII, she knew quite a lot about chopping off heads.

Would they hang Eve? She was really frightened when she thought of that, she was a child again, more like five than eleven, afraid of bad men coming and taking her mummy away. Like Eve and the spoiled woods, she wanted to hide herself and pretend it wasn't real. Besides, if she asked Eve about hanging it might make her think she had something more to worry about. Liza didn't ask. She and Eve worked at English literature and history and Latin from morning till night.

Until the day came when Eve didn't get up at all. She lay in bed with her face turned to the wall. Liza went out for the first time for days. It was the last day of October, the thirty-first, Halloween, a dry gray breezy morning.

The ruined wood looked different because all the leaves had died. They hadn't turned brown like the leaves on the remaining living trees, but still green, had dried up and curled and shriveled. As she pushed her way through the wreckage the dead leaves crackled. From the depths a pheasant gave its rattling cry and above her in the single standing tree she heard doves cooing. The birds had come back.

Her heart was in her mouth (as she had read) or perhaps she was only starting to feel sick again as she came to the clearing where the flat, smooth stump stood. But there was no fear of being sick this time or of smelling the smell of maggoty bone, for the bundle had gone.

She had a moment of absolute panic, of wanting to run and not knowing where to run to. Someone had come and found Bruno and taken him away. Then she saw what had happened. The body in the sack was still there, was somewhere down there, *inside* there. The leaning cherry tree had fallen and hidden it. The cherry tree she had clasped in her hands to test how stable it was had not been stable at all, had fallen next time the wind blew, and its broad solid trunk dropped on top of the bundle, driving it back into its grave.

Liza examined the place carefully. There wasn't a sign of that bundle unless you knew what to look for, unless you detected the corner of a sack protruding from where the lowest branch grew out of the cherry trunk. She tried pushing it under but it wouldn't go, so she dragged across branches and fetched armfuls of twigs, piling them up to conceal what remained of Bruno.

No one could find it now until men came to clear the wood. She hadn't thought of that at the time, she had simply been relieved, had believed it hidden forever, but no more than a few days after this a lot of workmen came in a lorry with chainsaws and axes. Jonathan came too. The men began by clearing the gatehouse garden and then they started work on the fallen and damaged trees in Shrove park.

That worried Liza a lot. She was sure they would move into the wood and begin shifting the logs and broken trees. For a whole day she worried about it until Jonathan—who sat for hours in the cottage with Eve, the two of them sighing and shaking their heads over what the hurricane had done— remarked in passing that the "little" wood was to be the last place to be cleared. It might be two years before they began to clear the "little" wood.

Eve got up for Jonathan and pulled herself together. She washed her hair and braided it on the back of her head, she put on her tight black top and her blue and purple skirt and smiled and made herself beautiful for Jonathan.

He came and he did what Liza hadn't seen him do for years, put his arms around Eve and kissed her. When Eve sent her away and said to write her history essay upstairs—she called it her "home-work" as if all her lessons weren't done at home—Liza listened outside the door. She heard Eve tell Jonathan it was half-term. Perhaps it was. In that case what she said wasn't really untrue. Of course, that depended on what you meant by a lie. It was a lie if by lying you meant intending to deceive. Eve certainly intended to deceive Jonathan into thinking Liza went to school.

They talked for a long time about the hurricane damage. Both knew a lot of statistics about this being the first hurricane in

England for so many hundred years and about so many million trees being destroyed. They talked about the Great Storm of 1703. It was all rather boring. After she'd heard the bit about delaying till last the clearing of the wood where Bruno's body lay, Liza decided to go upstairs and start writing about the rise of Napoleon Bonaparte. At that moment Jonathan changed the subject and told Eve quite abruptly that Victoria had left him for a lover and the two of them were living in Caracas. There was no hope of a reconciliation, this was what the court called "irretrievable breakdown."

Just as Eve began to say something Liza thought might be interesting there came a great thudding at the front door.

Eve said in a theatrical way, "What fresh hell is this?" and then explained with a laugh that someone called Dorothy Parker had said it first.

The person at the door was only one of the workmen looking for Jonathan to ask about some tree or other, whether to chop it down or leave it as it was, a torn-in-half tree. Liza went upstairs and, not being sure whether Caracas was the capital of Venezuela or Ecuador, looked it up in her atlas.

Jonathan stayed for less than a week. Just one night Liza was almost sure he'd spent in Eve's bedroom. It was a feeling she had, no more, for she hadn't heard them go to bed, had slept soundly all night, and when she came down in the morning there was no sign of him. But she was older, she was beginning to be very aware of things like that.

In January she was twelve.

Next time Liza went to Mrs. Spurdell's it was for one of the afternoon stints, so there was time to put up her hair the way Eve had for special occasions, in a thick braid on the back of her head.

It made her look several years older, she decided. She took with her the books she had borrowed.

Mr. Spurdell seldom got home before she left but he did that day, and he had been in no more than ten minutes when a woman arrived in a red car. Cleaning the bedroom windows, Liza saw her come up the path toward the front door. She was tall and good-looking in a masculine way, with dark hair tied back at the nape of her neck. Her trouser suit was dark gray with pinstripes and her shirt was red silk. But the most attractive thing about her was her warm and intelligent expression that made her look incapable of saying an unpleasant or stupid thing.

Liza waited for the doorbell to ring. Instead she heard the front door open. She must have a key of her own, she thought, and guessed who this was. Jane, who wrote in her books that they had been stolen from her. But she had been much younger then, of course. Jane, the daughter who had something to do with education. Now she could see a resemblance to the photograph.

How could a poor shriveled-up little man like Mr. Spurdell and a fat white-haired creature like his wife have a daughter as nice to look at as this? It was a great mystery. She finished her windows and went downstairs. No one bothered to introduce her, she wasn't surprised about that. Mr. and Mrs. Spurdell just went on talking as if she wasn't there, as if she were a robot cleverly programmed to sweep floors and dust furniture.

Liza said to Mrs. Spurdell that she had finished. Was there anything more she wanted her to do? Mrs. Spurdell said no, there wasn't, and gave her a look as from a feudal lady to a serf, so Liza went into the kitchen and sat at the table, waiting to get her money.

After a moment or two Mr. Spurdell appeared. He saw the books she had brought back on the kitchen table and began to interrogate her about their contents. Who was Miss Gradgrind?

What did Dickens mean by Mrs. Sparsit's Coriolanian nose? What did Mr. Boffin collect? Who was Silas Wegg? Liza was surprised but not disconcerted. She had had plenty of this from Eve and was answering his questions with the enthusiasm of the scholar who thoroughly knows her subject, when the good-looking education woman came into the kitchen.

She raised her eyebrows and gave Liza a wink. "Come off it, Dad, what d'you think you're doing, putting her through an examination? You're lucky she's too polite to tell you where you can put your questions." She held out her hand to Liza and said, "Jane Spurdell. You must excuse my father. He never really leaves school."

"That's all right," she said and, thinking quickly, gave Sean's name. The elder Spurdells had never asked her surname. "Liza Holford."

Mr. Spurdell wasn't at all put out. "This young lady is a dark horse, Jane. I caught her reading my Dickens. I suspect she is on sabbatical, or else she is in our house cleaning for purposes of research. What can they be, I ask myself. Shall we set out to discover her secret?"

"Speak for yourself, Dad," Jane Spurdell said, "and leave me out of it. Her secret, if she has one, is her own affair." She smiled at Liza in a very friendly way. "I say, I do like the way you've done your hair. Is it very difficult?"

Liza was explaining that while it wasn't very difficult to do, it took a long time, you had to allow yourself half an hour, when Mrs. Spurdell arrived with her purse in her left hand and a handful of loose change in the other. Liza could tell she didn't at all like finding her conversing on equal terms with her daughter.

"Perhaps you should have been a hairdresser," she said unpleasantly. "When you've finished the demonstration, I'd like to get through the business of your pay."

Jane Spurdell looked ashamed of her mother, as well she might, Liza thought, and even more embarrassed when she asked for a loan of two pound coins to bring the total up to twelve. Mr. Spurdell had gone upstairs but as she was going he appeared in the hall with paperbacks of *Little Dorrit* and *Vanity Fair.* Liza said nothing about having already read *Vanity Fair.* She was watching, with barely suppressed laughter, Mrs. Spurdell's face as Jane said good-bye and it had been nice to meet her.

In the car, going home, she thought of telling Sean about Jane, how nice-looking she was and how friendly. But she didn't tell him. Without quite knowing why, she sensed he wouldn't like it. He had hated school, alternatively called the teachers power mad and a bunch of snobs. He would think being an educationalist a job for a woman only if she couldn't get a man.

Instead, because he was curious to know, she spoke about the year at Shrove that followed the hurricane. It was strange how much he loved stories. How would he manage if he ever got a girlfriend who couldn't tell him stories? But, of course, he never would get another girlfriend, for they were to be together forever and ever.

"My TV was broken in the storm—well, I thought of it as mine—and I knew I'd never get another. I did lessons all the time instead and gradually Eve got better. It was a lovely summer that year, that was the start of all the lovely summers, the best we'd ever had."

"The greenhouse effect," said Sean.

She was surprised he knew and then angry with herself for being surprised. "Well, maybe," she said. "I wouldn't know. Eve said they had summers like that at the beginning of the century, before the First World War."

"How did she know? She wasn't old enough to know."

Liza shrugged, the way Eve did. "The milkman said, hot

enough for you? He said it every day, he must have picked it up somewhere. The heat didn't stop the men. They worked hard at Shrove, clearing up all the mess, and it didn't look so bad. They'd even planted some new trees in the park and down by the river. The trees did very well because it was like wetlands down there. Even Eve said things weren't as bad as she'd feared and Mr. Frost said every cloud has a silver lining and now with them big old trees gone you could see views you'd never seen before. I think that was the longest sentence I ever heard him speak.

"Jonathan came down to Shrove a lot that year. It was funny really, he never seemed to notice that I was home all the time. I mean, through May and June and July, when everyone else of my age was at school. And in the same sort of way he didn't seem to notice that Mrs. Cooper never came to clean while he was staying at Shrove, though once he was there for nearly two weeks. I suppose he'd had people waiting on him all his life, he took it for granted things got done, cleaning and meals got ready, and his clothes washed. He ate his meals with us, or Eve took them up to him at Shrove. She collected his washing too and washed and ironed it and took it back to him.

"I never heard him say thank-you or even mention it, though perhaps he did when I wasn't there. There were nights I think she spent at Shrove with him, then and at lots of times in the future. If she did, she left the gatehouse after I was asleep and came back very early in the morning. Things were back where they had been before he married Victoria, or she thought they were. She hoped they were.

"They talked for hours about his marriage. They forgot I was there, I didn't have to listen outside the door. She was always asking him about Victoria and the divorce, but I never heard him say a word about Bruno. And all the time Bruno's car was up in his stables and Bruno's dead body was lying in his wood. Rotting in his wood and the worms eating him."

"Liza," said Sean warningly. "Do you mind?"

"Sorry. You *are* squeamish. I don't think Jonathan was interested, I don't think he cared. He was only interested in Jonathan Tobias, and people were important to him only as being useful to Jonathan Tobias. Maybe we're all like that. Are we?"

"I'd put you first, I know that."

"Would you? That's nice. I kept remembering the story she'd told me about old Mr. Tobias and my grandmother and how Eve'd thought then that she and Jonathan were going to get married. It didn't matter about her mother not getting Shrove because she and Jonathan were going to be married. She'd thought like that when I was little and he came down for those three weeks and it was all happening again.

"She thought he'd marry her when he got his divorce. She'd been trying to get him for seventeen years."

s e v e n t e e n

W HEN you're telling someone a serial story you don't say that now you've come to a bit where nothing much happened. It makes your listener not care much about the outcome. Somehow Liza knew this and stopped herself saying it to Sean. Yet, when she was twelve and thirteen, nothing much had happened. Eve had made her work ferociously hard at English and history and languages. She had taught her to sew and to knit and unraveled old sweaters for Liza to knit up again. They had listened to music together, but there had been no drawing or painting, as this perhaps was a reminder of Bruno. Liza missed the television and felt sad on the day the council rubbish collectors came and she saw the old set thrown into the back of the truck.

But nothing of great moment happened. No one came to clear the wood. The British Rail workmen did take up the rails and sleepers where the line had been, but they didn't fill in or block up the tunnel, and the tunnel mouth now yawned like the opening of a cave.

Bruno's car remained locked up in the stable. Once every five or six weeks Liza went to make sure that it was still there. Occasionally, she checked Eve's jewel case to see if the gold ring was still there. It was, it always was. And when Eve wasn't wearing earrings, there were three pairs in the case.

Jonathan came and went. If he talked about Victoria it was only to complain about the amount of money she would expect from him when the divorce went through. Money and property. She would want the Ullswater house and no doubt would get it. He sent a postcard from Zimbabwe and that autumn brought two people with him to Shrove that she had never seen before, a man called David Cosby and his wife, Frances. They came down for the shooting.

"David is Jonathan's cousin," said Eve.

Liza knew about cousins, she had read about them in Victorian novels.

"He can't be his cousin," she objected. "Not if Caroline didn't have brothers or sisters and his father didn't."

"David is his second cousin. He is old Mr. Tobias's nephew's son. He loves Shrove, he loves it nearly as much as I do, I know he wishes it was his."

"If he loves it so much why hasn't he been before?"

"He's been living in Africa for twelve years but now he's come home for good."

David Cosby's face was as dark and shiny a brown as the

paneling in the library at Shrove while his wife's was wrinkled and yellow. The result of the suns of Africa, thought Liza, who had just read *King Solomon's Mines*. They stayed two weeks. This time Eve seemed to be in a rather different position. Liza noticed it without quite being able to say how it was different. Perhaps it was that the three of them at Shrove, unlike Victoria and her friends, didn't treat Eve in any way like a servant. She went up there for dinner three times—Jonathan had caterers to come in and cook the partridges they shot—and left the washing up for Mrs. Cooper to do in the morning.

The funny thing was, of course, that there was no Mrs. Cooper, so Eve had to run up there while they were all out with the guns or in their car and play her pretending-to-be-the-cleaner game. It was a strange thing to do and it made Liza uneasy.

Eve became altogether rather strange in those two uneventful years. Or perhaps she had always been strange and when she was a child Liza hadn't noticed. She had just been Mother. Now, although Liza still knew very few people, she knew more than she ever had before. She could make comparisons. She could begin to question their way of life at the gatehouse, particularly her own. Why did Eve never want to know anyone or go anywhere? Did other people have such a passionate attachment to a place as she had to Shrove? What was the purpose of doing such a lot of lessons, doing them all the time, on Saturdays and Sundays as well, Eve teaching and she learning for hours on end day in and day out? Why?

Eve had stopped going into town. She had found a grocer who would deliver once a week, and what he didn't bring the milkman would. When she did go, a rare once every two or three months, it was to buy books for Liza to learn from, and for another, stranger, reason: to take money out of the bank. Now

Jonathan's checks were sent to the bank by post and the money later drawn out to be hidden at home.

One day, after Eve had come back from town, having paid her only visit there of the entire winter, Liza saw her go into the little castle, carrying a small brown paper parcel. Eve, as far as she knew, had never possessed a handbag. Liza only knew handbags existed because she had seen Victoria and Claire and Frances Cosby carrying them. She saw Eve go into the little castle with the package and come out after a minute or two without it.

Later on, choosing a time when Eve was up at Shrove being Mrs. Cooper, Liza investigated the little castle. It appeared quite empty. There was nothing now to show it had ever been occupied, either by dog or man. She didn't take long to find the loose brick and thence the iron box and the money.

Dozens of notes filled the box, five-, ten-, twenty-, and even fifty-pound notes. She didn't try to count them, she could see there were hundreds of pounds. Besides, she had very little idea of what money was worth. She could have said what five pounds would buy in the time of Anthony Trollope but not what it would buy today, though she suspected a lot less. Eve had never hinted at the amount of money Jonathan gave her. All that Liza knew was that it came in checks. She sent these checks to the bank, brought back the money and hid it here in the wall.

Wasn't that the purpose of a bank, to look after your money? Liza didn't really know. Perhaps everyone behaved like this. Perhaps no one really trusted banks.

But Liza found herself often watching her mother after that, watching her behavior, anxious to see what she would do next. She watched her as once she had listened at doors. There was no listening anymore because Eve never talked to anyone but Liza and occasionally Jonathan on his rare appearances. Sometimes she tried to catch Eve unawares, watch her when she didn't know she was being watched. She would go to bed early, then creep downstairs to watch Eve unobserved from the stairs. But she never saw her do anything except ordinary expected things, reading and listening to music or marking one of Liza's essays or test papers.

She was fourteen before she began asking herself, what will become of me when I grow up? Shall I live here with Eve forever? When she has taught me all the English there is to learn and all the history and French and Latin, what will we do then? What shall I do with all of it?

"Be me," Eve had said, "me as I might have been if I stayed here, happy and innocent and good."

Did she want to be Eve? Did she want to be those things?

That spring, while Jonathan was staying at Shrove on his own, the woodsmen came back to clear the "little" wood.

"Bruno had been dead for nearly three years. I wanted to know how long it took before a body turned into a skeleton but I didn't know how to find out. There weren't any medical books at Shrove or any on forensics. You see, I thought that if he was bones by now, they might not notice so much if they dug him up. I was hoping the sack would have rotted and Bruno just be— well, scattered bones."

"It beats me," said Sean, "the way you can talk about it. A lovely young girl like you, it's weird. You're always the same, like talking about death and stuff that makes other people throw up, you talk about them like they're normal."

She smiled at him. "I suppose it is normal for me. Dead bodies don't upset me. I know I was sick when Bruno's hair came off in my hand but that wasn't *me*, it was a sort of reflex. I expect even doctors do that when they first start."

"You could have been a doctor, d'you know that?"

"I still could," said Liza. "But that's not the point. Maybe other people are taught as children to flinch from death and blood and all that, I mean they're conditioned, but I never was. You've got to remember Eve taught me everything she knew about academic things, but there must be thousands of things children know who lead an ordinary life and go to school that I never heard of. There can't," she said rather proudly, "be many people who've read the whole of Virgil's *Aeneid* in the original and seen two people murdered by the time they're sixteen."

He recoiled a little. The look on his face made her smile again. "Don't worry about it, Sean. It can't be changed, that's the way it is. I'm different from other girls and in some ways I expect I always will be."

"You've got me now," he said. It was something he liked saying and when he said it he always took hold of her hand.

"Yes, I've got you now. Anyway, as I was telling you, the men went up to start working in the wood and I was very anxious. I don't know if Eve was. She was always out and about with Jonathan when she wasn't teaching me. But as it turned out they never found anything. Jonathan had given them instructions to leave some of the logs lying and some dead trees to provide habitats for the wildlife. The cherry log was one they left. It was just chance or luck, whatever you like to call it."

"Luck?" said Sean.

"Luck for Eve, wasn't it? I think she'd been waiting to see what happened. As soon as she knew all was well up there, she got Jonathan to recharge the battery on Bruno's car."

"She did what?"

There hadn't been any real risk. Jonathan hadn't suspected

Bruno was dead. In his eyes, Bruno was just a young healthy man who had been living with Eve, who got tired of her or of whom she got tired, and who moved away. True, he had left his car behind, but Eve had furnished Jonathan with all sorts of reasons for that: it had been his mother's, it was old, where he would be living he had nowhere to park a car. Jonathan was no doubt pleased to be told the car was going at last, Bruno was coming for it, the Shrove stable would be vacated. Recharging the battery on jump leads from his own car engine was a small price to pay for that. Liza didn't know if this was how it was, she told Sean, but it seemed a fair guess.

Eve didn't say a word to Liza about Bruno. It was Liza who overheard her telling Jonathan that Bruno would come for the car tomorrow, the day incidentally that Jonathan himself was going back to London.

"I wondered what she'd do, how she was going to handle it. I even pretended to go out for a long walk in the afternoon to give her a chance to move the car. She did move it and she went off in it, but only to town. She came back an hour later with the boot full of groceries and left the car parked outside the cottage."

"What did she say when you asked when Bruno was coming?"

"I never did ask," said Liza. "She expected me to ask, but I didn't. I knew where Bruno was. I knew he couldn't be coming. I knew his body was up in the wood under the leaves I'd piled around it. We were absolutely silent with each other about it. There was Bruno's car and she was using it—*we* were using it, she drove me to the village once and into town, I had a rash and had to see the doctor—but she never mentioned Bruno and neither did I. Then one day the car wasn't there anymore."

"What d'you mean?"

"She got rid of it. I don't know how or where. But she must

have done. She must have driven it somewhere in the night. I've no idea what happened to it, I don't know about things like that, I don't know how you'd get rid of a car."

"Just leave it parked somewhere, I reckon. Hopefully some-one'd nick it." Sean considered. "If the police got it in the end they'd try to find the owner and they could, that'd be easy, they'd do it in seconds on the computer."

Liza said thoughtfully, "The owner was dead. I don't mean Bruno, I mean his mother. It was still in her name, he said so."

"I don't reckon they'd go to the trouble of tracing who the car'd been passed on to and if they tried they wouldn't find him, would they? And they wouldn't search either, not for a man of his age. They'd reason he'd gone off abroad somewhere. Your mum was clever."

"Oh, yes, she was. If they searched for him they never came near us. We never saw a policeman since that one came about Hugh with the beard. When Mr. Frost died it was an ambulance that came, not the police."

༺

Mrs. Spurdell greeted Liza with the news that her daughter Jane had just been appointed Senior Adviser for Secondary Education to the County Council. She was bursting with pride. Since Liza had very little idea what this appointment signified she could only smile and nod. Mrs. Spurdell said it was a team leadership role and payment was on the Soulbury Scale, information that served only to confuse Liza further.

Though she had said nothing about an errand of mercy two days before—and Mrs. Spurdell spoke constantly of her advance plans—she announced that she was on her way out to visit a friend in the hospital. Liza guessed the visit was taking place only because there was exciting news to impart and wondered just how ill the friend was when she saw her employer take some weary-looking grapes from the refrigerator as a gift and transfer them to a clean plastic bag.

As soon as Mrs. Spurdell had gone, Liza had a bath. Then she went into Mr. Spurdell's study to see if he had any new books and spent a happy half hour reading a short story by John Mortimer. It was about courts and barristers and judges and opened to her a whole unknown new world. It also made her think about Eve and wonder when there would be anything in the papers about her. How long must it be before she came to trial?

To save buying one, she always went quickly through Mr. Spurdell's newspaper. As usual, there was nothing. Time to get down to the cleaning, but before she started she looked up Jane Spurdell in the telephone directory. It was the first time she had ever looked up anyone in a phone book but it wasn't hard to do. She was listed twice, not as "Miss" but as Dr. J. A. Spurdell. Liza would never forget the address. By a curious coincidence that might be a good omen of something, the number was the year of her birth and the street name startlingly familiar: 76 Shrove Road.

She'd never forget it but why should she want it? Perhaps it was only that she'd liked her, she liked her better than any woman she'd ever known except Eve. Of course that wasn't difficult, seeing that the other women she'd known were Heather and Victoria and Frances Cosby and Mrs. Spurdell. When you liked people, Liza decided, you wanted to know everything you could about them.

Mrs. Spurdell kept her waiting while she rummaged about in one handbag after another for fifty pee. This made her late and Sean was already there, out on the pavement, when she got to Superway. He had news for her, he was quite excited, but insisted on saving it up until they were in the car on the way home.

"They want me to go on a training course."

"Who's they?"

"Superway. It's a management training course. They're pleased with me, the way I do my work and the way I always get in on time and all that. It's in Scotland, it's a six-month course, and hopefully at the end of it if I'm any good I'd go on to what they call Phase Two."

Liza didn't know what to say. She didn't really understand, so she listened.

"I've never said any of this to you, love. I've never talked about myself much. But I've always reckoned to not being much, if you know what I mean—well, rubbish, to be perfectly honest with you. I was useless at school and I left the day after I was sixteen. I'd been skiving off for months before that. No one ever suggested CSEs to me, I mean it'd have been a laugh. I never even saw myself doing nothing but unskilled laboring work, and that's what I did do. Then Mum got her new fella and they didn't want me, so I moved out. Well, I reckon I've told you all that. I got the car and the van and I took to the road and if I thought about it at all I reckoned I'd be living from one odd job to another until the time come to draw my pension. And now this has come up. It's sort of shook me. It's given me something to think about, I can tell you."

She was moved by him because she hadn't known he could be so articulate. He was so beautiful. It would mean something to her if he could speak and think as handsomely as he looked.

"What will you be?" she said slowly.

"I don't know about 'will.' I said it's given me something to think about. As for what I'd *be*—well, hopefully I'd *be* a manager one day. I'd sort of have my own store, maybe one of them big new ones on an estate."

"We went to one of those, Eve and Bruno and me."

He made a movement as if to brush this aside impatiently. "Yes, you said. I'd have a lot to learn. I'd be an assistant manager first. It'd take awhile. But I'm young, love, and I'm keen."

She wouldn't mind going to Scotland. Now she had begun, she liked traveling about and imagined moving from place to place during the next few years. "Are you going to, then?"

"I told them I'd like to think about it. I said to give me a couple of days."

The caravan was cold and damp. It usually was these evenings when they got home. Liza lit the burners on the oven, the oven itself, opening the door, and started the oil heater. Very soon the condensation began, the water running down the windows and lying in pools. She didn't much mind, as she said to Sean, you didn't have to look at it. So long as she had fish and chips or takeaway, books to read, and a warm bed with Sean to make love with, she didn't care much. Now that she had television and knew she could have it whenever she wanted, she seldom watched it. There was something to be said for being brought up without luxury, without many material possessions. Unlike Eve, she had never wanted Shrove or thought it might be hers.

One gloomy evening rather like this one when Jonathan was in a gloomy mood, she heard him tell her mother he had made his will and was leaving Shrove to David Cosby.

"It should remain in our family," he said like a character in a Victorian novel.

"He's ten years older than you," said Eve.

"His son can have it, then. They're all fond of the place. There's one thing, Victoria won't want it, she won't ask for this place in settlement, she hates it."

Aged fourteen, taller than Eve, looking like a young woman, Liza was developing a woman's understanding. She had begun to ask herself how it could be that Jonathan, who had known Eve since he was a boy, who had been close to her, her lover off and on (and now very probably on again), could have so little comprehension of how she felt about Shrove. He could talk with casual indifference about it to Eve, who loved it better than any person, better, perhaps, Liza sometimes thought, than her own child. He could talk about it to her as if it were just a piece of property, a parcel of land, even a nuisance. And he could talk about leaving it to a cousin whom, until this year, he hadn't seen for twelve years, without its apparently crossing his mind that he might leave it to Eve, as his grandfather had promised to leave it to Eve's mother.

Liza suspected that he too didn't like Shrove much. It was October now and this was only the second time he'd been down this year. His real life was elsewhere, doing things she and Eve knew nothing about. And he knew nothing about what they did. He never asked. It was as if Shrove was something to be packed up in a box when he was away from it and she and Eve puppets to be packed up with it.

Next day he was back again at the gatehouse telling Eve his divorce decree had at last been made absolute and Victoria had "taken him to the cleaners." He was free now. Liza heard him ask Eve if she ever heard from Bruno these days. She said she hadn't and she never would, that was all over and she was free as air. She was as free as he was.

Liza was listening outside the door and Eve and Jonathan were sitting in there in the dusk, the lamps unlit. She heard her mother say that about being free and then she heard the silence. Next morning Jonathan went off to London and thence to France, where his mother was dying.

A postcard with a picture of a French cathedral on it came after about a week to say that Caroline Ellison was dead. Smiling rather unpleasantly, Eve said she supposed he thought a churchy card was suitable for announcing a death while one with mountains or trees on it wouldn't be. Jonathan didn't sound grief-stricken, though it was hard to tell from a postcard. Eve was sure he would come back now, but he didn't and six months later they got a card from him in Penang.

Before that, before the winter started, Liza found Mr. Frost lying dead on the grass beside his tractor.

No one knew how old he was. Eve said very old because his daughter had been only a few years younger than her own mother, who would be seventy if she had lived. For the past few years he had done nothing beyond sitting on the tractor and driving it around the lawns. It was Eve who pulled out the weeds and put the mowings on the compost heap.

It was in early November, an exceptionally dry, sunny November, when Liza found him. He had been giving the grass its last cut before the winter. She was walking up from the river, taking the short cut across the Shrove garden. The sound of the mower had stopped ten minutes before and she thought he must have finished for the day. But the tractor was still there, in the middle of the sunny lawn, yellow leaves of lime and chestnut falling onto the grass, onto the tractor's black leather seat and scarlet bodywork, and onto the body of the old man lying beside it.

At first she didn't know he was dead. She was immensely curious. Her hand on his forehead encountered the coldness of marble. She could see that his veiny blue eyes were dead, they were quite lightless, and there was no breath from his slack mouth or movement of his chest. He no longer looked like a person but rather like one of the statues on the terrace, a prone figure in pale, cold stone.

The strange thought came to her that Eve would bury him. At once, immediately, she knew this was nonsense but she had thought it. She ran to the cottage and Eve came back with her and they went into Shrove House and phoned for an ambulance. They couldn't think what else to do even though they knew he was dead.

Mr. Frost had died of old age. His heart had broken—it had literally broken—with age. And who, now, was to do the Shrove garden?

No one, in the depths of winter. There was nothing to do when the snow came and the frost set hard. On the day Liza became fifteen, the snow fell so thickly and for so long they had to dig their way out of the front door.

But snow seldom lasts for long in England. In February, where it had lain were clumps of snowdrops, and by March the grass was starting to grow, there were catkins on the hazels, and the blackthorn was in bloom. Liza had her lessons in the morning and after lunch Eve went out on the tractor to cut the Shrove grass. The wide stretches of lawn were easy to mow. It wasn't much more than a matter of sitting on the seat and steering, but the edges had to be cut as well and the awkward bits between the new trees. Eve was on her knees pulling out the weeds after sunset, almost until dark.

Liza had never asked her why. She stopped asking questions of her mother after Bruno disappeared. It wasn't a conscious decision on her part not to ask but as if a voice inside her bade her be silent. Asking was dangerous, asking would only do damage, provoke lying, cause embarrassment. Don't ask. So she had never asked, why go on pretending to Jonathan that Mrs. Cooper exists? What harm can it do to you or me if a woman comes here to clean? She had never asked, what did you do with Bruno's car? And now she didn't ask, why are you doing this work in the garden? Why don't you find a successor to Mr. Frost?

Not only was she silent about these things, she also supported Eve in her subterfuges. It seemed natural to do so, it seemed right. For a long time now, when the rare people she saw asked her about school, how she was getting on, if she was on holiday, she had been saying, all right and yes, she was. Jonathan had once asked her, as he was leaving, if Mrs. Cooper was expected next day and Liza had said yes, knowing it would be Eve herself who would clear up at Shrove. She even told Eve he'd asked her. Wasn't she the crocodile bird who warned its host of impending danger?

It was now Eve who performed the tasks that had once been Mr. Frost's. Liza wondered if Jonathan even knew Mr. Frost was dead. Perhaps Eve herself simply kept the checks for his pay that Jonathan sent her. She now had the entire care of Shrove House, its gardens and its grounds in her hands, with Liza helping. Liza hated gardening but she couldn't be there and watch Eve do it all on her own, so she trimmed the edges with the long shears and pushed the little hand mower about, so bored she could have screamed.

Then, around midsummer, Eve found a man to do it. It was a very hot summer, the hottest of Liza's life except the one when she was a six-month-old baby. The grass stopped growing and the sun burned it brown, so there was watering to do instead of mowing. Sometimes Eve was so tired with carrying watering cans and pulling the hosepipe about that she fell asleep on their sofa and Liza had to get the supper. The weeds still grew too. Nothing stopped the nettles growing and the burdock.

Eve said, "I have to keep it going. I have to look after the young trees. It's so beautiful, I can't let it get in a mess. There's not a lovelier place in England. I can't bear to think of it all going to ruin."

Her hands were stained and cracked, the fingers ingrained with dirt, the nails broken. The sun had burned her face dark brown but her nose was peeling. Liza saw threads of gray in her dark hair, which had nothing to do with the sun but perhaps something to do with her hard life. Now that Liza was older she was beginning to see that Eve had made her life hard of her own volition, had made all kinds of difficulties for herself where there might have been ease and pleasantness. But she never asked why.

She did ask, why him? when the old man appeared at the gate saying he'd heard in the village they might be wanting someone to help out at Shrove. From whom had he heard? The postman perhaps, the milkman. Eve was to tell Jonathan he'd heard from Mrs. Cooper. He wasn't quite as old as Mr. Frost, his hair wasn't even gray, but his face was very lined and withered. A hump grew out of his back, which made Liza shrink a little when she saw it. She had always been accustomed to physical beauty or at least conformity. The old man's back was curved as if his spine had been bent into a bow the way you could bend a willow twig. He had strong arms and very large hands.

Eve said, yes, he could come twice a week. She sounded reluctant, grudging, and Liza understood that she had wanted to keep Shrove all to herself. It wasn't just a matter of not having people who might gossip or tell tales about the place, or it wasn't that *anymore*. She wanted exclusive possession of Shrove. If she was going to take Gib on—that was the only name they knew him by—it was because she was worn out, she had hurt her back and had to rest, she could no longer cope alone.

"But why him?" said Liza.

"He lives alone, he's not very bright, he won't try to take over. He can't talk much, didn't you notice?"

Gib had an impediment in his speech that made him hard to understand. He liked riding the mower, he worked hard, and if he couldn't tell a cultivated plant from a weed, he did his best, trimming the edges and sometimes proudly leaving in the midst of smoothly hoed earth a fine specimen of dandelion Eve said he had lovingly nourished up. She went around after he had gone, pulling up the weeds he had nurtured.

Jonathan came in August, while Gib was still with them, and talked a lot about the holiday he was about to take in British Columbia and the Rocky Mountains. He had no wife now and since his divorce he had brought no other woman to Shrove except his cousin's wife, Frances Cosby. But he didn't ask Eve to go with him to Canada. Once or twice Liza thought he came very near to doing this, but he didn't ask her. Perhaps he remembered the rebuff he had received all those years ago when Liza was little, or else he thought she wouldn't be able to leave Liza and they couldn't take Liza because she, of course, was at school.

Would Eve have gone if he'd asked her? Would they somehow have managed about Liza, said she could take time off school? Seeing her mother's sad, almost grim expression after Jonathan had gone, she thought that this time Eve would have said yes.

He didn't ask her but he did, at last, have the bathroom done. It was ten years since he had first promised to do it, but when Liza pointed this out Eve only shrugged and said they must be thankful for small mercies.

Jonathan had gone to the bathroom to wash his hands, only there was no bathroom, there was just the kitchen sink. Perhaps it wasn't pretense when he said he thought a bathroom had been put in years ago, he was sure of it, he thought Victoria had arranged it. Perhaps he really believed that. Eve only smiled and claimed she had forgotten his promises. But the builders came before he had left Shrove, built an annex onto the back of the gatehouse, and turned it into a bathroom.

One of the builders was Matt. They had always wondered what he did, Eve and Liza, and now they knew. He was a bricklayer, like Rainer Beck. The other one was some relation of his, a young man with yellow hair dyed pink at the front. The weather was so hot that Liza lay out in the back garden in the sun after bathing in the river. She had a black swimming costume that had been Eve's. The noise Matt made when he saw her was a whistle on two notes, the meaning of which was lost on Liza, who took no notice of it. She took almost no notice of either of them, for neither was handsome and she already knew that she preferred good-looking people.

The whistle was repeated and Eve came out and told her to cover herself up or come indoors. She explained that Matt and his cousin found Liza attractive, now she was growing up, and that was their low and vulgar way of showing it.

Liza digested this and pondered it for a long time. She wondered why there wasn't anything low and vulgar about the way Jonathan had made a similar sound when he saw Eve all prepared for him and dressed up in a black-and-scarlet skirt and black jumper from the good-as-new shop in town. But perhaps his laughing afterward and kissing Eve made it all right.

Gib was taken ill. The postman who brought Eve the message said he was often ill. He wasn't strong and the jobs he took on never lasted, though he tried, he did his best. By this time it was autumn and the grass at least no longer needed attention. And the rain came at last, day after day of it, until the river rose above its banks and flooded the wetlands, so that the trees stood in water to halfway up their trunks.

They were quite alone, Eve and Liza, in those last months of her sixteenth year. Gib didn't come back and there wasn't, anyway, much to be done in the garden. The oilman came and filled the tank while Eve and Liza were out walking, so they didn't see him, and the postman took to delivering their few letters before either of them was up. As for the milkman, he disappeared and was replaced by a man with red hair who whistled all the time. He told Eve *their* milkman had gone into a home because the dairy had found out about his mental age and said he could no longer work for them.

Jonathan was on the other side of the world, in Hawaii, as they knew from a not-at-all churchy card with a picture of a girl surfing on white waves. A card came from Heather on holiday in Cornwall and another one at Christmas with a note in it saying she'd moved to London and this was her new address.

Once the spring had come, Eve began to fret about the garden. She seldom went to town anymore, but she had to make the occasional visit. She had to go to buy Liza's jeans, her first pair, that Liza had been nagging her about for ages. When Eve came out of the jeans shop she saw an advertisement in the newsagent's window next door.

It said: "Strong man will do indoor and outdoor decorating, clearing sites, general laboring, gardening, and odd jobs." There was a box number, which Eve said meant he came into the shop and collected the replies he'd had. Liza didn't think much more about it because Eve hadn't been able to put a phone number on her reply and had said it would come to nothing, no one wrote letters anymore.

But he must have written and his letter come while Liza was still in bed in the morning because Eve announced one day that she thought she'd found a gardener and not, she hoped, a septuagenarian this time. She probably didn't guess how young he was, either.

"His name is Sean Holford," she said, "and he's coming for an interview on Tuesday."

SEEING her mother's picture in the paper was a shock, worse than seeing what the dogs did, much worse than finding Bruno. She was sitting in Mrs. Spurdell's kitchen waiting for her money and enjoying her own clean scented-soap smell. She had managed a bath and was screwing up her courage to ask Mr. Spurdell if she could borrow his *Morte d'Arthur,* which wasn't a paperback, when he came into the room carrying a newspaper.

He didn't say anything, he looked at her and, when his wife appeared, rummaging for change in two handbags, made her look at the paper too. They both stared at Liza. Then Mr. Spurdell said, "Isn't that an almost uncanny resemblance?"

Mrs. Spurdell said nothing. She was looking rather cross, the way she always did if Liza appeared to be briefly the focus of attention. Shaking his head as if in incredulity, Mr. Spurdell handed Liza the paper, pointing with one finger at a photograph.

Liza's heart began to beat very fast. The picture was of Eve. She stared at it. It showed a much younger Eve and had apparently been taken some years before and as she looked she remembered. Jonathan had taken it. Eve and she had taken the dogs back to Shrove one summer evening and Jonathan had come down the steps and taken a photograph. She should have been in it but she'd been shy and had hidden behind a tree.

The day that picture was taken was the Day of the Nightingale. How it came to be in a newspaper she had no idea.

"You're the spitting image of her, my dear," said Mr. Spurdell. "It struck me as soon as I saw it. Quite amusing, eh? I thought to myself, I'll run downstairs and show this to Liza before she goes. Not that I imagine she'll be overjoyed to find she looks like a murderess, eh?"

They didn't know then, they hadn't guessed. Liza forced herself to smile as she looked up and met his eyes.

"I don't see the likeness myself," Mrs. Spurdell was saying. "That creature, the one in the paper, is quite spectacularly good-looking, criminal or not. If you didn't know you'd take her for a film star."

Liza wanted to scream with laughter, though she knew it was hysteria, it hadn't much to do with amusement. She tried to read what the paper said, but the print swam and bobbed about. The headline she could make out: ALLEGED KILLER BURIED MAN'S BODY. She *must* get hold of this paper.

Mr. Spurdell was already holding out his hand for it. "I suppose, strictly speaking, we shouldn't call her a murderess or a criminal. She is still on trial, she hasn't been found guilty yet. Can I have my paper, please, my dear?"

Even if he thought it odd, she must have that paper. Knowing her voice must sound hoarse, she said, "Could I—do you think I could keep it?"

He gave his indulgent humoring laugh, a laugh she sometimes thought, seeking words for it, heavy with patronage and patriarchy. "And how am I to do my crossword puzzle?"

The problem was solved by Mrs. Spurdell's snatching the paper out of her hand and thrusting into it—for once in the form of one note and two coins—the twelve pounds for her four hours' work. Liza got up and left without another word, without even a good-bye. She had forgotten all about the *Morte d'Arthur*.

The nearest newsagent had no morning papers left. The next one was closed. On some previous occasion in Aspen Close she had heard Mr. Spurdell talking about the evening paper that used to be on sale but which had ceased to exist some months before. By the time she met Sean she was nearly distraught, pouring it all out to him in an incoherent stream.

Sean was always good in a crisis. He liked comforting her, keeping calm, showing his manly strength. He liked her weak and vulnerable. Tomorrow they would buy the newspapers, they would buy all the newspapers. Hadn't Mr. Spurdell said the trial wasn't over? It would have been going on again today. They would watch the television, every news there was.

When they got home he made tea for her. He hugged her and said not to worry, she had him, he would do all the worrying for her, leave it to him, and he began kissing her and stroking her. That led of course to making love and they were in bed for an hour, consequently missing the six o'clock news.

At nine there was nothing about Eve and nothing at ten.

Sean, who had seen hundreds of television programs and videos about murders and police investigations, said this might be because it wasn't a sensational enough case. It wasn't a child or a young girl who had been murdered or something that had attracted a lot of public attention when it happened.

"I just wish I knew more about it," said Liza, who was a lot calmer by now. "I wish I knew about the law."

"You can't know about everything."

"I'd like to be a lawyer. One day I'll *be* a lawyer."

Sean laughed. "Dream on, love. The other day you was going to be a doctor."

She was in a fever of anticipation when they drove into town the next morning. It wasn't one of her days in Aspen Close and she would either have to pass a solitary day wandering about the marketplace and spend hard-earned cash on the cinema or else go home on the bus. But she couldn't wait till Sean came home before seeing the papers.

They bought three, all so-called quality newspapers, but the story was almost identical in each of them. This time there was no picture of Eve. In the first one, which Liza read feverishly, still sitting in the car, the headline was: GATEHOUSE MURDER PREMEDITATED, SAYS QC.

The account was very long, filling nearly half a page. Try as she would, Liza couldn't take in more than the first two paragraphs.

"I don't understand it, Sean. I don't know what it means. It says she's been charged with the murder of Trevor Hughes. Who's Trevor Hughes? I've never heard of him."

"You better read it all. Read all three of them. Look, love, I've got to go or I'll be late. I wouldn't want to be late, not at this juncture. You can stay here in the car, no one'll see you."

She sat in the car in the Superway's underground car park

and read the accounts in all the papers. None of them had a word about the murders Liza knew Eve had committed. All the accounts were about this Trevor Hughes, a sales representative, aged thirty-one, who had been missing from home for twelve years. It appeared that he had quarreled with his wife and, instead of leaving for a holiday with her as they had planned, had gone off on his own.

Mrs. Eileen Hughes said she had identified her husband from his watch and his wedding ring, which had his name and hers inside it. A dentist had identified him by his teeth. How did they do that? Liza wondered. If she enquired of Sean he would ask if she wanted to be a dentist as well and tell her to dream on.

They had found shotgun pellets buried with the man. Buried in the wood? But surely only Bruno was up there. Now they were talking about this man being buried as well. It didn't seem as if Eve had said anything in the court or anyone had said anything on her behalf. But it was going on again today. At the end of the article it said the trial continues.

Liza felt bewildered. She wanted desperately to know, she wished there was someone she could ask, but the only person she could think of was Mr. Spurdell. Reading the newspaper accounts, she had been afraid of coming on her own name but she hadn't, her name wasn't mentioned. Would it be mentioned tomorrow?

She passed a tedious yet anxious day mooning about the town. The admiring manager was off today, so it wasn't even interesting taking a clandestine bath in the Duke's Head. She bought three paperback books, spending two-thirds of the twenty-four pounds she had earned that week. Sean would be cross. She sensed already that Sean was going to expect her to be pleased if her mother got sent to prison for years and years. How long would it be anyway? At least they'd stopped hanging people.

In the afternoon, after having a hamburger and a sundae in McDonald's, she went to the cinema and saw *Howards End*. Why had she never read any E. M. Forster? Because he was born too late to be in the Shrove library, she thought rather bitterly. Next week she'd buy *A Passage to India*, that was by him she was sure, and anything else he'd written. It took considerable strength of will to make herself leave the cinema and not sit there and watch the program all the way through again.

Sean was waiting. He was sure the trial would be on TV tonight. They switched on at six and again at nine and ten, but it wasn't on. Liza said, "I've been thinking. I know who Trevor Hughes was. He was the man with the beard. It says here he went missing twelve years ago and that was twelve years ago. I was four. I thought the policeman who came called him Hugh. D'you remember I said Hugh? But it wasn't, it was Trevor Hughes."

"The man the dogs went for," said Sean. "The one she shot."

"They must have searched the gatehouse and found the ring with the initials and the date inside. But why him?"

"It's a mystery," said Sean. "Like you say, why pick him? Why not the others?"

"I don't know. I don't know anything. I feel so ignorant." Liza thrust her hands through her hair and looked at him mutinously. "We can't go to the police, there's no one we can ask. It's beyond me, it's driving me mad."

When he saw the new books, Sean didn't say a word. She realized that she couldn't always predict how he would react. He was kind, he was good to her. She thought of the men in the books she'd read and the book she was reading now, she remembered Trevor Hughes and Bruno and Jonathan and thought she was lucky to have Sean. Once or twice she repeated it to convince herself, she was lucky to have Sean.

Quite a long time had passed after Eve told Jonathan the new gardener's name before Liza met him. She first saw him on the day he started, but didn't let him see her. It was mid-March and cold, she had been out for a long aimless walk and was coming back, her boots sinking into the marshy ground above the river. That winter she had been taking more and more of these walks, she had been growing increasingly frustrated with solitude, with sameness, with never seeing another face but Eve's. Lessons had become repetitive and she sensed that Eve had taught her almost all she knew. All that was left now was to write more essays about Shakespeare, examine more pieces of eighteenth-century prose, translate more de Maupassant, and do more Latin unseens. She had read all the books in the Shrove library she would ever want to read. Television was almost forgotten, what it had been like, why she had enjoyed it.

Was the whole of life going to be like this? Sean had asked her later on why she hadn't run away. He hadn't understood the extent of her learning and the depths of her ignorance. At the thought of running away, before she met him, she had felt almost faint with fear. She had never been on a bus or in a train, never bought anything in a shop herself, scarcely been in one, never made a phone call, and most important of all, never had any sort of relationship with a contemporary.

So she went for long walks, sometimes to the isolated villages, there to gaze at a village shop or the notice board inside a church porch, to read a bus timetable or stand outside a school and watch the children come out. She was teaching herself about the world Eve had kept from her. Once, anticipating Sean's question, she had even said, I could run away. But the very words, unspoken except in her mind, had terrified her. She saw herself standing in an empty street at night with no idea where to go, how to find food or a place to sleep. She imagined herself not running away but running *home*, throwing herself pathetically into Eve's arms.

But what was going to become of her? She often imagined the future and in the blackest way. She saw herself old, thirty or more, and Eve a really old woman, the two of them going on just the same, everything the same except that the new trees had grown tall with thick trunks and spreading crowns. Would she become the Shrove gardener when Eve was too old to do the work? Or the successor to Mrs. Cooper? She would be sent to town with the shopping basket and list, to cross the bridge and wait for the bus.

She saw herself crossing the marketplace, avoiding with fear the jostling teenagers, let out like effervescent water from an opened bottle. Stepping into the road to avoid them, keeping her eyes downcast like a nun she had seen in a picture. Afraid to speak to anyone but shopkeepers, and then only to ask in a whisper for what she wanted.

Thinking this way, she came dispiritedly up among those trees that were still saplings and saw someone in the Shrove garden. He was a long way off and for a moment she thought he must be Jonathan. But Jonathan wouldn't be clipping the yew hedge. Jonathan never did anything, he never pulled out a weed or plucked a dead head from a rose.

The man was working on the hedge with a pair of hand clippers. It must be the new gardener. She was still too far away from him to see much, but even from a hundred yards off she could tell he was young. Not young as Jonathan or Bruno were, but really young, the same sort of age as herself. She had never thought of hiding from Mr. Frost or Gib, but she was suddenly urgently sure that this man mustn't see her. He mustn't be allowed to see her casually approaching him.

It was easy to avoid his eye, a matter of keeping to the trees and, when the garden was reached, making her way toward the house. Why she was behaving so covertly she didn't ask herself, for she couldn't have replied.

She approached stealthily, careful not to step on a twig or, when she reached the path, let her feet make a sound on the gravel. Now he was no farther away from her than the length of their sitting room in the gatehouse. She looked at him between the branches and the dull pointed leaves of evergreens. He had finished the hedge and was lifting armfuls of clippings into a wheelbarrow, a tall, straight young man, a boy, with broad shoulders and narrow hips. His hair was raven black. She thought of it like that because that was the way the poets wrote. His face was turned away from her. She thought she might shriek with disappointment if she didn't see his face. But at the same time she knew she'd make no sound whatever he did, wherever he went.

Had she made a sound? She wasn't aware of it, unless her breathing itself had become noisy. There must have been something to make him turn from the barrow he was about to wheel away and look in her direction.

He couldn't see her. She could tell that. She stared. He was absolutely beautiful. His face was a pale olive color but with a flush on the cheeks, and his eyes were a dark bright blue. She saw a perfect nose and perfect lips and thought of the stars in those old films she had seen and of engravings of statues in ancient books and portraits by Titian.

His hands were long and brown. Once she had admired Jonathan's hands but no longer. This man had stars in his eyes and his gaze showed that he dreamed of wonderful things. The gods she read about lived in groves like this, half-concealed by leaves.

Because he couldn't see her and could now hear nothing, he shrugged a little and began wheeling the barrow away. He should have had a spear and a winged chariot but all he had were shears and a wheelbarrow. Liza didn't mind. She didn't even mind him going and she didn't want him to come back. In a strange way she had had as much as she could take for the present. An unexpected energy filled her and she ran all the way home, arriving breathless and throwing herself down on the sofa.

In a voice as casual as she could make it, she said to Eve, "Which days does the new gardener come?"

"Mondays, Wednesdays, and Fridays. Why?"

"Nothing. I just wondered."

The following afternoon she went to Shrove and searched for a picture he might resemble. She had done that when Bruno came, but this was different. That had been for the satisfaction of curiosity, this was an act of worship. Upstairs, next to the painting of Sodom and Gomorrah, was a portrait of a young man in black silk and silver lace. Eve called it "indifferent eighteenth-century two-a-penny stuff," but Liza had always liked it and now she gazed in wonder. Their new gardener in elegant fancy dress made her shiver, but pleasurably.

The next day was Friday and she watched for his car from Eve's bedroom window. It was a big old car, dark blue with patches of rust on the bodywork, and if she hadn't known a car had to have a driver she'd have thought it was moving along by its own volition. Rain fell all day on Monday, so he couldn't come, and it was Wednesday before she had a glimpse of him. His car was parked on the gravel by the coach house. She let herself into the house, went upstairs and into the bedroom with the fine views, the one Victoria had used and where she had left her clothes in the wardrobe. It made her jump to see him just outside the window, almost directly below her.

Clematis climbed across the garden front of Shrove House. He was on the steps, the old ones that used to be in the library, tying the clematis vines to the trellis. If he had turned his head to the right and lifted it a little he would have seen her. Any noise she might make wouldn't attract his attention today. He was wearing a headset and had a Walkman attached to the belt of his jeans.

In the week that had gone by she had sometimes wondered if she was remembering him as more beautiful than he actually was. Now she saw that he was even more beautiful than she remembered. Why did she care so much? She was dreadfully bewildered by it all. Was it just because he was the first person of her own age she had ever known? But she didn't know him.

He looked around suddenly and saw her. She was seized with shyness, with shame almost, and felt the blood rush into her face and burn her cheeks. He put up one hand in a salute and grinned. This made her retreat at once and run out of the bedroom. There was a mirror in a gilt frame hanging on the wall halfway down the stairs. Although she had never done this before, she stopped on the staircase and looked at herself in this mirror.

She thought she was—well, very pretty. Better than that perhaps. Nice eyes, big and dark, a full mouth, good skin, Eve always said, and lots of long dark hair. But—did all girls look like this? She need not be quite so naive. In the town she had seen others, but how could she judge? The old television images had grown vague and misty now. Why, anyway, did it matter? She continued to stare at herself, as if contemplating a great mystery.

For a moment or two, for five minutes perhaps, she had forgotten the boy on the steps. Narcissistically, she communed with herself, studying her smooth face and soft pink lips, the slim body and full breasts. How would she look in a dress like Caroline's? Red silk, low-cut. That almost made her laugh. She was wearing blue jeans, a black sweater with a polo neck, and Eve's old brown parka.

Because she knew he was in the back garden, she let herself out of the front door without a thought. She didn't peer from a window first but came straight out. And there he was, standing on the paving, studying the climbing hydrangea that clustered all across the front of Shrove House.

She stood quite still, staring at him, not knowing what to do, without a word to say.

He smiled. "Hi, there."

Something tied her tongue.

"D'you live here?"

She must speak. This time she wasn't blushing. She fancied she had gone pale.

"I saw you at the window, so I thought maybe you lived here. But the lady said no one did. At any rate you're not a ghost."

That should have made her laugh but she couldn't laugh. She found her tongue but not her poise. "That was my mother said that. We live at the Lodge."

"Out in the sticks, isn't it? It could give you the creeps."

Eve would hate him for "the creeps." "The sticks" she failed altogether to understand. "I have to go," she said. "I'm late."

"See you, then."

She didn't dare run. Guessing he was watching her, she walked down the drive, through the park, certain his eyes were on her. But when she looked back he was gone. His car passed her almost before she was aware of it and there he was waving to her. She was too confused to wave back.

At the gatehouse she read *Romeo and Juliet.* "Would that I were a glove upon that hand / That I might touch that cheek." Her future, the loneliness and the sameness, the oddities of Eve, all were forgotten. His was a face "to lose youth for / To occupy age with the dream of . . ." She turned to poetry, for she had no other comparisons and no other standards.

Talking to Eve, she longed to speak his name but was afraid to. Once she had uttered it, she wanted to talk about him all the time, yet she knew nothing about him.

"Where does Sean live?"

"In a caravan somewhere. What possible interest can it have for you?"

"I wanted to know where Gib lived." It was true. Let Eve believe that, knowing so few people, she was more interested in those she did know than others who had led different lives might be.

"Where does Sean keep his caravan?" This time she need not have used his name but she did use it.

"How should I know? Oh, yes, he said down by the old station. Have you been talking to him?"

Liza looked at her between the eyes and said, "No."

〜

This was the place where she had been so frightened. She had come through the station, carefree, enjoying the day, happy in the sunlight, and had seen Bruno sitting there with his painting things, in his lifted hand a brush loaded with gamboge. He had frightened her with his naked hatred.

"You've never told me why you came that day," Sean said. "D'you know, it was seven months ago. We've known each other seven months. What made you come?"

"I wanted to see where you lived. The way I felt, you want to know everything about a person, where they live, what they eat and drink, what they like doing, the way they are when they're alone. You want to see them against different backgrounds." She thought about it. "Against every possible background. You want to see how they'll be in the rain and what they do when the sun shines on them. How they comb their hair and fill a kettle and wash their hands and drink a glass of water. You want to see how they go about doing all the ordinary things."

Sean was nodding earnestly. "That's right, that's it. You're a clever girl, love, you sort of know it all."

That made her impatient. She waved him away. "I didn't mean to see you. I certainly didn't mean you to see me. I just meant to see where you lived and—well, creep away."

"But I saw you and I come out."

She said reflectively, as if talking of other people, another couple. "It was love at first sight."

"Right on. That's what it was."

"I wasn't hard to get. I didn't keep you guessing. I went into the caravan with you and when you asked if I'd got anyone, I didn't know what you meant. I said I'd got my mother. You tried again, you said, was I seeing anyone? It was hopeless. You had to ask me if I had a boyfriend. Then you said, would I come for a walk with you, and I knew it was all right because that's what people said in all those Victorian novels I'd read.'

"And the rest," said Sean, "like they say, is history."

"You must get the newspapers today. I won't be going in till the afternoon. I'm going to ask Mr. Spurdell to explain it to me. I mean, explain why Trevor Hughes."

"And what you going to do if he twigs?"

"If he guesses, d'you mean? He won't."

Later, when she had finished her work, and she made sure she finished in good time, she went along the passage and tapped on

Mr. Spurdell's study door. He had come in about a half hour before and gone straight up there.

He was wearing his half-glasses, gold-rimmed, and they made him look older and more scholarly than ever.

"If you haven't done my room, you'd better leave it," he said.

It angered her rather that he hadn't even noticed. She had taken particular care over the study, dusting his books and putting them back meticulously in the correct order.

"May I ask you something?"

"That rather depends on what it is. *What* is it?"

She plunged straight into the middle of things. "If someone murdered three people, A, B, and C, and the police knew about C, why would she—I mean he or she—be accused in court of murdering A only?"

"Is this some crime thriller you're reading?"

Easier to say it was, though she was doubtful as to what he meant. "Yes."

He loved explaining, he loved answering questions. She knew he did and that was why she had been so sure he wouldn't suspect anything. Anyway, he was far more interested in instructing than in her.

"It seems probable that though the police know about C, they cannot prove he or she murdered him. The same may apply to B. He or she is indicted for the murder of A because they are certain that is something they can prove in such a way as to make a case stand up in court. There, does that help you find whodunit?"

"Why not accuse—indict—the person with killing A *and* C?"

"Ah, well, they don't do that. You see, if your putative murderer were to be found not guilty by a jury and acquitted, the police could come back with C—or for that matter B—and bring him into court all over again on this different charge. If they

293

charged him with both and he was acquitted, they would have lost all hope of punishing him."

It was always "he" and "him," as if nothing ever happened to women and they did nothing. "I see," she said, and then, "Where would he—she—be while they were waiting to come into court?"

He began talking about something called the Criminal Justices Act 1991, a legal measure to do with sentencing and keeping people in prison, but when he got to the point of the Act just being implemented "now, while I speak, Liza," his phone began to ring. She turned to go but he motioned to her to stay while he picked up the phone.

"Hallo, Jane, my dear," she heard him say, "and what can I do for you?"

The conversation wasn't a long one. She felt that she would have liked to send some message to Jane Spurdell, something like her good wishes, but of course she couldn't do that. Replacing the receiver, Mr. Spurdell said, "I thought you might like to borrow another book." He added rather severely, "Something worthwhile."

This was perhaps a reference to what he believed she was reading at the moment. She took her opportunity.

"How long do they send a murderer to prison for?" Since her introduction to newspapers, she had heard, she thought, of quite short sentences for killing people. "I mean, does it vary according to how they've done it or why?"

"If someone is convicted of murder in this country, the mandatory sentence is imprisonment for life."

She grew cold. "Always?" she said, and he thought she didn't know what "mandatory" meant.

"The word signifies something of the nature of a command. Something mandatory is something which must be. We don't have degrees of murder here, though they do in the United States. If it was manslaughter, now, the sentence might be quite short."

The term meant nothing to her. It would look suspicious if she kept on questioning him. He had picked two Hardy novels in paperback off his shelves. She hadn't read them, she thanked him, and went downstairs to get her money.

T HAT day Eve had been in the witness box.

Liza was astonished to read that she admitted killing Trevor Hughes. Yet she had pleaded not guilty. Perhaps you could explain that when you understood her counsel was trying to get the charge changed from murder to that word Mr. Spurdell had used: "manslaughter." Sean seemed to know all about it.

Today there was a photograph of Trevor Hughes, a faceless man, his features buried in that thick, fair beard. Eve said she had killed him because he tried to rape her. She was quite alone in the house, there was no one living nearer than a mile away. She got away from him, ran into the house to get her gun, and shot him in self-defense.

Prosecuting counsel questioned her very closely. You could imagine there was a lot more than appeared in the paper. He asked her why she had a loaded shotgun in the house? Why did she not lock herself in the house and phone for help? She said she had no phone and he made much of a woman being nervous enough to have a loaded gun at hand but no phone. When she knew he was dead, why had she not phoned for help from Shrove House, where there was a phone? Why had she concealed the death by burying the man's body?

Before she had given her evidence someone called Matthew Edwards gave his. They didn't put things in order in the newspaper but arranged them in the most sensational way. It took Liza a moment to realize this was Matt, and reading what he had said took her back to that early morning long ago when she'd looked out of the window and seen him releasing the dogs from the little castle.

He told the court of the freshly dug earth he had seen and the dogs running about sniffing it and how Eve hadn't been able to answer when he asked if they'd been burying bones. Liza remembered it all. Eve hadn't answered, she'd just asked him if he knew what time it was and told him the time in an icy voice, six-thirty in the morning.

The trial would end next day. That meant this day, today. It would be over by now. Counsel for the Defense made a speech in which he spoke of Eva Beck's hard life. She had more cause than most women to fear rape, for she had already suffered it.

Liza stopped reading for a moment. She could feel the thudding of her own heartbeats. Unconsciously, she had covered the paper with her hand as if there was no one behind her, as if Sean wasn't there, reading it over her shoulder.

"You'll have to read it, love," Sean said gently.

"I know."

"Want me to read it to you? Shall I read it first and then read it to you?"

She shook her head and forced herself to take her hand away. The uncompromising words seemed blacker than the rest of the account, the paper whiter.

At the age of twenty-one, returning to Oxford from Heathrow, where she had been seeing a friend off on a flight to Rio, Eve Beck had hitched a lift from a truck driver. Two other men had been in the truck. It was driven to a lay-by where all three men raped her. As a result she had been very ill and had undergone prolonged psychiatric treatment. The rape had made her into a recluse who wanted nothing more from life than to be left alone and do her job as caretaker of the Shrove estate.

The society of other people she had eschewed and was virtually unknown in the nearby village. She had been living with a grown-up daughter who had since left home.

Liza sat very still and silent when she had finished reading. All her questions were answered. She could feel Sean's eyes on her. Presently he laid his hand on her shoulder and, when she didn't reject him, put his arm around her.

After a moment or two she said quietly, "Ever since I was about twelve, which was as soon as I could have ideas about it really, I've believed I was Jonathan Tobias's child. I didn't like it much, I'd stopped liking him much, but at least it meant I had a father."

"He still could have been."

"No. She never told me all that stuff, that in the paper, but she did say she hadn't seen Jonathan for two weeks before she went to see him off for America. One of those men in the truck was my father. There are three men about somewhere, they might be in the town here, or driving a lorry that we've passed on the road, and one of them's my father." She looked at him and away from him. "I expect I'll get used to it."

She could see Sean didn't know what to say. She made an effort. "It's mostly not true, what they said. She killed people because they threatened her living at Shrove. She killed them because they tried to stop her having what she wanted. No one's said anything about the way she loves Shrove. And as for me, I'm just the grown-up daughter who's left home."

He put his arms around her.

Grown up. Sean had asked her about that. Not the first time they met at the caravan or the second, but soon. She had gone for a walk with him, as promised, telling Eve she was spending the evening in Shrove library, there were books there she wanted that were too heavy to carry home. After the walk they sat in the caravan. He had a beer and she had a Coke.

That was when she started telling him how she'd lived, isolated, almost without society, in the little world of Shrove. "How old are you?" he'd asked, admitting she looked a year or two older than she was but still afraid she might say she was only fifteen.

That first time he didn't even kiss her. Two evenings later it was too hot to walk far, a close, humid, throbbing dusk, and they had flung themselves down in the long seed-headed grass by the maple hedge. She had looked at his face, six inches from her own, through the pale reedy stems. There was a scent of hay and of dryness. The feathery seedheads scattered brown dusty pollen on his hair. He parted the thin strands of grass and put his mouth on hers and kissed her.

She couldn't help herself, she had no control. Her arms were around his neck, she was clutching his hair in her hands, kissing him back with passion, putting everything she had read about love and desire into those kisses. It was he who restrained them, who jumped up and pulled her to her feet and began asking her if she was sure, did she know what she was doing, if they were going "all the way" she must be sure.

It wasn't possible for her to think about it. When she tried to think, all that happened was that she saw images of Sean and felt his kisses, growing hot and weak, growing wet in an unanticipated way that no instruction or reading had led her to expect. She tried to think calmly and reason it out but her mind became a screen of Sean pictures, Sean-and-herself-together pictures, her body shuddered with longing, and she got no further about being sure or knowing what she was doing than she had in the meadow. It came down to this: when next she saw him she would do everything and anything he wanted and everything she wanted, but if she never saw him again she would die.

She read *Romeo and Juliet* again but it no longer seemed to be about what she was feeling. On Monday evening it was raining, so they met in the caravan and made love as soon as they met, falling upon each other in a breathless joyful ecstasy.

It seemed a long time ago now.

Sean switched on the television and they watched the news. For the first time, so far as they knew, it contained something about Eve. They had to wait until almost the last item. The last was about attempts to put an end to bullfighting in Spain, but before that the newscaster announced laconically that Eva Beck, the killer in the Gatehouse Murder case, had been found guilty and sent to prison for life.

Sean held her, he kept his arm around her all night, hugging her tightly when she awoke whimpering. But still he didn't understand how she felt. She no longer had any identity. With Eve's denial—for whatever good purpose—she had ceased to be anyone, and, with the revelations of Eve's history, had been made worse than fatherless.

No words could be found to express what she felt. She had nothing to say to Sean, so she spoke about the everyday mundane things, what they would eat for supper, what food items he should bring back from the store. It was clear that he was relieved not to talk about Eve or the trial or Liza's own new vulnerability, and it pained her, it angered her. Once or twice, during their disturbed night, he had told her she must put "all that" behind her.

Just as he was leaving she surprised him by saying she was coming too.

"It's not your day for Mrs. S., is it?"

She shook her head. He must think she was coming into town because she didn't want to pass this day alone in the caravan. She sat beside him, saying how nice the weather was, a wonderful sunny day for the start of December. In just over a month's time she would be seventeen, but he didn't know when her birthday was, though he might have guessed. When they were first together they hadn't talked much. It had been all lovemaking and the aftermath of lovemaking and its renewal.

Anxious as ever not to be one minute late, he hurried into the store. The car keys were in his pocket, but she had brought the spare set. A map he never used, his sense of direction was so good, was tucked into the back of the glove compartment. She studied it, left it lying unfolded on the passenger seat.

They couldn't do much to her if they caught her driving without a license or insurance. The way she was feeling today she didn't much care what anyone did to her. It no longer mattered if they caught her and found out who she was, because she was no one, she had no identity. She was just the grown-up daughter who had since left home.

She drove past where the caravan was and out onto the big road. The world seemed entirely different here and had seemed so for the past three months, but for all that it was only about twenty miles from where she was going. Passing a garage, she glanced at the gas gauge. It was all right. The tank was nearly full. She began to wonder how she would feel when she came to the bridge and saw the river with the water meadows beyond and the house floating, as it seemed, above the white mists that lay low on the flat land, when she saw the domain that was the only place she had ever known until a mere ninety days ago.

But when the time came she experienced no startling reaction. It was a brisk breezy day without mist. The sun shone with a sharp winter brightness. Shrove House had never appeared so brilliantly unveiled. From halfway across the bridge, half a mile distant, she could pick out the dark spindly etching the clematis made on the rear walls and the features on the faces of the stone women in the alcoves.

The sun flashed sharply off the window from which she had watched Sean the second time she had seen him. She drove up the lane. Someone had been hedging along here, had mercilessly ripped back the high hawthorns. The gatehouse appeared suddenly, as it always did when the bend was passed. It looked the same as ever and the gateway to Shrove was the same except that the gates, for the first time that she could remember, were shut. The gates that, except on the day after the storm, had always stood folded back like permanently open shutters at a window were so firmly closed that the park could only be seen through their elaborate iron scrollwork and the curlicued letters: SHROVE HOUSE.

She walked up the garden path to the gatehouse. Her key she had always kept. She pushed it into the lock and opened the front door. Inside it was icy cold and smelling of damp. The smell was the stench of hollows in the roots of trees where fungus rotted.

The kitchen was dim and dark because the blind was pulled down. Raising it a little, she looked out, and then she let the string go and the blind spring up to its roller with a crack, she was so shocked by what she saw. The back garden, which had been neat with Eve's vegetable beds and flower borders, with the new tree planted to replace the fallen cherry, the small lawn, all of it was a wilderness of thin straggly weeds. These had not sprung up among the untended cultivated plants but were weeds growing on dug earth. The whole garden had been turned over with spades.

For a moment she couldn't imagine what had happened. Had someone else lived here temporarily, dug the garden and then departed? Had some new and zealous gardener taken over and left again?

Then she remembered what the paper had said about Eve burying the body of Trevor Hughes. Somewhere out there it must be that she had buried him, where Matt said the dogs had sniffed the earth. The police had excavated here, looking for more perhaps, looking for a graveyard. Their spades had made this wilderness. She thought of the numberless times they had sat out in the garden under the cherry tree, the work Eve had done, hoeing, planting, harvesting, but it affected her very little. It troubled her no more than walking in a cemetery.

She pulled the blind down once more and turned her attention to the interior of the gatehouse. Having been away from it for so long, she saw these rooms with new eyes, eyes educated enough by variety to find them strange: the vaulted ceilings, the pointed Gothic windows, the dark woodwork. It seemed remarkable now that she had lived here all her life, or as long as she could remember.

This room, the living room, was not as it had been when she left it. Of course, she couldn't tell how soon Eve had gone after her own departure. But she wouldn't have left it like this, the pictures crooked, the ornaments on the mantelpiece in the wrong order, the hearth rug out of alignment. It struck Liza that she had no idea who owned this furniture. Was it Eve's or did it belong in the lodge? Had it been there when Eve and she first came? The sofa had never stood quite like that, pushed flat against the wall. Someone had searched this room. The police had searched it. She had seen this sort of thing in a detective serial on television.

There was something missing from the room. A picture. A pale rectangle on the wall showed where it had once hung, her own portrait, the picture Bruno had painted of her.

It had never, in her opinion, looked much like her. The colors were too strong and her features too big. But Eve had liked it. Perhaps Eve had been allowed to take it with her, had it with her now, would keep it through those long years. The idea was comforting.

Had the police also searched the little castle?

The green studded door was still unlocked. If they had searched, surely they would have locked it after them. Liza loosened the brick at the foot of the wall between the lancet windows, pulled it out and found the iron box. The money was still there. She took the box with its contents.

Back in the gatehouse she went upstairs. She looked into Eve's bedroom, neat as a pin, desolate. The jewel case was there in the drawer, but it was empty. No gold wedding ring, of course, she had expected that, but no earrings, either, or jade necklace or brooches. She wondered what had become of them.

From the cupboard in her own bedroom she took her warm quilted coat, the two skirts Eve had made her, the red-and-blue sweater Eve had knitted.

The curtains were drawn in here, for no good reason that she could see. She drew them back and looked across the ruined gatehouse garden to the grounds of Shrove. It gave her a little shock to see David Cosby walking across the grass between the young trees. He had a dog with him, a red-and-white spaniel. Once she was sure he wasn't looking in this direction, she drew the curtains again.

His walk was taking him nowhere near the little wood. Liza put the metal box and the clothes into the boot of the car and locked it. She wondered if she dared leave it there for the ten minutes it would take her to do what she had to do and decided she must.

The sun still shone with unseasonable brightness. It was so late in the year that the shadows were long, even at noon. The ground was dry for early December, under her feet softly crackling strata, layer upon layer of them, of fallen leaves. She made her way into the little wood, not wanting to go but aware that she had to. This was as important a mission as the quest for the iron box of money.

Much of the clearing operations she had witnessed but not this replanting. It was unexpected, an unforeseen act. New trees with the deer and rabbit guards on their thin trunks stood everywhere in carefully planned groups. She took heart from the sight of the two dead larches left to stand as a feeding place for woodpeckers and the broken poplar that had put out new branches.

The cherry log lay where it had lain from the time of its fall, or she thought it lay like that. How could she be sure? It was deep now in dead leaves, awash with them almost, with a tide of brown beech leaves that hid two-thirds of the log. But all those leaves had fallen since October. . . .

She squatted down and began burrowing into the leaves with her hands. The relief at the feel of sacking against her fingers was so great she almost laughed aloud. Wedged beneath the log, the bundle was still in place, winter after winter was burying it deeper. Leaves would turn to leaf mold and leaf mold to earth. One day the log itself would be buried as the level of the ground gradually and very slowly rose, while Bruno slept on, undisturbed.

There were no policemen standing by the car taking notes, no David Cosby with his young inquisitive dog. She got into the driving seat and drove down the lane, over the bridge, and took the road to the village where Bruno had wanted to take Eve to live. There, in the village shop, she bought a pack of ham sandwiches, a can of Coke, and a Bounty bar for her lunch. It amused her a little that she had found buying these things in this shop so easy, she who had never dared go in there in former days.

But before that she investigated the contents of the iron box.

The previous time she had looked into the box, and helped herself from it, she had had very little idea of the value of money, what was a lot and what wasn't much. It was different now. She had lived a lifetime of experience in three months, had earned money and knew what things cost. Sitting in the driving seat in a secluded spot by the churchyard wall, she opened the box and counted the notes.

They amounted to something over a thousand pounds: to be precise, a thousand and seventy-five. Liza could hardly believe it. She must have made a mistake. But she counted again and again she reached the figure of a thousand and seventy-five. The money lay heavily on her, not on her hands, but like a burden on her back. She shook herself and tried to see it differently, as a blessing. No longer daring to leave it in the car, she carried the thousand pounds stuffed in her pockets as she went over to the shop. Because there was so much of it she felt she could afford a ham sandwich instead of cheese.

✍

The car restored to the Superway car park, she wandered about the town, afraid to steal a bath at the Duke's Head in case she got caught and they found all that money on her. There wasn't time to go to the cinema. Instead she went to the bookshop, acquiring undreamed-of marvels, among them *The Divine Comedy* in translation, Ovid's *Metamorphoses* in the original *and* translation, before telling herself she must be careful with the money, she must be prudent. They needed that money, she and Sean.

All the same, she postponed telling him about it. Later would do, another day would do. Nor did she show him the new books. She had been to Shrove, she said, she had fetched her clothes. All he was concerned about was her driving the car uninsured and without a license. He was rather angry about that. She hadn't dreamed, when first she knew him, that he would turn out so law-abiding.

The first hint of it she'd had was when the man who owned the land beside the old station discovered that the caravan was parked there and told him to move on. Liza, remembering that day when she had stood with the demonstrators and the last train had come down the line, said he need not move more than a dozen yards. If he parked it by the platform he would be on British Rail land and they never came near the place, they wouldn't find out. Sean wouldn't do it. He said he knew he was wrong being on that man's land without permission, he wasn't sticking his neck out again. He'd move over the bridge and up through the fields and woods to Ring Common, where anyone could be.

It was four or five miles away. Of course he went on coming to Shrove to do the garden. Liza never spoke to him while he was on the mower or doing the edges or weeding, it amused her to walk past him with a casual "hi" or even a shy "hallo" if Eve was with her, remembering their lovemaking of the previous evening. How had she known that her association with Sean wouldn't be acceptable to Eve? That Eve and she were Capulets and Sean a Montague? Instinctively, she had known it, and had kept their love an absolute secret.

At the same time it brought her enormous pleasure to watch him about the grounds of Shrove when he had no idea she was watching him. Observing his handsomeness and his grace, she liked to remember and to anticipate. She even enjoyed the pleasure-pain of needing to go up to him and touch him, kiss him and have him touch her, needing it passionately but still making herself resist.

One day she saw a man talking to him. It was a shock to realize that the man was Matt. The past couple of times Jonathan had been at Shrove he had brought Matt with him. It was a long time since they had seen Jonathan, she and Eve, though weeks rather than months. The years when he had scarcely come at all were gone by. He had been at Shrove in April and now it was June. Matt was talking to Sean about something or other, pointing at this and that in what seemed to Liza a hectoring way before going back to the house.

"What was he saying to you that day?" she asked Sean five months later. "Matt. When you had to stop the tractor and take off your visor?"

"I don't know. What does it matter? I reckon it was only to boss me about. Maybe it was to cut the tops off the lilacs, prune the lilacs. I never knew you was supposed to do that."

"We didn't know Jonathan was coming. He didn't warn us, but he often didn't. I told Eve I'd seen him. I knew she'd want me to do that so that she could get dressed up and wash her hair before he came. That was the evening he first started talking about the money he'd lost. He didn't mind me being there, he talked about it in front of me. He was what they call a Name at Lloyd's. D'you know what that means?"

"Sort of. I saw about it in the papers. They were a sort of insurance company, only very big and sort of important, and something happened so they had to fork out more than they'd got."

"It was to do with that Alaskan oil spill, that was the start of it. And they had more claims that they could—I think 'meet' is the word. Instead of making money, all the people who were Names found they had to pay money. Jonathan was one. He said he didn't know how much it would be yet but he thought a lot, and luckily he had the house in France to sell that had been Caroline's. He looked very miserable. But, you know, we didn't take it very seriously, Eve and I. Or Eve didn't. I wasn't interested. She was interested, she was interested in everything that concerned him, but even she didn't believe he was having a job finding money. She was so used to the Tobiases and the Ellisons having so much of it. They were the kind of people, she said to me, who'd say they were poor when they were down to their last million."

Sean shrugged. He put his arm around Liza. "Feeling a bit better, are you, love? About you-know-what?"

She knew what. The revelation in the paper. Eve's past life. "I'm all right. Only I'd like to go and see her."

"Your mum?"

"Not yet. Maybe after Christmas. I'll find out where she is, where they've put her, and then I'll go and see her."

"You're amazing, you really are. After what she done? After she murdered three blokes? After the way she brought you up? She's bad news, love."

"She never did me a bit of harm," said Liza. "She's my mother. You can understand why she killed those men. I can understand it. There was one place in the world she had a sanctuary, there was one kind of life she could live and stay, well, not mad, and they all wanted to take it away from her, one after the other."

"Not Trevor Hughes."

"Yes, he did. In a way. Jonathan had said she was there to see how she got on, but she knew he meant how it suited *him*. She was on *trial*. It wouldn't have suited him if his dogs had had to be destroyed because she'd set them on someone.

"And Bruno was going to make her leave unless she sent *me* away. You can understand why she killed them, she didn't have a choice. They'd got her in a corner and she acted like an animal would. And now I've read what happened to her before I was born, I know she was getting her revenge too, she was taking vengeance on three men for what three men had done to her."

"Not the same men," Sean objected.

"Oh, of *course* not. Don't you understand anything?" Immediately, she was remorseful. "I'm sorry. I'll tell you about the last one, shall I?"

He shrugged, then said a rather sullen, "Yes."

"I'll tell you about how she shot him."

t w e n t y

THIS would be the last of Scheherazade's stories, she said. Not a thousand and one nights but nearer a hundred. Three and a half months of nights to tell a life in.

"When did I run away, Sean?"

"It was August. No, it wasn't, it was September the first."

She began counting on her fingers. "That was something I never learned. I never learned much arithmetic. I make it a hundred and one nights tomorrow."

"Is that right?"

They were coming home from work on the following day, the hundredth day. Liza had carried the money with her to

Aspen Close, she dared not leave it in the caravan. Stopping work at lunchtime, she had walked around the town until she found a shop to sell her a money belt. In the public lavatory in the marketplace she packed all the notes into the belt and put it on over her jeans. She was so slim the belt looked smart, not cumbersome.

She still hadn't said anything about the money to Sean and he believed that all she had fetched from the lodge were her clothes. Glad of the quilted coat, she rubbed her cold hands together. The heater in the car worked only fitfully.

"I'd got to June, hadn't I?" she said. "It was when Jonathan first started going on about money. He'd brought Matt with him."

"He was always coming out in the garden telling me how to do my job," Sean grumbled.

"Did he? I didn't know that. Matt was a builder up in Cumbria but his business had failed. If it wasn't for him, Eve wouldn't be in prison. He hated us. I think it was because he'd once thought Eve beautiful but he disgusted *her.*"

Sean nodded. "That'd be it. She treated him like dirt."

"If it wasn't for him, the police wouldn't have suspected anything and Eve would still be at the gatehouse and so would I."

"I ought to thank him then, hadn't I?"

She smiled. "Jonathan sort of took him under his wing. Matt was getting married or he wanted to get married and Jonathan had some idea of getting him a place to live near Shrove and having him manage the grounds. While he was there he went out every night shooting rabbits by the car headlights. There was all this banging of guns night after night and the lights blazing over the fields. I hated it, I never liked Matt."

"Them little devils have to be kept down, love. I never seen so many rabbits as there was last summer. And pigeons, they tear the crops to bits."

"When he stayed at Shrove he slept in a room over the coach house. There are seventeen bedrooms at Shrove, but he had to sleep out there. He had to use the outside lavatory behind the stables and wash under the tap that was there for watering the horses."

Sean said seriously, "Tobias couldn't have him in the house, not a servant. Matt wouldn't have expected it."

Liza gave him a look. She shook her head a little at him, but he had his eye on the road. "Jonathan told Eve you were just a temporary measure. Those were his words. He was going to give you the sack at the end of the summer, at Michaelmas—whenever that is—and have Matt and his wife live over the coach house. He said he'd have things done to it to make it possible to live there. Put in one of his famous bathrooms, I expect."

"He did give me the sack. Well, he got Matt to do it."

"I was in a panic when he first said it. I thought he'd get rid of you and you'd have to go and I'd never see you again."

They had reached the place where the caravan was. Sean put his arms around Liza and hugged her.

"You didn't trust me."

"I don't think I trusted anyone by then, not even Eve."

Inside the caravan they lit the gas and the oil heater. The warmth came quickly, though it was a damp, smelly heat. Sean lit a cigarette, making the atmosphere worse, and opened the bottle of wine he had brought from Superway and began unwrapping the samosas and onion bhajis for their supper. Pulling off her coat, Liza hugged herself inside the comfort of the sweater Eve had made. She talked, drinking her wine.

Eve hadn't liked that idea of Matt and his wife living at

Shrove. Jonathan said it meant she could get rid of Mrs. Cooper, she wouldn't have to handle the wages and the organization, she'd have nothing to do but *be* there and, of course, she'd be in authority over them, they'd have to do as she said. Why can't we go on managing as we are? she wanted to know. It would be easier for her this way, Jonathan said, and besides, he had to find something for Matt, he had a duty to Matt.

Liza knew what her mother was really feeling. By this time she understood most of Eve's deeply emotional attitude toward Shrove. Eve didn't want anyone, anyone at all, coming between her and that house and that land, that domain. She even resented Sean's being there. Mr. Frost had been there before she came, was there when her own mother was, she accepted him like she did the train and the inevitable weekend guests, but Sean was new. Of course, she said none of this to Jonathan, and that night Jonathan stayed at the gatehouse. Liza felt very strange about that because she was deep in a sexual relationship of her own and she understood what went on beyond the wall dividing their bedrooms.

The next day she found Eve standing in front of the mirror, peering closely at her face, plucking out a gray hair. She came up behind Eve, not meaning to do this, not meaning to make the contrast. It all happened by chance that her face was reflected behind Eve's, a yard or so and twenty-two years between.

Eve turned around and said, *"Mater pulchra, filia pulchrior."*

Liza didn't know what to say. She could hardly reply that it was true the mother was beautiful but the daughter more so, or pretend not to understand. A lame "I think you look lovely" was all she could manage. But she wondered what the hectic light in Eve's eye portended and her wild behavior that day and her sudden bursts of too-loud laughter.

As it happened, she overheard what Eve said to Jonathan.

She'd got in the habit of listening at doors. It was a way of trying to save her life. Sometimes, these days, she felt her whole life was in jeopardy. If Matt came, would Eve stay? If she and Eve went, where could they go? If Sean went, what would she do? She would die. As soon as she sensed Eve or Jonathan or both of them wanted her out of the way, she knew they were going to talk secrets she should have been privy to, because it was she most of all that they threatened.

That evening she had been at the caravan with Sean. Well, more than the evening. She had been with him from the time he stopped work at four until nine, when he drove her back to Shrove. Home again at the gatehouse, she thought at first that they had gone out somewhere or to Shrove House.

Jonathan's jacket was hanging over the back of a chair but that meant nothing. She went to her bedroom and looked out of the open window toward the house, expecting to see them walking in the pale red light of the sunset afterglow. But they were much nearer at hand. They were sitting on a rug spread out on the grass in the garden just below her window. Or Eve was sitting, her knees drawn up and her arms wrapped around them, while Jonathan lay on his back, looking up at the thin moon that had appeared in the still-light sky.

They weren't speaking but Liza knew that once they did speak she would be able to hear every word. She crouched on the bed with her chin on the windowsill, thinking about Sean, how he had said to her that evening to come and live with him in the caravan. He had asked her, he had said he missed her too much when she wasn't with him, and what was there to keep her here? She couldn't answer that. She couldn't say, I'm frightened to go.

In a way she wanted to terribly and in another way she didn't want to at all. Yet it was only a couple of years before that she'd been always asking herself what would become of her and how would she ever get away? The silence down there was oppressive. When she was beginning to think she might as well go down there and join them, Eve spoke.

"Jonathan, will you marry me?"

It was a worse silence this time. Anything would have been better than this silence. He was was no longer looking at the moon but at Eve. She said with great bravery—how Liza admired her courage!—"I asked you to marry me. Women can do that, can't they? We were going to be married once, when we were very young. It all went wrong, we both know why, but is it too late to make it right?"

He sounded ashamed, Liza thought. "I'm afraid it is too late, Evie."

Eve made a little sound. She whispered, "Why is it?"

"The time for that's gone by, Evie. I'm sorry but it's just too late."

"But why is it? We're always happy when we're together. Don't I make you happy? Hasn't it always been—good with me?"

"I shan't marry again. I'm better alone and maybe you are too. I'll be frank, I don't want to be married. I've tried it and it didn't work. Victoria and I were all right until we got married. It was then that things started to fall apart. It would be the same with you and me."

"Then I have humiliated myself for nothing," Eve said in a hard voice, but almost at once she had turned back to him and suddenly cast herself upon him, clutching him in her arms and crying, "Jonathan, Jonathan, you know I love you, why won't you stay with me? Why have you kept me like this for all these years? I've waited for you for so long, I've waited forever and still I can't have you. Jonathan, please, please . . ."

Liza couldn't bear any more of it. She jumped off the bed and ran away into Eve's room, the way she had done when she was a child.

⁓

"She should have known better than that," said Sean.

"It was ironical, wasn't it? There was I being begged to go and live with you and not daring to and there was she begging Jonathan to marry her and being rejected."

She didn't like his reply, though it was complimentary to herself. "No, well, you're sixteen, aren't you, love? And she's a bit past her sell-by date."

"Jonathan was older than she."

"He's a man. It's different. I bet he didn't stay that night."

She digested the first part of these remarks. This was a point of view she hadn't previously come across and she found it deeply unsatisfactory. "He went back to Shrove about half an hour later, and he and Matt went off the next day. I thought he'd never come back but he did."

"Too right he did and that Matt with him. It was the end of August. Matt come up to me all smiles like he was going to give me a raise. It was ten minutes before I was due to leave and I was using that bit of time to thin out the plums. There was so many plums on that damn tree the branches was breaking. He said like he was my boss, Holford, we shan't need your services after the weekend, thanks very much. It was a Wednesday and he said he wouldn't need my services after the weekend. I said, is that what you call giving a person notice? He went on smiling. Take it or leave it, he says to me, you get paid up to Friday afternoon, and he just walked off."

Liza hadn't seen Sean on that Wednesday evening, so the news of his dismissal reached her secondhand. She was nearly frantic when she heard. They weren't in the lodge but at the house. It was such a rare thing for her and Eve to be asked up to the house when Jonathan was there that she had sensed something awful was going to happen.

Jonathan came to the gatehouse at about four in the afternoon. She and Eve were indoors, it was rather a chilly day for late August, and Jonathan talked to them from the window. He didn't come in. He just said, come up to the house for a drink about six, I've got something to tell you.

Eve was sore. She seemed truculent and sulky. No one but Liza would have guessed that what she was suffering from was simple unhappiness. Tell us what? she asked. He didn't answer. I'll take you both out for a meal afterward, if you like, he said.

Probably Eve was imagining all kinds of dreadful things— though nothing so dreadful as the truth. Jonathan received them in the drawing room, very grand. They sat in one of the groups of crimson-and-gold chairs and sofas that were arranged in each corner of the room around a marble or ormolu table. A good deal of the glory was lost when Matt came shambling in with bottles and glasses on a tray and peanuts in a packet. Matt's hair was down on his shoulders now but it had gone gray and he had grown a big belly, so Liza couldn't imagine what sort of a woman would think of marrying him. She had never seen a drunk person or heard the word Jonathan used and would have thought Matt ill if Eve hadn't explained later.

"How dare you come in here pissed? Put the bloody nuts in a dish and then get out."

Jonathan had been drinking too, she could smell it on his breath when he leaned toward her and asked her if she was allowed a glass of wine.

"I've just had Matt give that young man of yours the push," he said to Eve.

"What young man of mine?"

"The gardener."

"You've sacked him? Why?"

Liza could hear the relief in Eve's voice. She was aghast, but Eve was relieved because she was expecting something worse. So that was all Jonathan had got them up there for, Eve was no doubt thinking, to tell me he's got rid of Sean Holford to make room for Matt and Mrs. Matt, and now he'll be wanting me to get rid of Mrs. Cooper.

And what am I going to do? Liza thought feverishly. *Suppose he's gone, suppose he never comes back, suppose I never see him again?*

"I told you I'd got something to tell you, Eve. It's not that I've fired the gardener. It's not that Matt will be taking over. No one will be taking over. The fact is I'm going to have to sell the house. Shrove House will have to be sold."

∽

Trembling for her mother, Liza turned slowly to look at her. Eve was stone-still. She had gone white and suddenly she looked tremendously old, not thirty-eight but sixty-eight, an old woman with a lined forehead and mouth that has fallen in.

"Don't look like that, Evie," Jonathan said. "D'you think I want to do it? I've no choice. I told you about my financial difficulties. I've got to put more into Lloyd's than I dreamed was possible. It's been a frightful shock to me. But you must know what's happened to the Names, it's been all over the papers day after day—no, I forgot, you don't read the papers. The fact is I've got to find close to a million and I can't do it without selling Shrove. If I get fifty thousand for Mama's house in France I'll be doing well, it's more than I can hope for, thirty's more likely. I've been trying to sell it for two years. Again I was going to say you know what's happened to the property market but, no, I don't suppose you do know. I have to sell Shrove. When I do it will just cover me. I shall just keep my head above water."

Eve was staring at him. This was the first time Liza had ever drunk wine and she was making the most of it. It helped. She held out her glass for more and Jonathan filled it absently.

"For God's sake, Eve, say something." He tried, incredibly, facetiousness. "Say something if it's only good-bye."

Liza saw her make an effort. She saw her suck in her lips and raise her shoulders as if in pain. The voice, when it came, was breathless and thin. "You can sell Ullswater."

"The Ullswater house belongs to Victoria now—remember?"

"Why were you ever such a fool as to marry her?"

"D'you think I haven't asked myself that over and over?"

"Jonathan," said Eve, holding her hands tightly clenched together, "Jonathan, you can't sell Shrove, it's unthinkable, there has to be an alternative." She thought of one. "You can sell the London house."

"And where am I supposed to live?"

Eve, who hadn't taken her eyes off him, seemed to stare even more intently. Not liking the look in her mother's face, the glazed, hardly sane look, Liza shifted uncomfortably in her chair. Eve said, "You can live here."

"No, I can't." Jonathan was growing irritable. "I don't want to live here. Things are bad enough without my having to live in a place I dislike." He sounded like a petulant child. "All right, I know I've never told you I don't like this place, but the fact is I don't, I never have. It's isolated, it's miles from anywhere, and you mayn't have noticed this, but it's damp. Of course it is, stuck in a bloody river valley. Victoria got fibrositis through staying here."

"God damn Victoria to hell," said Eve in a voice to make Liza jump out of her skin.

Jonathan wasn't put out. "All right. Willingly. I wish she was in hell. I'm sure I've suffered from her more than you have, more than you dream of. Never mind her, anyway. I have to sell this house, I have to have the million it'll fetch."

"You won't be able to sell it. Even I know that. I may live out of the world but I've got a radio, I know what goes on. The house market's the worst it's been in my lifetime. You won't find a buyer. Not at the price you're asking you won't."

Jonathan refilled Eve's glass from the dry sherry bottle. She lifted the glass, watching him. For a moment Liza thought she was going to throw the contents of the glass at him but she didn't. Nor did she drink from it.

Jonathan said calmly, "I have. I have found a buyer."

Eve made a little pained sound.

"A hotel chain. They're embarking on a project called Country Heritage Hotels. Shrove will be their flagship, as they call it."

"I don't believe you."

"Come off it, Evie, of course you believe me. Why would I say it if it wasn't true?"

"The deal," said Eve, "the contract, whatever, I don't know about these things—is it settled?"

"Not yet. They've made an approach and I've told my solicitor to tell them a tentative yes. That's as far as we've got. You're the first person I've told."

"I should think so," Eve said scornfully.

"Of course I'd tell you first, Evie."

"What will become of me, of us? Have you thought of that?"

Jonathan began saying he would find her a house. Matt and

his wife would stay at Shrove until it was bought by Country Heritage and then they would have to have a home found for them. His idea was perhaps to find a pair of semidetached cottages. On the other side of the valley possibly, and he named the village where Bruno had nearly bought a house. Property was for sale all over the place and much of it going for a song.

There was no question of abandoning Eve. He hoped she knew his responsibility toward her. Unfortunately for her, the hotel chain wanted the gatehouse for use as their reception. They had specifically stated this in their offer.

Eve said flatly, "I will never leave here."

"That's all very well. I'm afraid you must. Do you think it's pleasant for me having to tell you this? Come to that, d'you think I like selling half my property? My grandfather would turn in his grave, I know that."

"He wouldn't," said Eve. "Not where he is, rotting in hell."

"I don't see the use of talking like that. It doesn't help."

"I will never leave here. They will have to take me away by force if they want me to leave here."

It was a prophecy soon to be fulfilled.

The next day, after a sleepless night, a night when she didn't go to bed at all, Eve went up to Shrove to plead with Jonathan. By that time Liza was already telling the news to Sean, and Sean was urging her to come to him, to leave her mother and Shrove and come and live with him. She was old enough, the law couldn't stop her.

Coming back, she encountered Matt in the stable yard with a fat middle-aged woman in an apron. The presence of his wife didn't stop him eyeing Liza up and down in a lecherous way—

just as he had eyed Eve all those years ago—and telling her she'd grown up into a lovely girl who'd soon have all the boys after her.

Jonathan came back with Eve and they spent the day arguing, Eve alternately pleading and shouting, occasionally weeping. As far as Liza knew, they spent the day like this. At four she went out to meet Sean and didn't get home till nearly ten. Eve didn't say anything, she uttered no word of reproach. Liza could hardly believe her eyes when Jonathan put his arm around Eve, lifted her off the sofa, and led her upstairs to her bedroom, where he closed the door on the pair of them for the rest of the night.

Outside, the usual banging started and the flaring lights as Matt went rabbit-hunting. Liza drew her curtains. She sat on the bed thinking about Sean. He would never come back to Shrove to work. Apple-picking had already begun in the Discovery orchards to the north of here. In less than a week he'd be moving on to earn as much as he could picking apples from dawn till dusk through September. How did two people communicate when neither had a phone? Sean didn't even have a postal address.

He said he'd drive over on Monday and they'd meet in the little wood. Why the little wood? she'd asked and he'd said because it was romantic. He'd also said she'd got to tell him if she was coming. Didn't she love him enough to come?

Secure in her love and companionship now, Sean said, interrupting the story, "I still don't know why you had to keep me on the hook so long."

"I've told you often enough. I was scared. I'd never been away. As far as I could remember, I'd never even slept in any bed but mine at the gatehouse."

He patted the bed they were sitting on. "We never slept much, did we, love?"

"Jonathan was practically living at the gatehouse that weekend," said Liza. "They were all over each other, more than I'd ever seen them. Eve'd never been demonstrative in public. Perhaps I wasn't public, perhaps she didn't care, I don't know. They were hugging and kissing in my presence but for all that, Jonathan could never be got to say he wouldn't sell Shrove. She'd plead and cajole and kiss him and at the end of it he'd just say, 'I've got to sell.'"

Then Eve gave up. On Sunday evening Liza heard her say, "If it must be, it must be."

She reached for Jonathan's hand and held it. Jonathan gave her a look that to Liza, who now knew about such things, seemed full of love.

"We'll find a nice house for you and Liza, you'll still have the countryside, the place itself . . ."

Jonathan stayed the night but left early in the morning before Liza was up. She came downstairs to find Eve seated at the breakfast table, glittery-eyed and galvanic with barely suppressed energy, her hands clasping and unclasping.

"He's going to sell Shrove, he's absolutely determined."

"I know," Liza said.

The tone of Eve's voice changed and became dreamy, reminiscing. "He's asked me to marry him."

"He hasn't!"

"The irony of it, Lizzie, the irony! Of course I said no. No, thanks, I said, you're too late. What's the good of him to me without Shrove?"

It was for Shrove she had wanted him. If he had married her a year ago he could have put Shrove in her name and kept it safe from his creditors. She laughed a little, not hysterically but madder than that, a manic laugh. Still, Liza couldn't believe she had been as abrupt with Jonathan as she implied, for he was back at the lodge in the late morning.

When she heard Eve say she'd go pigeon-shooting with him later, Liza thought the world was turning upside-down faster than she could cope with. Eve never killed birds or animals. Now she was saying the pigeons destroyed the vegetables she grew and would have to be kept down. Jonathan sounded quite happy to teach her to shoot with the four-ten, the gun, Liza thought, she had used to shoot the man with the beard. Only Jonathan, of course, had no idea of that.

Neither of them seemed deflected from their purpose by the fact that in a month or two Shrove would be sold, Eve would have left the gatehouse, and it would hardly matter to her whether the vegetables survived or not.

In the afternoon Liza went up into the little wood to meet Sean. In arranging where to meet she had been careful to arrange this trysting place a good distance from where Bruno's body lay. They made love on a bed of soft dry grass, walled-in by hawthorn bushes. But afterward, holding her in his arms, Sean grew grave. He had to work for his living. He wasn't going on benefit if he could help it. For the next two days he could take a job clearing a house of furniture for a dealer in town, but after that he'd have to move on to where the apples were. He wanted her. Would she come?

He couldn't wait forever, he couldn't really wait beyond Thursday. And after that how would they get in touch with each other?

She hadn't liked that, the fact that he wouldn't wait. In the romantic plays and books she had read, the true lover had been prepared to wait indefinitely, not make conditions and threats. She got him to say that he'd come back here next Saturday, same time, same place. By then she promised she'd have made up her mind. She would have separated herself from her mother and come to him or else she'd be staying. Was it her imagination that he had seemed reluctant? Instead of ardor, her request to him had been met with doubts about whether he could make it, much depended on where he was, he would do his best.

When he had gone and she had watched him go, heading for the place where he had parked the car, far up the lane, when she had seen the last of him as the trees absorbed him, the tears came into her eyes and she started to cry. They were tears of frustration, of impotence and self-pity at her own indecisiveness. Wiping her eyes on the backs of her hands, then rubbing them with her fists like a child, she walked slowly back the way she had come.

It was nearly six, she calculated, the sun still high in the sky but some of its heat departed. Sean and she had been together for three hours but it had seemed no more than three minutes. She was thinking about her dilemma once more, wondering if some middle way could be found, some compromise, whereby she could continue to be here with Eve and keep Sean nearby, when she heard the first shot.

Liza's instinct, whenever there was shooting on the grounds, was to take herself as far away from the neighborhood of those reports as possible, even to cover her ears. Her dread was of actually seeing a bird fall to the ground, bloody and with feathers flying, or a rabbit brought down as it fled for cover. But this time she was not exactly sure where the shot had come from, it was often hard to tell. At any rate, it wasn't in this wood and wouldn't be in their back garden.

She saw Matt first. Although she knew of Jonathan's intention to shoot pigeons, when she caught sight of Matt in the far distance, almost up by Shrove House, she thought it was he who was after the birds. Then she saw Jonathan and Eve standing together between the largest remaining cedar, the blue *atlantica glauca*, and the group of new young trees. They weren't very far from her, no more than a hundred yards, quite near enough for her to see that they had only one gun between them.

Jonathan had been demonstrating something and now he put the shotgun into Eve's hands. Holding it gingerly, she raised the barrel in a clumsy way, with what seemed an effort. He gave her a kindly glance, then adjusted her hands, moving them farther apart. Their shadows had lengthened as the sun sank and now streamed out thin and dark across the leaf-patterned grass. When Jonathan clapped his hands to make the pigeons fly Liza stopped looking, opened the gate, and let herself into the gatehouse garden.

She had forgotten to cover her ears. The gun went off, once, twice, three times. There came a cry no bird could have made, a high-pitched scream quite clearly audible from where she was. She stood still. For a moment a little child again, she saw in her mind's eye the bearded man as he died on the grass in the dusk.

Almost without realizing it, she had put up her hands over her ears. But there was to be no more firing. She took away her hands, she turned around and saw Matt running across the grass, waving his arms.

Between the trees, on the open green that the sun and shadows dappled, Jonathan lay sprawled on his back. Eve had dropped the gun and stood looking down at him, her hands clasped under her chin. Liza ran into the house.

HE'D shot him," Liza said. "I knew at once it was on purpose. If he was dead he couldn't sell Shrove and it would go to his cousin David Cosby, who loved the place and wouldn't dream of selling it. It was the only way to make sure she got it. Marrying him wouldn't have worked, he'd still have sold it.

"The way she looked at me, I read it all in her face. The trouble was Matt. Who knows what she'd have done if Matt hadn't been there? Pretended to find Jonathan dead that evening or next day and made people believe he'd been out shooting alone? But Matt had seen. I don't mean he'd seen her do it, but he'd seen them together firing at the pigeons.

"Eve said to me, tell the police you saw nothing, tell them you don't even live here, you're just visiting, and then she said, why tell them anything? You don't have to be here. Matt didn't see you. So I went and sat in the little castle and they didn't know I'd been there. I think I knew then that she wanted to handle it all on her own.

"The police knew she had killed Jonathan but they could never prove it wasn't an accident, no one saw it happen, you see. I've been thinking a lot about it since the trial and that's the conclusion I've come to, that once they knew she'd killed Jonathan they remembered Bruno going missing and then they started thinking about the man called Trevor Hughes. They'd actually questioned her about him and she'd denied ever seeing him, but they'd got a record of it, they never forgot. I expect that's what happened.

"When they searched the gatehouse they didn't find Bruno's earrings because she was wearing them. She was wearing them the night before I left so I'm sure she still had them on the next morning. They did find Trevor Hughes's wedding ring with his initials inside and his wife's.

"They must have asked Matt if he knew anything about Trevor Hughes. Or else Matt went to them of his own accord and told them what he remembered that morning when the dogs behaved in that strange way. If she'd killed him they wondered what she'd done with his body and eventually they started digging.

"I'm sure they'd have liked to indict her for shooting Jonathan, but they were afraid she'd be acquitted. And they got nowhere trying to trace Bruno. But when they found Trevor Hughes's bones they found shot among them that came from that four-ten shotgun, that same one Jonathan was using to teach her to shoot pigeons. And they must have found his watch too for his wife to identify. I expect it went on for weeks after they first arrested her. I'd really like to know how they managed that—I mean, did they charge her with murdering Jonathan and then give that up and charge her with manslaughter instead just to hold her? And when did they think they'd got enough evidence to be sure of getting a conviction on the Hughes murder charge?"

Sean was staring at her incredulously. Liza smiled at him. "I told you, I'd like to be a lawyer. I'm interested in the law."

"You're a bright girl. You shouldn't be cleaning for that old woman."

Liza shrugged. It didn't seem important, it was only temporary. She began clearing their takeaway containers off the table. "D'you want a cup of tea?"

"In a minute," he said. "I've got something to tell you first. Now it's my turn. *I've* got something to tell *you*."

She filled the kettle, lit the gas, and, catching sight of his expression, turned it low. "What, then?"

"I've been accepted for the management course."

As soon as the less than enthusiastic words were out, she regretted them, knew she should have congratulated him. But she had said, "Well, you knew you would be."

A flush darkened his face. "It's not been as straightforward as that. As a matter of fact, it was touch and go. They only took five out of two hundred applicants."

"And you're one of the five? Great."

She must have sounded kind but indifferent, maternally indulgent perhaps. He said, "Listen to me, Liza. Come and sit down."

Her sigh was audible but she sat down next to him.

"The course starts in the New Year but they want me up there next week. It's in Scotland, a place near Glasgow. They wanted to put me in a flat with the other four, that's the way they fix it, but I'll have you with me, so I said I'd see to my own accommodations. I never said caravan, I wasn't telling them all my private affairs."

"Glasgow?" she said. "That'll be a long way from wherever Eve is. But I don't suppose it'd be for long, would it? Didn't you say six months?"

"Liza, hopefully this is only the start. You've not been following me. This is a new way of life. It's great the things they'll do for you once you've shown you're up to the course. For one thing, the idea is to manage one of their stores and they're building new branches all the time. There's one they're putting up now on the M3. Hopefully I could be assistant manager of one of them by this time next year. They'll help you with a mortgage on a flat."

He must have seen she didn't know what he meant. While he explained what a mortgage was, she fidgeted about, suddenly wanting a cup of tea more than anything in the world but not quite liking to get up and make it. He took hold of her hand, imprisoning it.

"It's a great chance for me. It's sort of made me see myself differently, like I'm not the person I reckoned I was, I'm better, I could be my own man, a responsible person with a real career."

Yes, she thought, you even talk better. It's made you articulate, you can suddenly express yourself. Then he shocked her.

"There's something else I want to tell you, love. I want you to marry me, I want us to get married."

It was as much as she could do to speak. *"Married?"*

"I knew it'd be a surprise." He leaned toward her and gave her a quick kiss on the cheek. Fondly he said, "You silly nana, you've gone all red. If it's on account of your mum, I don't mind that. It'll be just the same to me as if you was any other girl with a normal family."

"Sean . . ." she began but it was as if she hadn't interrupted him.

"I'll get paid when I'm training, that's another great thing. Hopefully you won't have to work no more. I wouldn't want my wife going out cleaning anyway. And when the kids start coming you'll want to be at home . . ."

This time she shouted to break the flow. "I'm not yet seventeen years old!"

"That's okay. You have to be over sixteen to get married, not over seventeen. It's seventeen for a driving license."

She burst out laughing. It was too much. Unlike him though this would be, he had to be making some elaborate joke. It was a moment or two before she understood, before she saw from his hurt face that he was deadly serious. "Oh, Sean, don't look like that, don't be so *silly.*"

"Silly!"

"Well, of course it's silly talking about marrying and having children and one of those things, a what-d'you-call-it, a mortgage. We've got our lives to live first. I'm not even grown up really. In the law I can't sign a contract or make a will or anything."

"Shut up about the fucking law, will you?"

She flinched a little, got up and went to the stove. "I want my tea if you don't," she said in a chilly voice, Eve's voice. He was sullen as she had never seen him. Suddenly she realized that she had never crossed him, everything had gone pleasantly for him until this evening, but now the sultan was looking at her head and sharpening his sword.

"I don't mind coming to Scotland for a bit," she said in a

conciliating voice. "I'd quite like somewhere else for a change. We could try it. You might not like the course."

He took his tea without a thank-you. "You'd better listen to me, Liza. Have you thought where you'd be without me? You'd be lost, you'd be nothing. Thanks to the way that bitch brought you up, you wouldn't last five minutes on your own. You don't even know what a mortgage is! You never knew what the Pill was! The best you can do to earn your living is cleaning or picking apples. You don't know nothing except for rubbish out of books. She's crippled you for life, and you're going to need me to get you through it."

It was an echo of Bruno, Bruno's words outside the old station. She brought the teacup to her lips but the tea seemed tasteless.

"I'll be your husband, I'll look after you. There's some as'd say it was a pretty big thing I was doing, considering who and what your mother is. You don't reckon I'd rather live in this clapped-out old van than in a decent flat, do you? It'd be okay sharing with those guys, but I've a responsibility to you, I know that, and I'll be taking the car and the van up to Glasgow on Friday. I won't say I'll be taking them anyway, whether you come or not, because you'll have to come, you don't have no choice."

"Of course I have a choice."

"No, you don't. It's like this, you have to come with me just because you can't be left here with no place to live, no family, no friends, and—you have to face it, love—no skills. The truth is you're more like six than sixteen. It's not your fault but that's the way it is."

She said nothing. Taking her silence for acquiescence, he turned on the television. She thought he looked pleased with himself. The look on his face was Bruno's when he thought he had persuaded Eve to move into that house with him. After a little while he opened a can of beer and began to drink from the can. He must have been aware of her eyes on him, for he turned around, grinned, and made the thumbs-up sign, intended no doubt to reassure. She picked up the book Mr. Spurdell had lent her, *First Steps in English Law,* and found the place she had reached in it the day before.

That was the first broken night she had had since she shared a bed with Sean and almost the first that they hadn't made love. She lay awake, thinking how much she had loved him and wondering how that could have changed. How could you feel so passionately for a person and then, suddenly, not care anymore at all? A few words, a gross gesture, an insensitive assumption, and it was all gone. Had it been like that for Eve and Bruno?

She was out all day on Saturday, roaming the fields by herself, but on Sunday it rained and she lay in bed, reading. When she refused to get up and tidy the place, shake out the mats, help him fetch water, he accused her of sulking. They both went to work in the morning and met as usual at five. It was dark, pitch dark, when they reached the caravan, and there was no water. They had forgotten to fetch the water before they left. Liza took the bucket and a torch.

It struck her as somehow silly that it was pouring with rain yet they had no water. She held the bucket under the pipe that protruded from the hillside, filled it, and made her way back, once nearly falling on the slippery mud.

Once in the caravan she opened a can of Coke. She was washing her hands at the sink before she saw what he had done to the books. She glanced into the living area as she reached for the towel. A piece of book jacket, a torn-off triangle, red lettering on a black background, lay on the table. It brought a constriction to her throat. They had no wastebasket, only a plastic sack under the sink. The sight of its contents made her feel rather dizzy.

Sean wasn't looking at her, he was watching television, a can of beer beside him, a lighted cigarette in his left hand. She had the feeling he was consciously not looking at her, forcing his eyes to fix on the screen.

Easier than rummaging in that sack was to see what he had done by examining the books that remained. Mary Wollstonecraft was gone and *The Divine Comedy* and the *Metamorphoses*. *Middlemarch* was gone. With bile rising into her mouth, she saw that he had spared *First Steps in English Law* and the two Hardy novels. Those belonged to Mr. Spurdell and he knew it. Sean was always law-abiding. He wouldn't destroy "other people's" property. She didn't count as other people, she was his.

She walked across and switched off the television. He jumped up, and for a moment she thought he would hit her. But she had misjudged him there. Sean wouldn't hit a woman.

"Why?" she said, the single word.

"Come on, love, you know why. You've got to put all that behind you, that life. You've left the place, she's gone, you're out in the real world now. Them books, they was just a way of hiding yourself from real life. Hopefully you're not going to need them in the future. We've got our whole future before us. Isn't that what you said yourself?"

Had she? Not in that context, she was sure. He was triumphant, he was in charge. She felt as angry as she now guessed Eve must sometimes have felt.

"They were *my* books."

"They was *ours*, love. We've been through that before. Okay, so you bought them with the money you earned. How would you like it if I said that Coke you're drinking was mine because it was my money paid for it? It's the same thing."

It was illogical and Eve had taught her to be logical, to be reasonable. Eve must have felt like this when Bruno pretended to have a social conscience to cloak his need to possess her utterly. She must have felt like this when, after seventeen years of striving and repudiation, of hope and humiliation and desertion, Jonathan had at last asked her to marry him.

Liza was impotent, she had nothing to say, she could only imagine how he would twist what she said. She set their food out, she made tea, she put the television on again and was rewarded by his seizing her hand and squeezing it in his own. Together they watched an episode in a Hollywood miniseries. Or Sean watched it while she fixed her eyes on the screen and took her mind elsewhere.

She could clean a house and fetch water from a spring and read books but it was true what he said, in other ways she was more like six than sixteen. She couldn't manage on her own. Even if she worked eight hours a day for Mrs. Spurdell or someone like Mrs. Spurdell, she would still only earn £120 a week, and she doubted if she *could* do eight hours' housework a day. Where would she live? How would she afford anything?

Was there anyone in the world who would pay her to translate Latin into English for them? She knew nothing about it but that she doubted. Besides, she knew from investigating in Mr. Spurdell's study that you had to have certificates and things, diplomas, degrees, before people would employ you to do things which weren't housework or putting packets on a shelf in a supermarket.

She had nowhere to live. Jonathan Tobias might have helped her about that but he was dead. She had no father, only one of three men who knew nothing of her existence. Eve didn't seem to care for her. Eve didn't know where she was or what had happened to her, but perhaps, in Eve's position, she wouldn't care, either. Or Eve might care very much, might be in an agony of anxiety, when she found out, as she must have, that Liza had never got to Heather's. But no one had come looking for her, no one had put pieces in the paper about her or on the television. Liza knew there was no one to look after her but Sean. There was only Sean.

He held her hand. Soon he had his arm around her. She was full of cold dislike for him, which she somehow knew would have warmed into simple irritation after a night's sleep. If he would leave her alone. If he would leave her to come to terms with it in her own way. She had to, after all. She had to make the best of it because without him she was useless and helpless.

Only he wouldn't leave her alone. He must have been able to tell how hostile she was to him, he must have sensed her reluctance to be touched by him and understood something by the way she took his hand off her leg when he began running it up and down her thigh. They would have to share a bed, she was resigned to that, but when she realized he intended making love she spoke a firm, "No!" And then, "No, please, I don't want to."

But making love wasn't at all what happened. She had asked him once if he would ever force her and he had treated the question as ludicrous. But he took no notice when she told him she didn't want him, she didn't want to do it. He silenced her by clamping his mouth over hers. He held her hands down, tried to force her thighs apart with his knee, and when that didn't work, with his foot. To justify himself, he pretended she was playing coy and laughed into her mouth as he thrust like a dog in the street, as he shoved his penis hard inside her, held her arms stretched out the width of the bed, pinioning her.

She was powerless. It hurt, as it had never hurt even the first time. When it was over and he was whispering to her that he knew she had really enjoyed it, he could always tell if a girl liked it, she thought of Eve and Trevor Hughes. Eve had had a pair of dogs to call, but she had nothing.

He fell asleep immediately. She cried in silence. It was weak and foolish, she was a baby to do it, but she couldn't stop.

Eve would never have tolerated such treatment. Eve never permitted persecution. Not since what had happened on the way back from the airport. Her own suffering was nothing like as terrible, but bad enough, a foretaste of a possible future. Eve had revenged herself on three men for what three men had done to her. That was why she had done those things, for vengeance more than for fear or safety or gain. More for vengeance than for Shrove.

Was this then what her own life would be? Making love when she wanted to and also making love when she didn't want to. Or doing *that* when she didn't want to. After what had happened, she thought she would never want to again. She remembered the day of Jonathan Tobias's wedding and how Eve had used the occasion as an opportunity for a lesson, as she so often did. She had taught Liza about marriage and marriage customs but had said nothing of having to do what a man wanted when you didn't want to, of men getting their way because they were stronger, of working for them and waiting on them and submitting to their right to tell you what to do.

Perhaps she hadn't because Liza had been only a child then. It was a lifetime ago and she was a child no longer. But once more she was in a position where she couldn't run away. And it was worse than last time when all she needed was courage. Now she had nowhere to run to.

One other thing Eve had done for her, though, apart from teaching her so many of the things Sean said were useless, and that was to teach her to rough it. Life had never been soft. They made their own pleasures with the minimum of aid, without toys, television, videos, CD players, external amusements. Eventually, after years, they had got their bathroom. The gatehouse had an old fridge and an even older oven, but there was no heating upstairs, no down quilts or electric blankets of the kind she'd seen at Spurdells', no new clothes—those jeans and the padded coat were the only things she possessed not made by Eve or from the Oxfam shop—they'd had none of that takeaway or processed food she'd got used to with Sean but never really trusted. They'd made their own bread at the gatehouse, grown their own vegetables, made their own jam and even cream cheese. Everywhere they went they'd had to walk once Bruno was gone.

Her mother had given her a kind of endurance, a sort of toughness, but what use was that in the world of Spurdells and Superway? You didn't need to be tough, you needed certificates and diplomas, families and relations, a roof over your head and means of transport, you needed skills and money. Well, she had a thousand pounds.

She could see the money belt on the table where he had thrown it when he stripped her. If he knew about the money, he would want it. Once he wanted it, he would take it. He would say that what was hers was theirs and therefore his. She got up, washed all traces of him off her body, pulled on leggings and the blue-and-red sweater for warmth and, curling the money belt up as tightly as she could, thrust it inside one of her boots.

Keeping as far from him as she could, on the far edge of the bed, she went to sleep.

P ROUDLY showing Liza her box of decorations that had all come from Harrods, Mrs. Spurdell said it was too early to dress the tree yet. But there was no point in deferring the purchase of it until later when the best would be gone. Philippa and her children were coming for Christmas. Jane was coming. Having once told Liza Philippa's Christian name, Mrs. Spurdell had since then always referred to her as Mrs. Page while Jane was "my younger daughter."

It was the first Christmas tree Liza had ever seen. Indeed, it was the first she had ever heard of and the rationale for uprooting a fir tree, winding tinsel strings around it, and hanging glass balls on the branches was beyond her understanding. As for Christian customs, Eve had taught her no more about Christianity than she had about Buddhism, Judaism, and Islam.

She could hear Mr. Spurdell moving about in his study upstairs. His school had broken up for Christmas. With the two of them in the house she had no chance of a bath. She scrubbed out the tub and put caustic down the lavatory pan. While she was cleaning the basin it occurred to her to look in the medicine cabinet. There, among the denture-cleaning tablets, the vapor rub, and the corn solvent, she found a cylindrical container labeled: MRS. M. SPURDELL, SODIUM AMYTAL, ONE TO BE TAKEN AT NIGHT. Of its properties she knew nothing except that it evidently made you sleep. She put the container in her pocket.

If she didn't have her money in her hand before she gave notice, she thought it quite likely Mrs. Spurdell would refuse to pay her. While she pushed the vacuum cleaner up and down the passage, she worked out various strategies. Determined to be honest and not to prevaricate, she knocked on the study door.

"Do you want to come in here, Liza?" Mr. Spurdell put his head out. "I won't be a minute."

"I'll do the study last if you like," she said. "I've brought all your books back."

"That's a good girl. You're welcome to more. I've no objection to lending my dear old friends to a sensible person who knows how to take care of them. A good book, you know, Liza, 'is the precious lifeblood of a master spirit.'"

"Yes," said Liza, "but I don't want to borrow anymore. Can I ask you something?"

No doubt, he expected her to ask who said that about a good book but she already knew it was Milton and knew too, which was very likely more than he did, that it came from *Areopag-*

itica. He was all smiling invitation to having his brains picked.

"How can you find out where someone's in prison?"

"I beg your pardon?" The smile was swiftly gone.

Now for the honesty. "My mother has gone to prison and I want to know where she is."

"Your mother? Good heavens. This isn't a game, is it, Liza? You're being serious?"

She was weary with him. "I only want to know who to write to or who to phone and find out where they've put her. I want to write to her, I want to go and see her."

"Good heavens. You've really given me quite a shock." He took a step forward, glanced over the banisters, and spoke in a lowered voice, "Don't give Mrs. Spurdell a hint of this."

"Why would I tell *her*?" Liza made an impatient gesture with her hands. "Is there a place I could phone? An office, I mean, a police headquarters of some kind?" She was vaguely remembering American police serials.

"Oh, dear, I suppose it would be the Home Office."

"What's the Home Office?"

Questions that were requests for information always pleased him. Prefacing his explanation with a "You don't know what the Home Office is?" he proceeded to a little lecture on the police, prisons, immigration, and ministries of the interior. Liza took in what she needed.

She drew breath and braced herself. Sean's words came back to her, about being more like six than sixteen, about being helpless. "Please, may I use your phone? And may I look in the phone directory first?"

He was no longer the benevolent pedagogue, twinkling as he imparted knowledge. A frown appeared and a petulant tightening of the mouth. "No, I'm afraid you couldn't. No to both. I can't have that sort of thing going on here. Besides, this is the most expensive time. Have you any idea what it would cost to phone to London at eleven o'clock in the morning?"

"I'll pay."

"No, I'm sorry. It's not only the money. This isn't the kind of thing Mrs. Spurdell and I should wish to be involved in. I'm sorry but no, certainly not."

She gave a little bob of the head and immediately switched on the vacuum cleaner once more. When the bedrooms were done, she came back to the study and found him gone. Quickly she looked for Home Office in the phone book. Several numbers were listed. She wrote down three of them, knowing she didn't want Immigration or Nationality or Telecommunications.

The house was clean and tidy, her time up. It seemed harder than it had ever been to extract twelve pounds from Mrs. Spurdell, the last pound coming in the shape of fifteen separate coins. Liza thanked her and said she was leaving, she wouldn't be coming anymore. Mrs. Spurdell affected not to believe her ears. When she was convinced, she asked rhetorically how she was supposed to manage over Christmas. Liza said nothing but pocketed the money and put on her coat.

"I think you're very ungrateful," said Mrs. Spurdell, "and very foolish, considering how hard jobs are to come by."

She began shouting for her husband, presumably to come and stop Liza from leaving. Liza walked out of the front door and shut it behind her. All the way down Aspen Close she expected to have to run because one of them was pursuing her but nothing like that happened. If the manager who admired her had been on duty in the Duke's Head she would have asked him if she might use his phone, but there was a woman in reception. While she was occupied at the computer, Liza walked upstairs and had a bath.

Not waiting for Sean but going home on the bus, it occurred to her as she climbed to the front seat on the top, that for a six-year-old—like the milkman with a child's mental age?—she hadn't done badly. Surely she had been resourceful? She had acquired a soporific drug, discovered how to find her mother, had even found the phone number, had given in her notice, had a bath, and lacking a towel, dried herself on the hotel bathroom curtains.

Would she have done better if she'd grown up in a London street and been to boarding school?

Sean had finished at Superway. He had unpacked his last carton of cornflakes and last can of tomatoes. A little wary of her still but no longer sullen, he described how the manager had shaken hands with him and wished him well.

"Does anyone know about me?" Liza asked him. "I mean, the people at your work? Do they know you've got a girlfriend who lives with you and who I am and all that?"

"No, they don't. I keep my private affairs to myself. So far as they know, I'm all on my own."

"Will you drive to Scotland?"

"'Course I'll drive. What you got in mind? First-class train tickets and a stopover in a luxury hotel? You've got a lot to learn about money, love."

He began fretting about a new law that had come in, excluding caravans from all land except where the owner's express permission was given. The sooner they were gone the better. Would the law in Scotland be different? He'd heard it sometimes was. Liza knew more about it than he did, she had read it up in Mr. Spurdell's newspaper. For instance, she knew that if your caravan was turned off a piece of land and you weren't allowed to park it anywhere else, the local authority was bound to house you. It might not be a real house or a flat, it might be only a room, even a hotel room, but it would be *somewhere*. She wasn't going to say any of this to Sean and risk a sneer about her cleverness and her aspirations.

All the time they had been there she had kept the caravan very clean. Cleanliness was ingrained in her, Eve had seen to that, and she could no more have left her home dirty than she could have failed to wash herself. For all that, it was a poor place, everything about it shabby, worn, scraped, scuffed, chipped, broken, cracked, and makeshift-mended. But the gatehouse had been shabby too. Would she want anything like the "monstrosity" Bruno had picked or the Spurdells' house, she who had been spoiled for choice by Shrove?

The caravan and the car, a home and a means of transport. With those, life would be possible, some kind of future would be possible. She watched Sean speculatively. Spartan living wasn't all that Eve had taught her.

No one had known where Bruno was and no one had cared except an easily fobbed-off estate agent. Trevor Hughes had had an estranged wife, glad to see the back of him. No one knew Sean wasn't alone. Her existence, her presence in his life, all this he had kept secret. He had left Superway and at this branch they would think no more about him, no doubt he was already forgotten.

At the Glasgow end they would expect him to turn up for the course on Monday. If he didn't come they wouldn't set in motion a police alert but conclude that he had changed his mind. She knew little about life, but the experiences she had had were of a peculiar nature. Few could look back on a similar history. She knew from experience, from the disappearance of Trevor Hughes and Bruno Drummond, that the police do little about searching for missing men in their particular circumstances. In this case it was unlikely an absent man would even be reported missing.

Sean's mother had long since lost interest in him. His brothers and sisters were scattered in distant places, long out of touch. The chain-smoking grandfather was too ancient to bother. The people he called his friends were pub acquaintances and caravan-site neighbors like Kevin.

While Sean watched television, she looked at herself long in the glass, the cracked piece of mirror ten inches by six that was all she and Sean had to see their faces in. It had seemed to her that Eve had never changed. The woman she had run away from a hundred days and nights ago was in her eyes the same woman, looking just the same, as the mother who had brought her to Shrove when she was three, not older or heavier or less fresh. Yet now as she looked at her own face it was a youthful Eve that she saw, different from the Eve of the present, an Eve she had forgotten but who came back to her as herself. As Jonathan had once said, as Bruno had said, she was a clone of that Eve, fatherless, her mother's double, her mother all over again.

With her mother's methods, with her mother's instincts. What would Eve have done? Not put up with it. Never yielded. Eve would have argued, remonstrated, reasoned—as she had—and when all that was to no avail, when they wouldn't agree or see her point of view, appeared to give in and conciliate them.

Retreating to the kitchen where he couldn't see her, she reread the instructions on the label of the sodium amytal carton. One would evidently send him to sleep. Two, surely, would put him into a deep sleep. And while he slept? He had often reproached her for not being squeamish enough, for an ability to confront violence and blood and death.

She had never been taught a horror of these things. If she was horrified by any of violent death's aspects it was at her own weakness in vomiting when she found Bruno's body. Eve had taught her to be a perfectionist, to be good at everything she did. She would do this well, cleanly, efficiently, and without remorse.

"What time do we start in the morning?" she asked him.

"First thing. Hopefully we can be on our way by eight."

"At least it's stopped raining."

"The weather forecast says an area of high pressure's coming. It's going to get cold, cold and bright."

"Shouldn't you put the towing bar on tonight?"

"Christ," he said. "I forgot."

She doubted if she could do it herself. In the past, when he had done it, she hadn't bothered to watch him. This evening, of course, she watched him all the time, studying what he did, assessing him in every possible situation, as she had done in those early days when she was in love with him.

Perhaps, at sixteen, you were never in love with the same person for long. It was violent, it was intense, but of short duration. Did teachers like Mr. Spurdell, or people like Eve, ever ask if Juliet would have gone on being in love with Romeo?

Sean worked by the light of a Tilley lamp and a rechargeable battery torch. Wrapped in the thick padded coat, she sat on the caravan steps in the quiet and the darkness, appreciating for the first time how silent it was here and how remote. Like Shrove. This place had the advantages of Shrove. Not a single light was visible, not an isolated pinpoint in any direction across the miles of hills and meadowland. The black land rolled away to meet the nearly black sky. If she strained her ears the gentle chatter of the stream was just audible.

Above her now the stars were coming out, Charles's Wain pale and spread out and Orion bright and strong. The white planet, still and clear, was Venus. The air had that glittery feel to it, as of unseen frost in the atmosphere. Metal clinking against metal occasionally broke the silence as Sean worked, that and the soft ghostly cries of owls in the invisible trees.

She hooked her thumbs inside the money belt, feeling its thickness. How was it she knew that if she let Sean live and went up north with him he would sooner or later find out about that money and demand it himself? She did know. She could even create the scene in her mind with her telling him it was hers, hers by right of her mother, and Sean saying she wasn't fit to have charge of money, he'd look after it and put it toward the home they'd buy.

He finished coupling the car to the caravan. They went back inside and he washed his hands. It was late, past eleven, and as he kept saying, they had to get up early.

"Don't you worry, I'll wake you," he said. "You know what you are, sleep like the dead. I don't reckon you'd ever wake up without me to give you a shake."

She didn't argue. Her dissenting role was past and now she was all acquiescence. Eve had given in to Bruno over the house and to Jonathan over the sale of Shrove. Perhaps she had murmured, "Yes, all right," to Trevor Hughes before she bit his hand. You gave in, you smiled and said a sweet, "You win." You lulled them into believing theirs was the victory.

"Wake me up at seven and I'll make you tea."

It wasn't unusual for her to say that, she often said and did it. He never had a hot drink at night, always had one in the morning. She put the pill container behind the sugar basin, opened the drawer where they kept cutlery, their blunt knives and forks with bent tines, and checked that the one sharp knife was there, the carver. It was good to be the kind of person who didn't flinch from weapons or the consequences of using them.

He was already in bed. Her throat felt dry and her stomach muscles tightened as they had on the previous night and the night before. On neither of those nights had he touched her. Last evening he hadn't even kissed her. But she was afraid just the same, of his strength and her own weakness, knowing now something she'd never realized and would once have refused to believe: that a woman, however young and vigorous, is powerless against a determined man.

When she came to bed and switched off the light she fancied she could feel his eyes on her in the darkness. Gradually, as always happened, she became accustomed to the absence of light, and the darkness ceased to be absolute, became gray rather than black. The moon had risen out there, or half a moon to give so pale a light. It trickled thinly around the window blinds.

His eyes were on her and his lips tentatively touched her cheek. He must have felt her immediate tension for he sighed softly. An enormous relief relaxed her body as he rolled over on his side away from her. She withdrew to the side of the bed, to put as many inches as she could between herself and him.

She would sleep now and in the morning she would kill him.

DREAMING, she was herself and not herself. She was Eve, too. She looked down at her hands and they were Eve's hands, smaller than hers, the nails longer. A shrinking had reduced her to Eve's height.

Yet she was in the caravan where Eve had never been. She knew she was dreaming and that somehow, by taking thought, by a process of concentration, she could be herself again. It was dark. She could just make out the shape of Sean lying in bed and a hump in the bedclothes beside him as if another body lay there, *her* body. She had come out of her body the way the Ancient Egyptians believed the Ka did. But it felt solid, her hand tingled when she drew a nail across the palm. It was no longer Eve, for Eve had come in and was standing at the foot of the bed.

They looked at each other in silence. Eve's hands were chained, she had come out of prison, and Liza knew—though not how she knew—that she must go back there. In spite of the chains, painfully, with a great effort, Eve reached up and took the gun down from the caravan wall. There was no gun there but she reached up and took it down. A little moonlight gleamed on the metal. Long ago, years and years ago, Liza had known that her mother took the gun down from the wall but she had never seen her do it.

Eve came up to her, holding the gun in her manacled hands. She did not speak, yet her message communicated itself to Liza. It would be easy. Only the first time was hard. Sleep would still be possible and peace of mind and contentment. Long days of forgetfulness would pass. Eve smiled. She began to whisper confidingly how she had wrapped herself in a sheet, taken a kitchen knife, and crept upstairs to the sleeping Bruno.

Liza cried out then. She reached for Sean, for the bed, for the body of herself and entered it again, her body growing around her, waking as she woke. And then she was up, huddled and crouching in a far corner. The moon still shone and its greenish light still infiltrated the caravan, seeping between window frames and blinds. It was icy cold.

Gradually full wakefulness returned. The cold brought it back. Strangely, the dream had been quite warm. She fumbled around in the half dark, first for Mrs. Spurdell's pill container, then for the sweater Eve had knitted. As she pulled it over her head, the dreadful feeling came to her that once her eyes were uncovered again she would see Eve standing there, chained, smiling, advising.

She opened her eyes. They were alone, she and Sean. It

struck her as very strange, almost unbelievable, that she had meant to kill him.

More cold would come in but still she opened the caravan door. The steps glittered with frost. She prised the top off the pill carton and threw the pills into the long wet grass in the ditch. The frost burned her bare feet and when she was back inside again sharp pains shot through them.

Despair seemed to have been waiting for her in the caravan. It was there in the cold darkness and the smell of bodies and stale food. The world hadn't fallen apart when Eve told her to go. It was falling apart now, one staunch rock after another tumbling and landsliding, Eve, Sean, herself. Soon the ground beneath her feet would founder and split and swallow her up. She gave a little cry and in an agony of grief and loneliness, flung herself face-downward on the bed, breaking into sobs.

Sean woke up and put the light on. He didn't ask what was the matter but lifted her up in his arms, held his arms tightly around her, and pulled her close to him, burrowing them both under the covers. Murmuring that her hands were frozen, he squeezed them between their bodies, against his warm body.

"Don't cry, sweetheart."

"I can't help it, I can't stop."

"Yes, you can. You will in a minute. I know why you're crying."

"You don't, you can't." Because I can't kill you, because I'll never kill anyone, because I'm not Eve.

"I do know, Liza. It's because of what I done the other night, isn't it? It seemed funny at the time, like a joke, and then I got to remembering what you'd said to me when we first done it, back in the summer, like I'd never make you if you didn't want to, and I'd said I never would. I've been ashamed of myself. I've hated myself."

"Have you?" she whispered. "Have you really?"

"I didn't know how to say it. I was like embarrassed. In the light, in the daytime, I don't know, I couldn't say it. I'm not like you, I can't express myself like you. I've felt that too, maybe you never knew it but I have, you being like superior to me in everything."

"I'm not, I'm really not."

"It's so bloody cold in here I'm going to light the gas. I don't reckon we'll sleep no more. It's nearly six."

Wiping her wet face on the sheet, she watched him get up, wrap himself in the clothes that lay about, and then put a match to the open oven. Her eyes hurt with crying and she felt a little sick.

What he said next surprised her so much she sat bolt upright in bed.

"You don't want to come with me, do you?"

"What?"

He got back into bed and pulled her down under the bedclothes. He hugged her and held her head in the hollow of his shoulder. His hands were always warm. That hadn't really registered with her before, or she had taken it for granted. She remembered the sunny summer days and how she had watched him, that first time, from among the trees at Shrove and his puzzled look as he stared unseeing at her, aware as people mysteriously are of being observed.

He said it again, "You don't want to come with me," but not this time in the form of a question.

Shaking her head under the bedclothes, she realized that the movement indicated nothing to him and she whispered a small, "No."

"Is it because I—I forced myself on you?"

"No."

"I'd never do it again. I've learned my lesson."

"It's not because of that."

"No, I know." He sighed. She felt his chest move with the sigh and was aware of his heart beating under her cheek. "It's because we're not like the same kind of people," he said. "I'm an ordinary—well, I'm working class and you're—you may have been brought up in that cracked way but you're—you're light-years above me."

"No, no, Sean. No."

"You only got to listen to the way we talk. I know I get words wrong and I get grammar wrong. Hopefully that'll change when I get into management. I might say you could teach me, but that wouldn't work. In a funny sort of way, I knew it wouldn't work when it first started last summer, only I wouldn't admit it even to myself. I suppose I was in love—well, I know I was. I'd never been in love before."

"Nor I."

"No, I reckon you never had the chance. I had but I never was. Not till you. Only, love, how'll you make out on your own?"

"I'll manage."

"I do love you, Liza. It wasn't just for sex. I loved you from the first moment I saw you."

She put up her face to him and felt for his mouth with her mouth. The touch of his lips and the feel of his tongue on hers quickened her thawing body. She felt the quick familiar ripple of desire. He sighed with pleasure and relief. They made love half-clothed, buried under the piled covers, his hands warm and hers still icy, while the blue gas flared and the water from condensation flowed down the windows.

It was eight when they woke up, much later than he had intended. She was making tea, wearing her padded coat, when he said, "I'll tell you what I'll do, I'll leave you the van."

She turned around. "The caravan?"

He thought she was correcting him again. "Okay, teacher, the *cara*van. Always got to be right, haven't you? Always know best. That's what you'd better be, not a doctor or a lawyer, but a teacher."

"Did you really mean you'd leave me the caravan?"

"Sure I did. Look at it this way, I was going to take the van on account of you, but if you're not coming it'd be better for me to share with those guys, it'd be easier."

"You could sell it."

"What, this old wreck? Who'd buy it?"

Her hesitation lasted only a moment. "I've got some money," she said. "I found it when I went to Shrove. It was Eve's but she'd have wanted me to have it."

"You never said. Why didn't you tell me?"

"Because I'm horrible—or I thought you were. Don't be cross *now*. It's a lot, it's more than a thousand pounds."

She was ashamed because she'd thought he'd grab the money as soon as he got the chance and here he was shaking his head. "I always said I'd not live off my girlfriend and I won't. Even"— he smiled a bit ruefully—"if you're not my girlfriend no more. You'll need it, love, whatever you do. I'd get in touch with that Heather if I was you. Hopefully, she's been wondering what you've been up to. It'll be a relief to her. And then maybe you and her can go together to see your mum."

Liza gave him his tea. "I'll tell you what I'm going to do, Sean. I'm going to cook us a big breakfast of eggs and bacon and fried potatoes and fried bread and if it stinks out the caravan, who cares?"

"We'll meet again one day, won't we?" he said as he started on his first egg. "You never know, we might both be different."

"Of course we'll meet again."

She knew they never would. Whatever became of him, she would be different beyond recognition.

"You'll need someone to look after you." He fretted a bit as he packed his bags. They were Superway plastic carriers, the only luggage he had. Guilt over her made him fret. "You'll get hold of Heather, won't you? That money you've got, it's not all that much. I'll tell you what, I'll drive you into town, it's on my way. You can phone her from there."

"All right."

"I'll feel easier, love."

Instead of hating the new situation, he was relieved. Just a bit. She could tell that, she could see it in his eyes. Tomorrow it would be more than a bit, it would be overwhelming. He wouldn't be able to believe his luck. As it was, now, he was forcing himself to put up a big pretense of being sad.

"I'll worry about you."

"Write down where you'll be," she said, "and I'll write to you and tell you what's happened to me. I promise."

He gave her a sidelong look. "Don't put in too many long words."

The two phone boxes in the marketplace were both empty. Sean parked in front of them. He felt in his jacket pocket and gave her all the change he had: coins to phone Heather and coins to phone the Home Office. There were enough of them to last even if people at the other end kept her waiting while they went off to find someone. First, he said, she must get on to directory enquiries for Heather's number. She'd got the address still, hadn't she?

"But maybe you'd better come with me, after all, love. Just

for a week or two, until we've found someplace for you to go, until you're sure of this Heather."

She shook her head. "You've left the van behind, remember? You've left me the van."

That he was grateful for her use of his term she could see in his eyes. They seemed full of love, as they had been in those early days, at apple-picking time, in the warm sunny fields. She put up her face and kissed him, a long soft passionless kiss. It troubled her, and always would, that she had thought of killing him. Even if she hadn't really been serious, even if it was a fantasy created out of stress and memory, it would always be there. More than anything else, it would be responsible for making any further love or companionship or even contiguity between them impossible.

"Drive off," she said. "Don't wave. I'll be okay. Good luck."

But she watched the car go, she couldn't help herself. And he did wave. He did a funny thing, he blew her a kiss. She was left in the cold marketplace, on the pavement, with shoppers all around her.

The phone boxes weren't empty anymore. A woman had gone into one of them and a boy into the other. She sat down on the low brick wall built around a flower bed, an empty flower bed, the earth thinly sprinkled with frost. It didn't matter to her how many people went into those phone boxes, if a queue of fifty formed, if someone went in and vandalized them like they'd done to the one outside Superway, pulled the phones off the wall, it wouldn't matter to her because she didn't mean to phone anyone. What she had to do now was think of how to find out where a certain street was.

She thought about it. If she didn't fix her mind on something practical it would fill up with fear, with the realization of her utter aloneness. Sooner or later she was going to have to confront that, but not now. A picture of herself as a silly little ignorant girl sitting on a brick wall weeping rose before her eyes and she resolved not to let it become real. She would go into a shop and ask.

They didn't know. The shop was full of small objects Liza thought were called souvenirs, brooches and key rings and little boxes, fluffy animals and plastic dolls and china mugs, that she couldn't believe anyone would want to possess. The people who worked there all came from outside the town. You could get a street plan, one of them said. How do I, she asked, and if they looked at her strangely, they nevertheless said, a paper shop, yes, that's the best place, there's one three doors along.

And there was. And they had a street plan. They didn't seem to think it was a funny thing to ask for. It was a long way away, her destination, two miles she calculated from the rough scale.

On the way she passed street people who had been out all night on the pavement or in doorways if they were lucky. It brought back to her what Sean had said about "poor buggers sleeping rough." Would she be one of them? It was a possibility. A thousand pounds wasn't the fortune she had thought it when she first took the iron box. It didn't seem much when you could pay a twentieth part of it for that pair of shoes she saw in a shop window she passed.

The shops stopped soon after that and there came a place with a red fire engine half out of its door. Seeing one like it on television made identification possible. Next door was a big imposing building with a blue lamp over the door and a notice board on either side of the entrance. The blue lamp, like the one on the car, told her what it was before she read the County Police sign.

She stopped and stared at the poster on the notice board. The strange thing was that she recognized the painting in it as Bruno's before she knew it for her own portrait. The big features, the strong colors that had never been her features and colors. No one passing would know it for her. If anyone came by they would never connect the brown-and-yellow daub on the poster with the girl who stood looking at it.

No doubt, it was the best the police could do. It was all they had. Probably they had never before come upon a missing person who had never had her photograph taken. The poster said: HAVE YOU SEEN THIS GIRL? It said she was missing, gave her name and age, her height and weight and the color of her hair, that anyone knowing her whereabouts should be in touch with them.

Liza turned away. She felt enormously more cheerful, she felt full of hope. Eve hadn't forgotten her, Eve did need her. If no one had found her it was because the only likeness of her that existed was Bruno's strange daub. She began to walk fast along this street of small red houses, all linked together in a long row of roofs and chimneys and tiny gardens, each with its car at the pavement. Warmth began to spread through her and she felt the blood come into her cheeks.

The house she was going to wouldn't look like these, she had decided, but either like Mr. and Mrs. Spurdell's or else like the one Bruno had nearly bought, or a mixture of the two. That sort was beginning to appear now, prim, neat houses each hugging to itself its small, walled piece of land.

The name of the place where she had grown up and the year of her own birth. Shrove Road was on the edge of the town where the country started. Number 76 wasn't at all what she had expected but a house that looked as if left over from some distant past time when there were no other buildings but the church and the manor and the farms. This one had been a small farmhouse, she thought, which even now stood in a big piece of land with trees on it.

She was suddenly afraid. Of no one being at home, of her assumptions and assessments being all wrong, of walking back again to the bus stop past the street people. The bell by the front door didn't chime like the one in Aspen Close or toll like the bell on the door at Shrove. It buzzed. She took her finger away as if the insect that made the buzzing had stung it, then, more confidently, pressed again.

Jane Spurdell didn't recognize her. Liza could tell that and, inspired, she grasped a handful of her hair and pulled it to the back of her head.

"I know. It's Liza. Wait a minute, Liza Holford."

"Yes."

"Come in. You must be cold." A glance outside had told her Liza had come on foot. From where? "I'm miles from anywhere."

"I'm used to being miles from anywhere," Liza said, and that was the start of telling her. Not all, not a hundred nights of life story, just the essentials and an outline of her present state.

Jane Spurdell made coffee. They sat in her living room, which was a mess, but a nice mess with books on shelves and piled on tables and even on the floor.

"I want to study the law but I've a long way to go, I know that. I've got to get"—she couldn't remember the names of the examinations—"oh, GC Levels or something. And I want to find my mother and go and see her. I've got a thousand pounds and a caravan to live in."

"The law sounds a good idea. Why not?" Jane Spurdell said. "You can use my phone if you want to phone your mother." She looked a little wary. "I'm not sure about the caravan, I mean if you came to ask me if you could park it here, I'd have to think about that one."

"No, I've got it on a place where they'll make me move and when I can't they'll move me and find me somewhere to live. They have to." Liza finished her coffee. She was warm now and feeling strong. "I came to ask you one thing I know you can do for me."

"Yes?"

Liza didn't want to face it that for a moment she had sounded like her father. She said in a rush, "Please, can you arrange for me to go to school?"

It was relief that Jane felt. Liza could tell that. Whatever she had expected it hadn't been that. She had anticipated begging, requests for money, time, attention—even, perhaps, affection.

"Yes, of course I can," she said, relief beaming in her smile. "Nothing easier. It's not difficult. You can start somewhere in January. I only wish more people were like you. Is that all?"

Liza gave a great sigh. She was going to be all right and she wasn't going to burst into tears of relief or make confessions. A good time was beginning and she was going to think of that and be a Stoic.

"That's all I want. To go to school." She held out her cup. "And please may I have another cup of coffee?"